i

SOMEWHERE IN RED GAP

SOMEWHERE IN RED GAP

By
Harry Leon Wilson

ILLUSTRATED BY
JOHN R. NEILL, F. R. GRUGER, AND
HENRY RALEIGH

GARDEN CITY   NEW YORK
DOUBLEDAY, PAGE & COMPANY
1916

"THEY JUST CLENCHED THEIR HANDS AND HUNG ON WIL-
FRED'S WILD, FREE WORDS"

To
GEORGE HORACE LORIMER

CONTENTS

ILLUSTRATIONS

SOMEWHERE IN RED GAP

I

THE RED SPLASH OF ROMANCE

THE walls of the big living-room in the Arrowhead ranch house are tastefully enlivened here and there with artistic spoils of the owner, Mrs. Lysander John Pettengill. There are family portraits in crayon, photo-engravings of noble beasts clipped from the *Breeder's Gazette*, an etched cathedral or two, a stuffed and varnished trout of such size that no one would otherwise have believed in it, a print in three colours of a St. Bernard dog with a marked facial resemblance to the late William E. Gladstone, and a triumph of architectural perspective revealing two sides of the Pettengill block, corner of Fourth and Main streets, Red Gap, made vivacious by a bearded fop on horseback who doffs his silk hat to a couple of overdressed ladies with parasols in a passing victoria.

And there is the photograph of the fat man. He is very large—both high and wide. He has filled the lens and now compels the eye. His broad face beams a friendly interest. His moustache is a flourishing, uncurbed, riotous growth above his billowy chin.

The checked coat, held recklessly aside by a hand on each hip, reveals an incredible expanse of waistcoat,

the pattern of which raves horribly. From pocket
to pocket of this gaudy shield curves a watch chain
of massive links—nearly a yard of it, one guesses.

Often I have glanced at this noisy thing tacked to
the wall, entranced by the simple width of the man.
Now on a late afternoon I loitered before it while my
hostess changed from riding breeches to the gown of
lavender and lace in which she elects to drink tea
after a day's hard work along the valleys of the Arrowhead. And for the first time I observed a line of
writing beneath the portrait, the writing of my hostess, a rough, downright, plain fashion of script:
"Reading from left to right—Mr. Ben Sutton,
Popular Society Favourite of Nome, Alaska."

"Reading from left to right!" Here was the intent
facetious. And Ma Pettengill is never idly facetious.
Always, as the advertisements say, "There's a
reason!" And now, also for the first time, I noticed
some printed verses on a sheet of thickish yellow
paper tacked to the wall close beside the photograph
—so close that I somehow divined an intimate relationship between the two. With difficulty remov-
ing my gaze from the gentleman who should be read
from left to right, I scanned these verses:

SONG OF THE OPEN ROAD

A child of the road—a gypsy I—
My path o'er the land and sea;
With the fire of youth I warm my nights
And my days are wild and free.

Then ho! for the wild, the open road!
  Afar from the haunts of men.
The woods and the hills for my spirit untamed—
  I'm away to mountain and glen.

If ever I tried to leave my hills
  To abide in the cramped haunts of men,
The urge of the wild to her wayward child
  Would drag me to freedom again.

I'm slave to the call of the open road;
  In your cities I'd stifle and die.
I'm off to the hills in fancy I see—
  On the breast of old earth I'll lie.
          WILFRED LENNOX, *the Hobo Poet,*
            On a Coast-to-Coast Walking Tour.
These Cards for sale.

I briefly pondered the lyric. It told its own simple
story and could at once have been dismissed but for
its divined and puzzling relationship to the popular
society favourite of Nome, Alaska. What could
there be in this?

Mrs. Lysander John Pettengill bustled in upon my
speculation, but as usual I was compelled to wait for
the talk I wanted. For some moments she would be
only the tired owner of the Arrowhead Ranch—in the
tea gown of a débutante and with too much powder
on one side of her nose—and she must have at least
one cup of tea so corrosive that the Scotch whiskey

she adds to it is but a merciful dilution. She now drank eagerly of the fearful brew, dulled the bite of it with smoke from a hurriedly built cigarette, and relaxed gratefully into one of those chairs which are all that most of us remember William Morris for. Even then she must first murmur of the day's annoyances, provided this time by officials of the United States Forest Reserve. In the beginning I must always allow her a little to have her own way.

"The annual spring rumpus with them rangers," she wearily boomed. "Every year they tell me just where to turn my cattle out on the Reserve, and every year I go ahead and turn 'em out where I want 'em turned out, which ain't the same place at all, and then I have to listen patiently to their kicks and politely answer all letters from the higher-ups and wait for the official permit, which always comes—and it's wearing on a body. Darn it! They'd ought to know by this time I always get my own way. If they wasn't such a decent bunch I'd have words with 'em, giving me the same trouble year after year, probably because I'm a weak, defenceless woman. However!"

The lady rested largely, inert save for the hand that raised the cigarette automatically to her lips. My moment had come.

"What did Wilfred Lennox, the hobo poet, have to do with Mr. Ben Sutton, of Nome, Alaska?" I gently inquired.

"More than he wanted," replied the lady. Her glance warmed with memories; she hovered musingly on the verge of recital. But the cigarette was half done and at its best. I allowed her another moment, a moment in which she laughed confidentially to herself, a little dry, throaty laugh. I knew that laugh. She would be marshalling certain events in their just and diverting order. But they seemed to be many and of confusing values.

"Some said he not only wasn't a hobo but wasn't even a poet," she presently murmured, and smoked again. Then: "That Ben Sutton, now, he's a case. Comes from Alaska and don't like fresh eggs for breakfast because he says they ain't got any kick to 'em like Alaska eggs have along in March, and he's got to have canned milk for his coffee. Say, I got a three-quarters Jersey down in Red Gap gives milk so rich that the cream just naturally trembles into butter if you speak sharply to it or even give it a cross look; not for Ben though. Had to send out for canned milk that morning. I drew the line at hunting up case eggs for him though. He had to put up with insipid fresh ones. And fat, that man! My lands! He travels a lot in the West when he does leave home, and he tells me it's the fear of his life he'll get wedged into one of them narrow-gauge Pullmans some time and have to be chopped out. Well, as I was saying——" She paused.

"But you haven't begun," I protested. I sharply tapped the printed verses and the photograph reading from left to right. Now she became animated, speaking as she expertly rolled a fresh cigarette.

"Say, did you ever think what aggravating minxes women are after they been married a few years—after the wedding ring gets worn a little bit thin?"

This was not only brutal; it seemed irrelevant.

"Wilfred Lennox——" I tried to insist, but she commandingly raised the new cigarette at me.

"Yes, sir! Ever know one of 'em married for as long as ten years that didn't in her secret heart have a sort of contempt for her life partner as being a stuffy, plodding truck horse? Of course they keep a certain dull respect for him as a provider, but they can't see him as dashing and romantic any more; he ain't daring and adventurous. All he ever does is go down and open up the store or push back the roll-top, and keep from getting run over on the street. One day's like another with him, never having any wild, lawless instincts or reckless moods that make a man fascinating—about the nearest he ever comes to adventure is when he opens the bills the first of the month. And she often seeing him without any collar on, and needing a shave mebbe, and cherishing her own secret romantic dreams, while like as not he's prosily figuring out how he's going to make the next payment on the endowment policy.

"It's a hard, tiresome life women lead, chained to these here plodders. That's why rich widows generally pick out the dashing young devils they do for their second, having buried the man that made it for 'em. Oh, they like him well enough, call him

'Father' real tenderly, and see that he changes to the heavy flannels on time, but he don't ever thrill them, and when they order three hundred and fifty dollars' worth of duds from the Boston Cash Emporium and dress up like a foreign countess, they don't do it for Father, they do it for the romantic guy in the magazine serial they're reading, the handsome, cynical adventurer that has such an awful power over women. They know darned well they won't ever meet him; still it's just as well to be ready in case he ever should make Red Gap—or wherever they live—and it's easy with the charge account there, and Father never fussing more than a little about the bills.

"Not that I blame 'em. We're all alike—innocent enough, with freaks here and there that ain't. Why, I remember about a thousand years ago I was reading a book called 'Lillian's Honour,' in which the rightful earl didn't act like an earl had ought to, but went travelling off over the moors with a passel of gypsies, with all the she-gypsies falling in love with him, and no wonder—he was that dashing. Well, I used to think what might happen if he should come along while Lysander John was out with the beef round-up or something. I was well-meaning, understand, but at that I'd ought to have been laid out with a pick-handle. Oh, the nicest of us got specks inside us—if ever we did cut loose the best one of us would make the worst man of you look like nothing worse than a naughty little boy cutting up in Sunday-school. What holds us, of course—we always dream of being took off our feet; of being carried off by main force against our wills while we snuggle up to the romantic brute and plead with him to spare us—and the most reckless of 'em don't often get their nerve up to that. Well, as I was saying——"

But she was not saying. The thing moved too slowly. And still the woman paltered with her poisoned tea and made cigarettes and muttered inconsequently, as when she now broke out after a glance at the photograph:

"That Ben Sutton certainly runs amuck when be buys his vests. He must have about fifty, and the quietest one in the lot would make a leopard skin look like a piker." Again her glance dreamed off to visions.

I seated myself before her with some emphasis and said firmly: "Now, then!" It worked.

"Wilfred Lennox," she began, "calling himself the hobo poet, gets into Red Gap one day and makes the rounds with that there piece of poetry you see; pushes into stores and offices and hands the piece out, and like as not they crowd a dime or two bits onto him and send him along. That's what I done. I was waiting in Dr. Percy Hailey Martingale's office for a little painless dentistry, and I took Wilfred's poem and passed him a two-bit piece, and Doc Martingale does the same, and Wilfred blew on to the next office. A dashing and romantic figure he was, though kind of fat and pasty for a man that was walking from coast to coast, but a smooth talker with beautiful features and about nine hundred dollars' worth of hair and a soft hat and one of these flowing neckties. Red it was.

"So I looked over his piece of poetry—about the open road for his untamed spirit and him being stifled in the cramped haunts of men—and of course I get his number. All right about the urge of the wild to her wayward child, but here he was spending a lot of time in the cramped haunts of men taking their small change away from 'em and not seeming to stifle one bit.

"Ain't this new style of tramp funny? Now instead of coming round to the back door and asking for a hand-out like any self-respecting tramp had ought to, they march up to the front door, and they're somebody with two or three names that's walking round the world on a wager they made with one of the Vanderbilt boys or John D. Rockefeller. They've walked thirty-eight hundred miles already and got the papers to prove it—a letter from the mayor of Scranton, Pennsylvania, and the mayor of Davenport, Iowa, a picture post card of themselves on the courthouse steps at Denver, and they've bet forty thousand dollars they could start out without a cent and come back in twenty-two months with money in their pocket—and ain't it a good joke?—with everybody along the way entering into the spirit of it and passing them quarters and such, and thank you very much for your two bits for the picture post card—and they got another showing 'em in front of the Mormon

Tabernacle at Salt Lake City, if you'd like that, too—
and thank you again—and now they'll be off once
more to the open road and the wild, free life. Not!
Yes, two or three good firm Nots. Having milked
the town they'll be right down to the dee-po with their
silver changed to bills, waiting for No. 6 to come
along, and ho! for the open railroad and another
town that will skin pretty. I guess I've seen eight
or ten of them boys in the last five years, with their
letters from mayors.

"But this here Wilfred Lennox had a new graft.
He was the first I'd give up to for mere poetry. He
didn't have a single letter from a mayor, nor even a
picture card of himself standing with his hat off in
front of Pike's Peak—nothing but poetry. But, as I
said, he was there with a talk about pining for the
open road and despising the cramped haunts of men,
and he had appealing eyes and all this flowing hair
and necktie. So I says to myself: 'All right, Wilfred, you win!' and put my purse back in my bag and
thought no more of it.

"Yet not so was it to be. Wilfred, working the
best he could to make a living doing nothing, pretty
soon got to the office of Alonzo Price, Choice Improved Real Estate and Price's Addition. Lon was
out for the moment, but who should be there waiting
for him but his wife, Mrs. Henrietta Templeton
Price, recognized leader of our literary and artistic
set. Or I think they call it a 'group' or a 'coterie' or
something. Setting at Lon's desk she was, toying

petulantly with horrid old pens and blotters, and probably bestowing glances of disrelish from time to time round the grimy office where her scrubby little husband toiled his days away in unromantic squalor.

"I got to tell you about Henrietta. She's one of them like I just said the harsh things about, with the secret cry in her heart for romance and adventure and other forbidden things and with a kindly contempt for peaceful Alonzo. She admits to being thirty-six, so you can figure it out for yourself. Of course she gets her husband wrong at that, as women so often do. Alonzo has probably the last pair of side whiskers outside of a steel engraving and stands five feet two, weighing a hundred and twenty-six pounds at the ring side, but he's game as a swordfish, and as for being romantic in the true sense of the word—well, no one that ever heard him sell a lot in Price's Addition —three miles and a half up on the mesa, with only the smoke of the canning factory to tell a body they was still near the busy haunts of men, that and a mile of concrete sidewalk leading a life of complete idleness— I say no one that ever listened to Lon sell a lot up there, pointing out on a blue print the proposed site of the Carnegie Library, would accuse him of not being romantic.

"But of course Henrietta never sees Lon's romance and he ain't always had the greatest patience with hers—like the time she got up the Art Loan Exhibit to get new books for the M. E. Sabbath-school library and got Spud Mulkins of the El Adobe to lend

'em the big gold-framed oil painting that hangs over
his bar. Some of the other ladies objected to this—
the picture was a big pink hussy lying down beside
the ocean—but Henrietta says art for art's sake is
pure to them that are pure, or something, and they're
doing such things constantly in the East; and I'm
darned if Spud didn't have his oil painting down and
the mosquito netting ripped off it before Alonzo heard
about it and put the Not-at-All on it. He wouldn't
reason with Henrietta either. He just said his ob-
jection was that every man that saw it would put one
foot up groping for the brass railing, which would
be undignified for a Sabbath-school scheme, and that
she'd better hunt out something with clothes on like
Whistler's portrait of his mother, or, if she wanted
the nude in art, to get the Horse Fair or something
with animals.

"I tell you that to show you how they don't hit
it off sometimes. Then Henrietta sulks. Kind of
pinched and hungry looking she is, drapes her black
hair down over one side of her high forehead, wears
daring gowns—that's what she calls 'em anyway—
and reads the most outrageous kinds of poetry out
loud to them that will listen. Likes this Omar
Something stuff about your path being beset with
pitfalls and gin fizzes and getting soused out under a
tree with your girl.

"I'm just telling you so you'll get Henrietta when
Wilfred Lennox drips gracefully in with his piece of
poetry in one hand. Of course she must have looked

long and nervously at Wilfred, then read his poetry,
then looked again. There before her was Romance
against a background of Alonzo Price, who never had
an adventurous or evil thought in his life, and wore
rubbers! Oh, sure! He must have palsied her at
once, this wild, free creature of the woods who
couldn't stand the cramped haunts of men. And I
have said that Wilfred was there with the wild, free
words about himself, and the hat and tie and the
waving brown hair that give him so much trouble.
Shucks! I don't blame the woman. It's only a few
years since we been let out from under lock and key.
Give us a little time to get our bearings, say I. Wilfred was just one big red splash before her yearning
eyes; he blinded her. And he stood there telling how
this here life in the marts of trade would sure twist
and blacken some of the very finest chords in his
being. Something like that it must have been.

"Anyway, about a quarter to six a procession went
up Fourth Street, consisting of Wilfred Lennox, Henrietta, and Alonzo. The latter was tripping along
about three steps back of the other two and every
once in a while he would stop for a minute and simply
look puzzled. I saw him. It's really a great pity
Lon insists on wearing a derby hat with his side
whiskers. To my mind the two never seem meant
for each other.

"The procession went to the Price mansion up on
Ophir Avenue. And that evening Henrietta had in a
few friends to listen to the poet recite his verses and

tell anecdotes about himself. About five or six ladies in the parlour and their menfolks smoking out on the front porch. The men didn't seem to fall for Wilfred's open-road stuff the way the ladies did. Wilfred was a good reciter and held the ladies with his voice and his melting blue eyes with the long lashes, and Henrietta was envied for having nailed him. That is, the women envied her. The men sort of slouched off down to the front gate and then went down to the Temperance Billiard Parlour, where several of 'em got stewed. Most of 'em, like old Judge Ballard, who come to the country in '62, and Jeff Tuttle, who's always had more than he wanted of the open road, were very cold indeed to Wilfred's main proposition. It is probable that low mutterings might have been heard among 'em, especially after a travelling man that was playing pool said the hobo poet had come in on the Pullman of No. 6.

"But I must say that Alonzo didn't seem to mutter any, from all I could hear. Pathetic, the way that little man will believe right up to the bitter end. He said that for a hobo Wilfred wrote very good poetry, better than most hobos could write, he thought, and that Henrietta always knew what she was doing. So the evening come to a peaceful end, most of the men getting back for their wives and Alonzo showing up in fair shape and plumb eager for the comfort of his guest. It was Alonzo's notion that the guest would of course want to sleep out in the front yard on the breast of old earth where he could look up at the pretty stars and feel at home, and he was getting out a roll of blankets when the guest said he didn't want to make the least bit of trouble and for one night he'd manage to sleep inside four stifling walls in a regular bed, like common people do. So Lon bedded him down in the guest chamber, but opened up the four windows in it and propped the door wide open so the poor fellow could have a breeze and not smother. He told this downtown the next morning, and he was beginning to look right puzzled indeed. He said the wayward child of Nature had got up after about half an hour and shut all the windows and the door. Lon thought first he was intending to commit suicide, but he didn't like to interfere. He was telling Jeff Tuttle and me about it when we happened to pass his office.

" 'And there's another funny thing,' " he says. 'This chap was telling us all the way up home last night that he never ate meat—simply fruits and nuts with a mug of spring water. He said eating the carcasses of murdered beasts was abhorrent to him. But when we got down to the table he consented to partake of the roast beef and he did so repeatedly. We usually have cold meat for lunch the day after a rib roast, but there will be something else to-day; and along with the meat he drank two bottles of beer, though with mutterings of disgust. He said spring water in the hills was pure, but that water out of pipes was full of typhoid germs. He admitted that there were times when the grosser appetites assailed him. And they assailed him this morning, too. He said he might bring himself to eat some chops, and he did it without scarcely a struggle. He ate six. He said living the nauseous artificial life even for one night brought back the hateful meat craving. I don't know. He is undeniably peculiar. And of course you've heard about Pettikin's affair for this evening?'

"We had. Just before leaving the house I had received Henrietta's card inviting me to the country club that evening 'to meet Mr. Wilfred Lennox, Poet and Nature Lover, who will recite his original verses and give a brief talk on "The World's Debt to Poetry."' And there you have the whole trouble. Henrietta should have known better. But I've let out what women really are. I told Alonzo I would sure be among those present. I said it sounded good. And then Alonzo pipes up about Ben Sutton coming to town on the eleven forty-two from the West. Ben makes a trip out of Alaska every summer and never fails to stop off a day or two with Lon, they having been partners up North in '98.

"'Good old Ben will enjoy it, too,' says Alonzo; 'and, furthermore, Ben will straighten out one or two little things that have puzzled me about this poet. He will understand his complex nature in a way that I confess I have been unequal to. What I mean is,' he says, 'there was talk when I left this morning of the poet consenting to take a class in poetry for several weeks in our thriving little city, and Henrietta was urging him to make our house his home. I have a sort of feeling that Ben will be able to make several

suggestions of prime value. I have never known him
to fail at making suggestions.'

"Funny, the way the little man tried to put it over
on us, letting on he was just puzzled—not really
bothered, as he plainly was. You knew Henrietta
was still seeing the big red splash of Romance, behind which the figure of her husband was totally
obscured. Jeff Tuttle saw the facts, and he up and
spoke in a very common way about what would
quickly happen to any tramp that tried to camp in his
house, poet or no poet, but that's neither here nor
there. We left Alonzo looking cheerily forward to
Ben Sutton on the eleven forty-two, and I went on to
do some errands.

"In the course of these I discovered that others
besides Henrietta had fell hard for the poet of Nature.
I met Mrs. Dr. Percy Hailey Martingale and she just
bubbles about him, she having been at the Prices' the
night before.

"'Isn't he a glorious thing!' she says; 'and how
grateful we should be for the dazzling bit of colour
he brings into our drab existence!' She is a good
deal like that herself at times. And I met Beryl
Mae Macomber, a well-known young society girl of
seventeen, and Beryl Mae says: 'He's awfully good
looking, but do you think he's sincere?' And even
Mrs. Judge Ballard comes along and says: 'What a
stimulus he should be to us in our dull lives! How he
shows us the big, vital bits!' and her at that very
minute going into Bullitt & Fleishacker's to buy shoes

for her nine-year-old twin grandsons! And the Reverend Mrs. Wiley Knapp in at the Racquet Store wanting to know if the poet didn't make me think of some wild, free creature of the woods—a deer or an antelope poised for instant flight while for one moment he timidly overlooked man in his hideous commercialism. But, of course, she was a minister's wife. I said he made me feel just like that. I said so to all of 'em. What else could I say? If I'd said what I thought there on the street I'd of been pinched. So I beat it home in self-protection. I was sympathizing good and hearty with Lon Price by that time and looking forward to Ben Sutton myself. I had a notion Ben would see the right of it where these poor dubs of husbands wouldn't—or wouldn't dast say it if they did.

"About five o'clock I took another run downtown for some things I'd forgot, with an eye out to see how Alonzo and Ben might be coming on. The fact is, seeing each other only once a year that way they're apt to kind of loosen up—if you know what I mean.

"No sign of 'em at first. Nothing but ladies young and old—even some of us older ranching set—making final purchases of ribbons and such for the sole benefit of Wilfred Lennox, and talking in a flushed manner about him whenever they met. Almost every darned one of 'em had made it a point to stroll past the Price mansion that afternoon where Wilfred was setting out on the lawn in a wicker chair with some bottles of beer surveying Nature with a look of lofty approval and chatting with Henrietta about the real things of life.

"Beryl Mae Macomber had traipsed past four times, changing her clothes twice with a different shade of ribbon across her forehead and all her college pins on, and at last she'd simply walked right in and asked if she hadn't left her tennis racquet there last Tuesday. She says to Mrs. Judge Ballard and Mrs. Martingale and me in the Cut-Rate Pharmacy, she says: 'Oh, he's just awfully magnetic —but do you really think he's sincere?' Then she bought an ounce of Breath of Orient perfume and kind of two-stepped out. These other ladies spoke very sharply about the freedom Beryl Mae's aunt allowed her. Mrs. Martingale said the poet, it was true, had a compelling personality, but what was our young girls coming to? And if that child was hers——

"So I left these two lady highbinders and went on into the retail side of the Family Liquor Store to order up some cooking sherry, and there over the partition from the bar side what do I hear but Alonzo Price and Ben Sutton! Right off I could tell they'd been pinning a few on. In fact, Alonzo was calling the bartender Mister. You don't know about Lon, but when he calls the bartender Mister the ship has sailed. Ten minutes after that he'll be crying over his operation. So I thought quick, remembering that we had now established a grillroom at the country club, consisting of a bar and three tables with

bells on them, and a Chinaman, and that if Alonzo
and Ben Sutton come there at all they had better
come right—at least to start with. When I'd given
my order I sent Louis Meyer in to tell the two gentlemen a lady wished to speak to them outside.

"In a minute Ben comes out alone. He was awful
glad to see me and I said how well he looked, and he
did look well, sort of cordial and bulging—his forehead bulges and his eyes bulge and his moustache and
his chin, and he has cushions on his face. He beamed
on me in a wide and hearty manner and explained
that Alonzo refused to come out to meet a lady until
he knew who she was, because you got to be careful
in a small town like this where every one talks. 'And
besides,' says Ben, 'he's just broke down and begun
to cry about his appendicitis that was three years ago.
He's leaning his head on his arms down by the end of
the bar and sobbing bitterly over it. He seems to
grieve about it as a personal loss. I've tried to cheer
him up and told him it was probably all for the best,
but he says when it comes over him this way he
simply can't stand it. And what shall I do?'

"Well, of course I seen the worst had happened
with Alonzo. So I says to Ben: 'You know there's
a party to-night and if that man ain't seen to he will
certainly sink the ship. Now you get him out of that
swamp and I'll think of something.' 'I'll do it,' says
Ben, turning sideways so he could go through the
doorway again. 'I'll do it,' he says, 'if I have to use
force on the little scoundrel.'

"And sure enough, in a minute he edged out again with Alonzo firmly fastened to him in some way. Lon hadn't wanted to come and didn't want to stay now, but he simply couldn't move. Say, that Ben Sutton would make an awful grand anchor for a captive balloon. Alonzo wiped his eyes until he could see who I was. Then I rebuked him, reminding him of his sacred duties as a prominent citizen, a husband, and the secretary of the Red Gap Chamber of Commerce. 'Of course it's all right to take a drink now and then,' I says.

"Alonzo brightened at this. 'Good!' says he; 'now it's now and pretty soon it will be then. Let's go into a saloon or something like that!'

"'You'll come with me,' I says firmly. And I marched 'em down to the United States Grill, where I ordered tea and toast for 'em. Ben was sensible enough, but Alonzo was horrified at the thought of tea. 'It's tea or nice cold water for yours,' I says, and that set him off again. 'Water!' he sobs. 'Water! Water! Maybe you don't know that some dear cousins of mine have just lost their all in the Dayton flood—twenty years' gathering went in a minute, just like that!' and he tried to snap his fingers. All the same I got some hot tea into him and sent for Eddie Pierce to be out in front with his hack. While we was waiting for Eddie it occurs to Alonzo to telephone his wife. He come back very solemn and says: 'I told her I wouldn't be home to dinner because I was hungry and there probably wouldn't be enough meat, what with a vegetarian poet in the house. I told her I should sink to the level of a brute in the night life of our gay little city. I said I was a wayward child of Nature myself if you come right down to it.'

"'Good for you,' I says, having got word that Eddie is outside with his hack. 'And now for the open road!' 'Fine!' says Alonzo. 'My spirit is certainly feeling very untamed, like some poet's!' So I hustled 'em out and into the four-wheeler. Then I give Eddie Pierce private instructions. 'Get 'em out into the hills about four miles,' I says, 'out past the Catholic burying ground, then make an excuse that your hack has broke down, and as soon as they set foot to the ground have them skates of yours run away. Pay no attention whatever to their pleadings or their profane threats, only yelling to 'em that you'll be back as soon as possible. But don't go back. They'll wait an hour or so, then walk. And they need to walk.'

"'You said something there,' says Eddie, glancing back at 'em. Ben Sutton was trying to cheer Alonzo up by reminding him of the Christmas night they went to sleep in the steam room of the Turkish bath at Nome, and the man forgot 'em and shut off the steam and they froze to the benches and had to be chiselled off. And Eddie trotted off with his load. You'd ought to seen the way the hack sagged down on Ben's side. And I felt that I had done a good work, so I hurried home to get a bite to eat and dress and

make the party, which I still felt would be a good
party even if the husband of our hostess was among
the killed or missing.

"I reached the clubhouse at eight o'clock of that
beautiful June evening, to find the party already well
assembled on the piazza and the front steps or strolling about the lawn, about eight or ten of our prominent society matrons and near as many husbands.
And mebbe those dames hadn't lingered before their
mirrors for final touches! Mrs. Martingale had on
all her rings and the jade bracelet and the art-craft
necklace with amethysts, and Mrs. Judge Ballard
had done her hair a new way, and Beryl Mae Macomber, there with her aunt, not only had a new scarf
with silver stars over her frail young shoulders and a
band of cherry-coloured velvet across her forehead,
but she was wearing the first ankle watch ever seen in
Red Gap. I couldn't begin to tell you the fussy im-
provements them ladies had made in themselves—
and all, mind you, for the passing child of Nature
who had never paid a bill for 'em in his life.

"Oh, it was a gay, careless throng with the mad
light of pleasure in its eyes, and all of 'em milling
round Wilfred Lennox, who was eating it up. Some
bantered him roguishly and some spoke in chest
tones of what was the real inner meaning of life after
all. Henrietta Templeton Price hovered near with
the glad light of capture in her eyes. Silent but
proud Henrietta was, careless but superior, reminding me of the hunter that has his picture taken over in

Africa with one negligent foot on the head of a two-horned rhinoceros he's just killed.

"But again the husbands was kind of lurking in the background, bunched up together. They seemed abashed by this strange frenzy of their womenfolks. How'd they know, the poor dubs, that a poet wasn't something a business man had ought to be polite and grovelling to? They affected an easy manner, but it was poor work. Even Judge Ballard, who seems nine feet tall in his Prince Albert, and usually looks quite dignified and hostile with his long dark face and his moustache and goatee—even the good old judge was rattled after a brief and unhappy effort to hold a bit of converse with the guest of honour. Him and Jeff Tuttle went to the grillroom twice in ten minutes. The judge always takes his with a dash of pepper sauce in it, but now it only seemed to make him more gloomy.

"Well, I was listening along, feeling elated that I'd put Alonzo and Ben Sutton out of the way and wondering when the show would begin—Beryl Mae in her high, innocent voice had just said to the poet: 'But seriously now, are you sincere?' and I was getting some plenty of that, when up the road in the dusk I seen Bush Jones driving a dray-load of furniture. I wondered where in time any family could be moving out that way. I didn't know any houses beyond the club and I was pondering about this, idly as you might say, when Bush Jones pulls his team up right in front of the clubhouse, and there on the load is the two I had tried to lose. In a big armchair beside a varnished centre table sits Ben Sutton reading something that I recognized as the yellow card with Wilfred's verses on it. And across the dray from him on a red-plush sofa is Alonzo Price singing 'My Wild Irish Rose' in a very noisy tenor.

"Well, sir, I could have basted that fool Bush Jones with one of his own dray stakes. That man's got an intellect just powerful enough to take furniture from one house to another if the new address ain't too hard for him to commit to memory. That's Bush Jones all right! He has the machinery for thinking, but it all glitters as new as the day it was put in. So he'd come a mile out of his way with these two riots—and people off somewhere wondering where that last load of things was!

"The ladies all affected to ignore this disgraceful spectacle, with Henrietta sinking her nails into her bloodless palms, but the men broke out and cheered a little in a half-scared manner and some of 'em went down to help the newcomers climb out. Then Ben had words with Bush Jones because he wanted him to wait there and take 'em back to town when the party was over and Bush refused to wait. After suffering about twenty seconds in the throes of mental effort I reckon he discovered that he had business to attend to or was hungry or something. Anyway, Ben paid him some money finally and he drove off after calling out 'Good-night, all!' just as if nothing had happened.

"Alonzo and Ben Sutton joined the party without further formality. They didn't look so bad, either, so I saw my crooked work had done some good. Lon quit singing almost at once and walked good and his eyes didn't wabble, and he looked kind of desperate and respectable, and Ben was first-class, except he was slightly oratorical and his collar had melted the way fat men's do. And it was funny to see how every husband there bucked up when Ben came forward, as if all they had wanted was some one to make medicine for 'em before they begun the war dance. They mooched right up round Ben when he trampled a way into the flushed group about Wilfred.

"'At last the well-known stranger!' says Ben cordially, seizing one of Wilfred's pale, beautiful hands. 'I've been hearing so much of you, wayward child of the open road that you are, and I've just been reading your wonderful verses as I sat in my library. The woods and the hills for your spirit untamed and the fire of youth to warm your nights—that's the talk.' He paused and waved Wilfred's verses in a fat, freckled hand. Then he looked at him hard and peculiar and says: 'When you going to pull some of it for us?'

"Wilfred had looked slightly rattled from the beginning. Now he smiled, but only with his lips—he made it seem like a mere Swedish exercise or something, and the next second his face looked as if it had been sewed up for the winter.

"'Little starry-eyed gypsy, I say, when are you

going to pull some of that open-road stuff?' says Ben
again, all cordial and sinister.

"Wilfred gulped and tried to be jaunty. 'Oh, as
to that, I'm here to-day and there to-morrow,' he
murmurs, and nervously fixes his necktie.

"'Oh, my, and isn't that nice!' says Ben heartily—
'the urge of the wild to her wayward child'—I
know you're a slave to it. And now you're going to
tell us all about the open road, and then you and I are
going to have an intimate chat and I'll tell you
about it—about some of the dearest little open roads
you ever saw, right round in these parts. I've just
counted nine, all leading out of town to the cunning-
est mountains and glens that would make you write
poetry hours at a time, with Nature's glad fruits and
nuts and a mug of spring water and some bottled beer
and a ham and some rump steak——'

"The stillness of that group had become darned
painful, I want to tell you. There was a horrid fear
that Ben Sutton might go too far, even for a country
club. Every woman was shuddering and smiling in a
painful manner, and the men regarding Ben with
glistening eyes. And Ben felt it himself all at once.
So he says: 'But I fear I am detaining you,' and let
go of the end of Wilfred's tie that he had been toying
with in a somewhat firm manner. 'Let us be on
with your part of the evening's entertainment,' he
says, 'but don't forget, gypsy wilding that you are,
that you and I must have a chat about open roads the
moment you have finished. I know we are cramping

you. By that time you will be feeling the old, restless urge and you might take a road that wasn't open if I didn't direct you.'

"He patted Wilfred loudly on the back a couple of times and Wilfred ducked the third pat and got out of the group, and the ladies all began to flurry their voices about the lovely June evening but wouldn't it be pleasanter inside, and Henrietta tragically called from the doorway to come at once, for God's sake, so they all went at once, with the men only half trailing, and inside we could hear 'em fixing chairs round and putting out a table for the poet to stand by, and so forth.

"Alonzo, however, had not trailed. He was over on the steps holding Beryl Mae Macomber by her new scarf and telling her how flowerlike her beauty was. And old Judge Ballard was holding about half the men, including Ben Sutton, while he made a speech. I hung back to listen. 'Sir,' he was saying to Ben, 'Secretary Seward some years since purchased your territory from Russia for seven million dollars despite the protests of a clamorous and purblind opposition. How niggardly seems that purchase price at this moment! For Alaska has perfected you, sir, if it did not produce you. Gentlemen, I feel that we dealt unfairly by Russia. But that is in the dead past. It is not too late, however, to tiptoe to the grillroom and offer a toast to our young sister of the snows.'

"There was subdued cheers and they tiptoed. Ben

Sutton was telling the judge that he felt highly com-
plimented, but it was a mistake to ring in that snow
stuff on Alaska. She'd suffered from it too long. He
was going on to paint Alaska as something like Ala-
bama—cooler nights, of course, but bracing. Alonzo
still had Beryl Mae by the scarf, telling her how flowerlike her beauty was.

"I went into the big room, picking a chair over by
the door so I could keep tabs on that grillroom. Only
three or four of the meekest husbands had come with
us. And Wilfred started. I'll do him the justice
to say he was game. The ladies thought anything
bordering on roughness was all over, but Wilfred
didn't. When he'd try to get a far-away look in his
eyes while he was reciting his poetry he couldn't get
it any farther away than the grillroom door. He was
nervous but determined, for there had been notice
given of a silver offering for him. He recited the
verses on the card and the ladies all thrilled up at
once, including Beryl Mae, who'd come in without
her scarf. They just clenched their hands and hung
on Wilfred's wild, free words.

"And after the poetry he kind of lectured about
how man had ought to break away from the vile
cities and seek the solace of great Mother Nature,
where his bruised spirit could be healed and the
veneer of civilization cast aside and the soul come
into its own, and things like that. And he went on to
say that out in the open the perspective of life is
broadened and one is a laughing philosopher as long

as the blue sky is overhead and the green grass underfoot. 'To lie,' says he, 'with relaxed muscles on the carpet of pine needles and look up through the gently swaying branches of majestic trees at the fleecy white clouds, dreaming away the hours far from the sordid activities of the market place, is one of the best nerve tonics in all the world.' It was an unfortunate phrase for Wilfred, because some of the husbands had tiptoed out of the grillroom to listen, and there was a hearty cheer at this, led by Jeff Tuttle. 'Sure! Some nerve tonic!' they called out, and laughed coarsely. Then they rushed back to the grillroom without tiptoeing.

"The disgraceful interruption was tactfully covered by Wilfred and his audience. He took a sip from the glass of water and went on to talk about the world's debt to poetry. Then I sneaked out to the grillroom myself. By this time the Chinaman had got tangled up with the orders and was putting out drinks every which way. And they was being taken willingly. Judge Ballard and Ben Sutton was now planting cotton in Alaska and getting good crops every year, and Ben was also promising to send the judge a lovely spotted fawnskin vest that an Indian had made for him, but made too small—not having more than six or eight fawns, I judged. And Alonzo had got a second start. Still he wasn't so bad yet, with Beryl Mae's scarf over his arm, and talking of the unparalleled beauties of Price's Addition to Red Gap, which he said he wouldn't trade even for the

whole of Alaska if it was offered to him to-morrow—
not that Ben Sutton wasn't the whitest soul God ever
made and he'd like to hear some one say different—
and so on.

"I mixed in with 'em and took a friendly drink
myself, with the aim of smoothing things down, but I
saw it would be delicate work.   About all I could do
was keep 'em reminded there was ladies present and
it wasn't a barroom where anything could be rightly
started.   Doc Martingale's feelings was running high,
too, account, I suppose, of certain full-hearted things
his wife had blurted out to him about the hypnotic
eyes of this here Nature lover.   He was quiet enough,
but vicious, acting like he'd love to do some dental
work on the poet that might or might not be painless for all he cared a hoot.   He was taking his
own drinks all alone, like clockwork—moody but
systematic.

"Then we hear chairs pushed round in the other
room and the chink of silver to be offered to the poet,
and Henrietta come out to give word for the refreshments to be served.   She found Alonzo in the hall-
way telling Beryl Mae how flowerlike her beauty was
and giving her the elk's tooth charm off his watch
chain.   Beryl Mae was giggling heartily until she
caught Henrietta's eye—like a cobra's.

"The refreshments was handed round peaceful
enough, with the ladies pressing sardine sandwiches
and chocolate cake and cups of coffee on to Wilfred
and asking him interesting questions about his ad-

venturous life in the open. And the plans was all
made for his class in poetry to be held at Henrietta's
house, where the lady subscribers for a few weeks
could come into contact with the higher realities of
life, at eight dollars for the course, and Wilfred was
beginning to cheer up again, though still subject to
dismay when one of the husbands would glare in at
him from the hall, and especially when Ben Sutton
would look in with his bulging and expressive eyes
and kind of bark at him.

"Then Ben Sutton come and stood in the doorway
till he caught Wilfred's eye and beckoned to him.
Wilfred pretended not to notice the first time, but
Ben beckoned a little harder, so Wilfred excused himself to the six or eight ladies and went out. It
seemed to me he first looked quick round him to make
sure there wasn't any other way out. I was standing
in the hall when Ben led him tenderly into the grillroom with two fingers.

"'Here is our well-known poet and *bon vivant*,'
says Ben to Alonzo, who had followed 'em in. So
Alonzo bristles up to Wilfred and glares at him and
says: 'All joking aside, is that one of my new shirts
you're wearing or is it not?'

"Wilfred gasped a couple times and says: 'Why,
as to that, you see, the madam insisted——'

"Alonzo shut him off. 'How dare you drag a
lady's name into a barroom brawl?' says he.

"'Don't shoot in here,' says Ben. 'You'd scare the
ladies.'

"Wilfred went pasty, indeed, thinking his host was going to gun him.

"'Oh, very well, I won't then,' says Alonzo. 'I guess I can be a·gentleman when necessary. But all joking aside, I want to ask him this: Does he consider poetry to be an accomplishment or a vice?'

"'I was going to put something like that to him myself, only I couldn't think of it,' says Doc Martingale, edging up and looking quite restrained and nervous in the arms. I was afraid of the doc. I was afraid he was going to blemish Wilfred a couple of times right there.

"'An accomplishment or a vice? Answer yes or no!' orders the judge in a hard voice.

"The poet looks round at 'em and attempts to laugh merrily, but he only does it from the teeth out.

"'Laugh on, my proud beauty!' says Ben Sutton. Then he turns to the bunch. 'What we really ought to do,' he says, 'we ought to make a believer of him right here and now.'

"Even then, mind you, the husbands would have lost their nerve if Ben hadn't took the lead. Ben didn't have to live with their wives so what cared he? Wilfred Lennox sort of shuffled his feet and smiled a smile of pure anxiety. He knew some way that this was nothing to cheer about.

"'I got it,' says Jeff Tuttle with the air of a thinker. 'We're cramping the poor cuss here. What he wants is the open road.'

"'What he really wants,' says Alonzo, 'is about

six bottles of my pure, sparkling beer, but maybe he'll take the open road if we show him a good one.'

"'He wants the open road—show him a good one!' yells the other husbands in chorus. It was kind of like a song.

"'I had meant to be on my way,' says Wilfred very cold and lofty.

"'You're here to-day and there to-morrow,' says Ben; 'but how can you be there to-morrow if you don't start from here now?—for the way is long and lonely.'

"'I was about to start,' says Wilfred, getting in a couple of steps toward the door.

"''Tis better so,' says Ben. 'This is no place for a county recorder's son, and there's a bully road out here open at both ends.'

"They made way for the poet, and a sickening silence reigned. Even the women gathered about the door of the other room was silent. They knew the thing had got out of their hands. The men closed in after Wilfred as he reached the steps. He there took his soft hat out from under his coat where he'd cached it. He went cautiously down the steps. Beryl Mae broke the silence.

"'Oh, Mr. Price,' says she, catching Alonzo by the sleeve, 'do you think he's really sincere?'

"'He is at this moment,' says Alonzo. 'He's behaving as sincerely as ever I saw a man behave.' And just then at the foot of the steps Wilfred made a tactical error. He started to run. The husbands and Ben Sutton gave the long yell and went in pursuit. Wilfred would have left them all if he hadn't run into the tennis net. He come down like a sack of meal.

"'There!' says Ben Sutton. 'Now he's done it—broke his neck or something. That's the way with some men—they'll try anything to get a laugh.'

"They went and picked the poet up. He was all right, only dazed.

"'But that's one of the roads that ain't open,' says Ben. 'And besides, you was going right toward the nasty old railroad that runs into the cramped haunts of men. You must have got turned round. Here'—he pointed out over the golf links—'it's off that way that Mother Nature awaits her wayward child. Miles and miles of her—all open. Doesn't your gypsy soul hear the call? This way for the hills and glens, thou star-eyed woodling!' and he gently led Wilfred off over the links, the rest of the men trailing after and making some word racket, believe me. They was all good conversationalists at the moment. Doc Martingale was wanting the poet to run into the tennis net again, just for fun, and Jeff Tuttle says make him climb a tree like the monkeys do in their native glades, but Ben says just keep him away from the railroad, that's all. Good Mother Nature will attend to the rest.

"The wives by now was huddled round the side of the clubhouse, too scared to talk much, just muttering incoherently and wringing their hands, and Beryl

Mae pipes up and says: 'Oh, perhaps I wronged him after all; perhaps deep down in his heart he was sincere.'

"The moon had come up now and we could see the mob with its victim starting off toward the Canadian Rockies. Then all at once they began to run, and I knew Wilfred had made another dash for liberty. Pretty soon they scattered out and seemed to be beating up the shrubbery down by the creek. And after a bit some of 'em straggled back. They paid no attention to us ladies, but made for the grillroom.

"'We lost him in that brush beyond the fifth hole,' says Alonzo. 'None of us is any match for him on level ground, but we got some good trackers and we're guarding the line to keep him headed off from the railroad and into his beloved hills.'

"'We should hurry back with refreshment for the faithful watchers,' says Judge Ballard. 'The fellow will surely try to double back to the railroad.'

"'Got to keep him away from the cramped haunts of business men,' says Alonzo brightly.

"'I wish Clay, my faithful old hound, were still alive,' says the judge wistfully.

"'Say, I got a peach of a terrier down to the house right now,' says Jeff Tuttle, 'but he's only trained for bear—I never tried him on poets.'

"'He might tree him at that,' says Doc Martingale.

"'Percy,' cries his wife, 'have you forgotten your manhood?'

"'Yes,' says Percy.

"'Darling,' calls Henrietta, 'will you listen to reason a moment?'

"'No,' says Alonzo.

"'It's that creature from Alaska leading them on,' says Mrs. Judge Ballard—'that overdressed drunken rowdy!'

"Ben Sutton looked right hurt at this. He buttoned his coat over his checked vest and says: 'I take that unkindly, madam—calling me overdressed. I selected this suiting with great care. It ain't nice to call me overdressed. I feel it deeply.'

"But they was off again before one thing could lead to another, taking bottles of hard liquor they had uncorked. 'The open road! The open road!' they yelled as they went.

"Well, that's about all. Some of the wives begun to straggle off home, mostly in tears, and some hung round till later. I was one of these, not wishing to miss anything of an absorbing character. Edgar Tomlinson went early, too. Edgar writes 'The Lounger in the Lobby' column for the *Recorder*, and he'd come out to report the entertainment; but at one o'clock he said it was a case for the sporting editor and he'd try to get him out before the kill.

"At different times one or two of the hunters would straggle back for more drink. They said the quarry was making a long detour round their left flank, trying his darndest to get to the railroad, but they had hopes. And they scattered out. Ever and anon you would hear the long howl of some lone drunkard that had got lost from the pack.

"About sunup they all found themselves at the railroad track about a mile beyond the clubhouse, just at the head of Stender's grade. There they was voting to picket the track for a mile each way when along come the four-thirty-two way freight. It had slowed up some making the grade, and while they watched it what should dart out from a bunch of scrub oak but the active figure of Wilfred Lennox. He made one of them iron ladders all right and was on top of a car when the train come by, but none of 'em dast jump it because it had picked up speed again.

"They said Wilfred stood up and shook both fists at 'em and called 'em every name he could lay his tongue to—using language so coarse you'd never think it could have come from a poet's lips. They could see his handsome face working violently long after they couldn't hear him. Just my luck! I'm always missing something.

"So they come grouching back to the clubhouse and I took 'em home to breakfast. When we got down to the table old Judge Ballard says: 'What might have been an evening of rare enjoyment was converted into a detestable failure by that cur. I saw from the very beginning that he was determined to spoil our fun.'

"'The joke is sure on us,' says Ben Sutton, 'but I bear him no grudge. In fact, I did him an injustice.

I knew he wasn't a poet, but I didn't believe he was even a hobo till he jumped that freight.'

"Alonzo was out in the hall telephoning Henrietta. We could hear his cheerful voice: 'No, Pettikins, no! It doesn't ache a bit. What's that? Of course I still do! You are the only woman that ever meant anything to me. What? What's that? Oh, I may have errant fancies now and again, like the best of men—you know yourself how sensitive I am to a certain type of flowerlike beauty—but it never touches my deeper nature. Yes, certainly, I shall be right up the very minute good old Ben leaves—to-morrow or next day. What's that? Now, now! Don't do that! Just the minute he leaves—G'-by.'

"And the little brute hung up on her!"

II

MA PETTINGILL AND THE
SONG OF SONGS

T HE hammock between the two jack pines at the back of the Arrowhead ranch house had lured me to mid-afternoon slumber. The day was hot and the morning had been toilsome— four miles of trout stream, rocky, difficult miles. And my hostess, Mrs. Lysander John Pettengill, had ridden off after luncheon to some remote fastness of her domain, leaving me and the place somnolent.

In the shadowed coolness, aching gratefully in many joints, I had plunged into the hammock's Lethe, swooning shamelessly to a benign oblivion. Dreamless it must long have been, for the shadows of ranch house, stable, hay barn, corral, and bunk house were long to the east when next I observed them. But I fought to this wakefulness through one of those dreams of a monstrous futility that sometimes madden us from sleep. Through a fearsome gorge a stream wound and in it I hunted one certain giant trout. Savagely it took the fly, but always the line broke when I struck; rather, it dissolved; there would be no resistance. And the giant fish mocked

me each time, jeered and flouted me, came brazenly
to the surface and derided me with antics weirdly
human.

Then, as I persisted, it surprisingly became a
musical trout. It whistled, it played a guitar, it
sang. How pathetic our mildly amazed acceptance
of these miracles in dreams! I was only the more determined to snare a fish that could whistle and sing
simultaneously, and accompany itself on a stringed
instrument, and was six feet in length. It was that by
now and ever growing. It seemed only an attractive
novelty and I still believed a brown hackle would
suffice. But then I became aware that this trout, to
its stringed accompaniment, ever whistled and sang
one song with a desperate intentness. That song was
"The Rosary." The fish had presumed too far.
"This," I shrewdly told myself, "is almost certainly
a dream." The soundless words were magic. Gorge
and stream vanished, the versatile fish faded to blue
sky showing through the green needles of a jack pine.
It was a sane world again and still, I thought,
with the shadows of ranch house, stable, hay
barn, corral, and bunk house going long to the
east. I stretched in the hammock. I tingled with
a lazy well-being. The world was still; but was it—
quite?

On a bench over by the corral gate crouched Buck
Devine, doing something needful to a saddle. And
as he wrought he whistled. He whistled "The Rosary"
shrilly and with much feeling. Nor was the world

still but for this. From the bunk house came the
mellow throbbing of a stringed instrument, the guitar
of Sandy Sawtelle, star rider of the Arrowhead, tem-
porarily withdrawn from a career of sprightly endeavour by a sprained ankle and solacing his retire-
ment with music. He was playing "The Rosary"—
very badly indeed, but one knew only too well what
he meant. The two performers were distant enough
to be no affront to each other. The hammock, less
happily, was midway between them.

I sat up with groans. I hated to leave the hammock.

"The trout also sang it," I reminded myself.
Followed the voice, a voice from the stable, the
cracked, whining tenor of a very aged vassal of the
Arrowhead, one Jimmie Time. Jimmie, I gathered,
was currying a horse as he sang, for each bar of the
ballad was measured by the double thud of a currycomb against the side of a stall. Whistle, guitar, and
voice now attacked the thing in differing keys and at
varying points. Jimmie might be said to prevail.
There was a fatuous tenderness in his attack and the
thudding currycomb gave it spirit. Nor did he slur
any of the affecting words; they clave the air with an
unctuous precision:

The ow-wurs I spu-hend with thu-hee, dee-yur heart,
      (The currycomb: Thud, thud!)
Are as a stru-hing of pur-rulls tuh me-e-e,
      (The currycomb: Thud, thud!)

Came a dramatic and equally soulful interpolation: "Whoa, dang you! You would, would you? Whoa-a-a, now!"

Again the melody:

I count them o-vurr, ev-ry one apar-rut,
   (Thud, thud!)
My ro-sah-ree—my ro-sah-ree!
   (Thud, thud!)

Buck Devine still mouthed his woful whistle and Sandy Sawtelle valiantly strove for the true and just accord of his six strings. It was no place for a passive soul. I parted swiftly from the hammock and made over the sun-scorched turf for the ranch house. There was shelter and surcease; doors and windows might be closed. The unctuous whine of Jimmie Time pursued me:

Each ow-wur a pur-rull, each pur-rull a prayer,
   (Thud, thud!)
Tuh stu-hill a heart in absence wru-hung,
   (Thud, thud!)

As I reached the hospitable door of the living-room I observed Lew Wee, Chinese chef of the Arrowhead, engaged in cranking one of those devices with a musical intention which I have somewhere seen advertised. It is an important-looking device in a polished mahogany case, and I recall in the advertisement I saw it was surrounded by a numerous enthralled-looking family in a costly drawing-room, while the ghost of Beethoven simpered above it in ineffable benignancy. Something now told me the worst, even as Lew Wee adjusted the needle to the revolving disk. I waited for no more than the opening orchestral strains. It is a leisurely rhythmed cacophony, and I had time to be almost beyond range ere the voice took up a tale I was hearing too often in one day. Even so I distantly perceived it to be a fruity contralto voice with an expert sob.

A hundred yards in front of the ranch house all was holy peace, peace in the stilled air, peace dreaming along the neighbouring hills and lying like a benediction over the wide river-flat below me, through which the stream wove a shining course. I exulted in it, from the dangers passed. Then appeared Mrs. Lysander John Pettengill from the fringe of cottonwoods, jolting a tired horse toward me over the flat.

"Come have some tea," she cordially boomed as she passed. I returned uncertainly. Tea? Yes. But—— However, the door would be shut and the Asiatic probably diverted.

As I came again to the rear of the ranch house Mrs. Pettengill, in khaki riding breeches, flannel shirt, and the hat of her trade, towered bulkily as an admirable figure of wrath, one hand on her hip, one poising a quirt viciously aloft. By the corral gate Buck Devine drooped cravenly above his damaged saddle; at the door of the bunk house Sandy Sawtelle tottered precariously on one foot, his guitar under his arm, a

look of guilty horror on his set face. By the stable
door stood the incredibly withered Jimmie Time,
shrinking a vast dismay.

"You hear me!" exploded the infuriated chate-
laine, and I knew she was repeating the phrase.

"Ain't I got to mend this latigo?" protested Buck
Devine piteously.

"You'll go up the gulch and beyond the dry fork
and mend it, if you whistle that tune again!"

Sandy Sawtelle rumpled his pink hair to further
disorder and found a few weak words for his conscious guilt.

"Now, I wasn't aiming to harm anybody, what with
with my game laig and shet up here like I am——"

"Well, my Lord! Can't you play a sensible tune
then?"

Jimmie Time hereupon behaved craftily. He
lifted his head, showing the face of a boy who had
somehow got to be seventy years old without ever
getting to be more than a boy, and began to whistle
softly and innocently—an air of which hardly anything could be definitely said except that it was not
"The Rosary." It was very flagrantly not "The Rosary." His craft availed him not.

"Yes, and you, too!" thundered the lady. "You
was the worst—you was singing. Didn't I hear you?
How many times I got to tell you? First thing you
know, you little reprobate——"

Jimmie Time cowered again. Visibly he took on
unbelievable years.

"Yes, ma'am," he whispered.

"Yes, ma'am," meekly echoed the tottering instrumentalist.

"Yes, ma'am," muttered Buck Devine, "not knowing you was anywheres near——"

"Makes no difference where I be—you hear me!"

Although her back was toward me I felt her glare. The wretches winced. She came a dozen steps toward me, then turned swiftly to glare again. They shuddered, even though she spoke no word. Then she came on, muttering hotly, and together we approached the ranch house. A dozen feet from the door she bounded ahead of me with a cry of baffled rage. I saw why. Lew Wee, unrecking her approach, was cold-bloodedly committing an encore. She sped through the doorway, and I heard Lew Wee's frightened squeal as he sped through another. When I stood in the room she was putting violent hands to the throat of the thing.

"The hours I spend with th——" The throttled note expired in a very dreadful squawk of agony. It was as if foul murder had been done, and done swiftly. The maddened woman faced me with the potentially evil disk clutched in her hands. In a voice that is a notable loss to our revivals of Greek tragedy she declaimed:

"Ain't it the limit?—and the last thing I done was to hide out that record up behind the clock where he couldn't find it!"

In a sudden new alarm and with three long steps

she reached the door of the kitchen and flung it open. Through a window thus exposed we beheld the offender. One so seldom thinks of the Chinese as athletes! Lew Wee was well down the flat toward the cottonwoods and still going strong.

"Ain't it the limit?" again demanded his employer. "Gosh all—excuse me, but they got me into such a state. Here I am panting like a tuckered hound. And now I got to make the tea myself. He won't dare come back before suppertime."

It seemed to be not yet an occasion for words from me. I tried for a look of intelligent sympathy. In the kitchen I heard her noisily fill a teakettle with water. She was not herself yet. She still muttered hotly. I moved to the magazine-littered table and affected to be taken with the portrait of a smug-looking prize Holstein on the first page of the *Stock Breeder's Gazette.*

The volcano presently seethed through the room and entered its own apartment.

Ten minutes later my hostess emerged with recovered aplomb. She had donned a skirt and a flowered blouse, and dusted powder upon and about her sunburned and rather blobby nose. Her crinkly gray hair had been drawn to a knot at the back of her grenadier's head. Her widely set eyes gleamed with the smile of her broad and competent mouth.

"Tea in one minute," she promised more than audibly as she bustled into the kitchen. It really came in five, and beside the tray she pleasantly relaxed. The cups were filled and a breach was made upon the cake she had brought. The tea was advertising a sufficient strength, yet she now raised the dynamics of her own portion.

"I'll just spill a hooker of this here Scotch into mine," she said, and then, as she did even so: "My lands! Ain't I the cynical old Kate! And silly! Letting them boys upset me that way with that there fool song." She decanted a saucerful of the reenforced tea and raised it to her pursed lips. "Looking at you!" she murmured cavernously and drank deep. She put the saucer back where nice persons leave theirs at all times. "Say, it was hot over on that bench to-day. I was getting out that bunch of bull calves, and all the time here was old Safety First mumbling round——"

This was rather promising, but I had resolved differently.

"That song," I insinuated. "Of course there are people——"

"You bet there are! I'm one of 'em, too! What that song's done to me—and to other innocent bystanders in the last couple weeks——"

She sighed hugely, drank more of the fortified brew —nicely from the cup this time—and fashioned a cigarette from materials at her hand.

In the flame of a lighted match Mrs. Pettengill's eyes sparkled with a kind of savage retrospection. She shrugged it off impatiently.

"I guess you thought I spoke a mite short when you asked about Nettie's wedding yesterday."

It was true. She had turned the friendly inquiry with a rather mystifying abruptness. I murmured politely. She blew twin jets of smoke from the widely separated corners of her generous mouth and then shrewdly narrowed her gaze to some distant point of narration.

"Yes, sir, I says to her, 'Woman's place is the home.' And what you think she come back with? That she was going to be a leader of the New Dawn. Yes, sir, just like that. Five feet one, a hundred and eight pounds in her winter clothes, a confirmed pickle eater—pretty enough, even if she is kind of peaked and spiritual looking—and going to lead the New Dawn.

"Where'd she catch it? My fault, of course, sending her back East to school and letting her visit the W. B. Hemingways, Mrs. H. being the well-known clubwoman like the newspapers always print under her photo in evening dress. That's how she caught it all right.

"I hadn't realized it when she first got back, except she was pale and faraway in the eyes and et pickles heavily at every meal—oh, mustard, dill, sour, sweet, anything that was pickles—and not enough meat and regular victuals. Gaunted she was, but I didn't suspect her mind was contaminated none till I sprung Chester Timmins on her as a good marrying bet. You know Chet, son of old Dave that has the Lazy Eight

Ranch over on Pipe Stone—a good, clean boy that'll have the ranch to himself as soon as old Dave dies of meanness, and that can't be long now. It was then she come out delirious about not being the pampered toy of any male—*male*, mind you! It seems when these hussies want to knock man nowadays they call him a male. And she rippled on about the freedom of her soul and her downtrod sisters and this here New Dawn.

"Well, sir, a baby could have pushed me flat with one finger. At first I didn' know no better'n to argue with her, I was that affrighted. 'Why, Nettie Hosford,' I says, 'to think I've lived to hear my only sister's only child talking in shrieks like that! To think I should have to tell one of my own kin that women's place is the home. Look at me,' I says—we was down in Red Gap at the time—'pretty soon I'll go up to the ranch and what'll I do there?'" I says.

"'Well, listen,' I says, 'to a few of the things I'll be doing: I'll be marking, branding, and vaccinating the calves, I'll be classing and turning out the strong cattle on the range. I'll be having the colts rid, breaking mules for haying, oiling and mending the team harness, cutting and hauling posts, tattooing the ears and registering the thoroughbred calves, putting in dams, cleaning ditches, irrigating the flats, setting out the vegetable garden, building fence, swinging new gates, overhauling the haying tools, receiving, marking, and branding the new two-year-old bulls, plowing and seeding grain for our work stock

and hogs, breaking in new cooks and blacksmiths'—I
was so mad I went on till I was winded. 'And that
ain't half of it,' I says. 'Women's work is never
done; her place is in the home and she finds so much
to do right there that she ain't getting any time to
lead a New Dawn. I'll start you easy,' I says; 'learn
you to bake a batch of bread or do a tub of washing—
something simple—and there's Chet Timmins, waiting to give you a glorious future as wife and mother
and helpmeet.'

"She just give me one look as cold as all arctics and
says, 'It's repellent'—that's all, just 'repellent.' I
see I was up against it. No good talking. Sometimes it comes over me like a flash when not to talk.
It does to some women. So I affected a light manner
and pretended to laugh it off, just as if I didn't see
scandal threatening—think of having it talked about
that a niece of my own raising was a leader of the New
Dawn!

"'All right,' I says, 'only, of course, Chet Timmins is a good friend and neighbour of mine, even if
he is a male, so I hope you won't mind his dropping in
now and again from time to time, just to say howdy
and eat a meal.' And she flusters me again with her
coolness.

"'No,' she says, 'I won't mind, but I know what
you're counting on, and it won't do either of you any
good. I'm above the appeal of a man's mere presence,' she says, 'for I've thrown off the age-long sub-
jection; but I won't mind his coming. I shall delight

to study him.   They're all alike, and one specimen is as good as another for that.   But neither of you need expect anything,' she says, 'for the wrongs of my sisters have armoured me against the grossness of mere sex appeal.'   Excuse me for getting off such things, but I'm telling you how she talked.

"'Oh, shucks!' I says to myself profanely, for all at once I saw she wasn't talking her own real thoughts but stuff she'd picked up from the well-known lady friends of Mrs. W. B. Hemingway.   I was mad all right; but the minute I get plumb sure mad I get wily. 'I was just trying you out,' I says.   'Of course you are right!'   'Of course I am,' says she, 'though I hardly expected you to see it, you being so hardened a product of the ancient ideal of slave marriage.'

"At them words it was pretty hard for me to keep on being wily, but I kept all right.   I kept beautifully. I just laughed and said we'd have Chet Timmins up for supper, and she laughed and said it would be amusing.

"And it was, or it would have been if it hadn't been so sad and disgusting.   Chet, you see, had plumb crumpled the first time he ever set eyes on her, and he's never been able to uncrumple.   He always choked up the minute she'd come into the room, and that night he choked worse'n ever because the little devil started in to lead him on—aiming to show me how she could study a male, I reckon.   He couldn't even ask for some more of the creamed potatoes without choking up—with her all the time using her eyes on him, and telling him how a great rough man like him scared 'poor little me.'   Chet's tan bleaches out a mite by the end of winter, but she kept his face exactly the shade of that new mahogany sideboard I got, and she told him several times that he ought to go see a throat specialist right off about that choking of his.

"And after supper I'm darned if she didn't lure him out onto the porch in the moonlight, and stand there sad looking and helpless, simply egging him on, mind you, her in one of them little squashy white dresses that she managed to brush against him—all in the way of cold study, mind you.   Say, ain't we the lovely tame rattlesnakes when we want to be! And this big husky lummox of a Chester Timmins—him she'd called a male—what does he do but stand safely at a distance of four feet in the grand romantic light of the full moon, and tell her vivaciously all about the new saddle he's having made in Spokane. And even then he not only chokes but he giggles. They do say a strong man in tears is a terrible sight. But a husky man giggling is worse—take it from one who has suffered.   And all the time I knew his heart was furnishing enough actual power to run a feed chopper.   So did she!

"'The creature is so typical,' she says when the poor cuss had finally stumbled down the front steps. 'He's a real type.'   Only she called it 'teep,' having studied the French language among other things. 'He is a teep indeed!' she says.

"I had to admit myself that Chester wasn't any self-starter. I saw he'd have to be cranked by an outsider if he was going to win a place of his own in the New Dawn. And I kept thinking wily, and the next P. M. when Nettie and I was downtown I got my hunch. You know that music store on Fourth Street across from the Boston Cash Emporium. It's kept by C. Wilbur Todd, and out in front in a glass case he had a mechanical banjo that was playing 'The Rosary' with variations when we come by. We stopped a minute to watch the machinery picking the strings and in a flash I says to myself, 'I got it! Eureka, California!' I says, 'it's come to me!'

"Of course that piece don't sound so awful tender when it's done on a banjo with variations, but I'd heard it done right and swell one time and so I says, 'There's the song of songs to bring foolish males and females to their just mating sense.'"

The speaker paused to drain her cup and to fashion another cigarette, her eyes dreaming upon far vistas.

"Ain't it fierce what music does to persons," she resumed. "Right off I remembered the first time I'd heard that piece—in New York City four years ago, in a restaurant after the theatre one night, where I'd gone with Mrs. W. B. Hemingway and her husband. A grand, gay place it was, with an orchestra. I picked at some untimely food and sipped a highball—they wouldn't let a lady smoke there— and what interested me was the folks that come in. Folks always do interest me something amazing.

Strange ones like that, I mean, where you set and try to figure out all about 'em, what kind of homes they got, and how they act when they ain't in a swell restaurant, and everything. Pretty soon comes a couple to the table next us and, say, they was just plain Mr. and Mrs. Mad. Both of 'em stall-fed. He was a large, shiny lad, with pink jowls barbered to death and wicked looking, like a well-known clubman or villain. The lady was spectacular and cynical, with a cold, thin nose and eyes like a couple of glass marbles. Her hair was several shades off a legal yellow and she was dressed! She would have made handsome loot, believe me—aigrette, bracelets, rings, dog collar, gold-mesh bag, vanity case—— Oh, you could see at a glance that she was one of them Broadway social favourites you read about. And both grouchy, like I said. He scowled till you knew he'd just love to beat a crippled step-child to death, and she—well, her work wasn't so coarse; she kept her mad down better. She set there as nice and sweet as a pet scorpion.

"'A scrap,' I says to myself, 'and they've only half finished. She's threatened to quit and he, the cowardly dog, has dared her to.' Plain enough. The waiter knew it soon as I did when he come to take their order. Wouldn't speak to each other. Talked through him; fought it out to something different for each one. Couldn't even agree on the same kind of cocktail. Both slamming the waiter—before they fought the order to a finish each had wanted to call the head waiter, only the other one stopped it.

"So I rubbered awhile, trying to figure out why such folks want to finish up their fights in a restaurant, and then I forgot 'em, looking at some other persons that come in. Then the orchestra started this song and I seen a lady was getting up in front to sing it. I admit the piece got me. It got me good. Really, ain't it the gooey mess of heart-throbs when you come right down to it? This lady singer was a good-looking sad-faced contralto in a low-cut black dress—and how she did get the tears out of them low notes! Oh, I quit looking at people while her chest was oozing out that music. And it got others, too. I noticed lots of 'em had stopped eating when I looked round, and there was so much clapping she had to get up and do it all over again. And what you think? In the middle of the second time I look over to these fighters, and darned if they ain't holding hands across the table; and more, she's she's got a kind of pitiful, crying smile on and he's crying right out—crying into his cold asparagus, plain as day.

"What more would you want to know about the powers of this here piece of music? They both spoke like human beings to the scared waiter when he come back, and the lad left a five-spot on the tray when he paid his check. Some song, yes?

"And all this flashed back on me when Nettie and I stood there watching this cute little banjo. So I says to myself, 'Here, my morbid vestal, is where I put you sane; here's where I hurl an asphyxiating bomb into the trenches of the New Dawn.' Out loud I only says, 'Let's go in and see if Wilbur has got some new records.'

" 'Wilbur?' says she, and we went in. Nettie had not met Wilbur.

"I may as well tell you here and now that C. Wilbur Todd is a shrimp. Shrimp I have said and shrimp I always will say. He talks real brightly in his way—he will speak words like an actor or something—but for brains! Say, he always reminds me of the dub friend of the great detective in the magazine stories, the one that goes along to the scene of the crime to ask silly questions and make fool guesses about the guilty one, and never even suspects who done the murder, till the detective tells on the last page when they're all together in the library.

"Sure, that's Wilbur. It would be an ideal position for him. Instead of which he runs this here music store, sells these jitney pianos and phonographs and truck like that. And serious! Honestly, if you seen him coming down the street you'd say, 'There comes one of these here musicians.' Wears long hair and a low collar and a flowing necktie and talks about his technique. Yes, sir, about the technique of working a machinery piano. Gives free recitals in the store every second Saturday afternoon, and to see him set down and pump with his feet, and push levers and pull handles, weaving himself back and forth, tossing his long, silken locks back and looking dreamily off into the distance, you'd think he was a Paderewski. As a matter of fact, I've seen Paderewski play and he don't make a tenth of the fuss Wilbur does. And after this recital I was at one Saturday he comes up to some of us ladies, mopping his pale brow, and he says, 'It does take it out of one! I'm always a nervous wreck after these little affairs of mine.' Would that get you, or would it not?

"So we go in the store and Wilbur looks up from a table he's setting at in the back end.

"'You find me studying some new manuscripts,' he says, pushing back the raven locks from his brow. Say, it was a weary gesture he done it with—sort of languid and world-weary. And what you reckon he meant by studying manuscripts? Why, he had one of these rolls of paper with the music punched into it in holes, and he was studying that line that tells you when to play hard or soft and all like that. Honest, that was it!

"'I always study these manuscripts of the masters conscientiously before I play them,' says he.

"Such is Wilbur. Such he will ever be. So I introduced him to Nettie and asked if he had this here song on a phonograph record. He had. He had it on two records. 'One by a barytone gentleman, and one by a mezzo-soprano,' says Wilbur. I set myself back for both. He also had it with variations on one of these punched rolls. He played that for us. It took him three minutes to get set right at the piano and to dust his fingers with a white silk handkerchief which he wore up his sleeve. And he played with great expression and agony and bending exercises, ever and anon tossing back his rebellious locks and fixing us with a look of pained ecstasy. Of course it sounded better than the banjo, but you got to have the voice with that song if you're meaning to do any crooked work. Nettie was much taken with it even so, and Wilbur played it another way. What he said was that it was another school of interpretation. It seemed to have its points with him, though he favoured the first school, he said, because of a certain almost rugged fidelity. He said the other school was marked by a tendency to idealism, and he pulled some of the handles to show how it was done. I'm merely telling you how Wilbur talked.

"Nettie listened very serious. There was a new look in her eyes. 'That song has got to her even on a machinery piano,' I says, 'but wait till we get the voice, with she and Chester out in the mischievous moonlight.' Wasn't I the wily old hound! Nettie sort of lingered to hear Wilbur, who was going good by this time. 'One must be the soul behind the wood and wire,' he says; 'one rather feels just that, or one remains merely a brutal mechanic.'

"'I understand,' says Nettie. 'How you must have studied!'

"'Oh, studied!' says Wilbur, and tossed his mane back and laughed in a lofty and suffering manner.

Studied! He'd gone one year to a business college in Seattle after he got out of high school!

"'I understand,' says Nettie, looking all reverent and buffaloed.

"'It is the price one must pay for technique,' says Wilbur. 'And to-day you found me in the mood. I am not always in the mood.'

"'I understand,' says Nettie.

"I'm just giving you an idea, understand. Then Wilbur says, 'I will bring these records up this evening if I may. The mezzo-soprano requires a radically different adjustment from the barytone.' 'My God!' thinks I, 'has he got technique on the phonograph, too!' But I says he must come by all means, thinking he could tend the machine while Nettie and Chester is out on the porch getting wise to each other.

"'There's another teep for you,' I says to Nettie when we got out of the place. 'He certainly is marked by tendencies,' I says. I meant it for a nasty slam at Wilbur's painful deficiencies as a human being, but she took it as serious as Wilbur took himself—which is some!

"'Ah, yes, the artist teep,' says she, 'the most complex, the most baffling of all.'

"That was a kind of a sickish jolt to me—the idea that something as low in the animal kingdom as Wilbur could baffle any one—but I thinks, 'Shucks! Wait till he lines up alongside of a regular human man like Chet Timmins!'

"I had Chet up to supper again. He still choked on words of one syllable if Nettie so much as glanced at him, and turned all sorts of painful colours like a cheap rug. But I keep thinking the piece will fix that all right.

"At eight o'clock Wilbur sifted in with his records and something else flat and thin, done up in paper that I didn't notice much at the time. My dear heart, how serious he was! As serious as—well, I chanced to be present at the house of mourning when the barber come to shave old Judge Armstead after he'd passed away—you know what I mean—kind of like him Wilbur was, talking subdued and cat-footing round very solemn and professional. I thought he'd never get that machine going. He cleaned it, and he oiled it, and he had great trouble picking out the right fibre needle, holding six or eight of 'em up to the light, doing secret things to the machine's inwards, looking at us sharp as if we oughtn't to be talking even then, and when she did move off I'm darned if he didn't hang in a strained manner over that box, like he was the one that was doing it all and it wouldn't get the notes right if he took his attention off.

"It was a first-class record, I'll say that. It was the male barytone—one of them pleading voices that get all into you. It wasn't half over before I seen Nettie was strongly moved, as they say, only she was staring at Wilbur, who by now was leading the orchestra with one graceful arm and looking absorbed and sodden, like he done it unconsciously.

Chester just set there with his mouth open, like something you see at one of these here aquariums.

"We moved round some when it was over, while Wilbur was picking out just the right needle for the other record, and so I managed to cut that lump of a Chester out of the bunch and hold him on the porch till I got Nettie out, too. Then I said 'Sh-h-h!' so they wouldn't move when Wilbur let the mezzo-soprano start. And they had to stay out there in the golden moonlight with love's young dream and every-thing. The lady singer was good, too. No use in talking, that song must have done a lot of heart work right among our very best families. It had me going again so I plumb forgot my couple outside. I even forgot Wilbur, standing by the box showing the lady how to sing.

"It come to the last—you know how it ends— 'To kiss the cross, sweetheart, to kiss the cross!' There was a rich and silent moment and I says, 'If that Chet Timmins hasn't shown himself to be a regular male teep by this time——' And here come Chet's voice, choking as usual, 'Yes, paw switched to Durhams and Herefords over ten years ago—you see Holsteins was too light; they don't carry the meat——' Honest! I'm telling you what I heard. And yet when they come in I could see that Chester had had tears in his eyes from that song, so still I didn't give in, especially as Nettie herself looked very exalted, like she wasn't at that minute giving two whoops in the bad place for the New Dawn.

"Nettie made for Wilbur, who was pushing back his hair with a weak but graceful sweep of the arm—it had got down before his face like a portière—and I took Chet into a corner and tried to get some of the just wrath of God into his heart; but, my lands! You'd have said he didn't know there was such a thing as a girl in the whole Kulanche Valley. He didn't seem to hear me. He talked other matters.

"'Paw thinks,' he says, 'that he might manage to take them hundred and fifty bull calves off your hands.' 'Oh, indeed!' I says. 'And does he think of buying 'em—as is often done in the cattle business —or is he merely aiming to do me a favour?' I was that mad at the poor worm, but he never knew. 'Why, now, paw says "You tell Maw Pettengill I might be willing to take 'em off her hands at fifty dollars a head,"' he says. 'I should think he might be,' I says, 'but they ain't bothering my hands the least little mite. I like to have 'em on my hands at anything less than sixty a head,' I says. 'Your pa,' I went on, 'is the man that started this here safety-first cry. Others may claim the honour, but it belongs solely to him.' 'He never said anything about that,' says poor Chester. 'He just said you was going to be short of range this summer.' 'Be that all too true, as it may be,' I says, 'but I still got my business faculties——' And I was going on some more, but just then I seen Nettie and Wilbur was awful thick over something he'd unwrapped from the other package he'd brought. It was neither more nor less than a big photo of C. Wilbur Todd. Yes, sir, he'd brought her one.

"'I think the artist has caught a bit of the real just there, if you know what I mean,' says Wilbur, laying a pale thumb across the upper part of the horrible thing.

"'I understand,' says Nettie, 'the real you was expressing itself.'

"'Perhaps,' concedes Wilbur kind of nobly. 'I dare say he caught me in one of my rarer moods. You don't think it too idealized?'

"'Don't jest,' says she, very pretty and severe. And they both gazed spellbound.

"'Chester,' I says in low but venomous tones, 'you been hanging round that girl worse than Grant hung round Richmond, but you got to remember that Grant was more than a hanger. He made moves, Chester, moves! Do you get me?'

"'About them calves,' says Chester, 'pa told me it's his honest opinion——'

"Well, that was enough for once. I busted up that party sudden and firm.

"'It has meant much to me,' says Wilbur at parting.

"'I understand,' says Nettie.

"'When you come up to the ranch, Miss Nettie,' says Chester, 'you want to ride over to the Lazy Eight, and see that there tame coyote I got. It licks your hand like a dog.'

"But what could I do, more than what I had done?

Nettie was looking at the photograph when I shut the door on 'em. 'The soul behind the wood and wire,' she murmurs. I looked closer then and what do you reckon it was? Just as true as I set here, it was Wilbur, leaning forward all negligent and patronizing on a twelve-hundred-dollar grand piano, his hair well forward and his eyes masterful, like that there noble instrument was his bond slave. But wait! And underneath he'd writ a bar of music with notes running up and down, and signed his name to it—not plain, mind you, though he can write a good business hand if he wants to, but all scrawly like some one important, so you couldn't tell if it was meant for Dutch or English. Could you beat that for nerve—in a day, in a million years?

"'What's Wilbur writing that kind of music for?' I asks in a cold voice. 'He don't know that kind. What he had ought to of written is a bunch of them hollow slats and squares like they punch in the only kind of music he plays,' I says.

"'Hush!' says Nettie. 'It's that last divine phrase, "To kiss the cross!"'"

"I choked up myself then. And I went to bed and thought. And this is what I thought: When you think you got the winning hand, keep on raising. To call is to admit you got no faith in your judgment. Better lay down than call. So I resolve not to say another word to the girl about Chester, but simply to press the song in on her. Already it had made her act like a human person. Of course I didn't worry none about Wilbur. The wisdom of the ages couldn't have done that. But I seen I had got to have a real first-class human voice in that song, like the one I had heard in New York City. They'll just have to clench, I think, when they hear a good A-number-one voice in it.

"Next day I look in on Wilbur and say, 'What about this concert and musical entertainment the North Side set is talking about giving for the starving Belgians?'

"'The plans are maturing,' he says, 'but I'm getting up a Brahms concerto that I have promised to play—you know how terrifically difficult Brahms is—so the date hasn't been set yet.'

"'Well, set it and let's get to work,' I says. 'There'll be you, and the North Side Ladies' String Quartet, and Ed Bughalter with a bass solo, and Mrs. Dr. Percy Hailey Martingale with the "Jewel Song" from Faust, and I been thinking,' I says, 'that we had ought to get a good professional lady concert singer down from Spokane.'

"'I'm afraid the expenses would go over our receipts,' says Wilbur, and I can see him figuring that this concert will cost the Belgians money instead of helping 'em; so right off I says, 'If you can get a good-looking, sad-faced contralto, with a low-cut black dress, that can sing "The Rosary" like it had ought to be sung, why, you can touch me for that part of the evening's entertainment.'

"Wilbur says I'm too good, not suspicioning I'm

just being wily, so he says he'll write up and fix it. And a couple days later he says the lady professional is engaged, and it'll cost me fifty, and he shows me her picture and the dress is all right, and she had a sad, powerful face, and the date is set and everything.

"Meantime, I keep them two records het up for the benefit of my reluctant couple: daytime for Nettie —she standing dreamy-eyed while it was doing, showing she was coming more and more human, understand—and evenings for both of 'em, when Chester Timmins would call. And Chet himself about the third night begins to get a new look in his eyes, kind of absent and desperate, so I thinks this here lady professional will simply goad him to a frenzy. Oh, we had some sad musical week before that concert! That was when this crazy Chink of mine got took by the song. He don't know yet what it means, but it took him all right; he got regular besotted with it, keeping the kitchen door open all the time, so he wouldn't miss a single turn. It took his mind off his work, too. Talk about the Yellow Peril! He got so locoed with that song one day, what does he do but peel and cook up twelve dollars' worth of the Piedmont Queen dahlia bulbs I'd ordered for the front yard. Sure! Served 'em with cream sauce, and we et 'em, thinking they was some kind of a Chinese vegetable.

"But I was saying about this new look in Chester's eyes, kind of far-off and criminal, when that song was playing. And then something give me a pause, as they say. Chet showed up one evening with his nails all manicured; yes, sir, polished till you needed smoked glasses to look at 'em. I knew all right where he'd been. I may as well tell you that Henry Lehman was giving Red Gap a flash of form with his new barber shop—tiled floor, plate-glass front, exposed plumbing, and a manicure girl from Seattle; yes, sir, just like in the great wicked cities. It had already turned some of our very best homes into domestic hells, and no wonder! Decent, God-fearing men, who'd led regular lives and had whiskers and grown children, setting down to a little spindle-legged table with this creature, dipping their clumsy old hands into a pink saucedish of suds and then going brazenly back to their innocent families with their nails glittering like piano keys. Oh, that young dame was bound to be a social pet among the ladies of the town, yes—no? She was pretty and neat figured, with very careful hair, though its colour had been tampered with unsuccessfully, and she wore little, blue-striped shirtwaists that fitted very close—you know —with low collars. It was said that she was a good conversationalist and would talk in low, eager tones to them whose fingers she tooled.

"Still, I didn't think anything of Chester resorting to that sanitary den of vice. All I think is that he's trying to pretty himself up for Nettie and maybe show her he can be a man-about-town, like them she has known in Spokane and in Yonkers, New York, at the select home of Mrs. W. B. Hemingway and her

husband.   How little we think when we had ought to
be thinking our darndest!   Me?   I just went on
playing them two records, the male barytone and the
lady mezzo, and trying to curse that Chinaman into
keeping the kitchen door shut on his cooking, with
Wilbur dropping in now and then so him and Nettie
could look at his photo, which was propped up against
a book on the centre table—one of them large three-
dollar books that you get stuck with by an agent and
never read—and Nettie dropping into his store now
and then to hear him practise over difficult bits from
his piece that he was going to render at the musical
entertainment for the Belgians, with him asking her
if she thought he shaded the staccato passage a mite
too heavy, or some guff like that.

"So here come the concert, with every seat sold and
the hall draped pretty with flags and cut flowers.
Some of the boys was down from the ranch, and you
bet I made 'em all come across for tickets, and old
Safety First—Chet's father—I stuck him for a dollar
one, though he had an evil look in his eyes.   That's
how the boys got so crazy about this here song.   They
brought that record back with 'em.   And Buck Devine, that I met on the street that very day of the
concert, he give me another kind of a little jolt.   He'd
been gossiping round town, the vicious way men do,
and he says to me:

"'That Chester lad is taking awful chances for a
man that needs his two hands at his work.   Of course
if he was a foot-racer or something like that, where he

didn't need hands——' 'What's all this?' I asks.
'Why,' says Buck, 'he's had his nails rasped down to
the quick till he almost screams if they touch anything, and he goes back for more every single day.
It's a wonder they ain't mortified on him already; and
say, it costs him six bits a throw and, of course, he
don't take no change from a dollar—he leaves the
extra two bits for a tip. Gee! A dollar a day for
keeping your nails tuned up—and I ain't sure he
don't have 'em done twice on Sundays. Mine ain't
never had a file teched to 'em yet,' he says. 'I see
that,' I says. 'If any foul-minded person ever
accuses you of it, you got abundant proofs of your
innocence right there with you. As for Chester,' I
says, 'he has an object.' 'He has,' says Buck. 'Not
what you think,' I says. 'Very different from that.
It's true,' I concedes, 'that he ought to take that
money and go to some good osteopath and have his
head treated, but he's all right at that. Don't you
set up nights worrying about it.' And I sent Buck
slinking off shamefaced but unconvinced, I could see.
But I wasn't a bit scared.

"Chet et supper with us the night of the concert
and took Nettie and I to the hall, and you bet I
wedged them two close in next each other when we
got to our seats. This was my star play. If they
didn't fall for each other now—— Shucks! They
had to. And I noticed they was more confidential
already, with Nettie looking at him sometimes almost respectfully.

"Well, the concert went fine, with the hired lady professional singer giving us some operatic gems in various foreign languages in the first part, and Ed Bughalter singing "A King of the Desert Am I, Ha, Ha!" very bass—Ed always sounds to me like moving heavy furniture round that ain't got any casters under it— and Mrs. Dr. Percy Hailey Martingale with the "Jewel Song" from Faust, that she learned in a musical conservatory at Pittsburgh, Pennsylvania, and "Coming Through the Rye" for an encore—holding the music rolled up in her hands, though the Lord knows she knew every word and note of it by heart—and the North Side Ladies' String Quartet, and Wilbur Todd, of course, putting on more airs than as if he was the only son of old man Piano himself, while he shifted the gears and pumped, and Nettie whispering that he always slept two hours before performing in public and took no nourishment but one cup of warm milk —just a bundle of nerves that way—and she sent him up a bunch of lilies tied with lavender ribbon while he was bowing and scraping, but I didn't pay no attention to that, for now it was coming.

"Yes, sir, the last thing was this here lady professional, getting up stern and kind of sweetish sad in her low-cut black dress to sing the song of songs. I was awful excited for a party of my age, and I see they was, too. Nettie nudged Chet and whispered, 'Don't you just love it?' And Chet actually says, 'I love it,' so no wonder I felt sure, when up to that time he'd hardly been able to say a word except about his pa being willing to take them calves for almost nothing. Then I seen his eyes glaze and point off across the hall, and darned if there wasn't this manicure party in a cheek little hat and tailored gown, setting with Mrs. Henry Lehman and her husband. But still I felt all right, because him and Nettie was nudging each other intimately again when Professor Gluckstein started in on the accompaniment—I bet Wilbur thinks the prof is awful old-fashioned, playing with his fingers that way; I know they don't speak on the street.

"So this lady just floated into that piece with all the heart stops pulled out, and after one line I didn't begrudge her a cent of my fifty. I just set there and thrilled. I could feel Nettie and Chet thrilling, too, and I says, 'There's nothing to it—not from now on.'

"The applause didn't bust loose till almost a minute after she'd kissed the cross in that rich brown voice of hers, and even then my couple didn't join in. Nettie set still, all frozen and star-eyed, and Chester was choking and sniffling awful emotionally. 'I've sure nailed the young fools,' I thinks. And, of course, this lady had to sing it again, and not half through was she when, sure enough, I glanced down sideways and Chet's right hand and her left hand is squirming together till they look like a bunch of eels. 'All over but the rice,' I says, and at that I felt so good and thrilled! I was thinking back to my own time when I was just husband-high, though that wasn't so little, Lysander John being a scant six foot

three—and our wedding tour to the Centennial and
the trip to Niagara Falls—just soaking in old memories
that bless and bind that this lady singer was calling
up—well, you could have had anything from me right
then when she kissed that cross a second time, just
pouring her torn heart out. 'Worth every cent of
that fifty,' I says.

"Then everybody was standing up and moving out
—wiping their eyes a lot of 'em was—so I push on
ahead quick, aiming to be more wily than ever and
leave my couple alone. They don't miss me, either.
When I look back, darned if they ain't kind of shaking hands right there in the hall. 'Quick work!' I
says. 'You got to hand it to that song.' Even then
I noticed Nettie was looking back to where Wilbur
was tripping down from the platform, and Chester
had his eyes glazed over on this manicure party.
Still, they was gripping each other's hands right there
before folks, and I think they're just a bit embarrassed. My old heart went right on echoing that
song as I pushed forward—not looking back again, I
was that certain.

"And to show you the mushy state I was in, here is
old Safety First himself leering at me down by the
door, with a clean shave and his other clothes on, and
he says all about how it was a grand evening's musical
entertainment and how much will the Belgians get
in cold cash, anyway, and how about them hundred
and fifty head of bull calves that he was willing to
take off my hands, and me, all mushed up by that

song as I am telling you, saying to him in a hearty manner, 'They're yours, Dave! Take 'em at your own price, old friend.' Honest, I said it just that way, so you can see. 'Oh, I'll be stuck on 'em at fifty a head,' says Dave, 'but I knew you'd listen to reason, we being such old neighbours.' 'I ain't heard reason since that last song,' I says. 'I'm listening to my heart, and it's a grand pity yours never learned to talk.' 'Fifty a head,' says the old robber.

"So, thus throwing away at least fifteen hundred dollars like it was a mere bagatelle or something, I walk out into the romantic night and beat it for home, wanting to be in before my happy couple reached there, so they'd feel free to linger over their parting. My, but I did feel responsible and dangerous, directing human destinies so brashly the way I had."

There was a pause, eloquent with unworded emotions.

Then "Human destinies, hell!" the lady at length intoned.

Hereupon I amazingly saw that she believed her tale to be done. I permitted the silence to go a minute, perhaps, while she fingered the cigarette paper and loose tobacco.

"And of course, then," I hinted, as the twin jets of smoke were rather viciously expelled.

"I should say so—'of course, then'—you got it. But I didn't get it for near an hour yet. I set up to my bedroom window in the dark, waiting excitedly, and pretty soon they slowly floated up to the front

gate, talking in hushed tones and gurgles. 'Male
and female created He them,' I says, flushed with
triumph. The moon wasn't up yet, but you hadn't
any trouble making out they was such. He was
acting outrageously like a male and she was suffering
it with the splendid courage which has long distinguished our helpless sex. And there I set, warming my old heart in it and expanding like one of them
little squeezed-up sponges you see in the drug-store
window which swells up so astonishing when you put
it in water. I wasn't impatient for them to quit, oh,
no! They seemed to clench and unclench and clench
again, as if they had all the time in the world—with
me doing nothing but applaud silently.

"After spending about twenty years out there they
loitered softly up the walk and round to the side door
where I'd left the light burning, and I slipped over to
the side window, which was also open, and looked
down on the dim fond pair, and she finally opened the
door softly and the light shone out."

Again Ma Pettengill paused, her elbows on the
arms of her chair, her shoulders forward, her gray
old head low between them. She drew a long breath
and rumbled fiercely:

"And the mushy fool me, forcing that herd of
calves on old Dave at that scandalous price—after
all, that's what really gaffed me the worst! My
stars! If I could have seen that degenerate old
crook again that night—but of course a trade's a
trade, and I'd said it. Ain't I the old silly!"

"The door opened and the light shone out——"
I gently prompted.

She erected herself in the chair, threw back her shoulders, and her wide mouth curved and lifted at the corners with the humour that never long deserts this woman.

"Yep! That light flooded out its golden rays on the reprehensible person of C. Wilbur Todd," she crisply announced. "And like they say in the stories, little remains to be told.

"I let out a kind of strangled yell, and Wilbur beat it right across my new lawn, and I beat it downstairs. But that girl was like a sleepwalker—not to be talked to, I mean, like you could talk to persons.

"'Aunty,' she says in creepy tones, 'I have brought myself to the ultimate surrender. I know the chains are about me, already I feel the shackles, but I glory in them.' She kind of gasped and shivered in horrible delight. 'I've kissed the cross at last,' she mutters.

"I was so weak I dropped into a chair and I just looked at her. At first I couldn't speak, then I saw it was no good speaking. She was free, white, and twenty-one. So I never let on. I've had to take a jolt or two in my time. I've learned how. But finally I did manage to ask how about Chet Timmins.

"'I wronged dear Chester,' she says. 'I admit it freely. He has a heart of gold and a nature in a thousand. But, of course, there could never be anything between him and a nature like mine; our

egos function on different planes,' she says. 'Dear
Chester came to see it, too.   It's only in the last week
we've come to understand each other.   It was really
that wonderful song that brought us to our mutual
knowledge.   It helped us to understand our mutual
depths better than all the ages of eternity could have
achieved.'   On she goes with this mutual stuff, till
you'd have thought she was reading a composition
or something.   'And dear Chester is so radiant in
his own new-found happiness,' she says.   'What!'
I yells, for this was indeed some jolt.

"'He has come into his own,' she says.   'They
have eloped to Spokane, though I promised to observe secrecy until the train had gone.   A very
worthy creature I gather from what Chester tells me,
a Miss Macgillicuddy——'

"'Not the manicure party?' I yells again.

"'I believe she has been a wage-earner,' says
Nettie.   'And dear Chester is so grateful about
that song.   It was her favourite song, too, and it
seemed to bring them together, just as it opened my
own soul to Wilbur.   He says she sings the song very
charmingly herself, and he thought it preferable
that they be wed in Spokane before his father objected.   And oh, aunty, I do see how blind I was to
my destiny, and how kind you were to me in my
blindness—you who had led the fuller life as I shall
lead it at Wilbur's side.'

"'You beat it to your room,' I orders her, very
savage and disorganized.   For I had stood about

all the jolts in one day that God had meant me to. And so they was married, Chester and his bride attending the ceremony and Oscar Teetz' five-piece orchestra playing the——" She broke off, with a suddenly blazing glance at the disk, and seized it from the table rather purposefully. With a hand firmly at both edges she stared inscrutably at it a long moment.

"I hate to break the darned thing," she said musingly at last. "I guess I'll just lock it up. Maybe some time I'll be feeling the need to hear it again. I know I can still be had by it if all the circumstances is right."

Still she stared at the thing curiously.

"Gee! It was hot getting them calves out to-day, and old Safety First moaning about all over the place how he's being stuck with 'em, till more than once I come near forgetting I was a lady—and, oh, yes"— she brightened—"I was going to tell you. After it was all over, Wilbur, the gallant young tone poet, comes gushing up to me and says, 'Now, aunty, always when you are in town you must drop round and break bread with us.' Aunty, mind you, right off the reel. 'Well,' I says, 'if I drop round to break any bread your wife bakes I'll be sure to bring a hammer.' I couldn't help it. He'll make a home for the girl all right, but he does something sinful to my nerves every time he opens his face. And then coming back here, where I looked for God's peace and quiet, and being made to hear that darned song every time I turned round!

"I give orders plain enough, but say, it's like a brush fire—you never know when you got it stamped out."

From the kitchen came the sound of a dropped armful of stove wood. Hard upon this, the unctuous whining tenor of Jimmie Time:

Oh-h-h mem-o-reez thu-hat blu-hess and bu-hurn!

"You, Jimmie Time!" It is a voice meant for Greek tragedy and a theatre open to the heavens. I could feel the terror of the aged vassal.

"Yes, ma'am!" The tone crawled abasingly. "I forgot myself."

I was glad, and I dare say he had the wit to be, that he had not to face the menace of her glare.

III

THE REAL PERUVIAN DOUGHNUTS

THE affairs of Arrowhead Ranch are administered by its owner, Mrs. Lysander John Pettengill, through a score or so of hired experts. As a trout-fishing guest of the castle I found the retainers of this excellent feudalism interesting enough and generally explicable. But standing out among them, both as a spectacle and by reason of his peculiar activities, is a shrunken little man whom I would hear addressed as Jimmie Time. He alone piqued as well as interested. There was a tang to all the surmises he prompted in me.

I have said he is a man; but wait! The years have had him, have scoured and rasped and withered him; yet his face is curiously but the face of a boy, his eyes but the fresh, inquiring, hurt eyes of a boy who has been misused for years threescore. Time has basely done all but age him. So much for the wastrel as Nature has left him. But Art has furthered the piquant values of him as a spectacle.

In dress, speech, and demeanour Jimmie seems to be of the West, Western—of the old, bad West of informal vendetta, when a man's increase of years might lie squarely on his quickness in the "draw";

when he went abundantly armed by day and slept
lightly at night—trigger fingers instinctively crooked.
Of course such days have very definitely passed;
wherefore the engaging puzzle of certain survivals
in Jimmie Time—for I found him still a two-gun man.
He wore them rather consciously sagging from his
lean hips—almost pompously, it seemed.   Nor did he
appear properly unconscious of his remaining attire—
of the broad-brimmed hat, its band of rattlesnake
skin; of the fringed buckskin shirt, opening gallantly
across his pinched throat; of his corduroy trousers,
fitting bedraggled; of his beautiful beaded moccasins.

He was perfect in detail—and yet he at once
struck me as being too acutely aware of himself.
Could this suspicion ensue, I wondered, from the cir-
cumstance that the light duties he discharged in and
about the Arrowhead Ranch house were of a semi-
domestic character; from a marked incongruity in the
sight of him, full panoplied for homicide, bearing arm-
fuls of wood to the house; or, with his wicked hat
pulled desperately over a scowling brow, and still
with his flaunt of weapons, engaging a sinkful of
soiled dishes in the kitchen under the eyes of a mere
unarmed Chinaman who sat by and smoked an easy
cigarette at him, scornful of firearms?

There were times, to be sure, when Jimmie's behaviour was in nice accord with his dreadful appearance—as when I chanced to observe him late the
second afternoon of my arrival.   Solitary in front of
the bunk house, he rapidly drew and snapped his side

arms at an imaginary foe some paces in front of him.
They would be simultaneously withdrawn from their
holsters, fired from the hip and replaced, the performer snarling viciously the while. The weapons
were unloaded, but I inferred that the foe crumpled
each time.

Then the old man varied the drama, vastly in-
creasing the advantage of the foe and the peril of his
own emergency by turning a careless back on the
scene. The carelessness was only seeming. Swiftly
he wheeled, and even as he did so twin volleys
came from the hip. It was spirited—the weapons
seemed to smoke; the smile of the marksman was
evil and masterly. Beyond all question the foe had
crumpled again, despite his tremendous advantage of
approach.

I drew gently near before the arms were again
holstered and permitted the full exposure of my admiration for this readiness of retort under difficulties.
The puissant one looked up at me with suspicion,
hostile yet embarrassed. I stood admiring ingenu-
ously, stubborn in my fascination. Slowly I won
him. The coldness in his bright little eyes warmed
to awkward but friendly apology.

"A gun fighter lets hisself git stiff," he winningly
began; "then, first thing he knows, some fine day—
crack! Like that! All his own fault, too, 'cause he
ain't kep' in trim." He jauntily twirled one of the
heavy revolvers on a forefinger. "Not me, though,
pard! Keep m'self up and comin', you bet! Ketch

me not ready to fan the old forty-four! I guess not!
Some has thought they could. Oh, yes; plenty has
thought they could. Crack! Like that!" He
wheeled, this time fatally intercepting the foe as he
treacherously crept round a corner of the bunk house.
"Buryin' ground for you, mister! That's all—buryin' ground!"

The desperado replaced one of the weapons and
patted the other with grisly affection. In the excess
of my admiration I made bold to reach for it. He re-
linquished it to me with a mother's yearning. And
all too legible in the polished butt of the thing were
notches! Nine sinister notches I counted—not
fresh notches, but emphatic, eloquent, chilling. I
thrust the bloody record back on its gladdened
owner.

"Never think it to look at me?" said he as our eyes
hung above that grim bit of bookkeeping.

"Never!" I warmly admitted.

"Me—I always been one of them quiet, mild-
mannered ones that you wouldn't think butter would
melt in their mouth—jest up to a certain point. Lots
of 'em fooled that way about me—jest up to a certain
point, mind you—then, crack! Buryin' ground—
that's all! Never go huntin' trouble—understand?
But when it's put on me—say!"

He lovingly replaced the weapon—with its mortu-
ary statistics—doffed the broad-brimmed hat with its
snake-skin garniture, and placed a forefinger athwart
an area of his shining scalp which is said by a certain

pseudo-science to shield several of man's more spiritual attributes. The finger traced an ancient but still evil-looking scar.

"One creased me there," he confessed—"a depity marshal—that time they had a reward out for me, dead or alive."

I was for details.

"What did you do?"

Jimmie Time stayed laconic.

"Left him there—that's all!"

It was arid, yet somehow informing. It conveyed to me that a marshal had been cleverly put to needing a new deputy.

"Burying ground?" I guessed.

"That's all!" He laughed venomously—a short, dry, restrained laugh. "They give me a nickname," said he. "They called me Little Sure Shot. No wonder they did! Ho! I should think they would of called me something like that." He lifted his voice. "Hey! Boogles!"

I had been conscious of a stooping figure in the adjacent vegetable garden. It now became erect, a figure of no distinction—short, rounded, decked in carelessly worn garments of no elegance. It slouched inquiringly toward us between rows of sprouted corn. Then I saw that the head surmounting it was a noble head. It was uncovered, burnished to a half-circle of grayish fringe; but it was shaped in the grand manner and well borne, and the full face of it was beautified by features of a very Roman perfection.

It was the face of a judge of the Supreme Court or the face of an ideal senator. His large grave eyes bathed us in a friendly regard; his full lips of an orator parted with leisurely and promising unction. I awaited courtly phrases, richly rounded periods.

"A regular hell-cat—what he is!"

Thus vocalized the able lips. Jimmie Time glowed modestly.

"Show him how I can shoot," said he.

The amazing Boogles waddled—yet with dignity— to a point ten paces distant, drew a coin from the pocket of his dingy overalls, and spun it to the blue of heaven. Ere it fell the deadly weapon bore swiftly on it and snapped.

"Crack!" said the marksman grimly.

His assistant recovered the coin, scrutinized it closely, rubbed a fat thumb over its supposedly dented surface, and again spun it. The desperado had turned his back. He drew as he wheeled, and again I was given to understand that his aim had been faultless.

"Good Little Sure Shot!" declaimed Boogles fulsomely.

"Hold it in your hand oncet," directed Little Sure Shot. The intrepid assistant gallantly extended the half dollar at arm's length between thumb and finger and averted his statesman's face with practiced apprehension. "Crack!" said Little Sure Shot, and the coin seemed to be struck from the unscathed hand. "Only nicked the aidge of it," said he, genially deprecating. "I don't like to take no chancet with the lad's mitt."

It had indeed been a pretty display of sharpshooting—and noiseless.

"Had me nervous, you bet, first time he tried that," called Boogles. "Didn't know his work then. Thought sure he'd wing me."

Jimmie Time loftily ejected imaginary shells from his trusty firearm and seemed to expel smoke from its delicate interior. Boogles waddled his approach.

"Any time they back Little Sure Shot up against the wall they want to duck," said he warmly. "He has 'em hard to find in about a minute. Tell him about that fresh depity marshal, Jimmie."

"I already did," said Jimmie.

"Ain't he the hell-cat?" demanded Boogles, mopping a brow that Daniel Webster would have observed with instant and perhaps envious respect.

"I been a holy terror in my time, all right, all right!" admitted the hero. "Never think it to look at me though. One o' the deceivin' kind till I'm put upon; then—good-night!"

"Jest like that!" murmured Boogles.

"Buryin' ground—that's all." The lips of the bad man shut grimly on this.

"Say," demanded Boogles, "on the level, ain't he the real Peruvian doughnuts? Don't he jest make 'em all hunt their——" The tribute was unfinished.

"You ol' Jim! You ol' Jim Time!" Shrilly this came from Lew Wee, Chinese cook of the Arrowhead framed in the kitchen doorway of the ranch house. He brandished a scornful and commanding dish towel at the bad man, who instantly and almost cravenly cowered under the distant assault. The garment of his old bad past fell from him, leaving him as one exposed in the market-place to the scornful towels of Chinamen. "You run, ol' Jim Time! How you think catch 'um din' not have wood?"

"Now I was jest goin' to," mumbled Jimmie Time; and he amazingly slunk from the scene of his late triumphs toward the open front of a woodhouse.

His insulter turned back to the kitchen with a final affronting flourish of the towel. The whisper of Boogles came hoarsely to me: "Some of these days Little Sure Shot'll put a dose o' cold lead through that Chink's heart."

"Is he really dangerous?" I demanded.

"Dangerous!" Boogles choked warmly on this. "Let me tell you, that old boy is the real Peruvian doughnuts, and no mistake! Some day there won't be so many Chinks round this dump. No, sir-ee! That little cutthroat'll have another notch in his gun."

The situation did indeed seem to brim with the cheerfullest promise; yet something told me that Little Sure Shot was too good, too perfect. Something warned me that he suffered delusions of grandeur—that he fell, in fact, somewhat short of being the real doughnuts, either of a Peruvian or any other valued sort.

Nor had many hours passed ere it befell emphatically even so. There had been the evening meal, followed by an hour or so of the always pleasing and often instructive talk of my hostess, Mrs. Lysander John Pettengill, who has largely known life for sixty years and found it entertaining and good. And we had parted at an early nine, both tired from the work and the play that had respectively engaged us the day long.

My candle had just been extinguished when three closely fired shots cracked the vast stillness of the night. Ensued vocal explosions of a curdling shrillness from the back of the house. One instantly knew them to be indignant and Chinese. Caucasian ears gathered this much. I looked from an open window as the impassioned cries came nearer. The lucent moon of the mountains flooded that side of the house, and starkly into its light from round the nearest corner struggled Lew Wee, the Chinaman. He shone refulgent, being yet in the white or full-dress uniform of his calling.

In one hand he held the best gun of Jimmie Time; in the other—there seemed to be a well-gripped connection with the slack of a buckskin shirt— writhed the alleged real doughnuts of a possibly Peruvian character. The captor looked aloft and remained vocal, waving the gun, waving Jimmie Time, playing them together as cymbals, never loosening them. It was fine. It filled the eye and appeased the deepest longings of the ear.

Then from a neighbouring window projected the heroic head and shoulders of my hostess, and there boomed into the already vivacious libretto a passionate barytone, or thereabout, of sterling timbre.

"What in the name of——"

I leave it there. To do so is not only kind but necessary. The most indulgent censor that ever guarded the columns of a print intended for young and old about the evening lamp would swiftly delete from this invocation, if not the name of Deity itself, at least the greater number of the attributes with which she endowed it. A few were conventional enough, but they served only to accentuate others that were too hastily selected in the heat of this crisis. Enough to say that the lady overbore by sheer mass of tone production the strident soprano of Lew Wee, controlling it at length to a lucid disclosure of his grievance.

From the doorway of his kitchen, inoffensively proffering a final cigarette to the radiant night, he had been the target of three shots with intent to kill. He submitted the weapon. He submitted the writhing assassin.

"I catch 'um!" he said effectively, and rested his case.

"Now—I aimed over his head." It was Jimmie Time alias Little Sure Shot, and he whimpered the words. "I jest went to play a sell on him."

The voice of the judge boomed wrathfully on this:

"You darned pestering mischief, you! Ain't I

forbid you time and again ever to load them guns?
Where'd you get the ca'tridges?"

"Now—I found 'em," pleaded the bad man. "I
did so; I found 'em."

"Cooned 'em, you mean!" thundered the judge.
"You cooned 'em from Buck or Sandy. Don't tell
me, you young reprobate!"

"He all like bad man," submitted the prosecution.
"I tell 'um catch stlovewood; he tell 'um me: 'You
go to haitch!' I tell 'um: 'You ownself go to haitch!
He say: 'I flan you my gun plitty soon!' He do."

"I aimed over the coward's head," protested the
defendant.

"Can happen!" sanely objected the prosecution.

"Ain't I told you what I'd do if you loaded them
guns?" roared the judge. "Gentle, limping, bald-
headed——" [Deleted by censor.] "How many
more times I got to tell you? Now you know what
you'll get. You'll get your needings—that's what
you'll get! All day to-morrow! You hear me?
You'll wear 'em all day to-morrow! Put 'em on
first thing in the morning and wear 'em till sundown.
No hiding out, neither! Wear 'em where folks can
see what a bad boy you are. And swearing, too!
I got to be 'shamed of you! Yes, sir! Everybody'll
know how 'shamed I am to have a tough kid like
you on the place. I won't be able to hold my head
up. You wear 'em!"

"I—I—I aimed above——" Jimmie Time broke
down. He was weeping bitterly. His captor re-

leased him with a final shake, and he brought a fore-
arm to his streaming eyes.

"You'll wear 'em all day to-morrow!" again thundered the judge as the culprit sobbed a stumbling
way into obscurity.

"You'self go to haitch!" the unrelenting com-
plainant called after him.

The judge effected a rumbling withdrawal. The
night was again calm. Then I slept on the problem
of the Arrowhead's two-gun bad man. It seemed
now pretty certain that the fatuous Boogles had
grossly overpraised him. I must question his being
the real doughnuts of any sort—even the mildest—
much less the real Peruvian. But what was "'em"
that in degrading punishment and to the public
shame of the Arrowhead he must wear on the morrow?
What, indeed, could "'em" be?

I woke, still pondering the mystery. Nor could
I be enlightened during my breakfast, for this was
solitary, my hostess being long abroad to far places
of the Arrowhead, and the stolid mask of Lew Wee
inviting no questions.

Breakfast over, I stationed myself in the bracing
sunlight that warmed the east porch and aimlessly
overhauled a book of flies. To three that had proved
most popular in the neighbouring stream I did small
bits of mending, ever with a questing eye on adjacent
outbuildings, where Little Sure Shot—*née* Time—
might be expected to show himself, wearing "'em."

A blank hour elapsed. I no longer affected occu-

pation with the flies. Jimmie Time was irritating me.
Had he not been specifically warned to "wear 'em"
full shamefully in the public eye? Was not the
public eye present, avid? Boogles I saw intermit-
tently among beanpoles in the garden. He appeared
to putter, to have no care or system in his labour.
And at moments I noticed he was dropping all pretense of this to stand motionless, staring intently at
the shut door of the stable.

Could his fallen idol be there,. I wondered? Purposefully I also watched the door of the stable.
Presently it opened slightly; then, with evident infinite caution, it was pushed outward until it hung
half yawning. A palpitant moment we gazed, Boogles
and I. Then shot from the stable gloom an as-
tounding figure in headlong flight. Its goal appeared to be the bunk house fifty yards distant; but
its course was devious, laid clearly with a view to
securing such incidental brief shelter as would be
afforded by the corral wall, by a meagre clump of
buck-brush, by a wagon, by a stack of hay. Good
time was made, however. The fugitive vanished
into the bunk house and the door of that structure
was slammed to. But now the small puzzle I had
thought to solve had grown to be, in that brief space
—easily under eight seconds—a mystery of enormous,
of sheerly inhuman dimensions. For the swift and
winged one had been all too plainly a correctly uniformed messenger boy of the Western Union Telegraph Company—that blue uniform with metal

buttons, with the corded red at the trouser sides, the flat cap fronted by a badge of nickel—unthinkable, yet there. And the speedy bearer of this scenic investiture had been the desperate, blood-letting, two-gun bad man of the Arrowhead.

It was a complication not to be borne with any restraint. I hastened to stand before the shut door of the sanctuary. It slept in an unpromising stillness. Invincibly reticent it seemed, even when the anguished face of Jimmie Time, under that incredible cap with its nickeled badge, wavered an instant back of the grimy window—wavered and vanished with an effect of very stubborn finality. I would risk no defeat there. I passed resolutely on to Boogles, who now most diligently trained up tender young bean vines in the way they should go.

"Why does he hide in there?" I demanded in a loud, indignant voice. I was to have no nonsense about it.

Boogles turned on me the slow, lofty, considering regard of a United States senator submitting to photography for publication in a press that has no respect for private rights. He lacked but a few clothes and the portico of a capitol. Speech became immanent in him. One should not have been surprised to hear him utter decorative words meant for the rejoicing and incitement of voters. Yet he only said—or started to say:

"Little Sure Shot'll get that Chink yet! I tell you, now, that old boy is sure the real Peruvian——"

This was absurdly too much. I then and there opened on Boogles, opened flooding gates of wrath and scorn on him—for him and for his idol of clay who, I flatly told him, could not be the real doughnuts of any sort. As for his being the real Peruvian—— Faugh!

Often I had wished to test in speech the widely alleged merits of this vocable. I found it do all that has been claimed for it. Its effect on Boogles was so withering that I used it repeatedly in the next three minutes. I even faughed him twice in succession, which is very insulting and beneficial indeed, and has a pleasant feel on the lips.

"And now then," I said, "if you don't give me the truth of this matter here and now, one of us two is going to be mighty sorry for it."

In the early moments of my violence Boogles had protested weakly; then he began to quiver perilously. On this I soothed him, and at the precisely right moment I cajoled. I lured him to the bench by the corral gate, and there I conferred costly cigarettes on him as man to man. Discreetly then I sounded for the origins of a certain bad man who had a way— even though they might crease him—of leaving deputy marshals where he found them. Boogles smoked one of the cigarettes before he succumbed; but first:

"Let me git my work," said he, and was off to the bunk house.

I observed his part in an extended parley before

the door was opened to him. He came to me on the bench a moment later, bearing a ball of scarlet yarn, a large crochet hook of bone, and something begun in the zephyr but as yet without form.

"I'm making the madam a red one for her birthday," he confided.

He bent his statesman's head above the task and wrought with nimble fingers the while he talked. It was difficult, this talk of his, scattered, fragmentary; and his mind would go from it, his voice expire untimely. He must be prompted, recalled, questioned. His hands worked with a very certain skill, but in his narrative he dropped stitches. Made to pick these up, the result was still a droning monotony burdened with many irrelevancies. I am loath to transcribe his speech. It were better reported with an eye strictly to salience.

You may see, then—and I hope with less difficulty than I had in seeing—Jimmie Time and Boogles on night duty at the front of the little Western Union Office off Park Row in the far city of New York. The law of that city is tender to the human young. Night messenger boys must be adults. It is one of the preliminary shocks to the visitor—to ring for the messenger boy of tradition and behold in his uniform a venerable gentleman with perhaps a flowing white beard. I still think Jimmie Time and Boogles were beating the law—on a technicality. Of course Jimmie was far descended into the vale of years, and even Boogles was forty—but adults!

It is three o'clock of a warm spring morning. The two legal adults converse in whispers, like bad boys kept after school. They whisper so as not to waken the manager, a blasé, mature youth of twenty who sleeps expertly in the big chair back of the railing. They whisper of the terrific hazards and the precarious rewards of their adventurous calling. The hazards are nearly all provided by the youngsters who come on the day watch—hardy ruffians of sixteen or so who not only "pick on" these two but, with sportive affectations, often rob them, when they change from uniform to civilian attire, of any spoil the night may have brought them. They are powerless against these aggressions. They can but whisper their indignation.

Boogles eyed the sleeping manager.

"I struck it fine to-night, Jimmie!" he whispered. Jimmie mutely questioned. "Got a whole case note. You know that guy over to the newspaper office—the one that's such a tank drama—he had to send a note up to a girl in a show that he couldn't be there."

"That tank drama? Sure, I know him. He kids me every time he's stewed."

"He kids me, too, something fierce; and he give me the case note."

"Them strong arms'll cop it on you when they get here," warned Jimmie.

"Took my collar off and hid her on the inside of it. Oh, I know tricks!"

"Chee! You're all to the Wall Street!"

"I got to look out for my stepmother, too. She'd crown me with a chair if she thought I held out on her. Beans me about every day just for nothing anyway."

"Don't you stand for it!"

"Yah! All right for you to talk. You're the lucky guy. You're an orphan. S'pose you had a stepmother! I wish I was an orphan."

Jimmie swelled with the pride of orphanship.

"Yes; I'd hate to have any parents knocking me round," he said. "But if it ain't a stepmother then it's somebody else that beans you. A guy in this burg is always getting knocked round by somebody."

"Read some more of the novel," pleaded Boogles, to change the distressing topic.

Jimmie drew a tattered paper romance from the pocket of his faded coat and pushed the cap back from his seamed old forehead. It went back easily, having been built for a larger head than his. He found the place he had marked at the end of his previous half-hour with literature. Boogles leaned eagerly toward him. He loved being read to. Doing it himself was too slow and painful:

"'No,' said our hero in a clear, ringing voice; 'all your tainted gold would not keep me here in the foul, crowded city. I must have the free, wild life of the plains, the canter after the Texas steers, and the fierce battles with my peers. For me the boundless, the glorious West!'"

"Chee! It must be something grand—that wild

life!" interrupted Boogles. "That's the real stuff—
the cowboy and trapper on them peraries, hunting
bufflers and Injuns. I seen a film——"

Jimmie Time frowned at this. He did not like
interruptions. He firmly resumed the tale:

"With a gesture of disdain our hero waved aside
the proffered gold of the scoundrelly millionaire and
dashed down the stairway of the proud mansion to
where his gallant steed, Midnight, was champing
at the hitching post. At that moment——"

Romance was snatched from the hands of Jimmie
Time. The manager towered above him.

"Ain't I told you guys not to be taking up the
company's time with them novels?" he demanded.
He sternly returned to his big chair behind the railing, where he no less sternly took up his own perusal
of the confiscated tale.

"The big stiff!" muttered Jimmie. "That's the
third one he's copped on me this week. A kid in
this choint ain't got no rights! I got a good notion
to throw 'em down cold and go with the Postal
people."

"Never mind! I'll blow you to an ice cream after
work," consoled Boogles.

"Ice cream!" Jimmie Time was contemptuous.
"I want the free, wild life of the boundless peraries.
I want b'ar steaks br'iled on the glowing coals of the
camp fire. I want to be Little Sure Shot, trapper,
scout, and guide——"

"Next out!" yelled the manager. "Hustle now!"

Jimmie Time was next out. He hustled sullenly.

Boogles, alone, slept fitfully on his bench until the young thugs of the day watch straggled in. Then he achieved the change of his uniform to civilian garments, with only the accustomed minor maltreatment at the hands of these tormentors. True, with sportive affectations—yet with deadly intentness—they searched him for possible loot; but only his pockets. His dollar bill, folded inside his collar, went unfound. With assumed jauntiness he strolled from the outlaws' den and safely reached the street.

The gilding on the castellated towers of the tallest building in the world dazzled his blinking, foolish eyes. That was a glorious summit which sang to the new sun, but no higher than his own elation at the moment. Had he not come off with his dollar? He found balm and a tender stimulus in the morning air —an air for dreams and revolt. Boogles felt this as thousands of others must have felt it who were yet tamely issuing from subway caverns and the Brooklyn Bridge to be wage slaves.

A block away from the office he encountered Jimmie Time, who seemed to await him importantly. He seethed with excitement.

"I got one, too!" he called. "That tank drama he sent another note uptown to a restaurant where a party was, and he give me a case note, too."

He revealed it; and when Boogles withdrew his own treasure the two were lovingly compared and admired. Nothing in all the world can be so foul to the touch as the dollar bill that circulates in New York, but these two were intrepidly fondled.

"I ain't going back to change," said Jimmie Time. "Them other kids would cop it on me."

"Have some cigarettes," urged Boogles, and royally bought them—with gilded tips, in a beautiful casket.

"I had about enough of their helling," declared Jimmie, still glowing with a fine desperation.

They sought the William Street Tunnel under the Brooklyn Bridge. It was cool and dark there. One might smoke and take his ease. And plan! They sprawled on the stone pavement and smoked largely.

"Chee! If we could get out West and do all them fine things!" mused Boogles.

"Let's!" said Jimmie Time.

"Huh!" Boogles gasped blankly at this.

"Let's beat it!"

"Chee!" said Boogles. He stared at this bolder spirit with startled admiration.

"Me—I'm going," declared Jimmie Time stoutly, and waited.

Boogles wavered a tremulous moment.

"I'm going with you," he managed at last.

He blurted the words. They had to rush out to beat down his native caution with quick blows.

"Listen!" said Jimmie Time impressively. "We got money enough to start. Then we just strike out for the peraries."

"Like the guy in the story!" Boogles glowed at the

adept who before his very eyes was turning a beautiful dream into stark reality. He was praying that his own courage to face it would endure.

"You hurry home," commanded Jimmie, "and cop an axe and all the grub you can lay your hands on."

Boogles fell from the heights as he had feared he would.

"Aw, chee!" he said sanely. "And s'pose me stepmother gets her lamps on me! Wouldn't she bean me? Sure she would!"

"Bind her and gag her," said Jimmie promptly. "What's one weak woman?"

"Yah! She's a hellion and you know it."

"Listen!" said Jimmie sternly. "If you're going into the wild and lawless life of the peraries with me you got to learn to get things. Jesse James or Morgan's men could get me that axe and that grub, and not make one-two-three of it."

"Them guys had practice—and likely they never had to go against their stepmothers."

"Do I go alone, then?"

"Well, now——"

"Will you or won't you?"

Boogles drew a fateful breath.

"I'll take a chance. You wait here. If I ain't back in one hour you'll know I been murdered."

"Good, my man!" said Jimmie Time with the air of an outlaw chief. "Be off at once."

Boogles was off. And Boogles was back in less

than the hour with a delectable bulging meal sack. He was trembling but radiant.

"She seen me gitting away and she yelled her head off," he gasped; "but you bet I never stopped. I just thought of Jesse James and General Grant, and run like hell!"

"Good, my man!" said Jimmie Time; and then, with a sudden gleam of the practical, he inventoried the commissary and quartermaster supplies in the sack. He found them to be: One hatchet; one well-used boiled hambone; six greasy sugared crullers; four dill pickles; a bottle of catchup; two tomatoes all but obliterated in transit; two loaves of bread; a flatiron.

Jimmie cast the last item from him.

"Wh'd you bring that for?" he demanded.

"I don't know," confessed Boogles. "I just put it in. Mebbe I was afraid she'd throw it at me when I was making my get-away. It'll be good for cracking nuts if we find any on the peraries. I bet they have nuts!"

"All right, then. You can carry it if you want to, pard."

Jimmie thrust the bundle into Boogles' arms and valiantly led a desperate way to the North River. Boogles panted under his burden as they dodged impatient taxicabs. So they came into the maze of dock traffic by way of Desbrosses Street. The eyes of both were lit by adventure. Jimmie pushed through the crowd on the wharf to a ticket office. A glimpse through a door of the huge shed had given him inspiration. No common ferryboats for them! He had seen the stately river steamer, *Robert Fulton*, gay with flags and bunting, awaiting the throng of excursionists. He recklessly bought tickets. So far, so good. A momentous start had been made.

At this very interesting point in his discourse to me, however, Boogles began to miss explosions too frequently. From the disorderly jumble of his narrative to this moment I believe I have brought something like the truth; I have caused the widely scattered parts to cohere. After this I could make little of his maunderings.

They were on the crowded boat and the boat steamed up the Hudson River; and they disembarked at a thriving Western town—which, I gather, was Yonkers—because Boogles feared his stepmother might trace him to this boat, and because Jimmie Time became convinced that detectives were on his track, wanting him for the embezzlement of a worn but still practicable uniform of the Western Union Telegraph Company. So it was agreed that they should take to the trackless forest, where there are ways of throwing one's pursuers off the scent; where they would travel by night, guided by the stars, and lay up by day, subsisting on spring water and a little pemmican—source undisclosed. They were not going to be taken alive—that was understood.

They hurried through the streets of this thriving Western town, ultimately boarding an electric car

—with a shrewd eye out for the hellhounds of the law; and the car took them to the beginning of the frontier, where they found the trackless forest. They reached the depths of this forest after climbing a stone wall; and Jimmie Time said the West looked good to him and that he could already smell the "b'ar steaks br'iling."

Plain enough still, perhaps; but immediately it seemed that a princess had for some time been sharing this great adventure. She was a beautiful golden-haired princess, though quite small, and had flowers in her hair and put some in the cap of Jimmie Time—behind the nickel badge—and said she would make him her court dwarf or jester or knight, or something; only the scout who was with her said this was rather silly and that they had better be getting home or they knew very well what would happen to them. But when they got lost Jimmie Time looked at this scout's rifle and said it was a first-class rifle, and would knock an Indian or a wild animal silly.

And the scout smoked a cigarette and got sick by it, and cried something fierce; so they made a fire, and the princess didn't get sick when she smoked hers, but told them a couple of bully stories, like reading in a book, and ate every one of the greasy sugared crullers, because she was a genuine princess, and Boogles thought at this time that maybe the boundless West wasn't what it was cracked up to be; so, after they met the madam, the madam said, well, if they was wanting to go out West they might as well come along

here; and they said all right—as long as they was
wanting to go out West anyway, why, they might as
well come along with her as with anybody else.

And that Chink would mighty soon find out if
Little Sure Shot wasn't the real Peruvian doughnuts,
because that old murderer would sure have him hard
to find, come sundown; still, he was glad he had come
along with the madam, because back there it wasn't
any job for you, account of getting too fat for the
uniform, with every one giving you the laugh that
way—and they wouldn't get you a bigger one——

I left Boogles then, though he seemed not to know
it. His needle worked swiftly on the red one he was
making for the madam, and his aimless, random
phrases seemed to flow as before; but I knew now
where to apply for the details that had been too many
for his slender gift of narrative.

At four that afternoon Mrs. Lysander John Pettengill, accompanied by one Buck Devine, a valued re-
tainer, rode into the yard and dismounted. She at
once looked searchingly about her. Then she raised
her voice, which is a carrying voice even when not
raised: "You, Jimmie Time!"

Once was enough. The door of the bunk house
swung slowly open and the disgraced one appeared
in all his shameful panoply. The cap was pulled
well down over a face hopelessly embittered. The
shrunken little figure drooped.

"None of that hiding out!" admonished his judge.
"You keep standing round out here where decent

folks can look at you and see what a bad boy you are."

With a glance she identified me as one of the decent she would have edified. Jimmie Time muttered evilly in undertones and slouched forward, head down.

"Ain't he the hostile wretch?" called Buck Devine, who stood with the horses. He spoke with a florid but false admiration.

Jimmie Time, snarling, turned on him:

"You go to——"

I perceived that Lew Wee the night before had delicately indicated by a mere initial letter a bad word that could fall trippingly from the lips of Jimmie.

"Sure!" agreed Buck Devine cordially. "And say, take this here telegram up to the corner of Broadway and Harlem; and move lively now—don't you stop to read any of them nickel liberries."

I saw what a gentleman should do. I turned my back on the piteous figure of Jimmie Time. I moved idly off, as if the spectacle of his ignominy had never even briefly engaged me.

"Shoot up a good cook, will you?" said the lady grimly. "I'll give you your needings." She followed me to the house.

On the west porch, when she had exchanged the laced boots, khaki riding breeches, and army shirt for a most absurdly feminine house gown, we had tea. Her nose was powdered, and her slippers were bronzed leather and monstrous small. She mingled Scotch whiskey with the tea and drank her first cupful from a capacious saucer.

"That fresh bunch of campers!" she began. "What you reckon they did last night? Cut my wire fence in two places over on the west flat—yes, sir!—had a pair of wire clippers in the whip socket. What I didn't give 'em! Say, ain't it a downright wonder I still retain my girlish laughter?"

But then, after she had refused my made cigarette for one of her own deft handiwork, she spoke as I wished her to:

"Yes; three years ago. Me visiting a week at the home of Mrs. W. B. Hemingway and her husband, just outside of Yonkers, back in York State. A very nice swell home, with a nice front yard and everything. And also Mrs. W. B.'s sister and her little boy, visiting her from Albany, the sister's name being Mrs. L. H. Cummins, and the boy being nine years old and named Rupert Cummins, Junior; and very junior he was for his age, too—I will say that. He was a perfectly handsome little boy; but you might call him a blubberhead if you wanted to, him always being scared silly and pestered and roughhoused out of his senses by his little girl cousin, Margery Hemingway—Mrs. W. B.'s little girl, you understand—and her only seven, or two years younger than Junior, but leading him round into all kinds of musses till his own mother was that demoralized after a couple of days she said if that Mar-

gery child was hers she'd have her put away in some
good institution.

"Of course she only told that to me, not to Margery's mother. I don't know—mebbe she would of
put her away, she was that frightened little Margery
would get Junior killed off in some horrible manner,
like the time she got him to see how high he dast jump
out of the apple tree from, or like the time she told
him, one ironing day, that if he drank a whole bowl-
ful of starch it would make him have whiskers like his
pa in fifteen minutes. Things like that—not fatal,
mebbe, but wearing.

"Well, this day come a telegram about nine A. M.
for Mrs. W. B., that her aunt, with money, is very
sick in New Jersey, which is near Yonkers; so she and
Mrs. L. H. Cummins, her sister, must go to see about
this aunt—and would I stay and look after the two
kids and not let them get poisoned or killed or anything serious? And they might have to stay overnight, because the aunt was eccentric and often
thought she was sick; but this time she might be
right. She was worth all the way from three to four
hundred thousand dollars.

"So I said I'd love to stay and look after the little
ones. I wanted to stay. Shopping in New York
City the day before, two bargain sales—one being
hand-embroidered Swiss waists from two-ninety-eight
upward—I felt as if a stampede of longhorns had
caught me. Darned near bedfast I was! Say, talk
about the pale, weak, nervous city woman with ex-

hausted vitality! See 'em in action first, say I.
There was a corn-fed hussy in a plush bonnet with
forget-me-nots, two hundred and thirty or forty on
the hoof, that exhausted my vitality all right—no
holds barred, an arm like first-growth hick'ry across
my windpipe, and me up against a solid pillar of
structural ironwork! Once I was wrastled by a cin-
namon bear that had lately become a mother; but
the poor old thing would have lost her life with this
dame after the hand-embroidereds. Gee! I was
lame in places I'd lived fifty-eight years and never
knew I had.

"So off went these ladies, with Mrs. L. H. Cummins giving me special and private warning to be sure
and keep Junior well out of it in case little mischievous Margery started anything that would be
likely to kill her. And I looked forward to a quiet
day on the lounge, where I could ache in peace and
read the "Famous Crimes of History," which the W.
B.'s had in twelve volumes—you wouldn't have
thought there was that many, would you? I dressed
soft, out of respect to my corpse, and picked out a
corking volume of these here Crimes and lay on the
big lounge by an open window where the breeze could
soothe me and where I could keep tabs on the little
ones at their sports; and everything went as right as
if I had been in some A-Number-One hospital where
I had ought to of been.

"Lunchtime come before I knew it; and I had mine
brought to my bed of pain by the Swede on a tray,

while the kids et theirs in an orderly and uproarious manner in the dining-room. Rupert, Junior, was dressed like one of these boy scouts and had his air gun at the table with him, and little Margery was telling him there was, too, fairy princes all round in different places; and she bet she could find one any day she wanted to. They seemed to be all safe enough, so I took up my Crimes again. Really, ain't history the limit?—the things they done in it and got away with—never even being arrested or fined or anything!

"Pretty soon I could hear the merry prattle of the little ones again out in the side yard. Ain't it funny how they get the gambling spirit so young? I'd hear little Margery say: 'I bet you can't!' And Rupert, Junior, would say: 'I bet I can, too!' And off they'd go ninety miles on a straight track: 'I bet you'd be afraid to!'—'I bet I wouldn't be!'—'I bet you'd run as fast!'—'I bet I never would!' Ever see such natural-born gamblers? And it's all about what Rupert, Junior, would do if he seen a big tiger in some woods—Rupert betting he'd shoot it dead, right between the eyes, and Margery taking the other end. She has by far the best end of it, I think, it being at least a forty-to-one shot that Rupert, the boy scout, is talking high and wide. And I drop into the Crimes again at a good, murderous place with stilettos.

"I can't tell even now how it happened. All I know is that it was two o'clock, and all at once it was five-thirty P. M. by a fussy gold clock over on the mantel with a gold young lady, wearing a spear, standing on top of it. I woke up without ever suspicioning that I'd been asleep. Anyway, I think I'm feeling better, and I stretch, though careful, account of the dame in the plush bonnet with forget-me-nots; and I lie there thinking mebbe I'll enter the ring again to-morrow for some other truck I was needing, and thinking how quiet and peaceful it is—how awful quiet! I got it then, all right. That quiet! If you'd known little Margery better you'd know how sick that quiet made me all at once. My gizzard or something turned clean over.

"I let out a yell for them kids right where I lay. Then I bounded to my feet and run through the rooms downstairs yelling. No sign of 'em! And out into the kitchen—and here was Tillie, the maid, and Yetta, the cook, both saying it's queer, but they ain't heard a sound of 'em either, for near an hour. So I yelled out back to an old hick of a gardener that's deef, and he comes running; but he don't know a thing on earth about the kids or anything else. Then I am sick! I send Tillie one way along the street and the gardener the other way to find out if any neighbours had seen 'em. Then in a minute this here Yetta, the cook, says: 'Why, now, Miss Margery was saying she'd go downtown to buy some candy,' and Yetta says: 'You know, Miss Margery, your mother never lets you have candy.' And Margery says: 'Well, she might change her mind any minute—you can't tell; and it's best to have some on hand in case she does.' And she'd got some poker chips out of the box to buy the candy with—five blue chips she had, knowing they was nearly money anyway.

"And when Yetta seen it was only poker chips she knew the kid couldn't buy candy with 'em—not even in Yonkers; so she didn't think any more about it until it come over her—just like that—how quiet everything was. Oh, that Yetta would certainly be found bone clear to the centre if her skull was ever drilled—the same stuff they slaughter the poor elephants for over in Africa—going so far away, with Yetta right there to their hands, as you might say. And I'm getting sicker and sicker! I'd have retained my calm mind, mind you, if they had been my own kids—but kids of others I'd been sacredly trusted with!

"And then down the back stairs comes this here sandy-complected, horse-faced plumber that had been frittering away his time all day up in a bathroom over one little leak, and looking as sad and mournful as if he hadn't just won eight dollars, or whatever it was. He must have been born that way—not even being a plumber had cheered him up.

"'Blackhanders!' he says right off, kind of brightening a little bit.

"I like to fainted for fair! He says they had lured the kids off with candy and popcorn, and would hold 'em in a tenement house for ten thousand dollars, to be left on a certain spot at twelve P. M. He seemed to know a lot about their ways.

"'They got the Honourable Simon T. Griffen-
baugh's youngest that way,' he says, 'only a month
ago.   Likely the same gang got these two.'

"'How do you know?' I asks him.

"'Well,' he says, 'they's a gang of over two hundred of these I-talian Blackhanders working right
now on a sewer job something about two miles up the
road.   That's how I know,' he says.   'That's plain
enough, ain't it?   It's as plain as the back of my
hand.   What chance would them two defenceless
little children have with a gang of two hundred
Blackhanders?'

"But that looked foolish, even to me.   'Shucks!' I
says.   'That don't stand to reason.'   But then I got
another scare.   'How about water?' I says.   'Any
places round here they could fall into and get
drownded?'

"He'd looked glum again when I said two hundred
Blackhanders didn't sound reasonable; but he cheers
up at this and says: 'Oh, yes; lots of places they could
drownd—cricks and rivers and lakes and ponds and
tanks—any number of places they could fall into and
never come up again.'   Say, he made that whole
neighbourhood sound like Venice, Italy.   You wondered how folks ever got round without gondolas or
something.   'One of Dr. George F. Maybury's two
kids was nearly drownded last Tuesday—only the
older one saved him; a wonder it was they didn't have
to drag the river and find 'em on the bottom locked in
each other's arms!   And a boy by the name of

Clifford Something, only the other day, playing down
by the railroad tracks——'

"I shut him off, you bet! I told him to get out
quick and go to his home if he had one.

"'I certainly hope I won't have to read anything
horrible in to-morrow's paper!' he says as he goes
down the back stoop. 'Only last week they was a
nigger caught——'

"I shut the door on him. Rattled good and plenty
I was by then. Back comes this silly old gardener—
he'd gone with his hoe and was still gripping it. The
neighbours down that way hadn't seen the kids.
Back comes Tillie. One neighbour where she'd been
had seen 'em climb on to a street car—only it wasn't
going downtown but into the country; and this
neighbour had said to herself that the boy would be
likely to let some one have it in the eye with his gun,
the careless way he was lugging it.

"Thank the Lord, that was a trace! I telephoned
to the police and told 'em all about it. And I telephoned for a motor car for me and got into some
clothes. Good and scared—yes! I caught sight of
my face in the looking-glass, and, my! but it was
pasty—it looked like one of these cheap apple pies
you see in the window of a two-bit lunch place! And
while I'm waiting for this motor car, what should
come but a telegram from Mr. W. B. himself saying
that the aunt was worse and he would go to New
Jersey himself for the night! Some said this aunt
was worth a good deal more than she was supposed to

be. And I not knowing the name of this town in
Jersey where they would all be!—it was East Some-
thing or West Something, and hard to remember, and
I'd forgot it.

"I called the police again and they said descrip-
tions was being sent out, and that probably I'd better
not worry, because they often had cases like this.
And I offered to bet them they hadn't a case since
Yonkers was first thought of that had meant so much
spot cash to 'em as this one would mean the minute
I got a good grip on them kids. So this cop said
mebbe they had better worry a little, after all, and
they'd send out two cars of their own and scour the
country, and try to find the conductor of this street
car that the neighbour woman had seen the kids get
on to.

"I r'ared round that house till the auto come that
I'd ordered. It was late coming, naturally, and
nearly dark when it got there; but we covered a lot of
miles while the daylight lasted, with the man looking sharp out along the road, too, because he had
three kids of his own that would do any living thing
sometimes, though safe at home and asleep at that
minute, thank God!

"It was moisting when we started, and pretty soon
it clouded up and the dark came on, and I felt beat.
We got fair locoed. We'd go down one road and
then back the same way. We stopped to ask everybody. Then we found the two autos sent out by the
police. I told the cops again what would happen to

'em from me the minute the kids was found—the kids or their bodies. I was so despairing—what with that damned plumber and everything! I'll bet he's the merry chatterbox in his own home. The police said cheer up—nothing like that, with the country as safe as a church. But we went over to this Black-handers' construction camp, just the same, to make sure, and none of the men was missing, the boss said, and no children had been seen; and anyway his men was ordinary decent wops and not Blackhanders— and blamed if about fifty of 'em didn't turn out to help look! Yes, sir, there they was—foreigners to the last man except the boss, who was Irish—and acting just like human beings.

"It was near ten o'clock now; so we went to a country saloon to telephone police headquarters, and they had found the car conductor, he remembering because he had threatened to put the boy scout off the car if he didn't quit pointing his gun straight at an old man with gold spectacles setting across the aisle. And finally they had got off themselves about three miles down the road; he'd watched 'em climb over a stone wall and start up a hill into some woods that was there. And he was Conductor Number Twenty-seven, if we wanted to know that.

"We beat it to that spot after I'd powdered my nose and we'd had a quick round of drinks. The po-licemen knew where it was. It wasn't moisting any more—it was raining for fair; and we done some ground-and-lofty skidding before we got there. We found the stone wall all right and the slope leading up to the woods; but, my Lord, there was a good half mile of it! We strung out—four cops and my driver and me—hundreds of yards apart and all yelling, so maybe the poor lost things would hear us.

"We made up to the woods without raising a sign; and, my lands, wasn't it dark inside the woods! I worked forward, trying to keep straight from tree to tree; but I stumbled and tore my clothes and sprained my wrist, and blacked one eye the prettiest you'd want to see—mighty near being a blubberhead myself, I was—it not being my kids, you understand. Oh, I kept to it though! I'd have gone straight up the grand old state of New York into Lake Erie if something hadn't stopped me.

"It was a light off through the pine and oak trees, and down in a kind of little draw—not a lamplight but a fire blazing up. I yelled to both sides toward the others. I can yell good when I'm put to it. Then I started for the light. I could make out figures round the fire. Mebbe it's a Blackhanders' camp, I think; so I didn't yell any more. I cat-footed. And in a minute I was up close and seen 'em —there in the dripping rain.

"Rupert, Junior, was asleep, leaned setting up against a tree, with a messenger boy's cap on. And Margery was asleep on a pile of leaves, with her cheek on one hand and something over her. And a fat man was asleep on his back, with his mouth open, making an awful fuss about it. And the only one that wasn't asleep was a funny little old man setting against another tree. He had on the scout's campaign hat and he held the gun across his chest in the crook of his arm. He hadn't any coat on. Then I see his coat was what was over Margery; and I looked closer and it was a messenger boy's coat.

"I was more floored than ever when I took that in. I made a little move, and this funny old man must have heard me—he looked like one of them silly little critters that play hob with Rip Van Winkle out on the mountain before he goes to sleep. And he cocks his ears this way and that; then he jumped to his feet, and I come forward where he could see me. And darned if he didn't up with this here air gun of Rupert's, like a flash, and plunk me with a buckshot it carried—right on my sprained wrist, too!

"Say, I let out a yell, and I had him by the neck of his shirt in one grab. I was still shaking him when the others come to. The fat man set up and rubbed his eyes and blinked. That's all he done. Rupert woke up the same minute and begun to cry like a baby; and Margery woke up, but she didn't cry. She took a good look at me and she says: 'You let him alone! He's my knight—he slays all the dragons. He's a good knight!'

"There I was, still shaking the little old man—I'd forgot all about him. So I dropped him on the ground and reached for Margery; and I was so afraid I was going to blubber like Rupert, the scout, that I

let out some words to keep from it.   Yes, sir; I admit
it.

"'Oh! Oh! Oh! Swearing!' says Rupert. I
shall tell mother and Aunt Hilda just what you said!'

"Mebby you can get Rupert's number from that.
I did anyway. I stood up from Margery and cuffed
him. He went on sobbing, but not without reason.

"'Margery Hemingway,' I says, 'how dare you!'
And she looks up all cool and cunning, and says:
'Ho! I bet I know worse words than what you said!
See if I don't.' So then I shut her off mighty quick.
But still she didn't cry. 'I s'pose I must go back
home,' she says. 'And perhaps it is all for the best.
I have a very beautiful home. Perhaps I should stay
there oftener.'

"I turned on the Blackhanders.

"'Did these brutes entice you away with candy?'
I demanded. 'Was they holding you here for ran-
som?'

"'Huh! I should think not!' she says. 'They
are a couple of 'fraid-cats. They were afraid as anything when we all got lost in these woods and wanted
to keep on finding our way out. And I said I bet
they were awful cowards, and the fat one said of
course he was; but this old one became very, very indignant and said he bet he wasn't any more of a
coward than I am, but we simply ought to go where
there were more houses. And so I consented and we
got lost worse than ever—about a hundred miles, I
think—in this dense forest and we couldn't return to

our beautiful homes. And this one said he was a trapper, scout, and guide; so he built this lovely fire and I ate a lot of crullers the silly things had brought with them. And then this old one flung his robe over me because I was a princess, and it made me invisible to prowling wolves; and anyway he sat up to shoot them with his deadly rifle that he took away from Cousin Rupert. And Cousin Rupert became very tearful indeed; so we took his hat away, too, because it's a truly scout hat.'

"'And she smoked a cigarette,' says Rupert, still sobbing.

"'He smoked one, too, and I mean to tell his mother,' says Margery. 'It's something I think she ought to know.'

"'It made me sick,' says Rupert. 'It was a poison cigarette; I nearly died.'

"'Mine never made me sick,' says Margery—'only it was kind of sting-y to the tongue and I swallowed smoke through my nose repeatedly. And first, this old one wouldn't give us the cigarettes at all, until I threatened to cast a spell on him and turn him into a toad forever. I never did that to any one, but I bet I could. And the fat one cried like anything and begged me not to turn the old one into a toad, and the old one said he didn't think I could in a thousand years, but he wouldn't take any chances in the Far West; so he gave us the cigarettes, and Rupert only smoked half of his and then he acted in a very common way, I must say. And this old one said we would have br'iled b'ar steaks for breakfast. What is a br'iled b'ar steak? I'm hungry.'

"Such was little angel-faced Margery. Does she promise to make life interesting for those who love her, or does she not?

"Well, that's all. Of course these cops when they come up said the two men was desperate crooks wanted in every state in the Union; but I swore I knew them both well and they was harmless; and I made it right with 'em about the reward as soon as I got back to a check book. After that they'd have believed anything I said. And I sent something over to the Blackhanders that had turned out to help look, and something to Conductor Number Twenty-seven. And the next day I squared myself with Mrs. W. B. Hemingway and her husband, and Mrs. L. H. Cummins, when they come back, the aunt not having been sick but only eccentric again.

"And them two poor homeless boys—they kind of got me, I admit, after I'd questioned 'em awhile. So I coaxed 'em out here where they could lead the wild, free life. Kind of sad and pathetic, almost, they was. The fat one I found was just a kind of natural-born one—a feeb you understand—and the old one had a scar that the doctor said explained him all right —you must have noticed it up over his temple. It's where his old man laid him out once, when he was a kid, with a stovelifter. It seemed to stop his works.

"Yes; they're pretty good boys. Boogles was never bad but once, account of two custard pies off the kitchen window sill. I threatened him with his stepmother and he hid under the house for twenty-four hours. The other one is pretty good, too. This is only the second time I had to punish him for fooling with live ca'tridges. There! It's sundown and he's got on his Wild Wests again."

Jimmie Time swaggered from the bunk house in his fearsome regalia. Under the awed observation of Boogles he wheeled, drew, and shot from the hip one who had cravenly sought to attack him from the rear.

"My, but he's hostile!" murmured my hostess. "Ain't he just the hostile little wretch?"

IV

ONCE A SCOTCHMAN, ALWAYS

TERRIFIC sound waves beat upon the Arrowhead ranch house this night. At five o'clock a hundred and twenty Hereford calves had been torn from their anguished mothers for the first time and shut into a too adjacent feeding pen. Mothers and offspring, kept a hundred yards apart by two stout fences, unceasingly bawled their grief, a noble chorus of yearning and despair. The calves projected a high, full-throated barytone, with here and there a wailing tenor against the rumbling bass of their dams. And ever and again pealed distantly into the chorus the flute obbligato of an emotional coyote down on the flat. There was never a diminuendo. The fortissimo had been steadily maintained for three hours and would endure the night long, perhaps for two other nights.

At eight o'clock I sleepily wondered how I should sleep. And thus wondering, I marvelled at the indifference to the racket of my hostess, Mrs. Lysander John Pettengill. Through dinner and now as she read a San Francisco newspaper she had betrayed no consciousness of it. She read her paper and from time to time she chuckled.

"How do you like it?" I demanded, referring to the monstrous din.

"It's great," she said, plainly referring to something else. "One of them real upty-up weddings in high life, with orchestras and bowers of orchids and the bride a vision of loveliness——"

"I mean the noise."

"What noise?" She put the paper aside and stared at me, listening intently. I saw that she was honestly puzzled, even as the chorus swelled to unbelievable volume. I merely waved a hand. The coyote was then doing a most difficult tremolo high above the clamour.

"Oh, that!" said my enlightened hostess. "That's nothing; just a little bunch of calves being weaned. We never notice that—and say, they got the groom's mother in here, too. Yes, sir, Ellabelle in all her tiaras and sunbursts and dog collars and diamond chest protectors—Mrs. Angus McDonald, mother of groom, in a stunning creation! I bet they didn't need any flashlight when they took her, not with them stones all over her person. They could have took her in a coal cellar."

"How do you expect to sleep with all that going on?" I insisted.

"All what? Oh, them calves. That's nothing! Angus says to her when they first got money: 'Whatever you economize in, let it not be in diamonds!' He says nothing looks so poverty-stricken as a person that can only afford a few. Better wear

none at all than just a mere handful, he says. What
do you think of that talk from a man named Angus
McDonald? You'd think a Scotchman and his
money was soon parted, but I heard him say it from
the heart out. And yet Ellabelle never does seem
to get him. Only a year ago, when I was at this
here rich place down from San Francisco where they
got the new marble palace, there was a lovely blow-
up and Ellabelle says to me in her hysteria: 'Once a
Scotchman, always a Scotchman!' Oh, she was
hysteric all right! She was like what I seen about
one of the movie actresses, 'the empress of stormy
emotion.' Of course she feels better now, after the
wedding and all this newspaper guff. And it was a
funny blow-up. I don't know as I blamed her at the
time."

I now closed a window and a door upon the noisy
September night. It helped a little. I went back to
a chair nearer to this woman with ears trained in re-
jection. That helped more. I could hear her now,
save in the more passionate intervals of the chorus.

"All right, then. What was the funny blow-up?"
She caught the significance of the closed door and
window.

"But that's music," she insisted. "Why, I'd like
to have a good record of about two hundred of them
white-faced beauties being weaned, so I could play
it on a phonograph when I'm off visiting—only it
would make me too homesick." She glanced at the
closed door and window in a way that I found sinister.

"I couldn't hear you," I suggested.

"Oh, all right!" She listened wistfully a moment to the now slightly dulled oratorio, then: "Yes, Angus McDonald is his name; but there are two kinds of Scotch, and Angus is the other kind. Of course he's one of the big millionaires now, with money enough to blind any kind of a Scotchman, but he was the other kind even when he first come out to us, a good thirty years ago, without a cent. He's a kind of second or third cousin of mine by marriage or something—I never could quite work it out—and he'd learned his trade back in Ohio; but he felt that the East didn't have any future to speak of, so he decided to come West. He was a painter and grainer and kalsominer and paperhanger, that kind of thing —a good, quiet boy about twenty-five, not saying much, chunky and slow-moving but sure, with a round Scotch head and a snub nose, and one heavy eyebrow that run clean across his face—not cut in two like most are.

"He landed on the ranch and slowly looked things over and let on after a few days that he mebbe would be a cowboy on account of it taking him outdoors more than kalsomining would. Lysander John was pretty busy, but he said all right, and gave him a saddle and bridle and a pair of bull pants and warned him about a couple of cinch-binders that he mustn't try to ride or they would murder him. And so one morning Angus asked a little bronch-squeezer we had, named Everett Sloan, to pick him out something

safe to ride, and Everett done so. Brought him up
a nice old rope horse that would have been as safe as
a supreme-court judge, but the canny Angus says:
'No, none of your tricks now! That beast has the
very devil in his eye, and you wish to sit by and
laugh your fool head off when he displaces me.'
'Is that so?' says Everett. 'I suspect you,' says
Angus. 'I've read plentifully about the tricks of
you cowlads.' 'Pick your own horse, then,' says
Everett. 'I'd better,' says Angus, and picks one
over by the corral gate that was asleep standing up,
with a wisp of hay hanging out of his mouth like
he'd been too tired to finish eating it. 'This steed
is more to my eye,' says Angus. 'He's old and
withered and he has no evil ambitions. But maybe
I can wake him up.' 'Maybe you can,' says Everett,
'but are you dead sure you want to?' Angus
was dead sure. 'I shall thwart your murderous design,' says he. So Everett with a stung look helped
him saddle this one. He had his alibi all right, and
besides, nothing ever did worry that buckaroo as
long as his fingers wasn't too cold to roll a cigarette.

"The beast was still asleep when Angus forked
him. Without seeming to wake up much he at once
traded ends, poured Angus out of the saddle, and
stacked him up in some mud that was providentially
there—mud soft enough to mire your shadow. Angus got promptly up, landed a strong kick in the ribs
of the outlaw which had gone to sleep again before he

lit, shook hands warmly with Everett and says: 'What does a man need with two trades anyway? Good-bye!'

"But when Lysander John hears about it he says Angus has just the right stuff in him for a cowman. He says he has never known one yet that you could tell anything to before he found it out for himself, and Angus must sure have the makings of a good one, so he persuades him to stay round for a while, working at easy jobs that couldn't stack him up, and later he sent him to Omaha with the bunch in charge of a trainload of steers.

"The trip back was when his romance begun. Angus had kept fancy-free up to that time, being willing enough but thoroughly cautious. Do you remember the eating-house at North Platte, Nebraska? The night train from Omaha would reach there at breakfast time and you'd get out in the frosty air, hungry as a confirmed dyspeptic, and rush into the big red building past the man that was rapidly beating on a gong with one of these soft-ended bass-drum sticks. My, the good hot smells inside! Tables already loaded with ham and eggs and fried oysters and fried chicken and sausage and fried potatoes and steaks and hot biscuits and corn bread and hotcakes and regular coffee—till you didn't know which to begin on, and first thing you knew you had your plate loaded with too many things—but how you did eat!—and yes, thank you, another cup of coffee, and please pass the sirup this way. And no

worry about the train pulling out, because there the
conductor is at that other table and it can't go without him, so take your time—and about three more of
them big fried oysters, the only good fried ones I ever
had in the world! To this day I get hungry thinking
of that North Platte breakfast, and mad when I go
into the dining-car as we pass there and try to get the
languid mulatto to show a little enthusiasm.

"Well, they had girls at that eating-house. Of
course no one ever noticed 'em much, being too
famished and busy. You only knew in a general
way that females was passing the food along. But
Angus actually did notice Ellabelle, though it must
have been at the end of the meal, mebbe when she
was pouring the third cup. Ellabelle was never
right pretty to my notion, but she had some figure
and kind of a sad dignity, and her brown hair lacked
the towers and minarets and golden domes that the
other girls built with their own or theirs by right of
purchase. And she seems to have noticed Angus
from the very first. Angus saw that when she wasn't
passing the fried chicken or the hot biscuits along,
even for half a minute, she'd pick up a book from the
window sill and glance studiously at its pages. He
saw the book was called 'Lucile.' And he looked her
over some more—between mouthfuls, of course—the
neat-fitting black dress revealing every line of her
lithe young figure, like these magazine stories say,
the starched white apron and the look of sad dignity
that had probably come of fresh drummers trying

to teach her how to take a joke, and the smooth
brown hair—he'd probably got wise to the other
kind back in the social centres of Ohio—and all at
once he saw there was something about her. He
couldn't tell what it was, but he knew it was there.
He heard one of the over-haired ones call her Ellabelle,
and he committed the name to memory.

"He also remembered the book she was reading.
He come back with a copy he'd bought at Spokane
and kept it on his bureau. Not that he read it
much. It was harder to get into than 'Peck's
Bad Boy,' which was his favourite reading just
then.

"Pretty soon another load of steers is ready—my
sakes, what scrubby runts we sent off the range in
them days compared to now!—and Angus pleads to
go, so Lysander John makes a place for him and, coming back, here's Ellabelle handing the hot things
along same as ever, with 'Lucile' at hand for idle
moments. This time Angus again made certain
there was something about her. He cross-examined
her, I suppose, between the last ham and eggs and
the first hot cakes. Her folks was corn farmers over
in Iowa and she'd gone to high school and had meant
to be a teacher, but took this job because with her it
was anything to get out of Iowa, which she spoke of
in a warm, harsh way.

"Angus nearly lost the train that time, making
certain there was something about her. He told
her to be sure and stay there till he showed up again.

He told me about her when he got back. 'There's
something about her,' he says. 'I suspect it's her
eyes, though it might be something else.'

"Me? I suspected there was something about her,
too; only I thought it was just that North Platte
breakfast and his appetite. No meal can ever be
like breakfast to them that's two-fisted, and Angus
was. He'd think there was something about any
girl, I says to myself, seeing her through the romantic
golden haze of them North Platte breakfast victuals.
Of course I didn't suggest any such base notion to
Angus, knowing how little good it does to talk sense
to a man when he thinks there's something about a
girl. He tried to read 'Lucile' again, but couldn't
seem to strike any funny parts.

"Next time he went to Omaha, a month later, he
took his other suit and his new boots. 'I shall fling
caution to the winds and seal my fate,' he says.
'There's something about her, and some depraved
scoundrel might find it out.' 'All right, go ahead
and seal,' I says. 'You can't expect us to be shipping
steers every month just to give you twenty minutes
with a North Platte waiter girl.' 'Will she think me
impetuous?' says he. 'Better that than have her
think you ain't,' I warns him. 'Men have been
turned down for ten million reasons, and being impetuous is about the only one that was never num-
bered among them. It will be strange o'clock when
that happens.' 'She's different,' says Angus. 'Of
course,' I says. 'We're all different. That's what

makes us so much alike.' 'You might know,' says he doubtfully.

"He proved I did, on the trip back. He marched up to Ellabelle's end of the table in his other suit and his new boots and a startling necktie he'd bought at a place near the stockyards in South Omaha, and proposed honourable marriage to her, probably after the first bite of sausage and while she was setting his coffee down. 'And you've only twenty minutes,' he says, 'so hurry and pack your grip. We'll be wed when we get off the train.' 'You're too impetuous,' says Ellabelle, looking more than ever as if there was something about her. 'There, I was afraid I'd be,' says Angus, quitting on some steak and breaking out into scarlet rash. 'What did you think I am?' demands Ellabelle. 'Did you think I would answer your beck and call or your lightest nod as if I were your slave or something? Little you know me,' she says, tossing her head indignantly. 'I apologize bitterly,' says Angus. 'The very idea is monstrous,' says she. 'Twenty minutes—and with all my packing! You will wait over till the four-thirty-two this afternoon,' she goes on, very stern and nervous, 'or all is over between us.' 'I'll wait as long as that for you,' says Angus, going to the steak again. 'Are the other meals here as good as breakfast?' 'There's one up the street,' says Ellabelle; 'a Presbyterian.' 'I would prefer a Presbyterian,' says Angus. 'Are those fried oysters I see up there?'

"That was about the way of it, I gathered later.

Anyway, Angus brought her back, eating on the way a whole wicker suitcase full of lunch that she put up. And she seemed a good, capable girl, all right. She told me there was something about Angus. She'd seen that from the first. Even so, she said, she hadn't let him sweep her off her feet like he had meant to, but had forced him to give her time to do her packing and consider the grave step she was taking for better or worse, like every true, serious-minded woman ought to.

"Angus now said he couldn't afford to fritter away any more time in the cattle business, having a wife to support in the style she had been accustomed to, so he would go to work at his trade. He picked out Wallace, just over in Idaho, as a young and growing town where he could do well. He rented a nice four-room cottage there, with an icebox out on the back porch and a hammock in the front yard, and begun to paper and paint and grain and kalsomine and made good money from the start. Ellabelle was a crackajack housekeeper and had plenty of time to lie out in the hammock and read 'Lucile' of afternoons.

"By and by Angus had some money saved up, and what should he do with bits of it now and then but grubstake old Snowstorm Hickey, who'd been scratching mountainsides all his life and never found a thing and likely never would—a grouchy old hardshell with white hair and whiskers whirling about his head in such quantities that a body just naturally called him Snowstorm without thinking.

It made him highly indignant, but he never would get the things cut. Well, and what does this old snow-scene-in-the-Alps do after about a year but mush along up the cañon past Mullan and find a high-grade proposition so rich it was scandalous! They didn't know how rich at first, of course, but Angus got assays and they looked so good they must be a mistake, so they sunk a shaft and drifted in a tunnel, and the assays got better, and people with money was pretty soon taking notice.

"One day Snowstorm come grouching down to Angus and tells about a capitalist that had brought two experts with him and nosed over the workings for three days. Snowstorm was awful dejected. He had hated the capitalist right off. 'He wears a gold watch chain and silk underclothes like one of these fly city dames,' says Snowstorm, who was a knowing old scoundrel, 'and he says his syndicate on the reports of these two thieving experts will pay twelve hundred for it and not a cent more. What do you think of that for nerve?'

"'Is that all?' says Angus, working away at his job in the new International Hotel at Wallace. Graining a door in the dining-room he was, with a ham rind and a stocking over one thumb nail, doing little curlicues in the brown wet paint to make it look like what the wood was at first before it was painted at all. 'Well,' he says, 'I suspected from the assays that we might get a bit more, but if he had experts with him you better let him have it for twelve hun-

dred.   After all, twelve hundred dollars is a good bit
of money.'

"'Twelve hundred thousand,' says Snowstorm,
still grouchy.

"'Oh,' says Angus. 'In that case don't let him
have it.   If the shark offers that it'll be worth more.
I'll go into the mining business myself as soon as I've
done this door and the wainscoting and give them
their varnish.'

"He did so.   He had the International finished
in three more days, turned down a job in the new
bank building cold, and went into the mining business
just like he'd do anything else—slow and sure, yet
impetuous here and there.   It wasn't a hard proposition, the stuff being there nearly from the grass roots,
and the money soon come a-plenty.   Snowstorm
not only got things trimmed up but had 'em dyed
black as a crow's wing and retired to a life of sinful
ease in Spokane, eating bacon and beans and cocoanut
custard pie three times a day till the doctors found
out what a lot of expensive things he had the matter
with him.

"Angus not only kept on the job but branched out
into other mines that he bought up, and pretty soon
he quit counting his money.   You know what that
would mean to most of his race.   It fazed him a mite
at first.   He tried faithfully to act like a crazy fool
with his money, experimenting with revelry and
champagne for breakfast, and buying up the Sans
Soosy dance hall every Saturday night for his friends

and admirers. But he wasn't gaited to go on that track long. Even Ellabelle wasn't worried the least bit, and in fact she thought something of the kind was due his position. And she was busy herself buying the things that are champagne to a woman, only they're kept on the outside. That was when Angus told her if she was going in for diamonds at all to get enough so she could appear to be wasteful and contemptuous of them. Two thousand she give for one little diamond circlet to pin her napkin up on her chest with. It was her own idea.

"Then Angus for a time complicated his amateur debauchery with fast horses. He got him a pair of matched pacing stallions that would go anywhere, he said. And he frequently put them there when he had the main chandelier lighted. In driving them over a watering-trough one night an accident of some sort happened. Angus didn't come to till after his leg was set and the stitches in—eight in one place, six in another, and so on; I wonder why they're always so careful to count the stitches in a person that way—and he wished to know if his new side-bar buggy was safe and they told him it wasn't, and he wanted to know where his team was, but nobody knew that for three days, so he says to the doctors and Ellabelle: 'Hereafter I suspect I shall take only soft drinks like beer and sherry. Champagne has a bonnier look but it's too enterprising. I might get into trouble some time.' And he's done so to this day. Oh, I've seen him take a sip or two of champagne

to some one's health, or as much Scotch whiskey in a
tumbler of water as you could dribble from a medium-
boilered fountain pen. But that's a high riot with
him. He'll eat one of these corned peaches in
brandy, and mebbe take a cream pitcher of beer on
his oatmeal of a morning when his stomach don't feel
just right, but he's never been a willing performer
since that experiment in hurdling.

"When he could walk again him and Ellabelle
moved to the International Hotel, where she wouldn't
have to cook or split kindling and could make a
brutal display of diamonds at every meal, and we
went down to see them. That was when Angus give
Lysander John the scarfpin he'd sent clear to New
York for—a big gold bull's head with ruby eyes and
in its mouth a nugget of platinum set with three
diamonds. Of course Lysander John never dast
wear it except when Angus was going to see it.

"Then along comes Angus, Junior, though poor
Ellabelle thinks for several days that he's Elwin.
We'd gone down so I could be with her.

"'Elwin is the name I have chosen for my son,'
says she to Angus the third day.

"'Not so,' says Angus, slumping down his one
eyebrow clear across in a firm manner. 'You're too
late. My son is already named. I named him
Angus the night before he was born.'

"'How could you do that when you didn't know
the sex?' demands Ellabelle with a frightened air of
triumph.

"'I did it, didn't I?' says Angus. 'Then why ask how I could?' And he curved the eyebrow up one side and down the other in a fighting way.

"Ellabelle had been wedded wife of Angus long enough to know when the Scotch curse was on him. 'Very well,' she says, though turning her face to the wall. Angus straightened the eyebrow. 'Like we might have two now, one of each kind,' says he quite soft, 'you'd name your daughter as you liked, with perhaps no more than a bit of a suggestion from me, to be taken or not by you, unless we'd contend amiably about it for a length of time till we had it settled right as it should be. But a son—my son— why, look at the chest on him already, projecting outward like a clock shelf—and you would name him —but no matter! I was forehanded, thank God.' Oh, you saw plainly that in case a girl ever come along F   elle would have the privilege of naming it any- thing in the world she wanted to that Angus thought suitable.

"So that was settled reasonably, and Angus went on showing what to do with your mine instead of selling it to a shark, and the baby fatted up, being stall-fed, and Ellabelle got out into the world again, with more money than ever to spend, but fewer things to buy, because in Wallace she couldn't think of any more. Trust her, though! First the Inter- national Hotel wasn't good enough. Angus said they'd have a mansion, the biggest in Wallace, only without slippery hardwood floors, because he felt

brittle after his accident. Ellabelle says Wallace
itself ain't big enough for the mansion that ought to
be a home to his only son. She was learning how to
get to Angus without seeming to. He thought there
might be something in that, still he didn't like to
trust the child away from him, and he had to stick
there for a while.

"So Ellabelle's health broke down. Yes, sir, she
got to be a total wreck. Of course the fool doctor
in Wallace couldn't find it out. She tried him and he
told her she was strong as a horse and ought to be
doing a tub of washing that very minute. Which
was no way to talk to the wife of a rich mining man,
so he lost quite a piece of money by it. Ellabelle
then went to Spokane and consulted a specialist.
That's the difference. You only see a doctor, but a
specialist you consult. This one confirmed her fears
about herself in a very gentlemanly way and re rd
his reward on the spot. Ellabelle's came after she had
convinced Angus that even if she did have such a good
appetite it wasn't a normal one, but it was, in fact,
one of her worst symptoms and threatened her with
a complete nervous breakdown. After about a year
of this, when Angus had horned his way into a few
more mines—he said he might as well have a bunch
of them since he couldn't be there on the spot anyway—they went to New York City. Angus had
never been there except to pass from a Clyde liner
to Jersey City, and they do say that when he heard
the rates, exclusive of board, at the one Ellabelle

had picked out from reading the papers, he timidly asked her if they hadn't ought to go to the other hotel. She told him there wasn't any other—not for them. She told him further it was part of her mission to broaden his horizon, and she firmly meant to do it if God would only vouchsafe her a remnant of her once magnificent vitality.

"She didn't have to work so hard either. Angus begun to get a broader horizon in just a few days, corrupting every waiter he came in contact with, and there was a report round the hotel the summer I was there that a hat-boy had actually tried to reason with him, thinking he was a foreigner making mistakes with his money by giving up a dollar bill every time for having his hat snatched from him. As a matter of fact, Angus can't believe to this day that dollar bills are money. He feels apologetic when he gives 'em away. All the same I never believed that report about the hat-boy till some one explained to me that he wasn't allowed to keep his loot, not only having clothes made special without pockets but being searched to the hide every night like them poor unfortunate Zulus that toil in the diamond mines of Africa. Of course I could see then that this boy had become merely enraged like a wildcat at having a dollar crowded onto him for some one else every time a head waiter grovelled Angus out of the restaurant.

"The novelty of that life wore off after about a year, even with side trips to resorts where the prices were sufficiently outrageous to charm Ellabelle. She'd begun right off to broaden her own horizon. After only one week in New York she put her diamond napkin pincher to doing other work, and after six months she dressed about as well as them prominent society ladies that drift round the corridors of this hotel waiting for parties that never seem on time, and looking none too austere while they wait.

"So Ellabelle, having in the meantime taken up art and literature and gone to lectures where the professor would show sights and scenes in foreign lands with his magic lantern, begun to feel the call of the Old World. She'd got far beyond 'Lucile'— though 'Peck's Bad Boy' was still the favourite of Angus when he got time for any serious reading— and was coming to loathe the crudities of our so-called American civilization. So she said. She begun to let out to Angus that they wasn't doing right by the little one, bringing him up in a hole like New York City where he'd catch the American accent—though God knows where she ever noticed that danger there!—and it was only fair to the child to get him to England or Paris or some such place where he could have decent advantages. I gather that Angus let out a holler at first so that Ellabelle had to consult another specialist and have little Angus consult one, too. They both said: 'Certainly, don't delay another day if you value the child's life or your own,' and of course Angus had to give in. I reckon that was the last real fight he ever put up till the time I'm going to tell you about.

"They went to England and bought a castle that had never known the profane touch of a plumber, having been built in the time of the first earl or something, and after that they had to get another castle in France, account of little Angus having a weak throat that Ellabelle got another gentlemanly specialist to find out about him; and so it went, with Ellabelle hovering on the very edge of a nervous breakdown, and taking up art and literature at different spots where fashion gathered, going to Italy and India's coral strand to study the dead past, and so forth, and learning to address her inferiors in a refined and hostile manner, with little Angus having a maid and a governess and something new the matter with him every time Ellabelle felt the need of a change.

"At first Angus used to make two trips back every year, then he cut them down to one, and at last he'd only come every two or three years, having his hirelings come to him instead. He'd branched out a lot, even at that distance, getting into copper and such, and being president of banks and trusts here and there and equitable coöperative companies and all such things that help to keep the lower classes trimmed proper. For a whole lot of years I didn't see either of 'em. I sort of lost track of the outfit, except as I'd see the name of Angus heading a new board of directors after the reorganization, or renting the north half of Scotland for the sage-hen and coyote

shooting, or whatever the game is there. Of course
it took genius to do this with Angus, and I've never
denied that Ellabelle has it. I bet there wasn't a
day in all them years that Angus didn't believe himself to be a stubborn, domineering brute, riding
roughshod over the poor little wreck of a woman.
If he didn't it wasn't for want of his wife accusing
him of it in so many words—and perhaps a few more.

"I guess she got to feeling so sure of herself she let
her work coarsen up. Anyway, when little Angus
come to be eighteen his pa shocked her one day by
saying he must go back home to some good college.
'You mean England,' says Ellabelle, they being at
the time on some other foreign domains.

"'I do not,' says Angus, 'nor Sweden nor Japan
nor East Africa. I mean the United States.' 'You're
jesting,' says she. 'You wrong me cruelly,' says
Angus. 'The lad's eighteen and threatening to be a
foreigner. Should he stay here longer it would set in
his blood.' 'Remember his weak throat,' says Ellabelle. 'I did,' says Angus. 'To save you trouble
I sent for a specialist to look him over. He says the
lad has never a flaw in his throat. We'll go soon.'

"Of course it was dirty work on the part of Angus,
getting to the specialist first, but she saw she had to
take it. She knew it was like the time they agreed on
his name—she could see the Scotch blood leaping in
his veins. So she gave in with never a mutter that
Angus could hear. That's part of the genius of Ellabelle, knowing when she can and when she positively

cannot, and making no foolish struggle in the latter
event.

"Back they come to New York and young Angus
went to the swellest college Ellabelle could learn
about, and they had a town house and a country
house and Ellabelle prepared to dazzle New York
society, having met frayed ends of it in her years
abroad. But she couldn't seem to put it over. Lots
of male and female society foreigners that she'd met
would come and put up with her and linger on in the
most friendly manner, but Ellabelle never fools herself so very much. She knew she wasn't making the
least dent in New York itself. She got uncomfortable there. I bet she had that feeling you get when
you're riding your horse over soft ground and all at
once he begins to bog down.

"Anyway, they come West after a year or so,
where Angus had more drag and Ellabelle could feel
more important. Not back to Wallace, of course.
Ellabelle had forgotten the name of that town, and
also they come over a road that misses the thriving
little town of North Platte by several hundred miles.
And pretty soon they got into this darned swell little
suburb out from San Francisco, through knowing one
of the old families that had lived there man and boy
for upward of four years. It's a town where I believe they won't let you get off the train unless you
got a visitor's card and a valet.

"Here at last Ellabelle felt she might come into her
own, for parties seemed to recognize her true worth at

once. Some of them indeed she could buffalo right
on the spot, for she hadn't lived in Europe and such
places all them years for nothing. So, camping in a
miserable rented shack that never cost a penny over
seventy thousand dollars, with only thirty-eight
rooms and no proper space for the servants, they set
to work building their present marble palace—there's
inside and outside pictures of it in a magazine somewhere round here—bigger than the state insane
asylum and very tasty and expensive, with hand-
painted ceilings and pergolas and cafés and hot and
cold water and everything.

"It was then I first see Ellabelle after all the years,
and I want to tell you she was impressive. She
looked like the descendant of a long line of ancestry
or something and she spoke as good as any reciter you
ever heard in a hall. Last time I had seen her she
was still forgetting about the r's—she'd say: 'Oh,
there-urr you ah!' thus showing she was at least
half Iowa in breed—but nothing like that now. She
could give the English cards and spades and beat
them at their own game. Her face looked a little bit
overmassaged and she was having trouble keeping
her hips down, and wore a patent chin-squeezer
nights, and her hair couldn't be trusted to itself long
at a time; but she knew how to dress and she'd
learned decency in the use of the diamond except
when it was really proper to break out all over with
'em. You'd look at her twice in any show ring.
Ain't women the wonders! Gazing at Ellabelle when

she had everything on, you'd never dream that she'd
come up from the vilest dregs only a few years before
—helping cook for the harvest hands in Iowa, feeding
Union Pacific passengers at twenty-two a month, or
splitting her own kindling at Wallace, Idaho, and
dreaming about a new silk dress for next year, or
mebbe the year after if things went well.

"Men ain't that way. Angus had took no care of
his figure, which was now pouchy, his hair was gray,
and he was either shedding or had been roached, and
he had lines of care and food in his face, and took no
pains whatever with his accent—or with what he
said, for that matter. I never saw a man yet that
could hide a disgraceful past like a woman can.
They don't seem to have any pride. Most of 'em act
like they don't care a hoot whether people find it out
on 'em or not.

"Angus was always reckless that way, adding to his
wife's burden of anxiety. She'd got her own vile
past well buried, but she never knew when his was
going to stick its ugly head up out of its grave. He'd
go along all right for a while like one of the best set
had ought to—then Zooey! We was out to dinner at
another millionaire's one night—in that town you're
either a millionaire or drawing wages from one—and
Angus talked along with his host for half an hour
about the impossibility of getting a decent valet on
this side of the water, Americans not knowing their
place like the English do, till you'd have thought he
was born to it, and then all at once he breaks out

about the hardwood finish to the dining-room, and how the art of graining has perished and ought to be revived. 'And I wish I had a silver dollar,' he says, 'for every door like that one there that I've grained to resemble the natural wood so cunningly you'd never guess it—hardly.'

"At that his break didn't faze any one but Ella-belle. The host was an old train-robber who'd cut your throat for two bits—I'll bet he couldn't play an honest game of solitaire—and he let out himself right off that he had once worked in a livery stable and was proud of it; but poor Ellabelle, who'd been talking about the dear Countess of Comtessa or somebody, and the dukes and earls that was just one-two-three with her on the other side, she blushed up till it almost showed through the second coating. Angus was certainly poison ivy to her on occasion, and he'd refuse to listen to reason when she called him down about it. He'd do most of the things she asked him to about food and clothes and so forth—like the time he had the two gold teeth took out and replaced by real porcelain nature fakers—but he never could understand why he wasn't free to chat about the days when he earned what money he had.

"It was this time that I first saw little Angus since he had changed from a governess to a governor—or whatever they call the he-teacher of a millionaire's brat. He was home for the summer vacation. Naturally I'd been prejudiced against him not only by his mother's praise but by his father's steady coppering of the same. Judiciously comparing the two, I was led to expect a kind of cross between Little Lord Fauntleroy and the late Sitting Bull, with the vices of each and the virtues of neither. Instead of which I found him a winsome whelp of six-foot or so with Scotch eyes and his mother's nose and chin and a good, big, straight mouth, and full of the most engaging bedevilments for one and all. He didn't seem to be any brighter in his studies than a brute of that age should be, and though there was something easy and grand in his manner that his pa and ma never had, he wasn't really any more foreign than what I be. Of course he spoke Eastern American instead of Western, but you forgive him that after a few minutes when you see how nice he naturally meant to be. I admit we took to each other from the start. They often say I'm a good mixer, but it took no talent to get next to that boy. I woke up the first night thinking I knew what old silly would do her darndest to adopt him if ever his poor pa and ma was to get buttered over the right of way in some railroad accident.

"And yet I didn't see Angus, Junior, one bit the way either of his parents saw him. Ellabelle seemed to look on him merely as a smart dresser and social know-it-all that would be a 98 cent credit to her in the position of society queen for which the good God had always intended her. And his father said he wasn't any good except to idle away his time and spend money, and would come to a bad end by manslaughter in a high-powered car; or in the alcoholic ward of some hospital; that he was, in fact, a mere helling scapegrace that would have been put in some good detention home years before if he hadn't been born to a father that was all kinds of a so-and-so old Scotch fool. There you get Angus, *fills*, from three different slants, and I ain't saying there wasn't justification for the other two besides mine. The boy could act in a crowd of tea-drinking women with a finish that made his father look like some one edging in to ask where they wanted the load of coal dumped. But also Angus, *peer*, was merely painting the lily, as they say, when he'd tell all the different kinds of Indian the boy was. That very summer before he went back to the educational centre where they teach such arts, he helped wreck a road house a few miles up the line till it looked like one of them pictures of what a Zeppelin does to a rare old English drug store in London. And a week later he lost a race with the Los Angeles flyer, account of not having as good a roadbed to run on as the train had, and having to take too short a turn with his new car.

"I remember we three was wondering where he could be that night the telephone rung from the place where kindly strangers had hauled him for first aid to the foolish. But it was the boy himself that was able to talk and tell his anxious parents to forget all about it. His father took the message and as soon as he got the sense of it he begun to get hopeful that the kid had broke at least one leg—thinking, he must have been, of the matched pacing stallions that once did himself such a good turn without meaning to. His disappointment was pitiful as he turned to us after learning that he had lit on his head but only sustained a few bruises and sprains and concussions, with the wall-paper scraped off here and there.

"'Struck on his head, the only part of him that seems invulnerable,' says the fond father. 'What's that?' he yells, for the boy was talking again. He listened a minute, and it was right entertaining to watch his face work as the words come along. It registered all the evil that Scotland has suffered from her oppressors since they first thought up the name for it. Finally he begun to splutter back—it must have sounded fine at the other end—but he had to hang up, he was that emotional. After he got his face human again he says to us:

"'Would either of you think now that you could guess at what might have been his dying speech? Would you guess it might be words of cheer to the bereaved mother that nursed him, or even a word of comfort to the idiot father that never touched whip-leather to his back while he was still husky enough to get by with it? Well, you'd guess wild. He's but inflamed with indignation over the state of the road where he passed out for some minutes. He says it's a disgrace to any civilized community, and he means to make trouble about it with the county supervisor, who must be a murderer at heart, and then he'll take it up to the supreme court and see if we can't have roads in this country as good as Napoleon the First made them build in France, so a gentleman can speed up a bit over five miles an hour without breaking every bone in his body, to say nothing of totally ruining a car costing forty-eight hundred dollars of his good money, with the ink on the check for it scarce dry. He was going on to say that he had the race for the crossing as good as won and had just waved mockingly at the engineer of the defeated train who was pretending to feel indifferent about it—but I hung up on him. My strength was waning. Was he here this minute I make no doubt I'd go to the mat with him, unequal as we are in prowess.' He dribbled off into vicious mutterings of what he'd say to the boy if he was to come to the door.

"Then dear Ellabelle pipes up: 'And doesn't the dear boy say who was with him in this prank?'

"Angus snorted horribly at the word 'prank,' just like he'd never had one single advantage of foreign travel. 'He does indeed—one of those Hammersmith twin louts was with him—the speckled devil with the lisp, I gather—and praise God his bones, at least, are broke in two places!'

"Ellabelle's eyes shined up at this with real delight. 'How terrible!' she says, not looking it. 'That's Gerald Hammersmith, son of Mrs. St. John Hammersmith, leader of the most exclusive set here—oh, she's quite in the lead of everything that has class! And after this we must know each other far, far better than we have in the past. She has nevei called up to this time. I must inquire after her poor boy directly to-morrow comes.' That is Ellabelle. Trust her not to overlook a single bet.

"Angus again snorted in a common way. 'St. John Hammersmith!' says he, steaming up. 'When he trammed ore for three-fifty a day and went to bed with his clothes on any night he'd the price of a quart of gin-and-beer mixed—liking to get his quick—his name was naked 'John' with never a Saint to it, which his widow tacked on a dozen years later. And speaking of names, Mrs. McDonald, I sorely regret you didn't name your own son after your first willful fancy. It was no good day for his father when you put my own name to him.'

"But Ellabelle paid no attention whatever to this rough stuff, being already engaged in courting the Hammersmith dame for the good of her social importance. I make no doubt before the maid finished rubbing in the complexion cream that night she had reduced this upstart to the ranks and stepped into her place as leader of the most exclusive social set between South San Francisco and old Henry Miller's ranch house at Gilroy. Anyway, she kept talking to herself about it, almost over the mangled remains of her own son, as you might say.

"A year later the new mansion was done, setting in the centre of sixty acres of well-manicured land as flat as a floor and naturally called Hillcrest. Angus asked me down for another visit. There had been grand doings to open the new house, and Ellabelle

felt she was on the way to ruling things social with an
iron hand if she was just careful and didn't overbet
her cards. Angus, not being ashamed of his scandalous past, was really all that kept her nerves
strung up. It seems he'd give her trouble while the
painters and decorators was at work, hanging round
'em fascinated and telling 'em how he'd had to work
ten hours a day in his time and how he could grain a
door till it looked exactly like the natural wood, so
they'd say it wasn't painted at all. And one day he
become so inflamed with evil desire that Ellabelle,
escorting a bunch of the real triple-platers through the
mansion, found him with his coat off learning how to
rub down a hardwood panel with oil and pumice
stone. Gee! Wouldn't I like to of been there! I
suppose I got a lower nature as well as the rest of us.

"After I'd been there a few days, along comes
Angus, *fills*, out into the world from college to make a
name for himself. By ingenuity or native brute
force he had contrived to graduate. He was nice as
ever and told me he was going to look about a bit until he could decide what his field of endeavour should
be. Apparently it was breaking his neck in outdoor
sports, including loop-the-loop in his new car on roads
not meant for it, and delighting Ellabelle because he
was a fine social drag in her favour, and enraging his
father by the same reasons. Ellabelle was especially
thrilled by his making up to a girl that was daughter
to this here old train-robber I mentioned. It was
looking like he might form an alliance, as they say,

with this old family which had lived quite a decent life since they actually got it. The girl looked to me nice enough even for Angus, Junior, but his pa denounced her as a yellow-haired pest with none but frivolous aims in life, who wouldn't know whether a kitchen was a room in a house or a little woolly animal from Paraguay. We had some nice, friendly breakfasts, I believe not, whilst they discussed this poisonous topic, old Angus being only further embittered when it comes out that the train-robber is also dead set against this here alliance because his only daughter needs a decent, reputable man who would come home nights from some low mahogany den in a bank building, and not a worthless young hound that couldn't make a dollar of his own and had displayed no talent except for winning the notice of head waiters and policemen. Old Angus says he knows well enough his son can be arrested out of most crowds just on that description alone, but who is this So-and-So old thug to be saying it in public?

"And so it went, with Ellabelle living in high hopes and young Angus busy inventing new ways to bump himself off, and old Angus getting more and more seething—quiet enough outside, but so desperate inside that it wasn't any time at all till I saw he was just waiting for a good chance to make some horrible Scotch exhibition of himself.

"Then comes the fatal polo doings, with young Angus playing on the side that won, and Ellabelle being set up higher than ever till she actually begins to snub people here and there at the game that look like they'd swallow it, and old Angus ashamed and proud and glaring round as if he'd like to hear some one besides himself call his son a worthless young hound—if they wanted to start something.

"And the polo victory of course had to be celebrated by a banquet at the hotel, attended by all the players and their huskiest ruffian friends. They didn't have the ponies there, but I guess they would of if they'd thought of it. It must have been a good banquet, with vintages and song and that sort of thing—I believe they even tried to have food at first—and hearty indoor sports with the china and silver and chairs that had been thoughtlessly provided and a couple of big mirrors that looked as if you could throw a catsup bottle clear through them, only you couldn't, because it would stop there after merely breaking the glass, and spatter in a helpless way.

"And of course there was speeches. The best one, as far as I could learn, was made by the owner of the outraged premises at a late hour—when the party was breaking up—as you might put it. He said the bill would be about eighteen hundred dollars, as near as he could tell at first glance. He was greeted with hearty laughter and applause from the high-spirited young incendiaries and retired hastily through an unsuspected door to the pantry as they rushed for him. It was then they found out what to do with the rest of the catsup—and did it—so the walls and ceiling wouldn't look so monotonous, and fixed the windows so they would let out the foul tobacco smoke, and completed a large painting of the Yosemite that hung on the wall, doing several things to it that hadn't occurred to the artist in his hurry, and performed a serious operation on the piano without the use of gas. The tables, I believe, was left flat on their backs.

"Angus, *fills*, was fetched home in a car by a gang of his roguish young playmates. They stopped down on the stately drive under my window and a quartet sung a pathetic song that run:

> "*Don't forget your parents,*
> *Think all they done for you!*

"Then young Angus ascended the marble steps to the top one, bared his agreeable head to the moonlight, and made them a nice speech He said the campaign now in progress, fellow-citizens, marked the gravest crisis in the affairs of our grand old state that an intelligent constituency had ever been called upon to vote down, but that he felt they were on the eve of a sweeping victory that would sweep the corrupt hell-hounds of a venal opposition into an ignominy from which they would never be swept by any base act of his while they honoured him with their suffrages, because his life was an open book and he challenged any son-of-a-gun within sound of his voice to challenge this to his face or take the consequences of being swept into oblivion by the high tide

of a people's indignation that would sweep everything
before it on the third day of November next, having
been aroused in its might at last from the debasing
sloth into which the corrupt hell-hounds of a venal
opposition had swept them, but a brighter day had
dawned, which would sweep the onrushing hordes
of petty chicanery to where they would get theirs;
and, as one who had heard the call of an oppressed
people, he would accept this fitting testimonial, not
for its intrinsic worth but for the spirit in which it
was tendered. As for the nefarious tariff on watch
springs, sawed lumber, and indigo, he would defer
his masterly discussion of these burning issues to a
more fitting time because a man had to get a little
sleep now and then or he wasn't any good next day.
In the meantime he thanked them one and all, and
so, gentlemen, good-night.

"The audience cheered hoarsely and drove off.
I guess the speech would have been longer if a light
hadn't showed in the east wing of the castle where
Angus, *peer*, slept. And then all was peace and
quiet till the storm broke on a rocky coast next day.
It didn't really break until evening, but suspicious
clouds no bigger than a man's hand might have been
observed earlier. If young Angus took any breakfast that morning it was done in the privacy of his
apartment under the pitying glances of a valet or
something. But here he was at lunch, blithe as ever,
and full of merry details about the late disaster. He
spoke with much humour about a wider use for

tomato catsup than was ever encouraged by the old school of house decorators. Old Angus listened respectfully, taking only a few bites of food but chewing them long and thoughtfully. Ellabelle was chiefly interested in the names of the hearty young vandals. She was delighted to learn that they was all of the right set, and her eyes glowed with pride. The eyes of Angus, *peer*, was now glowing with what I could see was something else, though I couldn't make out just what it was. He never once exploded like you'd of thought he was due to.

"Then come a note for the boy which the perfect-mannered Englishman that was tending us said was brought by a messenger. Young Angus glanced at the page and broke out indignantly. 'The thieving old pirate!' he says. 'Last night he thought it would be about eighteen hundred dollars, and that sounded hysterical enough for the few little things we'd scratched or mussed up. I told him he would doubtless feel better this morning, but in any event to send the bill to me and I would pay it.'

"'Quite right of you,' says Ellabelle proudly.

"'And now the scoundrel sends me one for twenty-three hundred and odd. He's a robber, net!'

"Old Angus said never a word, but chewed slowly, whilst various puzzling expressions chased themselves acrost his eloquent face. I couldn't make a thing out of any of them.

"'Never patronize the fellow again,' says Ellabelle warmly.

"'As to that,' says her son, 'he hinted something last night about having me arrested if I ever tried to patronize him again, but that isn't the point. He's robbing me now.'

"'Oh, money!' says Ellabelle in a low tone of disgust and with a gesture like she was rebuking her son for mentioning such a thing before the servant.

"'But I don't like to be taken advantage of,' says he, looking very annoyed and grand. Then old Angus swallowed something he'd been chewing for eight minutes and spoke up with an entirely new expression that puzzled me more than ever.

"'If you're sure you have the right of it, don't you submit to the outrage.'

"Angus, Junior, backed up a little bit at this, not knowing quite how to take the old man's mildness. 'Oh, of course the fellow might win out if he took it into court,' he says. 'Every one knows the courts are just a mass of corruption.'

"'True, I've heard gossip to that effect,' says his father. 'Yet there must be some way to thwart the crook. I'm feeling strangely ingenious at the moment.' He was very mild, and yet there was something sinister and Scotch about him that the boy felt.

"'Of course I'd pay it out of my own money,' he remarks generously.

"'Even so, I hate to see you cheated,' says his father kindly. 'I hate to have you pay unjust extortions out of the mere pittance your tight-fisted old father allows you.'

"Young Angus said nothing to this, but blushed and coughed uncomfortably.

"'If you hurt that hotel anything like twenty-three hundred dollars' worth, it must be an interesting sight,' his father goes on brightly.

"'Oh, it was funny at the time,' says Angus boy, cheering up again.

"'Things often are,' says old Angus. 'I'll have a look.'

"'At the bill?'

"'No, at the wreck,' says he. The old boy was still quiet on the outside, but was plainly under great excitement, for he now folded his napkin with care, a crime of which I knew Ellabelle had broken him the first week in New York, years before. I noticed their butler had the fine feeling to look steadily away at the wall during this obscenity. The offender then made a pleasant remark about the beauty of the day and left the palatial apartment swiftly. Young Angus and his mother looked at each other and strolled after him softly over rugs costing about eighty thousand dollars. The husband and father was being driven off by a man he could trust in a car they had let him have for his own use. Later Ellabelle confides to me that she mistrusts old Angus is contemplating some bit of his national deviltry. 'He had a strange look on his face,' says she, 'and you know—once a Scotchman, always a Scotchman! Oh, it would be pitiful if he did anything peculiarly Scotch just at our most crit-

ical period here!' Then she felt of her face to see
if there was any nervous lines come into it, and there
was, and she beat it for the maid to have 'em rubbed
out ere they set.

"Yet at dinner that night everything seemed fine,
with old Angus as jovial as I'd ever seen him, and the
meal come to a cheerful end and we was having coffee
in the Looey de Medisee saloon, I think it is, before a
word was said about this here injured hotel.

"'You were far too modest this morning, you sly
dog!' says Angus, *peer*, at last, chuckling delightedly.
'You misled me grievously. That job of wrecking
shows genius of a quality that was all too rare in my
time. I suspect it's the college that does it. I
shouldn't wonder now if going through college is as
good as a liberal education. I don't believe mere
uneducated house-wreckers could have done so
pretty a job in twice the time, and there's clever
little touches they never would have thought of at
all.'

"'It did look thorough when we left,' says young
Angus, not quite knowing whether to laugh.

"'It's nothing short of sublime,' says his father
proudly. 'I stood in that deserted banquet hall,
though it looks never a bit like one, with ruin and
desolation on every hand as far as the eye could reach.
It inspired such awe in the bereaved owner and
me that we instinctively spoke in hushed whispers.
I've had no such gripping sensation as that since I
gazed upon the dead city of Pompeii. No longer can

it be said that Europe possesses all the impressive ruins.'

"Angus boy grinned cheerfully now, feeling that this tribute was heartfelt.

"'I suspect now,' goes on the old boy, 'that when the wreckage is cleared away we shall find the mangled bodies of several that perished when the bolts descended from a clear sky upon the gay scene.'

"'Perhaps under the tables,' says young Angus, chirking up still more at this geniality. 'Two or three went down early and may still be there.'

"'Yet twenty-three hundred for it is a monstrous outrage,' says the old man, changing his voice just a mite. 'Too well I know the cost of such repairs. Fifteen hundred at most would make the place better than ever—and to think that you, struggling along to keep up appearances on the little I give you, should be imposed upon by a crook that undoubtedly has the law on his side! I could endure no thought of it, so I foiled him.'

"'How?' says young Angus, kind of alarmed.

"Angus, *peer*, yawned and got up. 'It's a long story and would hardly interest you,' says he, moving over to the door. 'Besides, I must be to bed against the morrow, which will be a long, hard day for me.' His voice had tightened up.

"'What have you done?' demands Ellabelle passionately.

"'Saved your son eight hundred dollars,' says Angus, 'or the equivalent of his own earnings for something like eight hundred years at current prices for labour.'

"'I've a right to know,' says Ellabelle through her teeth and stiffening in her chair.   Young Angus just set there with his mouth open.

"'So you have,' says old Angus, and he goes on as crisp as a bunch of celery: 'I told you I felt ingenious. I've kept this money in the family by the simple device of taking the job. I've engaged two other painters and decorators besides myself, a carpenter, an electrician, a glazier, and a few proletariats of minor talent for clearing away the wreckage.   I shall be on the job at eight.   The loafers won't start at seven, as I used to.   Don't think I'd see any son of mine robbed before my very eyes.   My new overalls are laid out and my valet has instructions to get me into them at seven, though he persists in believing I'm to attend a fancy-dress ball at some strangely fashionable hour.   So I bid you all good evening.'

"Well, I guess that was the first time Ellabelle had really let go of herself since she was four years old or thereabouts.   Talk about the empress of stormy emotion!   For ten minutes the room sounded like a torture chamber of the dark Middle Ages.   But the doctor reached there at last in a swift car, and him and the two maids managed to get her laid out all comfortable and moaning, though still with outbreaks about every twenty minutes that I could hear clear over on my side of the house.

"And down below my window on the marble porch Angus, *fils*, was walking swiftly up and down for about one hour. He made no speech like the night before. He just walked and walked. The part that struck me was that neither of them had ever seemed to have the slightest notion of pleading old Angus out of his mad folly. They both seemed to know the Scotch when it did break out.

"At seven-thirty the next morning the old boy in overalls and jumper and a cap was driven to his job in a car as big as an apartment house. The curtains to Ellabelle's Looey Seez boudoir remained drawn, with hourly bulletins from the two Swiss maids that she was passing away in great agony. Angus, Junior, was off early, too, in his snakiest car. A few minutes later they got a telephone from him sixty miles away that he would not be home to lunch. Old Angus had taken his own lunch with him in a tin pail he'd bought the day before, with a little cupola on top for the cup to put the bottle of cold coffee in.

"It was a joyous home that day, if you don't care how you talk. All it needed was a crêpe necktie on the knob of the front door. That ornery old hound, Angus, got in from his work at six, spotty with paint and smelling of oil and turpentine, but cheerful as a new father. He washed up, ridding himself of at least a third of the paint smell, looked in at Ellabelle's door to say, 'What! Not feeling well, mamma? Now, that's too bad!' ate a hearty dinner with me, young Angus not having been heard from further, and fell asleep in a gold armchair at ten minutes past nine.

"He was off again next morning. Ellabelle's health was still breaking down, but young Angus sneaked in and partook of a meagre lunch with me. He was highly vexed with his pa. 'He's nothing but a scoundrelly old liar,' he says to me, 'saying that he gives me but a pittance. He's always given me a whale of an allowance. Why, actually, I've more than once had money left over at the end of the quarter. And now his talk about saving money! I tell you he has some other reason than money for breaking the mater's heart.' The boy looked very shrewd as he said this.

"That night at quitting time he was strangely down at the place with his own car to fetch his father home. 'I'll trust you this once,' says the old man, getting in and looking more then ever like a dissolute working man. On the way they passed this here yellow-haired daughter of the old train-robber that there had been talk of the boy making a match with. She was driving her own car and looked neither to right nor left.

"'Not speaking?' says old Angus.

"'She didn't see us,' says the boy.

"'She's ashamed of your father,' says the old man.

"'She's not,' says the boy.

"'You know it,' says the old scoundrel.

"'I'll show her,' says his son.

"Well, we had another cheerful evening, with

Ellabelle sending word to old Angus that she wanted me to have the necklace of brilliants with thê sapphire pendant, and the two faithful maids was to get suitable keepsakes out of the rest of her jewels, and would her son always wear the seal ring with her hair in it that she had given him when he was twenty? And the old devil started in to tell how much he could have saved by taking charge of the work in his own house, and how a union man nowadays would do just enough to keep within the law, and so on; but he got to yawning his head off and retired at nine, complaining that his valet that morning had cleaned and pressed his overalls. Young Angus looked very shrewd at me and again says: 'The old liar! He has some other reason than money. He can't fool me.'

"I kind of gathered from both of them the truth of what happened the next day. Young Angus himself showed up at the job about nine A. M., with a bundle under his arm. 'Where's the old man?' his father heard him demand of the carpenter, he usually speaking of old Angus as the governor.

"'Here,' says he from the top of a stepladder in the entry which looked as if a glacier had passed through it.

"'Could you put me to work?' says the boy.

"'Don't get me to shaking with laughter up here,' says the old brute. 'Can't you see I'd be in peril of falling off?'

"Young Angus undoes his bundle and reveals

overalls and a jumper which he gets into quickly.
'What do I do first?' says he.

"His father went on kalsomining and took never
a look at him more. 'The time has largely passed
here,' says he, 'for men that haven't learned to do
something, but you might take some of the burnt
umber there and work it well into a big gob of that
putty till it's brown enough to match the woodwork.
Should you display the least talent for that we may
see later if you've any knack with a putty knife.'

"The new hand had brought no lunch with him,
but his father spared him a few scraps from his own,
and they all swigged beer from a pail of it they sent
out for. So the scandal was now complete in all its
details. The palatial dining-room that night, being
a copy of a good church or something from ancient
Italy, smelled like a paint shop indeed—and sounded
like one through dinner. 'That woodwork will be
fit to second-coat first thing in the morning,' says old
Angus. 'I'll have it sandpapered in no time,' says
the boy. 'Your sandpapering ain't bad,' says the
other, 'though you have next to no skill with a brush.'
'I thought I was pretty good with that flat one
though.' 'Oh, fair; just fair! First-coating needs
little finesse. There! I forgot to order more rubbing
varnish. Maybe the men will think of it.' And so
on till they both yawned themselves off to their
Scotch Renaysence apartments. Ellabelle had not
yet learned the worst. It seemed to be felt that she
had a right to perish without suffering the added

ignominy of knowing her son was acting like a common wage slave.

"They was both on the job next day. Of course the disgraceful affair had by now penetrated to the remotest outlying marble shack. Several male millionaires this day appeared on the scene to josh Angus, *peer*, and Angus, *fills*, as they toiled at their degrading tasks. Not much attention was paid to 'em, it appears, not even to the old train-robber who come to jest and remained to cross-examine Angus about how much he was really going to clear on the job, seriously now. Anything like that was bound to fascinate the old crook.

"And next day, close to quitting time, what happens but this here robber chieftain's petted daughter coming in and hanging round and begging to be let to help because it was such jolly fun. I believe she did get hold of a square of sandpaper with which she daintily tried to remove some fresh varnish that should have been let strictly alone; and when they both ordered her out in a frenzy of rage, what does she do but wait for 'em with her car which she made them enter and drove them to their abode like they belonged to the better class of people that one would care to know. The two fools was both kind of excited about this that night.

"The next day she breezes in again and tries to get them to knock off an hour early so she can take them to the country club for tea, but they refuse this, so she makes little putty statues of them both and drove a few nails where they would do no good and upset a bucket of paste and leaned a two-hundred-dollar lace thing against a varnished wall to the detriment of both, and fell off a stepladder. Old Angus caught her and boxed her ears soundly. And again she drove them through the avenues of a colony of fine old families with money a little bit older, by a few days, and up the drive to their own door.

"Ellabelle was peeking between the plush curtains on this occasion, for some heartless busybody during the day had told her that her son and husband was both renegades now. And strangely enough, she begun to get back her strength from that very moment—seeing that exclusive and well-known young debby-tant consorting in public with the reprobates. I'm darned if she didn't have the genius after that to treat the whole thing as a practical joke, especially when she finds out that none of them exclusives had had it long enough to look down on another millionaire merely for pinching a penny now and then. Old Angus as a matter of fact had become just a little more important than she had ever been and could have snubbed any one he wanted to. The only single one in the whole place that throwed him down was his own English valet. He was found helpless drunk in a greenhouse the third day, having ruined nine thousand dollars' worth of orchids he'd gone to sleep amongst, and he resigned his position with bitter dignity the moment he recovered consciousness.

"Moreover, young Angus and this girl clenched

without further opposition. Her train-robber father said the boy must have something in him even if he didn't look it, and old Angus said he still believed the girl to be nothing but a yellow-haired soubrette; but what should we expect of a woman, after all?

"The night the job was finished we had the jolliest dinner of my visit, with a whole gang of exclusive-setters at the groaning board, including this girl and her folks, and champagne, of which Angus, *peer*, consumed near one of the cut-glass vases full.

"I caught him with young Angus in the deserted library later, while the rest was one-stepping in the Henry Quatter ballroom or dance hall. The old man had his arms pretty well upon the boy's shoulders. Yes, sir, he was almost actually hugging him. The boy fled to this gilded café where the rest was, and old Angus, with his eyes shining very queer, he grabs me by the arm and says, 'Once when he was very small—though unusually large for his age of three, mind you—he had a way of scratching my face something painful with his little nails, and all in laughing play, you know. I tried to warn him, but he couldn't understand, of course; so, not knowing how else to instruct him, I scratched back one day, laughing myself like he was, but sinking my nails right fierce into the back of his little fat neck. He relaxed the tension in his own fingers. He was hurt, for the tears started, but he never cried. He just looked puzzled and kept on laughing, being bright to see I could play the game, too. Only he saw it wasn't so good a game as he'd thought. I wonder what made me think of that, now! I don't know. Come—from yonder doorway we can see him as he dances.'

"And Ellabelle was saying gently to one and all, with her merry peal of laughter, 'Ah, yes—once a Scotchman, always——'

"My land! It's ten o'clock. Don't them little white-faced beauties make the music! Honestly I'd like to have a cot out in the corral. We miss a lot of it in here."

V

NON PLUSH ULTRA

SUNDAY and a driving rain had combined to keep Ma Pettengill within the Arrowhead ranch house. Neither could have done this alone. The rain would merely have added a slicker to her business costume of khaki riding breeches, laced boots, and flannel shirt as she rode abroad; while a clement Sabbath would have seen her "resting," as she would put it, in and round the various outbuildings, feeding-pens, blacksmith shop, harness-room, branding-chute, or what not, issuing orders to attentive henchmen from time to time; diagnosing the gray mule's barbed-wire cut; compounding a tonic for Adolph, the big milk-strain Durham bull, who has been ailing; wishing to be told why in something the water hadn't been turned into that south ditch; and, like a competent general, disposing her forces and munitions for the campaign of the coming week. But Sunday—and a wildly rainy Sunday—had housed her utterly.

Being one who can idle with no grace whatever she was engaged in what she called putting the place to rights. This meant taking out the contents of bureau drawers and wardrobes and putting them back

174

again, massing the litter on the big table in the living-
room into an involved geometry of neat piles that
would endure for all of an hour, straightening pictures on the walls, eliminating the home-circles of
spiders long unmolested, loudly calling upon Lew
Wee, the Chinaman, who affrightedly fled farther and
farther after each call, and ever and again booming
pained surmises through the house as to what fearful
state it would get to be in if she didn't fight it to a
clean finish once in a dog's age.

The woman dumped a wastebasket of varied rub-
bish into the open fire, leaned a broom against the
mantel, readjusted the towel that protected her gray
hair from the dust—hair on week days exposed with
never a qualm to all manner of dust—cursed all
Chinamen on land or sea with an especial and piquant
blight invoked upon the one now in hiding, then took
from the back of a chair where she had hung it the
moment before a riding skirt come to feebleness and
decrepitude. She held it up before critical eyes as
one scanning the morning paper for headlines of
significance.

"Ruined!" she murmured. Even her murmur
must have reached Lew Wee, how remote soever his
isle of safety. "Worn one time and all ruined up!
That's what happens for trying to get something for
nothing. You'd think women would learn. You
would if you didn't know a few. Hetty Daggett, her
that was Hetty Tipton, orders this by catalogue, No.
3456 or something, from the mail-order house in

Chicago. I was down in Red Gap when it come. 'Isn't it simply wonderful what you can get for three thirty-eight!' says she with gleaming eyes, laying this thing out before me. 'I don't see how they can ever do it for the money.' She found out the next day when she rode up here in it with me and Mr. Burchell Daggett, her husband. Nothing but ruin! Seams all busted, sleazy cloth wore through. But Hetty just looks it over cheerfully and says: 'Oh, well, what can you expect for three thirty-eight?' Is that like a woman or is it like something science has not yet discovered?

"That Hetty child is sure one woman. This skirt would never have held together to ride back in, so she goes down as far as the narrow gauge in the wagon with Buck Devine, wearing a charming afternoon frock of pale blue charmeuse rather than get into a pair of my khakis and ride back with her own lawful-wedded husband; yes, sir; married to him safe as anything, but wouldn't forget her womanhood. Only once did she ever come near it. I saved her then because she hadn't snared Mr. Burchell Daggett yet, and of course a girl has to be a little careful. And she took my counsels so much to heart she's been careful ever since. 'Why, I should simply die of mortification if my dear mate were to witness me in those,' says she when I'm telling her to take a chance for once and get into these here riding pants of mine because it would be uncomfortable going down in that wagon. 'But what is my com-

fort compared to dear Burchell's peace of mind?'
says she.

"Ain't we the goods, though, when we do once
learn a thing? Of course most of us don't have to
learn stuff like this. Born in us. I shouldn't wonder if they was something in the talk of this man
Shaw or Shavian—I see the name spelled both ways
in the papers. I can't read his pieces myself because
he rasps me, being not only a smarty but a vegetarian.
I don't know. I might stand one or the other pure-
bred, but the cross seems to bring out the worst
strain in both. I once got a line on his beliefs and
customs though—like it appears he don't believe
anything ought to be done for its own sake but only
for some good purpose. It was one day I got caught
at a meeting of the Onward and Upward Club in Red
Gap and Mrs. Alonzo Price read a paper about his
meaning. I hope she didn't wrong him. I hope she
was justified in all she said he really means in his
secret heart. No one ought to talk that way about
any one if they ain't got the goods on 'em. One
thing I might have listened to with some patience if
the man et steaks and talked more like some one
you'd care to have in your own home. In fact, I
listened to it anyway. Maybe he took it from some
book he read—about woman and her true nature.
According to Henrietta Templeton Price, as near as
I could get her, this Shaw or Shavian believes that
women is merely a flock of men-hawks circling above
the herd till they see a nice fat little la b of a man,

then one fell swoop and all is over but the screams of
the victim dying out horribly. They bear him off to
their nest in a blasted pine and pick the meat from his
bones at leisure. Of course that ain't the way ladies
was spoken of in the Aunt Patty Little Helper Series
I got out of the Presbyterian Sabbath-school library
back in Fredonia, New York, when I was thirteen—
and yet—and yet—as they say on the stage in these
plays of high or English life."

It sounded promising enough, and the dust had
now settled so that I could dimly make out the noble
lines of my hostess. I begged for more.

"Well, go on—Mrs. Burchell Daggett once nearly
forgot her womanhood. Certainly, go on, if it's anything that would be told outside of a smoking-car."

The lady grinned.

"Many of us has forgot our womanhood in the
dear, dead past," she confessed. "Me? Sure!
Where's that photo album. Where did I put that
album anyway? That's the way in this house. Get
things straightened up once, you can't find a single
one you want. Look where I put it now!" She
demolished an obelisk of books on the table, one she
had lately constructed with some pains, and brought
the album that had been its pedestal. "Get me
there, do you?"

It was the photograph of a handsome young woman
in the voluminous riding skirt of years gone by, before
the side-saddle became extinct. She held a crop and
wore an astoundingly plumed bonnet. Despite the

offensive disguise, one saw provocation for the course
adopted by the late Lysander John Pettengill at
about that period.

"Very well—now get me here, after I'd been on the
ranch only a month." It was the same young
woman in the not too foppish garb of a cowboy. In
wide-brimmed hat, flannel shirt, woolly chaps, quirt
in hand, she bestrode a horse that looked capable and
daring.

"Yes, sir, I hadn't been here only a month when I
forgot my womanhood like that. Gee! How good it
felt to get into 'em and banish that sideshow tent of a
skirt. I'd never known a free moment before and I
blessed Lysander John for putting me up to it. Then,
proud as Punch, what do I do but send one of these
photos back to dear old Aunt Waitstill, in Fredonia,
thinking she would rejoice at the wild, free life I was
now leading in the Far West. And what do I get for it
but a tear-spotted letter of eighteen pages, with a
side-kick from her pastor, the Reverend Abner
Hemingway, saying he wishes to indorse every word
of Sister Baxter's appeal to me—asking why do I
parade myself shamelessly in this garb of a fallen
woman, and can nothing be said to recall me to the
true nobility that must still be in my nature but which
I am forgetting in these licentious habiliments, and
so on! The picture had been burned after giving
the Reverend his own horrified flash of it, and they
would both pray daily that I might get up out of this
degradation and be once more a good, true woman

that some pure little child would not be ashamed to call the sacred name of mother.

"Such was Aunt Waitstill—what names them poor old girls had to stand for! I had another aunt named Obedience, only she proved to be a regular cinch-binder. Her name was never mentioned in the family after she slid down a rainspout one night and eloped to marry a depraved scoundrel who drove through there on a red wagon with tinware inside that he would trade for old rags. I'm just telling you how times have changed in spite of the best efforts of a sanctified ministry. I cried over that letter at first. Then I showed it to Lysander John, who said 'Oh, hell!' being a man of few words, so I felt better and went right on forgetting my womanhood in that shameless garb of a so-and-so—though where aunty had got her ideas of such I never could make out— and it got to be so much a matter of course and I had so many things to think of besides my woman-hood that I plumb forgot the whole thing until this social upheaval in Red Gap a few years ago.

"I got to tell you that the wild and lawless West, in all matters relating to proper dress for ladies, is the most conservative and hidebound section of our great land of the free and home of the brave—if you can get by with it. Out here the women see by the Sunday papers that it's being wore that way publicly in New York and no one arrested for it, but they don't hardly believe it at that, and they wouldn't show themselves in one, not if you begged them to on your bended knees, and what is society coming to anyway? You might as well dress like one of them barefooted dancers, only calling 'em barefooted must be meant like sarcasm—and they'd die before they'd let a daughter of theirs make a show of herself like that for odious beasts of men to leer at, and so on—until a couple years later Mrs. Henrietta Templeton Price gets a regular one and wears it down Main Street, and nothing objectionable happens; so then they all hustle to get one—not quite so extreme, of course, but after all, why not, since only the evil-minded could criticise? Pretty soon they're all wearing it exactly like New York did two years ago, with mebbe the limit raised a bit here and there by some one who makes her own. But again they're saying that the latest one New York is wearing is so bad that it must be confined to a certain class of women, even if they do get taken from left to right at Asbury Park and Newport and other colonies of wealth and fashion, because the vilest dregs can go there if they have the price, which they often do.

"Red Gap is like that. With me out here on the ranch it didn't matter what I wore because it was mostly only men that saw me; but I can well remember the social upheaval when our smartest young matrons and well-known society belles flung modesty to the chinook wind and took to divided skirts for horseback riding. My, the brazen hussies! It ain't so many years ago. Up to that time any female over the age of nine caught riding a horse cross-saddle

would have lost her character good and quick. And
these pioneers lost any of theirs that wasn't cemented
good and hard with proved respectability. I remember hearing Jeff Tuttle tell what he'd do to any
of his womenfolks that so far forgot the sacred names
of home and mother. It was startling enough, but
Jeff somehow never done it. And if he was to hear
Addie or one of the girls talking about a side-saddle
to-day he'd think she was nutty or mebbe wanting
one for the state museum. So it goes with us. My
hunch is that so it will ever go.

"The years passed, and that thrill of viciousness at
wearing divided skirts in public got all rubbed off—
that thrill that every last one of us adores to feel if
only it don't get her talked about—too much—by
evil-minded gossips. Then comes this here next upheaval over riding pants for ladies—or them that set
themselves up to be such. Of course we'd long
known that the things were worn in New York and
even in such modern Babylons as Spokane and
Seattle; but no woman in Red Gap had ever forgot
she had a position to keep up, until summer before
last, when we saw just how low one of our sex could
fall, right out on the public street.

"She was the wife of a botanist from some Eastern
college and him and her rode a good bit and dressed
just alike in khaki things. My, the infamies that
was intimated about that poor creature! She was
bony and had plainly seen forty, very severe-featured,
with scraggly hair and a sharp nose and spectacles,

and looked as if she had never had a moment of the most innocent pleasure in all her life; but them riding pants fixed her good in the minds of our lady porch-knockers. And the men just as bad, though they could hardly bear to look twice at her, she was that discouraging to the eye; they agreed with their wives that she must be one of that sort.

"But things seem to pile up all at once in our town. That very summer the fashion magazines was handed round with pages turned down at the more daring spots where ladies were shown in such things. It wasn't felt that they were anything for the little ones to see. But still, after all, wasn't it sensible, now really, when you come right down to it? and as a matter of fact isn't a modest woman modest in any-thing?—it isn't what she wears but how she conducts herself in public, or don't you think so, Mrs. Ballard? —and you might as well be dead as out of style, and would Lehman, the Square Tailor, be able to make up anything like that one there?—but no, because how would he get your measure?—and surely no modest woman could give him hers even if she did take it her-self—anyway, you'd be insulted by all the street rowdies as you rode by, to say nothing of being ogled by men without a particle of fineness in their natures —but there's always something to be said on both sides, and it's time woman came into her own, any-way, if she is ever to be anything but man's toy for his idle moments—still it would never do to go to ex-tremes in a narrow little town like this with every one just looking for an excuse to talk—but it would be different if all the best people got together and agreed to do it, only most of them would probably back out at the last moment and that smarty on the *Recorder* would try to be funny about it—now that one with the long coat doesn't look so terrible, does it? or do you think so?—of course it's almost the same as a skirt except when you climb on or something—a woman has to think of those things—wouldn't Daisy Estelle look rather stunning in that?—she has just the figure for it. Here's this No. 9872 with the Norfolk jacket in this mail-order catalogue—do you think that looks too theatrical, or don't you? Of course for some figures, but I've always been able to wear —— And so forth, for a month or so.

"Late in the fall Henrietta Templeton Price done it. You may not know what that meant to Alonzo Price, Choice Villa Sites and Price's Addition to Red Gap. Alonzo is this kind: I met him the day Gussie Himebaugh had her accident when the mules she was driving to the mowing machine run away out on Himebaugh's east forty. Alonzo had took Doc May- bury out and passes me coming back. 'How bad was she hurt?' I asks. The poor thing looks down greatly embarrassed and mumbles: 'She has broken a limb.' 'Leg or arm?' I blurts out, forgetting all delicacy. You'd think I had him pinned down, wouldn't you? Not Lon, though. 'A lower limb,' says he, coughing and looking away.

"You see how men are till we put a spike collar and

chain on 'em. When Henrietta declared herself
Alonzo read the riot act and declared marital law.
But there was Henrietta with the collar and chain and
pretty soon Lon was saying: 'You're quite right,
Pettikins, and you ought to have the thanks of the
community for showing our ladies how to dress
rationally on horseback. It's not only sensible and
safe but it's modest—a plain pair of riding breeches,
no coquetry, no frills, nothing but stern utility—of
course I agree.'

"'I hoped you would, darling,' says Henrietta.
She went to Miss Gunslaugh and had her make the
costume, being one who rarely does things by halves.
It was of blue velvet corduroy, with a fetching little
bolero jacket, and the things themselves were fitted,
if you know what I mean. And stern utility! That
suit with its rosettes and bows and frogs and braid
had about the same stern utility as those pretty little
tin tongs that come on top of a box of candy—ever
see anybody use one of those? When Henrietta got
dressed for her first ride and had put on the Cuban
Pink Face Balm she looked like one of the gypsy
chorus in the Bohemian Girl opera.

"Alonzo gulped several times in rapid succession
when he saw her, but the little man never starts anything he don't aim to finish, and it was too late to
start it then. Henrietta brazened her way through
Main Street and out to the country club and back,
and next day she put them on again so Otto Hirsch,
of the E-light Studio, could come up and take her

standing by the horse out in front of the Price mansion. Then they was laid away until the Grand Annual Masquerade Ball of the Order of the Eastern Star, which is a kind of hen Masons, when she again gave us a flash of what New York society ladies was riding their horse in. As a matter of fact, Henrietta hates a horse like a rattlesnake, but she had done her pioneer work for once and all.

"Every one was now laughing and sneering at the old-fashioned divided skirt with which woman had endangered her life on a horse, and wondering how they had endured the clumsy things so long; and come spring all the prominent young society buds and younger matrons of the most exclusive set who could stay on a horse at all was getting theirs ready for the approaching season, Red Gap being like London in having its gayest season in the summer, when people can get out more. Even Mis' Judge Ballard fell for it, though hers was made of severe black with a long coat. She looked exactly like that Methodist minister, the old one, that we had three years ago.

"Most of the younger set used the mail-order catalogue, their figures still permitting it. And maybe there wasn't a lot of trying on behind drawn blinds pretty soon, and delighted giggles and innocent girlish wonderings about whether the lowest type of man really ogles as much under certain circumstances as he's said to. And the minute the roads got good the telephone of Pierce's Livery, Feed, and Sale Stable was kept on the ring. Then the social upheaval was on. Of course any of 'em looked quiet after Henrietta's costume, for none of the girls but Beryl Mae Macomber, a prominent young society bud, aged seventeen, had done anything like that. But it was the idea of the thing.

"A certain element on the South Side made a lot of talk and stirred things up and wrote letters to the president of the Civic Purity League, who was Mis' Judge Ballard herself, asking where this unspeakable disrobing business was going to end and calling her attention to the fate that befell Sodom and Gomorrah. But Mis' Ballard she's mixed on names and gets the idea these parties mean Samson and Delilah instead of a couple of twin cities, like St. Paul and Minneapolis, and she writes back saying what have these Bible characters got to do with a lady riding on horseback—in trousers, it is true, but with a coat falling modestly to the knee on each side, and certain people had better be a little more fussy about things that really matter in life before they begin to talk. She knew who she was hitting at all right, too. Trust Mis' Ballard!

"It was found that there was almost the expected amount of ogling from sidewalk loafers, at first. As Daisy Estelle Maybury said, it seemed as if a girl couldn't show herself on the public thoroughfare without being subjected to insult. Poor Daisy Estelle! She had been a very popular young society belle, and was considered one of the most attractive girls in Red Gap until this happened. No one had ever suspected it of her in the least degree up to that time. Of course it was too late after she was once seen off her horse. Them that didn't see was told in full detail by them that did. Most of the others was luckier. Beryl Mae Macomber in her sport shirt and trouserettes complained constantly about the odious wretches along Main Street and Fourth, where the post office was. She couldn't stop even twenty minutes in front of the post office, minding her own business and waiting for some one she knew to come along and get her mail for her, without having dozens of men stop and ogle her. That, of course, was during the first two weeks after she took to going for the mail, though the eternal feminine in Beryl Mae probably thought the insulting glances was going to keep up forever.

"I watched the poor child one day along in the third week, waiting there in front of the post office after the four o'clock mail, and no one hardly ogled her at all except some rude children out from school. What made it more pitiful, leaning right there against the post office front was Jack Shiels, Sammie Hamilton, and little old Elmer Cox, Red Gap's three town rowdies that ain't done a stroke of work since the canning factory closed down the fall before, creatures that by rights should have been leering at the poor child in all her striking beauty. But, no; the brutes stand there looking at nothing much until Jack Shiels stares a minute at this horse Beryl Mae is on and pipes up: 'Why, say, I thought Pierce let that little bay runt go

to the guy that was in here after polo ponies last
Thursday. I sure did.' And Sam Hamilton wakes
up and says: 'No, sir; not this one. He got rid of a
little mare that had shoulders like this, but she was a
roan with kind of mule ears and one froze off.' And
little old Elmer Cox, ignoring this defenceless young
girl with his impudent eyes, he says: 'Yes, Sam's
right for once. Pierce tried to let this one go, too,
but ain't you took a look at his hocks!' Then along
comes Dean Duke, the ratty old foreman in Pierce's
stable, and he don't ogle a bit, either, like you'd expect one of his debased calibre to, but just stops and
talks this horse over with 'em and says yes, it was his
bad hocks that lost the sale, and he tells 'em how he
had told Pierce just what to do to get him shaped up
for a quick sale, but Pierce wouldn't listen to him,
thinking he knew it all himself; and there the four
stood and gassed about this horse without even seeing
Beryl Mae, let alone leering at her. I bet she was
close to shedding tears of girlish mortification as she
rode off without ever waiting for the mail. Things
was getting to a pretty pass. If low creatures lost to
all decent instincts, like these four, wouldn't ogle a
girl when she was out for it, what could be expected
of the better element of the town? Still, of course,
now and then one or the other of the girls would have
a bit of luck to tell of.

"Well, now we come to the crookedest bit of
work I ever been guilty of, though first telling you
about Mr. Burchell Daggett, an Eastern society man

from Cedar Rapids, Iowa, that had come to Red Gap that spring to be assistant cashier in the First National, through his uncle having stock in the thing. He was a very pleasant kind of youngish gentleman, about thirty-four, I reckon, with dark, parted whiskers and gold eyeglasses and very good habits. He took his place among our very best people right off, teaching the Bible class in the M. E. Sabbath-school and belonging to the Chamber of Commerce and the City Beautiful Association, of which he was made vice-president, and being prominent at all functions held in our best homes. He wasn't at all one of them that lead a double life by stopping in at the Family Liquor Store for a gin fizz or two after work hours, or going downtown after supper to play Kelly pool at the Temperance Billiard Parlours and drink steam beer, or getting in with the bunch that gathers in the back room of the Owl Cigar Store of an evening and tells these here suggestive stories. Not that he was hide-bound. If he felt the need for a shot of something he'd go into the United States Grill and have a glass of sherry and bitters brought to him at a table and eat a cracker with it, and he'd take in every show, even the Dizzy Belles of Gotham Big Blonde Beauty Show. He was refined and even moral in the best sense of the word, but still human.

"Our prominent young society buds took the keenest notice of him at once, as would naturally happen, he being a society bachelor of means and by long odds

the best catch in Red Gap since old Potter Knapp, of
the Loan and Trust Company, had broke his period
of mourning for his third wife by marrying Myrtle
Wade that waited on table at the Occidental Hotel,
with the black band still on his left coat sleeve.   It's
no exaggeration to say that Mr. Burchell Daggett became the most sought-after social favourite among
Reg Gap's hoot mondy in less than a week after he
unpacked his trunk.   But it was very soon discovered
by the bright-eyed little gangsters of the best circles
that he wasn't going to be an easy one to disable.
Naturally when a man has fought 'em off to his age he
has learned much of woodcraft and the hunter's cunning wiles, and this one had sure developed timber
sense.   He beat 'em at their own game for three
months by the simple old device of not playing any
favourite for one single minute, and very, very seldom getting alone with one where the foul stroke can
be dealt by the frailest hand with muscular precision.   If he took Daisy Estelle Maybury to the
chicken pie supper to get a new carpet for the Presbyterian parsonage, he'd up and take Beryl Mae and her
aunt, or Gussie Himebaugh, or Luella Stultz, to the
lawn feet at Judge Ballard's for new uniforms for the
band boys.   At the Bazaar of All Nations he bought
as many chances of one girl as he did of another, and
if he hadn't any more luck than a rabbit and won
something—a hanging lamp or a celluloid manicure
set in a plush-lined box—he'd simply put it up to be
raffled off again for the good of the cause.   And none

of that moonlight loitering along shaded streets for him, where the dirk is so often drove stealthily between a man's ribs, and him thinking all the time he's only indulging in a little playful nonsense. Often as not he'd take two girls at once, where all could be merry without danger of anything happening.

"It was no time at all till this was found out on him. It was seen that under a pleasing exterior, looking all too easy to overcome by any girl in her right mind, he had powers of resistance and evasion that was like steel. Of course this only stirred the proud beauties on to renewed and crookeder efforts. Every darned one of 'em felt that her innocent young girlhood was challenged, and would she let it go at that? Not so. My lands! What snares and deadfalls was set for this wise old timber wolf that didn't look it, with his smiling ways and seemingly careless response to merry banter, and so forth!

"And of course every one of these shrinking little scoundrels thought at once of her new riding costume, so no time at all was lost in organizing the North Side Riding and Sports Club, which Mr. Burchell Daggett gladly joined, having, as he said, an eye for a horse and liking to get out after banking hours to where all Nature seems to smile and you can let your mount out a bit over the firm, smooth road. Them that had held off until now, on account of the gossip and leering, hurried up and got into line with No. 9872 in the mail-order catalogue, or went to Miss Gunslaugh, who by this time had a female wax dummy in her window

in a neat brown suit and puttees, with a coat just
opening and one foot advanced carelessly, with
gauntlets and a riding crop, and a fetching little cap
over the wind-blown hair and the clear, wonderful
blue eyes. Oh, you can bet every last girl of the
bunch was seeing herself send back picture postals to
her rivals telling what a royal time they was having
at Palm or Rockaway Beach or some place, and seeing the engraved cards—'Mr. and Mrs. Burchell Daggett, at Home After the Tenth, Ophir Avenue, Red
Gap, Wash.'

"Ain't we good when you really get us, if you ever
do—because some don't. Many, indeed! I reckon
there never was a woman yet outside of a feeb' home
that didn't believe she could be an A. No. 1 siren if she
only had the nerve to dress the part; never one that
didn't just ache to sway men to her lightest whim,
and believe she could—not for any evil purpose,
mind you, but just to show her power.   Think of the
tender hearts that must have shuddered over the
damage they could and actually might do in one of
them French bathing suits like you are said to witness
in Paris and Atlantic City and other sinks of iniquity.
And here was these well-known society favourites
wrought up by this legible party, as the French say,
till each one was ready to go just as far as the Civic
Purity League would let her in order to sweep him off
his feet in one mad moment.   Quite right, too.   It
all depends on what the object is, don't it; and wasn't
theirs honourable matrimony with an establishment

and a lawn in front of it with a couple of cast-iron moose, mebbe?

"And amid all this quaint girlish enterprise and secret infamy was the problem of Hetty Tipton. Hetty had been a friend and a problem of mine for seven years, or ever since she come back from normal to teach in the third-grade grammar school; a fine, clean, honest, true-blue girl, mebbe not as pretty you'd say at first as some others, but you like her better after you look a few times more, and with not the slightest nonsense about her. That last was Hetty's one curse. I ask you, what chance has a girl got with no nonsense about her? Hetty won my sympathy right at the start by this infirmity of hers, which was easily detected, and for seven years I'd been trying to cure her of it, but no use. Oh, she was always took out regular enough and well liked, but the gilded youth of Red Gap never fought for her smiles. They'd take her to parties and dances, turn and turn about, but they always respected her, which is the greatest blight a man can put on one of us, if you know what I mean. Every man at a party was always careful to dance a decent number of times with Hetty and see that she got back to her seat; and wasn't it warm in here this evening, yes, it was; and wouldn't she have a glass of the punch—No, thank you—then he'd gallop off to have some fun with a mere shallow-pated fool that had known how from the cradle. It was always a puzzle to me, because Hetty dressed a lot better than most of them, knowing what to wear and how, and could take a joke if it come slow, and laid herself out to be amiable to one and all. I kind of think it must be something about her mentality. Maybe it is too mental. I can't put her to you any plainer than to say that every single girl in town, young and old, just loved her, and not one of them up to this time had ever said an unkind or feminine thing about her. I guess you know what that would mean of any woman.

"Hetty was now coming twenty-nine—we never spoke of this, but I could count back—and it's my firm belief that no man had ever proposed marriage or anything else on earth to her. Wilbur Todd had once endeavoured to hold her hand out on the porch at a country-club dance and she had repulsed him in all kindness but firmly. She told him she couldn't bring herself to permit a familiarity of that sort except to the man who would one day lead her to the altar, which is something I believe she got from writing to a magazine about a young girl's perplexities. And here, in spite of her record, this poor thing had dared to raise her eyes to none other than this Mr. Burchell Daggett. There was something kind of grand and despairing about the impudence of it when you remember these here trained efficiency experts she was competing with. Yet so it was. She would drop in on me after school for a cup of tea and tell me frankly how distinguished his manner was and what shapely features he had and what fine eyes, and how there was a certain note in his voice at times, and had I ever noticed that one stubborn lock of hair that stuck out back of his left ear? Of course that last item settled it. When they notice that lock of hair you know the ship has struck the reef and all hands are perishing.

"And it seemed that the cuss had not only shown her more than a little attention at evening functions but had escorted her to the midspring production of 'Hamlet' by the Red Gap Amateur Theatrical and Dramatic Society. True, he had conducted himself like a perfect gentleman every minute they was alone together, even when they had to go home in Eddie Pierce's hack because it was raining when the show let out—but would I, or would I not, suspect from all this that he was in the least degree thinking of her in a way that—you know!

"Poor child of twenty-eight, with her hungry eyes and flushed face while she was showing down her hand to me! I seen the scoundrel's play at once. Hetty was the one safe bet for him in Red Gap's social whirl. He was wise, all right—this Mr. D. He'd known in a second he could trust himself alone with that girl and be as safe as a babe in its mother's arms. Of course I couldn't say this to Hetty. I just said he was a man that seemed to know his own mind very clearly, whatever it was, and Hetty blushed some more and said that something within her responded to a certain note in his voice. We let it go at that.

"So I think and ponder about poor Hetty, trying to invent some conspiracy that would fix it right, because she was the ideal mate for an assistant cashier that had a certain position to keep up. For that matter she was good enough for any man. Then I hear she has joined the riding club, and an all day's ride has been planned for the next Saturday up to Stender's Spring, with a basket lunch and a romantic ride back by moonlight. Of course, I don't believe in any of this spiritualist stuff, but you can't tell me there ain't something in it, mind-reading or something, with the hunches you get when parties is in some grave danger.

"Stella Ballard it was tells me about the picnic, calling me in as I passed their house to show me her natty new riding togs that had just come from the mail-order house. She called from back of a curtain, and when I got into the parlour she had them on, pleased as all get-out. Pretty they was, too—riding breeches and puttees and a man's flannel shirt and a neat-fitting Norfolk jacket, and Stella being a fine, upstanding figure.

"'They may cause considerable talk,' says she, smoothing down one leg where it wrinkled a bit, 'but really I think they look perfectly stunning on me, and wasn't it lucky they fit me so beautifully? They're called the Non Plush Ultra.'

"'The what?' I says.

"'The Non Plush Ultra,' she answers. 'That's the name of them sewed in the band.'

"'What's that mean?' I wanted to know.

"'Why,' says Stella, 'that's Latin or Greek, I

forget which, and it means they're the best, I believe. Oh, let me see! Why, it means nothing beyond, or something like that; the farthest you can go, I think. One forgets all that sort of thing after leaving high school.'

"'Well,' I says, 'they fit fine, and it's the only modest rig for a woman to ride a horse in, but they certainly are non plush, all right. That thin goods will never wear long against saddle leather, take my word for it.'

"But of course this made no impression on Stella— she was standing on the centre table by now, so she could lamp herself in the glass over the mantel—and then she tells me about the excursion for Saturday and how Mr. Burchell Daggett is enthused about it, him being a superb horseman himself, and, if I know what she means, don't I think she carries herself in the saddle almost better than any girl in her set, and won't her style show better than ever in this duck of a costume, and she must get her tan shoes polished, and do I think Mr. Daggett really meant anything when he said he'd expect her some day to return the masonic pin she had lifted off his vest the other night at the dance, and so on.

"It was while she was babbling this stuff that I get the strange hunch that Hetty Tipton is in grave danger and I ought to run to her; it seemed almost I could hear her calling on me to save her from some horrible fate. So I tell Stella yes, she's by far the finest rider in the whole Kulanche Valley, and she ought to get anything she wants with that suit on, and then I beat it quick over to the Ezra Dutton house where Hetty boards.

"You can laugh all you want to, but that hunch of mine was the God's truth. Hetty was in the gravest danger she'd faced since one time in early infancy when she got give morphine for quinine. What made it more horrible, she hadn't the least notion of her danger. Quite the contrary.

"'Thank the stars I've come in time!' I gasps as I rushes in on her, for there's the poor girl before her mirror in a pair of these same Non Plush Ultras and looking as pleased with herself as if she had some reason to be.

"'Back into your skirts quick!' I says. 'I'm a strong woman and all that, but still I can be affected more than you'd think.'

"Poor Hetty stutters and turns red and her chin begins to quiver, so I gentled her down and tried to explain, though seeing quick that I must tell her everything but the truth. I reckon nothing in this world can look funnier than a woman wearing them things that had never ought to for one reason or another. There was more reasons than that in Hetty's case. Dignity was the first safe bet I could think of with her, so I tried that.

"'I know all you would say,' says the poor thing in answer, 'but isn't it true that men rather like one to be—oh, well, you know—just the least bit daring?'

"'Truest thing in the world,' I says, 'but bless your

heart, did you suspicion riding breeches was daring on a woman? Not so. A girl wearing 'em can't be any more daring after the first quick shock is over than—well, you read the magazines, don't you? You've seen those pictures of family life in darkest Africa that the explorers and monkey hunters bring home, where the wives, mothers, and sweethearts, God bless 'em! wear only what the scorching climate demands. Didn't it strike you that one of them women without anything on would have a hard time if she tried to be daring—or did it? No woman can be daring without the proper clothes for it,' I says firmly, 'and as for you, I tell you plain, get into the most daring and immodest thing that was ever invented for woman—which is the well-known skirt.'

"'Oh, Ma Pettengill,' cries the poor thing, 'I never meant anything horrid and primitive when I said daring. As a matter of fact, I think these are quite modest to the intelligent eye.'

"'Just what I'm trying to tell you,' I says. 'Exactly that; they're modest to any eye whatever. But here you are embarked on a difficult enterprise, with a band of flinty-hearted cutthroats trying to beat you to it, and, my dear child, you have a staunch nature and a heart of gold, but you simply can't afford to be modest.'

"'I don't understand,' says she, looking at herself in the glass again.

"'Trust me, anyway,' I implores. 'Let others wear their Non Plush Ultras which are No. 9872'—

she tries to correct my pronunciation, but I wouldn't stop for that. 'Never mind how it's pronounced,' I says, 'because I know well the meaning of it in a foreign language. It means the limit, and it's a very desirable limit for many, but for you,' I says plainly, 'it's different. Your Non Plush Ultra will have to be a neat, ankle-length riding skirt. You got one, haven't you?'

"'I have,' says she, 'a very pretty one of tan corduroy, almost new, but I had looked forward to these, and I don't see yet——'

"Then I thought of another way I might get to her without blurting out the truth. 'Listen, Hetty,' I says, 'and remember not only that I'm your friend but that I know a heap more about this fool world than you do. I've had bitter experiences, and one of them got me at the time I first begun to wear riding pants myself, which must have been about the time you was beginning to bite dents into your silver mug that Aunt Caroline sent. I was a handsome young hellion, I don't mind telling you, and they looked well on me, and when Lysander John urged me to be brave and wear 'em outside I was afraid all the men within a day's ride was going to sneak round to stare at me. My! I was so embarrassed, also with that same feeling you got in your heart this minute that it was taking an unfair advantage of any man—you know! I felt like I was using all the power of my young beauty for unworthy ends.

"'Well, do you know what I got when I first rode

out on the ranch? I got just about the once-over
from every brute there, and that was all. If one of
them ranch hands had ever ogled me a second time
I'd have known it all right, but I never caught one
of the scoundrels at it. First I said: "Now, ain't
that fine and chivalrous?" Then I got wise. It
wasn't none of this here boasted Western chivalry,
but just plain lack of interest. I admit it made me
mad at first. Any man on the place was only too
glad to look me over when I had regular clothes on,
but dress me like Lysander John and they didn't
look at me any oftener than they did him. Not as
often, of course, because as a plain human being and
man's equal I wasn't near as interesting as he was.'

"'But then, too,' says Hetty, who had only been
about half listening to my lecture, 'I thought it
might be striking a blow at the same time for the
freedom of woman.'

"Well, you know how that freedom-of-the-sex
talk always gets me going. I was mad enough for a
minute to spank her just as she stood there in them
Non Plush Ultras she was so proud of. And I did
let out some high talk. Mrs. Dutton told her afterward she thought sure we was having words.

"'Freedom from skirts,' I says, 'is the last thing
your sex wants. Skirts is the final refuge of im-
modesty, to which women will cling like grim death.
They will do any possible thing to a skirt—slit it,
thin it, shorten it, hike it up one side—people are
setting up nights right now thinking up some new

thing to do to it—but women won't give it up and dress modestly as men do because it's the only unfair drag they got left with the men. I see one of our offended sex is daily asking right out in a newspaper: "Are women people?" I'd just like to whisper to her that no one yet knows.

"'If they'll quit their skirts, dress as decently as a man does so they won't have any but a legitimate pull with him, we'd have a chance to find out if they're good for anything else. As a matter of fact, they don't want to be people and dress modestly and wear hats you couldn't pay over eight dollars for. I believe there was one once, but the poor thing never got any notice from either sex after she became—a people, as you might say.'

"Well, I was going on to get off a few more things I'd got madded up to, but I caught the look in poor Hetty's face, and it would have melted a stone. Poor child! There she was, wanting a certain man and willing to wear or not wear anything on earth that would nail him, and not knowing what would do it, and complicating her ignorance with meaningless worries about modesty and daringness and the freedom of her poor sex, that ain't ever even deuce-low with one woman in a million.

"And right then, watching her distress, all at once I get my big inspiration—it just flooded me like the sun coming up. I don't know if I'm like other folks, but things do come to me that way. And not only was it a great truth, but it got me out of the hole

of having to tell Hetty certain truths about herself
that these Non Plush Ultras made all too glaring.

"'Listen,' I says: 'You believe I'm your friend,
don't you? And you believe anything I tell you is
from the heart out and will probably have a grain of
sense in it. Well, here is an inspired thought:
Women won't ever dress modestly like men do because men don't want 'em to. I never saw a man
yet that did if he'd tell the truth, and so this here dark
city stranger won't be any exception. Now, then,
what do we see on Saturday next? Why, we see this
here gay throng sally forth for Stender's Spring, the
youth and beauty of Red Gap, including Mr. D.,
with his nice refined odour of Russia leather and
bank bills of large size—from fifties up—that haven't
been handled much. The crowd is of all sexes,
technically, like you might say; a lot of nice, sweet
girls along but dressed to be mere jolly young roughnecks, and just as interesting to the said stranger as
the regular boys that will be present—hardly more
so. And now, as for poor little meek you—you will
look wild and Western, understand me, but feminine;
exactly like the coloured cigarette picture that says
under it "Rocky Mountain Cow Girl." You will
be in your pretty tan skirt—be sure to have it pressed
—and a blue-striped sport bloose that I just saw in
the La Mode window, and you'll get some other
rough Western stuff there, too: a blue silk neckerchief
and a natty little cow-girl sombrero—the La Mode
is showing a good one called the La Parisienne for

four fifty-eight—and the daintiest pair of tan kid gauntlets you can find, and don't forget a pair of tan silk stockings——'

"'They won't show in my riding boots,' says Hetty, looking as if she was coming to life a little.

"'Tush for the great, coarse, commonsense riding boots,' I says firmly; 'you will wear precisely that neat little pair of almost new tan pumps with the yellow bows that you're standing in now. Do you get me?'

"'But that would be too dainty and absurd,' says Hetty.

"'Exactly!' I says, shutting my mouth hard.

"'Why, I almost believe I do get you,' says she, looking religiously up into the future like that lady saint playing the organ in the picture.

"'Another thing,' I says: 'You are deathly afraid of a horse and was hardly ever on one but once when you were a teeny girl, but you do love the open life, so you just nerved yourself up to come.'

"'I believe I see more clearly than ever,' says Hetty. She grew up on a ranch, knows more about a horse than the horse himself does, and would be a top rider most places, with the cheap help we get nowadays that can hardly set a saddle.

"'Also from time to time,' I goes on, 'you want to ask this Mr. D. little, timid, silly questions that will just tickle him to death and make him feel superior. Ask him to tell you which legs of a horse the chaps go on, and other things like that; ask him if the sash that holds the horrid old saddle on isn't so tight it's hurting your horse. After the lunch is et, go over to the horse all alone and stroke his nose and call him a dear and be found by the gent when he follows you over trying to feed the noble animal a hard-boiled egg and a couple of pickles or something. Take my word for it, he'll be over all right and have a hearty laugh at your confusion, and begin to wonder what it is about you.

"'How about falling off and spraining my ankle on the way back?' demands the awakening vestal with a gleam in her eye.

"'No good,' I says; 'pretty enough for a minute, but it would make trouble if you kept up the bluff, and if there's one thing a man hates more than another it's to have a woman round that makes any trouble.'

"'You have me started on a strange new train of thought,' says Hetty.

"'I think it's a good one,' I tells her, 'but remember there are risks. For one thing, you know how popular you have always been with all the girls. Well, after this day none of 'em will hardly speak to you because of your low-lifed, deceitful game, and the things they'll say of you—such things as only woman can say of woman!'

"'I shall not count the cost,' says she firmly. 'And now I must hurry down for that sport bloose—blue-striped, you said?'

"'Something on that order,' I says, 'that fits only

too well. You can do almost anything you want to
with your neck and arms, but remember strictly—
a skirt is your one and only Non Plush Ultra.'

"So I went home all flushed and eager, thinking
joyously how little men—the poor dubs—ever suspect
how it's put over on 'em, and the next day, which
was Friday, I thought of a few more underhand
things she could do. So when she run in to see me
that afternoon, the excitement of the chase in her
eye, she wanted I should go along on this picnic.
I says yes, I will, being that excited myself and wanting to see really if I was a double-faced genius or
wasn't I? Henrietta Price couldn't go on account of
being still lame from her ride of a week ago, so I
could go as chaperone, and anyway I knew the dear
girls would all be glad to have me because I would
look so different from them—like a genial old ranch
foreman going out on rodeo—and the boys was
always glad to see me along anyway. 'I'll be there,'
I says to Hetty. 'And here—don't forget at all
times to-morrow to carry this little real lace handkerchief I'm giving you.'

"I was at the meeting-place next morning at nine.
None of the other girls was on time, of course, but
that was just as well, because Aggie Tuttle had got
her father to come down to the sale yard to pack a
mule with the hampers of lunch. Jeff Tuttle is a
good packer all right, but too inflamed in the case of a
mule, which he hates. They always know up and
down that street when he's packing one; ladies drag

their children by as fast as they can. But Jeff had
the hitch all throwed before any of the girls showed
up, and all began in a lovely manner, the crowd of
about fifteen getting off not more than an hour late;
Mr. Burchell in the lead and a bevy of these jolly
young rascals in their Non Plush Ultras riding herd on
him.

"Every girl cast cordial glances of pity at poor
Hetty when she showed up in her neat skirt and silly
tan pumps with the ridiculous silk stockings and the
close-fitting blue-striped thing, free at the neck, and
her pretty hair all neated under the La Parisienne
cow-girl hat. Oh, they felt kinder than ever before
to poor old Hetty when they saw her as little daring
as that, cheering her with a hearty uproar, slapping
their Non Plush Ultras with their caps or gloves,
and then giggling confidentially to one another.
Hetty accepted their applause with what they call a
pretty show of confusion and gored her horse with
her heel on the off side so it looked as if the vicious
brute was running away and she might fall off any
minute, but somehow she didn't, and got him soothed
with frightened words and by taking the hidden heel
out of his slats—though not until Mr. D. had noticed
her good and then looked again once or twice.

"And so the party moved on for an hour or two,
with the roguish young roughnecks cutting up merrily
at all times, pretending to be cowboys coming to
town on pay day, swinging their hats, giving the
long yell, and doing roughriding to cut each other

away from the side of Mr. D. every now and then, with a noisy laugh of good nature to hide the poisoned dagger. Daisy Estelle Maybury is an awful good rider, too, and got next to the hero about every time she wanted to. Poor thing, if she only knew that once she gets off a horse in 'em it makes all the difference in the world.

"The dark city stranger seemed to enjoy it fine, all this noise and cutting up and cowboy antics like they was just a lot of high-spirited young men together, but I never weakened in my faith for one minute. 'Laugh on, my proud beauties,' I says, 'but a time will come, just as sure as you look and act like a passel of healthy boys.' And you bet it did.

"We hadn't got halfway to Stender's Spring till Mr. D. got off to tighten his cinch, and then he sort of drifted back to where Hetty and I was. I dropped back still farther to where a good chaperone ought to be and he rode in beside Hetty. The trail was too narrow then for the rest to come back after their prey, so they had to carry on the rough work among themselves.

"Hetty acted perfect. She had a pensive, withdrawn look—'aloof,' I guess the word is—like she was too tender a flower, too fine for this rough stuff, and had ought to be in the home that minute telling a fairy story to the little ones gathered at her decently clad knee. I don't know how she done it, but she put that impression over. And she tells Mr. D. that in spite of her quiet, studious tastes she had re-

solved to come on this picnic because she loves
Nature oh! so dearly, the birds and the wild flowers
and the great rugged trees that have their message
for man if he will but listen with an understanding
heart—didn't Mr. D. think so, or did he? But not
too much of this dear old Nature stuff, which can be
easy overdone with a healthy man; just enough to
show there was hidden depths in her nature that
every one couldn't find.

"Then on to silly questions about does a horse lie
down when it goes to sleep each night after its hard
day's labour, and isn't her horse's sash too tight, and
what a pretty fetlock he has, so long and thick and
brown—— Oh, do you call that the mane? How absurd of poor little me! Mr. Daggett knows just everything, doesn't he? He's perfectly terrifying. And
where in the world did he ever learn to ride so stun-
ningly, like one of those dare-devils in a Wild West
entertainment? If her own naughty, naughty horse
tries to throw her on the ground again where he can
bite her she'll just have Mr. D. ride the nassy ole
sing and teach him better manners, so she will.
There now! He must have heard that—just see
him move his funny ears—don't tell her that horses
can't understand things that are said. And, seriously now, where did Mr. D. ever get his superb
athletic training, because, oh! how all too rare it is
to see a brain-worker of strong mentality and a splendid athlete in one and the same man. Oh, how pathetically she had wished and wished to be a man and

take her place out in the world fighting its battles, instead of poor little me who could never be anything but a homebody to worship the great, strong, red-blooded men who did the fighting and carried on great industries—not even an athletic girl like those dear things up ahead—and this horse is bobbing up and down like that on purpose, just to make poor little me giddy, and so forth. Holding her bridle rein daintily she was with the lace handkerchief I'd give her that cost me twelve fifty.

"Mr. D. took it all like a real man. He said her ignorance of a horse was adorable and laughed heartily at it. And he smiled in a deeply modest and masterful way and said 'But, really, that's nothing—nothing at all, I assure you,' when she said about how he was a corking athlete—and then kept still to see if she was going on to say more about it. But she didn't, having the God-given wisdom to leave him wanting. And then he would be laughing again at her poor-little-me horse talk.

"I never had a minute's doubt after that, for it was the eyes of one fascinated to a finish that he turned back on me half an hour later as he says: 'Really, Mrs. Pettengill, our Miss Hester is feminine to her finger tips, is she not?' 'She is, she is,' I answers. 'If you only knew the trouble I had with the chit about that horrible old riding skirt of hers when all her girl friends are wearing a sensible costume!' Hetty blushed good and proper at this, not knowing how indecent I might become, and Mr. D.

caught her at it. Aggie Tuttle and Stella Ballard
at this minute is pretending to be shooting up a town
with the couple of revolvers they'd brought along
in their cunning little holsters. Mr. D. turns his
glazed eyes to me once more. 'The real womanly
woman,' says he in a hushed voice, 'is God's best
gift to man.' Just like that.

"'Landed!' I says to myself. 'Throw him up on
the bank and light a fire.'

"And mebbe you think this tet-à-tet had not been
noticed by the merry throng up front. Not so.
The shouting and songs had died a natural death,
and the last three miles of that trail was covered in a
gloomy silence, except for the low voices of Hetty
and the male she had so neatly pronged. I could see
puzzled glances cast back at them and catch mutterings of bewilderment where the trail would turn on
itself. But the poor young things didn't yet realize
that their prey was hanging back there for reasons
over which he hadn't any control. They thought,
of course, he was just being polite or something.

"When we got to the picnic place, though, they
soon saw that all was not well. There was some
resumption of the merrymaking as they dismounted
and the girls put one stirrup over the saddle-horn
and eased the cinch like the boys did, and proud
of their knowledge, but the glances they now shot
at Hetty wasn't bewildered any more. They was
glances of pure fright. Hetty, in the first place,
had to be lifted off her horse, and Mr. D. done it in

a masterly way to show her what a mere feather she was in his giant's grasp. Then with her feet on the ground she reeled a mite, so he had to support her. She grasped his great strong arm firmly and says: 'It's nothing—I shall be right presently—leave me please, go and help those other girls.' They had some low, heated language about his leaving her at such a crisis, with her gripping his arm till I bet it showed for an hour. But finally they broke and he loosened her horse's sash, as she kept quaintly calling it, and she recovered completely and said it had been but a moment's giddiness anyway, and what strength he had in those arms, and yet could use it so gently, and he said she was a brave, game little woman, and the picnic was served to one and all, with looks of hearty suspicion and rage now being shot at Hetty from every other girl there.

"And now I see that my hunch has been even better than I thought. Not only does the star male hover about Hetty, cutely perched on a fallen log with her dainty, gleaming ankles crossed, and looking so fresh and nifty and feminine, but I'm darned if three or four of the other males don't catch the contagion of her woman's presence and hang round her, too, fetching her food of every kind there, feeding her spoonfuls of Aggie Tuttle's plum preserves, and all like that, one comical thing after another. Yes, sir; here was Mac Gordon and Riley Hardin and Charlie Dickman and Roth Hyde, men about town of the younger dancing set, that had knowed Hetty for years and hardly ever looked at her—here they was paying attentions to her now like she was some prize beauty, come down from Spokane for over Sunday, to say nothing of Mr. D., who hardly ever left her side except to get her another sardine sandwich or a paper cup of coffee. It was then I see the scientific explanation of it, like these high-school professors always say that science is at the bottom of everything. The science of this here was that they was all devoting themselves to Hetty for the simple reason that she was the one and only woman there present.

"Of course these girls in their modest Non Plush Ultras didn't get the scientific secret of this fact. They was still too obsessed with the idea that they ought to be ogled on account of them by any male beast in his right senses. But they knew they'd got in wrong somehow. By this time they was kind of bunching together and telling each other things in low tones, while not seeming to look at Hetty and her dupes, at which all would giggle in the most venemous manner. Daisy Estelle left the bunch once and made a coy bid for the notice of Mr. D. by snatching his cap and running merrily off with it about six feet. If there was any one in the world—except Hetty—could make a man hate the idea of riding pants for women, she was it. I could see the cold, flinty look come into his eyes as he turned away from her to Hetty with the pitcher of lemonade. And then Beryl Mae Macomber, she gets over close

enough for Mr. D. to hear it, and says conditions is
made very inharmonious at home for a girl of her
temperament, and she's just liable any minute to
chuck everything and either take up literary work
or go into the movies, she don't know which and
don't care—all kind of desperate so Mr. D. will feel
alarmed about a beautiful young thing like that out
in the world alone and unprotected and at the mercy
of every designing scoundrel. But I don't think
Mr. D. hears a word of it, he's so intently listening to
Hetty who says here in this beautiful mountain glade
where all is peace how one can't scarcely believe that
there is any evil in the world anywhere, and what a
difference it does make when one comes to see life
truly. Then she crossed and recrossed her silken
ankles, slightly adjusted her daring tan skirt, and
raised her eyes wistfully to the treetops, and I bet
there wasn't a man there didn't feel that she belonged
in the home circle with the little ones gathered about,
telling 'em an awfully exciting story about the
naughty, naughty, bad little white kitten and the
ball of mamma's yarn.

"Yes, sir; Hetty was as much of a revelation to
me in one way as she would of been to that party
in another if I hadn't saved her from it. She must
have had the correct female instinct all these years,
only no one had ever started her before on a track
where there was no other entries. With those other
girls dressed like she was Hetty would of been leaning
over some one's shoulder to fork up her own sand-

wiches, and no one taking hardly any notice whether
she'd had some of the hot coffee or whether she hadn't.
And the looks she got throughout the afternoon!
Say, I wouldn't of trusted that girl at the edge of a
cliff with a single pair of those No. 9872's anywhere
near.

"After the lunch things was packed up there was
faint attempts at fun and frolic with songs and chorus
—Riley Hardin has a magnificent bass voice at times
and Mac Gordon and Charlie Dickman and Roth
Hyde wouldn't be so bad if they'd let these Turkish
cigarettes alone—and the boys got together and sung
some of their good old business-college songs, with
the girls coming in while they murdered Hetty with
their beautiful eyes. But Hetty and Mr. D. sort
of withdrew from the noisy enjoyment and talked
about the serious aspects of life and how one could
get along almost any place if only they had their
favourite authors. And Mr. D. says doesn't she
sing at all, and she says, Oh! in a way; that her voice
has a certain parlour charm, she has been told, and
she sings at—you can't really call it singing—two or
three of the old Scotch songs of homely sentiment like
the Scotch seem to get into their songs as no other
nation can, or doesn't he think so, and he does, indeed.
And he's reading a wonderful new novel in which
there is much of Nature with its lessons for each of us,
but in which love conquers all at the end, and the
girl in it reminds him strongly of her, and perhaps
she'll be good enough to sing for him—just for him

alone in the dusk—if he brings this book up to-
morrow night so he can show her some good places
in it.

"At first she is sure she has a horrid old engagement for to-morrow night and is so sorry, but another time, perhaps—— Ain't it a marvel the
crooked tricks that girl had learned in one day! And
then she remembers that her engagement is for Tuesday night—what could she have been thinking of!—
and come by all means—only too charmed—and
how rarely nowadays does one meet one on one's
own level of culture, or perhaps that is too awful a
word to use—so hackneyed—but anyway he knows
what she means, or doesn't he? He does.

"Pretty soon she gets up and goes over to her
horse, picking her way daintily in the silly little tan
pumps, and seems to be offering the beast something.
The stricken man follows her the second he can without being too raw about it, and there is the adorably
feminine thing with a big dill pickle, two deviled
eggs, and a half of one of these Camelbert cheeses for
her horse. Mr. D. has a good masterly laugh at her
idea of horse fodder and calls her 'But, my dear
child!' and she looks prettily offended and offers this
chuck to the horse and he gulps it all down and noses
round for more of the same. It was an old horse
named Croppy that she'd known from childhood and
would eat anything on earth. She rode him up here
once and he nabbed a bar of laundry soap off the
back porch and chewed the whole thing down with

tears of ecstasy in his eyes and frothing at the mouth like a mad dog. Well, so Hetty gives mister man a look of dainty superiority as she flicks crumbs from her white fingers with my real lace handkerchief, and he stops his hearty laughter and just stares, and she says what nonsense to think the poor horses don't like food as well as any one. Them little moments have their effect on a man in a certain condition. He knew there probably wasn't another horse in the world would touch that truck, but he couldn't help feeling a strange new respect for her in addition to that glorious masculine protection she'd had him wallowing in all day.

"The ride home, at least on the part of the Non Plush Ultra cut-ups, was like they had laid a loved one to final rest out there on the lone mountainside. The handsome stranger and Hetty brought up the rear, conversing eagerly about themselves and other serious topics. I believe he give her to understand that he'd been pretty wild at one time in his life and wasn't any too darned well over it yet, but that some good womanly woman who would study his ways could still take him and make a man of him; and her answering that she knew he must have suffered beyond human endurance in that horrible conflict with his lower nature. He said he had.

"Of course the rabid young hoydens up ahead made a feeble effort now and then to carry it off lightly, and from time to time sang 'My Bonnie Lies Over the Ocean,' or 'Merrily We Roll Along,' with the high, squeaky tenor of Roth Hyde sounding above the others very pretty in the moonlight, but it was poor work as far as these enraged vestals was concerned. If I'd been Hetty and had got a strange box of candy through the mail the next week, directed in a disguised woman's hand, I'd of rushed right off to the police with it, not waiting for any analysis. And she, poor thing, would get so frightened at bad spots, with the fierce old horse bobbing about so dangerous, that she just has to be held on. And once she wrenched her ankle against a horrid old tree on the trail—she hadn't been able to resist a little one—and bit her under lip as the spasm of pain passed over her refined features. But she was all right in a minute and begged Mr. D. not to think of bathing it in cold water because it was nothing—nothing at all, really now—and he would embarrass her frightfully if he said one more word about it. And Mr. D. again remarked that she was feminine to her finger tips, a brave, game little woman, one of the gamest he ever knew. And pretty soon—what was she thinking about now? Why, she was merely wondering if horses think in the true sense of the word or only have animal instinct, as it is called. And wasn't she a strange, puzzling creature to be thinking on deep subjects like that at such a time! Yes, she had been called puzzling as a child, but she didn't like it one bit. She wanted to be like other girls, if he knew what she meant. He seemed to.

"They took Hetty home first on account of her

poor little ankle and sung 'Good Night, Ladies,' at the gate. And so ended a day that was wreck and ruin for most of our sex there present.

"And to show you what a good, deep, scientific cause I had discovered, the next night at Hetty's who shows up one by one but these four men about town, each with a pound of mixed from the Bon Ton Kandy Kitchen, and there they're all setting at the feet of Hetty, as it were, in her new light summer gown with the blue bows, when Mr. D. blows in with a two-pound box and the novel in which love conquered all. So excited she was when she tells me about it next day. The luck of that girl! But after all it wasn't luck, because she'd laid her foundations the day before, hadn't she? Always look a little bit back of anything that seems to be luck, say I.

"And Hetty with shining eyes entertained one and all with the wit and sparkle a woman can show only when there's four or five men at her at once—it's the only time we ever rise to our best. But she got a chance for a few words alone with Mr. D., who took his hat finally when he sees the other four was going to set him out; enough words to confide to him how she loathed this continual social racket to which she was constantly subjected, with never a let-up so one could get to one's books and to one's real thoughts. But perhaps he would venture up again some time next week or the week after—not getting coarse in her work, understand, even with him flopping around there out on the bank—and he give her one long, meaning look and said why not to-morrow night, and she carelessly said that would be charming, she was sure—she didn't think of any engagement at this minute—and it was ever so nice of him to think of poor little me.

"Then she went back and gave the social evening of their life to them four boys that had stayed. She said she couldn't thank them enough for coming this evening—which is probably the only time she had told the truth in thirty-six hours—and they all made merry. Roth Hyde sang 'Sally in Our Alley' so good on the high notes that the Duttons was all out in the hall listening; and Riley Hardin singing 'Down, Diver, Down, 'Neath the Deep Blue Waves!' and Mac Gordon singing his everlasting German songs in their native language, and Charlie Dickman singing a new sentimental one called 'Ain't There at Least One Gentleman Here?' about a fair young lady dancer being insulted in a gilded café in some large city; and one and all voted it was a jolly evening and said how about coming back to-morrow night, but Hetty said no, it was her one evening for study and she couldn't be bothered with them, which was a plain, downright so-and-so and well she knew it, because that girl's study was over for good and all.

"Well, why string it out? I've give you the facts. And my lands! Will you look at that clock now? Here's the morning gone and this room still looking like the inside of a sheep-herder's wagon! Oh, yes, and when Hetty was up here this time that she wouldn't wear my riding pants down, she says, 'Not only that, but I'm scrupulously careful in all ways. Why, I never even allow dear Burchell to observe me in one of those lace boudoir caps that so many women cover up their hair with when it's their best feature but they won't take time to do it.'

"Now was that spoken like a wise woman or like the two-horned Galumpsis Caladensis of East India, whose habits are little known to man? My Lord! Won't I ever learn to stop? Where did I put that dusting cloth?"

VI

COUSIN EGBERT INTERVENES

IT TAKES all kinds of foreigners to make a world," said Ma Pettengill—irrelevantly I thought, because the remark seemed to be inspired merely by the announcement of Sandy Sawtelle that the mule Jerry's hip had been laid open by a kick from the mule Alice, and that the bearer of the news had found fourteen stitches needed to mend the rent.

Sandy brought his news to the owner of the Arrowhead as she relaxed in my company on the west veranda of the ranch house and scented the golden dusk with burning tobacco of an inferior but popular brand. I listened but idly to the minute details of the catastrophe, discovering more entertainment in the solemn wake of light a dulled sun was leaving as it slipped over the sagging rim of Arrowhead Pass. And yet, through my absorption with the shadows that now played far off among the folded hills, there did come sharply the impression that this Sawtelle person was dwelling too insistently upon the precise number of stitches required by the breach in Jerry's hide.

"Fourteen—yes, ma'am; fourteen stitches. That there Alice mule sure needs handling. Fourteen regular ones. I'd certainly show her where to head in at, like now she was my personal property. Me, I'd abuse her shamefully. Only eleven I took last time in poor old Jerry; and here now it's plumb fourteen—yes, ma'am; fourteen good ones. Say, you get fourteen of them stitches in your hide, and I bet—thought, at first, I could make twelve do, but it takes full fourteen, with old Jerry nearly tearing the chute down while I was taking these fourteen——"

I began to see numbers black against that glowing panorama in the west. A monstrous 14 repeated itself stubbornly along the gorgeous reach of it.

"Yes, ma'am—fourteen; you can go out right now and count 'em yourself. And like mebbe I'll have to go down to town to-morrow fur some more of that King of Pain Liniment, on account of Lazarus and Bryan getting good and lamed in this same mix-up, and me letting fall the last bottle we had on the place and busting her wide open——"

"Don't you bother to bust any more!" broke in his employer in a tone that I found crisp with warning. "There's a whole new case of King of Pain in the storeroom."

"Huh!" exclaimed the surgeon, ably conveying disappointment thereby. "And like now if I did go down I could get the new parts for that there mower——"

"That's something for me to worry about exclusively. I'll begin when we got something to mow." There was finished coldness in this.

"Huh!" The primitive vocable now conveyed a lively resentment, but there was the pleading of a patient sufferer in what followed. "And like at the same time, having to make the trip anyway for these here supplies and things, I could stop just a minute at Doc Martingale's and have this old tooth of mine took out, that's been achin' like a knife stuck in me fur the last fourteen—well, fur about a week now— achin' night and day—no sleep at all now fur seven, eight nights; so painful I get regular delirious, let me tell you. And, of course, all wore out the way I am, I won't be any good on the place till my agony's relieved. Why, what with me suffering so horrible, I just wouldn't hardly know my own name sometimes if you was to come up and ask me!"

The woman's tone became more than ever repellent.

"Never you mind about not knowing your own name. I got it on the pay roll, and it'll still be there to-morrow if you're helping Buck get out the rest of them fence posts like I told you. If you happen to get stuck for your name when I ain't round, and the inquiring parties won't wait, just ask the Chinaman; he never forgets anything he's learned once. Or I'll write it out on a card, so you can show it to anybody who rides up and wants to know it in a hurry!"

"Huh!"

The powers of this brief utterance had not yet been exhausted. It now conveyed despair. With bowed head the speaker dully turned and withdrew from our presence. As he went I distinctly heard him mutter:

"Huh! Four-teen! Four-teen! And seven! And twenty-eight!"

"Say, there!" his callous employer called after him. "Why don't you get Boogles to embroider that name of yours on the front of your shirt? He'd adore to do it. And you can still read, can't you, in the midst of your agonies?"

There was no response to this taunt. The suffering one faded slowly down the path to the bunk house and was lost in its blackness. A light shone out and presently came sombre chords from a guitar, followed by the voice of Sandy in gloomy song: "There's a broken heart for every light on Broadway——"

I was not a little pained to discover this unsuspected vein of cruelty in a woman I had long admired. And the woman merely became irrelevant with her apothegm about foreigners. I ignored it.

"What about that sufferer down there in the bunk house?" I demanded. "Didn't you ever have toothache?"

"No; neither did Sandy Sawtelle. He ain't a sufferer; he's just a liar."

"Why?"

"So I'll let him go to town and play the number of them stitches on the wheel. Sure! He'd run a horse to death getting there, make for the back room of the Turf Club Saloon, where they run games whenever the town ain't lidded too tight, and play roulette till either him or the game had to close down.

Yes, sir; he'd string his bets along on fourteen and seven and twenty-eight and thirty-five, and if he didn't make a killing he'd believe all his life that the wheel was crooked. Stitches in a mule's hide is his bug. He could stitch up any horse on the place and never have the least hunch; but let it be a mule—— Say! Down there right now he's thinking about the thousand dollars or so I'm keeping him out of. I judge from his song that he'd figured on a trip East to New York City or Denver. At that, I don't know as I blame him. Yes, sir; that's what reminded me of foreigners and bazaars and vice, and so on—and poor Egbert Floud."

My hostess drew about her impressive shoulders a blanket of Indian weave that dulled the splendours of the western sky, and rolled a slender cigarette from the tobacco and papers at her side. By the ensuing flame of a match I saw that her eyes gleamed with the light of pure narration.

"Foreigners, bazaars, vice, and Egbert Floud?" I murmured, wishing these to be related more plausibly one to another.

"I'm coming to it," said the lady; and, after two sustaining inhalations from the new cigarette, forthwith she did:

It was late last winter, while I was still in Red Gap. The talk went round that we'd ought to have another something for the Belgians. We'd had a concert, the proceeds of which run up into two figures after all ex-

penses was paid; but it was felt something more could
be done—something in the nature of a bazaar, where
all could get together. The Mes-dames Henrietta
Templeton Price and Judge Ballard were appointed a
committee to do some advance scouting.

That was where Egbert Floud come in, though
after it was all over any one could see that he was
more to be pitied than censured. These well-known
leaders consulted him among others, and Cousin
Egbert says right off that, sure, he'll help 'em get up
something if they'll agree to spend a third of the loot
for tobacco for the poor soldiers, because a Belgian or
any one else don't worry so much about going hungry
if they can have a smoke from time to time, and he's
been reading about where tobacco is sorely needed in
the trenches. He felt strong about it, because one
time out on the trail he lost all his own and had to
smoke poplar bark or something for two weeks, nearly
burning his flues out.

The two Mes-dames agreed to this, knowing from
their menfolk that tobacco is one of the great human
needs, both in war and in peace, and knowing that
Cousin Egbert will be sure to donate handsomely
himself, he always having been the easiest mark in
town; so they said they was much obliged for his
timely suggestion and would he think up some novel
feature for the bazaar; and he said he would if he
could, and they went on to other men of influence.

Henrietta's husband, when he heard the money
wouldn't all be spent for mere food, said he'd put up a

choice lot in Price's Addition to be raffled off—a lot that would at some future date be worth five thousand dollars of anybody's money, and that was all right; and some of the merchants come through liberal with articles of use and adornment to be took chances on.

Even old Proctor Knapp, the richest man in town, actually give up something after they pestered him for an hour. He owns the People's Traction Company and he turned over a dollar's worth of street-car tickets to be raffled for, though saying he regarded gambling as a very objectionable and uncertain vice, and a person shouldn't go into anything without being sure they was dead certain to make something out of it, war or no war, he knowing all about it. Why wouldn't he, having started life as a poor, ragged boy and working his way up to where parties that know him is always very careful indeed when they do any business with him?

Some of the ladies they consulted was hostile about the tobacco end of it. Mrs. Tracy Bangs said that no victim of the weed could keep up his mentality, and that she, for one, would rather see her Tracy lying in his casket than smoking vile tobacco that would destroy his intellect and make him a loathsome object in the home. She said she knew perfectly well that if the countries at war had picked their soldiers from non-smokers it would have been all over in just a few days—and didn't that show you that the tobacco demon was as bad as the rum demon?

Mrs. Leonard Wales was not only bitter about tobacco but about any help at all. She said our hard
storms of that winter had been caused by the general
hatred in Europe which created evil waves of ma-
lignity; so let 'em shoot each other till they got sense
enough to dwell together in love and amity—only we
shouldn't prolong the war by sending 'em soup and
cigarettes, and so on. Her idea seemed to be that if
Red Gap would just stand firm in the matter the war
would die a natural death. Still, if a bazaar was
really going to be held, she would consent to pose in a
tableau if they insisted on it, and mebbe she could
thus inject into the evil atmosphere of Europe some
of the peace and good will that sets the United States
apart from other nations.

Trust Cora Wales not to overlook a bet like that.
She's a tall, sandy-haired party, with very extrava-
gant contours, and the thing she loves best on earth
is to get under a pasteboard crown, with gilt stars on
it, and drape herself in the flag of her country, with
one fat arm bare, while Maine, New Hampshire,
Vermont, Massachusetts, and the rest is gathered
about and looking up to her for protection. Mebbe
she don't look so bad as the Goddess of Liberty on a
float in the middle of one of our wide streets when the
Chamber of Commerce is giving a Greater Red Gap
pageant; but take her in a hall, where you set close
up to the platform, and she looks more like our
boasted liberty has degenerated into license, or something like that. Anyway, the committee had to

promise her she could do something in her flag and
crown and talcum powder, because they knew she'd
knock the show if they didn't.

This reminded 'em they had to have a program of
entertainment; so they got me on the committee with
the other Mes-dames to think up things, me always
being an easy mark. I find out right off that we're a
lot of foreigners and you got to be darned careful not to
hurt anybody's feelings. Little Bertha Lehman's pa
would let her be a state—Colorado or Nebraska, or
something—but he wouldn't let her sing unless it would
be a German song in the original; and Hobbs, the English baker, said his Tillie would have to sing " Britannia
Rules the Waves," or nothing; and two or three others
said what they would and wouldn't do, and it looked
like Red Gap itself was going to be dug up into trenches.
I had to get little Magnesia Waterman, daughter of the
coons that work in the U. S. Grill, to do the main
singing. She seemed to be about the only American
child soprano we had. She sings right well for a kid,
mostly these sad songs about heaven; but we picked
out a good live one for her that seemed to be neutral.

It was delicate work, let me tell you, turning down
folks that wanted to sing patriotic songs or recite war
poetry that would be sure to start something, with Professor Gluckstein wishing to get up and tell how the
cowardly British had left the crew of a German sub-
marine to perish after shooting it up when it was only
trying to sink their cruiser by fair and lawful meth-

ods; and Henry Lehman wanting to read a piece from a German newspaper about how the United States was a nation of vile money-grubbers that would sell ammunition to the enemy just because they had the ships to take it away, and wouldn't sell a dollar's worth to the Fatherland, showing we had been bought up by British gold—and so on.

But I kept neutral. I even turned down an Englishman named Ruggles, that keeps the U. S. Grill and is well thought of, though he swore that all he would do was to get off a few comical riddles, and such. He'd just got a new one that goes: "Why is an elephant like a corkscrew? Because there's a 'b' in both." I didn't see it at first, till he explained with hearty laughter—because there's a "b" in both—the word "both." See? Of course there's no sense to it. He admitted there wasn't, but said it was a jolly wheeze just the same. I might have took a chance with him, but he went on to say that he'd sent this wheeze to the brave lads in the trenches, along with a lot of cigars and tobacco, and had got about fifty postcards from 'em saying it was the funniest thing they'd heard since the war begun. And in a minute more he was explaining, with much feeling, just what lowdown nation it was that started the war—it not being England, by any means—and I saw he wasn't to be trusted on his feet.

So I smoothed him down till he promised to donate all the lemonade for Aggie Tuttle, who was to be Rebekkah at the Well; and I smoothed Henry Leh-

man till he said he'd let his folks come and buy
chances on things, even if the country was getting
overrun by foreigners, with an Italian barber shop
just opened in the same block with his sanitary shav-
ing parlour; though—thank goodness—the Italian
hadn't had much to do yet but play on a mandolin.
And I smoothed Professor Gluckstein down till he
agreed to furnish the music for us and let the war take
care of itself.

The Prof's a good old scout when he ain't got his
war bonnet on. He was darned near crying into his
meerschaum pipe with a carved fat lady on it when I
got through telling him about the poor soldiers in the
wet and cold without a thing to smoke. He says:
"You're right, madam; with Jake Frost in the
trenches and no tobacco, all men should be brothers
under their hides." And I got that printed in the
Recorder for a slogan, and other foreigners come into
line; and things looked pretty good.

Also, I got Doc Sulloway, who happened to be in
town, to promise he'd come and tell some funny
anecdotes. He ain't a regular doctor—he just took
it up; a guy with long black curls and a big moustache
and a big hat and diamond pin, that goes round
selling Indian Snake Oil off a wagon. Doc said he'd
have his musician, Ed Bemis, come, too. He said
Ed was known far and wide as the world's challenge
cornetist. I says all right, if he'll play something
neutral; and Doc says he'll play "Listen to the
Mocking Bird," with variations, and play it so

swell you'll think you're perched right up in the
treetops listening to Nature's own feathered song-
sters.

That about made up my show, including, of course,
the Spanish dance by Beryl Mae Macomber. Red
Gap always expects that and Beryl Mae never dis-
appoints 'em—makes no difference what the occasion is. Mebbe it's an Evening with Shakespeare,
or the Landing of the Pilgrim Fathers, or that
Oratorio by Elijah somebody, but Beryl Mae is right
there with her girlish young beauty and her tam-
bourine. You see, I didn't want it a long show—just
enough to make the two-bits admission seem a little
short of robbery. Our real graft, of course, was to be
where the young society débutantes and heiresses in
charge of the booths would wheedle money out of
the dazed throng for chances on the junk that would
be donated.

Well, about three days before the show I went up
to Masonic Hall to see about the stage decorations,
and I was waiting while some one went down to the
Turf Exchange to get the key off Tim Mahoney, the
janitor—Tim had lately had to do janitor work for a
B'nai B'rith lodge that was holding meetings there,
and it had made him gloomy and dissolute—and,
while I was waiting, who should come tripping along
but Egbert Floud, all sunned up like a man that
knows the world is his oyster and every month's got
an "r" in it. Usually he's a kind of sad, meek coot,
looking neglected and put upon; but now he was

actually giggling to himself as he come up the stairs two at a time.

"Well, Old-Timer, what has took the droop out of your face?" I ask him.

"Why," he says, twinkling all over the place, "I'm aiming to keep it a secret, but I don't mind hinting to an old friend that my part of the evening's entertainment is going to be so good it'll make the whole show top-heavy. Them ladies said they'd rely on me to think up something novel, and I said I would if I could, and I did—that's all. I'd seen enough of these shows where you ladies pike along with pincushions and fancy lemonade and infants' wear—and mebbe a red plush chair, with gold legs, that plays 'Alice, Where Art Thou?' when a person sets down on it—with little girls speaking a few pieces about the flowers and lambs, and so on, and cleaning up about eleven-twenty-nine on the evening's revel—or it would be that, only you find you forgot to pay the Golden Rule Cash Store for the red-and-blue bunting, and they're howling for their money like a wildcat. Yes, sir; that's been the way of it with woman at the hellum. I wouldn't wish to be a Belgian at all under present circumstances; but if I did have to be one I'd hate to think my regular meals was depending on any crooked work you ladies has done up to date."

"You'd cheer me strangely," I says, "only I been a diligent reader of history, and somehow I can't just recall your name being connected up with any cat-

aclysms of finance.   I don't remember you ever starting one of these here panics—or stopping one, for
that matter.   I did hear that you'd had your pocket
picked down to the San Francisco Fair."

I was prodding him along, understand, so he'd flare
up and tell me what his secret enterprise was that
would make women's operations look silly and feminine.   I seen his eyes kind of glisten when I said this
about him being touched.

"That's right," he says.   "Some lad nicked me for
my roll and my return ticket, and my gold watch and
chain, and my horseshoe scarfpin with the diamonds
in it."

"You stood a lot of pawing over," I says, "for a
man that's the keen financial genius you tell about
being.   This lad must of been a new hand at it.
Likely he'd took lessons from a correspondence
school.   At least, with you standing tied and blinded
that way, a good professional one would have tried
for your gold tooth—or, anyway, your collar button.
I see your secret though," I go on as sarcastically
as possible: "You got the lad's address and you're
going to have him here Saturday night to glide
among the throng and ply his evil trade.   Am I right
or wrong?"

"You are not," he says.   "I never thought of that.
But I won't say you ain't warm in your guess.   Yes,
you certainly are warm, because what I'm going to
do is just as dastardly, without being so darned illegal, except to an extent."

Well, it was very exasperating, but that was all I could get out of him. When I ask for details he just clams up.

"But, mark my words," says the old smarty, "I'll show you it takes brains in addition to woman's wiles and artwork to make a decent clean-up in this little one-cylinder town."

"If you just had a little more self-confidence," I says, "you might of gone to the top; lack of faith in yourself is all that's kept you back. Too bad!"

"All right for you to kid me," he says; "but I'd be almost willing to give you two dollars for every dollar that goes out of this hall Saturday night."

Well, it was kind of pathetic and disgusting the way this poor old dub was leaning on his certainty; so I let him alone and went on about my work, thinking mebbe he really had framed up something crooked that would bring at least a few dollars to the cause.

Every time I met him for the next three days after that he'd be so puffed up, like a toad, with importance and low remarks about woman that, at last, I just ignored him, pretending I hadn't the least curiosity about his evil secret. It hurt his feelings when I quit pestering him about it, but he'd been outraging mine right along; so we split even.

He'd had a good-sized room just down the hall turned over to him, and a lot of stuff of some kind carried in there in the night, and men working, with the door locked all the time; so I and the other ladies

went calmly on about our own business, decorating
the main hall with the flags of all nations, fixing up the
platform and the booths very pretty, and giving Mr.
Smarty Egbert Floud nothing but haughty glances
about his hidden novelty.   Even when his men was
hammering away in there at their work he'd have
something hung over the keyhole—as insulting to us
as only a man can be.

Saturday night come and we had a good crowd.
Cousin Egbert was after me the minute I got my
things off to come and see his dastardly secret; but I
had my revenge.   I told him I had no curiosity about
it and was going to be awful busy with my show, but
I'd try as a personal favour to give him a look over
before I went home.   Yes, sir; I just turned him
down with one superior look, and got my curtains
slid back on Mrs. Leonard Wales, dressed up like a
superdreadnought in a naval parade and surrounded
by every little girl in town that had a white dress.
They wasn't states this time, but Columbia's
Choicest Heritage, with a second line on the program
saying, "Future Buds and Débutantes From Society's Home Galleries."   It was a line we found
under some babies' photos on the society page of a
great newspaper printed in New York City.   Professor Gluckstein and his son Rudolph played the "Star-
Spangled Banner" on the piano and fiddle during this
feature.

Then little Magnesia Waterman, dressed to repre-
sent the Queen of Sheba, come forward and sung the

song we'd picked out for her, with the people joining
in the chorus:

We're for you, Woodrow Wilson,
One Hundred Million Strong!
We put you in the White House
And we know you can't do wrong.

It was very successful, barring hisses from all the
Germans and English present; but they was soon
hushed up.   Then Doc Sulloway come out and told
some funny anecdotes about two Irishmen named Pat
and Mike, lately landed in this country and looking
for work, and imitated two cats in a backyard, and
drawing a glass of soda water, and sawing a plank in
two; and winding up with the announcement that he
had donated a dozen bottles of the great Indian
Snake Oil Remedy for man and beast that had been
imparted to him in secret by old Rumpatunk, the
celebrated medicine man, who is supposed to have
had it from the Great Spirit; and Ed Bemis, the
World's Challenge Cornetist, entertained one and all;
and Beryl Mae done her Spanish dance that I'd last
seen her give at the Queen Esther Cantata in the M.
E. Church.   And that was the end of the show; just
enough to start 'em buying things at the booths.

At least, we thought it would be.   But what does a
lot of the crowd do, after looking round a little, but
drift out into the hall and down to this room where
Cousin Egbert had his foul enterprise, whatever it

was. I didn't know yet, having held aloof, as you might say, owing to the old hound's offensive manner. But I had heard three or four parties kind of gasping to each other, had they seen what that Egbert Floud was doing in the other room?—with looks of horror and delight on their faces. That made me feel more superior than ever to the old smarty; so I didn't go near the place yet, but herded people back to the raffles wherever I could.

The first thing was Lon Price's corner lot, for which a hundred chances had been sold. Lon had a blueprint showing the very lot; also a picture of a choice dwelling or bungalow, like the one he has painted on the drop curtain of Knapp's Opera House, under the line, "Price's Addition to Red Gap; Big Lots, Little Payments." It's a very fancy house with porches and bay windows and towers and front steps, and everything, painted blue and green and yellow; and a blond lady in a purple gown, with two golden-haired tots at her side, is waving good-bye to a tall, handsome man with brown whiskers as he hurries out to the waiting street car—though the car line ain't built out there yet by any means.

However, Lon got up and said it was a Paradise on earth, a Heaven of Homes; that in future he would sell lots there to any native Belgian at a 20 per cent. discount; and he hoped the lucky winner of this lot would at once erect a handsome and commodious mansion on it, such as the artist had here depicted; and it would be only nine blocks from the swell little

Carnegie Library when that, also, had been built, the
plans for it now being in his office safe.

Quite a few of the crowd had stayed for this, and
they cheered Lon and voted that little Magnesia
Waterman was honest enough to draw the numbers
out of a hat. They was then drawn and read by
Lon in an exciting silence—except for Mrs. Leonard
Wales, who was breathing heavily and talking to herself after each number. She and Leonard had took a
chance for a dollar and everybody there knew it by
now. She was dead sure they would get the lot.
She kept telling people so, right and left. She said
they was bound to get it if the drawing was honest.
As near as I could make out, she'd been taking a
course of lessons from a professor in Chicago about
how to control your destiny by the psychic force
that dwells within you. It seems all you got to
do is to will things to come your way and they have
to come. No way out of it. You step on this here
psychic gas and get what you ask for.

"I already see our little home," says Mrs. Wales
in a hoarse whisper. "I see it objectively. It is
mine. I claim it out of the boundless all-good. I
have put myself in the correct mental attitude of
reception; I am holding to the perfect All. My own
will come to me."

And so on, till parties round her begun to get nervous. Yes, sir; she kept this stuff going in low, tense
tones till she had every one in hearing buffaloed;
they was ready to give her the lot right there and

tear up their own tickets.   She was like a crapshooter
when he keeps calling to the dice: "Come, seven—
come on, come on!"   All right for the psychics, but
that's what she reminded me of.

And in just another minute everybody there
thought she'd cheated by taking these here lessons
that she got from Chicago for twelve dollars; for
you can believe it or not but her number won the lot.
Yes, sir; thirty-three took the deed and Lon filled
in her name on it right there.   Many a cold look was
shot at her as she rushed over to embrace her husband, a big lump of a man that's all right as far up
as his Adam's apple, and has been clerking in the Owl
Cigar Store ever since he can remember.   He tells
her she is certainly a wonder and she calls him a silly
boy; says it's just a power she has developed through
concentration, and now she must claim from the all-
good a dear little home of seven rooms and bath, to
be built on this lot; and she knows it will come if she
goes into the silence and demands it.   Say!   People
with any valuables on 'em begun to edge off, not
knowing just how this strange power of hers might
work.

Then I look round and see the other booths ain't
creating near the excitement they had ought to be,
only a few here and there taking two-bit chances on
things if Mrs. Wales ain't going in on 'em, too;
several of the most attractive booths was plumb
deserted, with the girls in charge looking mad or
chagrined, as you might say.   So I remember this

hidden evil of Egbert Floud's and that the crowd
has gone there; and while I'm deciding to give in and
gratify my morbid curiosity, here comes Cousin
Egbert himself, romping along in his dinner-jacket
suit and tan shoes, like a wild mustang.

"What was I telling you?" he demands.   "Didn't
I tell you the rest of this show was going to die standing up? Yes, sir; she's going to pass out on her
feet." And he waved a sneering arm round at the
deserted booths.   "What does parties want of this
truck when they can come down to my joint and get
real entertainment for their money? Why, they're
breaking their ankles now to get in there!"

It sure looked like he was right for once in his
life; so I says:

"What is it you've done?"

"Simple enough," says he, "to a thinking man. It
comes to me like a flash or inspiration, or something,
from being down to that fair in San Francisco, California. Yes, sir; they had a deadfall there, with
every kind of vice rampant that has ever been legal-
ized any place, and several kinds that ain't ever been;
they done everything, from strong-arm work to
short changing, and they was getting by with it by
reason of calling it Ye Olde Tyme Mining Camp of
'49, or something poetical like that. That was where
I got nicked for my roll, in addition to about fifty
I lost at a crooked wheel. I think the workers was
mostly ex-convicts, and not so darned ex- at that.
Anyway, their stuff got too raw even for the mana-

gers of an exposition, so they had to close down in spite of their name. That's where I get my idee when these ladies said think up something novel and pleasing. Just come and see how I'm taking it off of 'em." And, with that, he grabs me by the arm and rushes me down to this joint of his.

At the side of the doorway he had two signs stuck up. One says, Ye Olde Tyme Saloone; and the other says, Ye Olde Tyme Gambling Denne. You could of pushed me over with one finger when I looked in. He'd drew the crowd, all right. I knew then that Aggie Tuttle might just as well close down her Rebekkah-at-the-Well dive, and that no one was going to take any more chances on pincushions and tidies and knitted bed slippers.

About a third of the crowd was edged up to the bar and keeping Louis Meyer and his father busy with drink orders, and the other two-thirds was huddled round a roulette layout across the room. They was wedged in so tight I couldn't see the table, but I could hear the little ball click when it slowed up, and the rattle of chips, and squeals from them that won, and hoarse mutters from the losers.

Cousin Egbert rubbed his hands and giggled, waiting for me to bedeck him with floral tributes.

"I suppose you got a crooked wheel," I says.

"Shucks, no!" says he. "I did think of it, but I'd of had to send out of town for one and they're a lot of trouble to put in, what with the electric wiring and all; and besides, the straightest roulette

wheel ever made is crooked enough for any man of
decent instincts. I don't begrudge 'em a little excitement for their money. I got these old bar fixings
out of the Spilmer place that was being tore down,
and we're charging two bits a drink for whatever,
and that'll be a help; and it looks to me like you ladies
would of thought you needed a man's brain in these
shows long before this. Come on in and have a shot.
I'll buy."

So we squeezed in and had one. It was an old-
time saloon, all right—that is, fairly old; about
1889, with a brass foot rail, and back of the bar a
stuffed eagle and a cash register. A gang of ladies
was taking claret lemonades and saying how delight-
fully Bohemian it all was; and Miss Metta Bigler,
that gives lessons in oil painting and burnt wood,
said it brought back very forcibly to her the Latin
Quarter of Chicago, where she finished her art course.
Henrietta Templeton Price, with one foot on the
railing, was shaking dice with three other prominent
society matrons for the next round, and saying she
had always been a Bohemian at heart, only you
couldn't go very far in a small town like this without causing unfavourable comment among a certain
element.

It was a merry scene, with the cash register playing like the Swiss Family Bellringers. Even the new
Episcopalian minister come along, with old Proctor
Knapp, and read the signs and said they was undeniably quaint, and took a slug of rye and said it was

undeniably delightful; though old Proctor roared like a maddened bull when he found what the price was. I guess you can be an Episcopalian one without its interfering much with man's natural habits and innocent recreations. Then he went over and lost a two-bit piece on the double-o, and laughed heartily over the occurrence, saying it was undeniably piquant with old Proctor plunging ten cents on the red and losing it quick, and saying a fool and his money was soon parted—yes, and I wish I had as much money as that old crook ain't foolish; but no matter.

Beryl Mae Macomber was aiding the Belgians by running out in the big room to drum up the stragglers. She was now being Little Nugget, the Miners' Pet; and when she wasn't chasing in easy money she'd loll at one end of the bar with a leer on her flowerlike features to entice honest workingmen in to lose their all at the gaming tables. There was chuck-a-luck and a crap game going, and going every minute, too, with Cousin Egbert trying to start three-card monte at another table—only they all seemed wise to that. Even the little innocent children give him the laugh.

I went over to the roulette table and lost a few dollars, not being able to stick long, because other women would keep goring me with their elbows. Yes, sir; that layout was ringed with women four deep. All that the men could do was stand on the outside and pass over their loose silver to the fair ones. Sure! Women are the only real natural-born

gamblers in the world. Take a man that seems to be
one and it's only because he's got a big streak of
woman in him, even if it don't show any other way.
Men, of course, will gamble for the fun of it; but it
ain't ever funny to a woman, not even when she wins.
It brings out the natural wolf in her like nothing
else does. It was being proved this night all you'd
want to see anything proved. If the men got near
enough and won a bet they'd think it was a good joke
and stick round till they lost it. Not so my own sex.
Every last one of 'em saw herself growing rich on
Cousin Egbert's money—and let the Belgians look
out for themselves.

Mrs. Tracy Bangs, for instance, fought her way
out of the mob, looking as wild as any person in a
crazy house, choking twenty-eight dollars to death in
her two fists that she win off two bits. She crowds
this onto Tracy and makes him swear by the sacred
memory of his mother that he will positively not give
her back a cent of it to gamble with if the fever comes
on her again—not even if she begs him to on her
bended knees. And fifteen minutes later the poor
little shark nearly has hysterics because Tracy won't
give her back just five of it to gamble again with.
Sure! A very feminine woman she is.

Tracy is a pretty good little sport himself. He
says, No, and that'll be all, please, not only on account of the sacred memory of his mother but because
the poor Belgians has got to catch it going if they
don't catch it coming; and he's beat it out to a booth

and bought the twenty-five-dollar gold clock with chimes, with the other three dollars going for the dozen bottles of Snake Oil and the twenty street-car tickets.

And now let there be no further words about it, but there was when she hears this horrible disclosure —lots of words, and the brute won't even give her the street-car tickets, which she could play in for a dollar, and she has to go to the retiring room to bathe her temples, and treats Tracy all the rest of the evening like a crippled stepchild, thinking of all she could of won if he hadn't acted like a snake in the grass toward her!

Right after this Mrs. Leonard Wales, in her flag and powder, begun to stick up out of the scene, though not risking any money as yet. She'd just stand there like one petrified while cash was being paid in and out, keeping away about three women of regular size that would like to get their silver down. I caught the gleam in her eye, and the way she drawed in her breath when the lucky number was called out, kind of shrinking her upper lip every time in a blood-thirsty manner. Yes, sir; in the presence of actual money that dame reminded me of the great saber-toothed tiger that you see terrible pictures of in the animal books.

Pretty soon she mowed down a lot of her sister gamblers and got out to where Leonard was standing, to tell him all about how she'd have won a lot of money if she'd only put some chips down at the right

time, the way she would of done if she'd had any;
and Leonard said what a shame! And they drifted
into a corner, talking low. I bet she was asking
him if she couldn't make a claim to these here bets
she'd won in her mind, and if this wasn't the magic
time to get the little home or bungalow on the new
lot she'd won by finding out from the Chicago professor how to mould her destiny.

Then I lose track of the two for a minute, because
Judge Ballard comes in escorting his sister from
South Carolina, that's visiting them, and invites
every one to take something in her honour. She was
a frail little old lady, very old-fashioned indeed, with
white hair built up in a waterfall and curls over both
ears, and a flowered silk dress that I bet was made in
Civil War times, and black lace mitts. Say! She
looked like one of the ladies that would of been setting
in the front of a box at Ford's Theatre the night
President Lincoln was shot up!

She seemed a mite rattled when she found herself
in a common barroom, having failed to read Cousin
Egbert's undeniably quaint signs; but the Judge
introduced her to some that hadn't met her yet, and
when he asked her what her refreshment would be
she said in a very brazen way that she would take a
drop of anisette cordial. Louis Meyer says they
ain't keeping that, and she says, Oh, dear! she's too
old-fashioned! So Cousin Egbert says, why, then she
should take an old-fashioned cocktail, which she does
and sips it with no sign of relish. Then she says she

will help the cause by wagering a coin on yonder game of chance.

The Judge paws out a place for her and I go along to watch. She pries open a bead reticule that my mother had one like and gets out a knitted silk purse, and takes a five-dollar gold piece into her little bony white fingers and drops it on a number, and says: "Now that is well over!" But it wasn't over. There was excitement right off, because, outside of some silver dollars I'd lost myself, I hadn't seen anything bigger than a two-bit piece played there that night. Right over my shoulder I heard heavy breathing and I didn't have to turn round to know it was Cora Wales. When the ball slowed up she quit breathing entirely till it settled.

It must of been a horrible strain on her, for the man was raking in all the little bets and leaving the five-dollar one that win. Say! That woman gripped an arm of mine till I thought it was caught in machinery of some kind! And Mrs. Doc Martingale, that she gripped on the other side, let out a yell of agony. But that wasn't the worst of Cora Wales' torture. No, sir! She had to stand there and watch this little old-fashioned sport from South Carolina refuse the money!

"But I can't accept it from you good people," says she in her thin little voice. "I intended to help the cause of those poor sufferers, and to profit by the mere inadvertence of your toy there would be un-speakable—really no!"

And she pushed back the five and the hundred and seventy-five that the dealer had counted out for her, dusted her little fingers with a little lace handkerchief smelling of lavender, and asked the Judge to show her a game that wasn't so noisy.

I guess Cora Wales was lost from that moment. She had Len over in a corner again, telling him how easy it was to win, and how this poor demented creature had left all hers there because Judge Ballard probably didn't want to create a scene by making her take it; and mustn't they have a lot of trouble looking after the weak-minded thing all the time! And I could hear her say if one person could do it another could, especially if they had learned how to get in tune with the Infinite. Len says all right, how much does she want to risk? And that scares her plumb stiff again, in spite of her uncanny powers. She says it wouldn't be right to risk one cent unless she could be sure the number was going to win.

Of course if you made your claim on the Universal, your own was bound to come to you; still, you couldn't be so sure as you ought to be with a roulette wheel, because several times the ball had gone into numbers that she wasn't holding for with her psychic grip, and the uncertainty was killing her; and why didn't he say something to help her, instead of standing there silent and letting their little home slip from her grasp?

Cousin Egbert comes up just then, still happy and

puffed up; so I put him wise to this Wales conspiracy against his game.

"Mebbe you can win back that lot from her," I says, "and raffle it over again for the fund. She's getting worked up to where she'll take a chance."

"Good work!" says he. "I'll approach her in the matter."

So over he goes and tries to interest her in the dice games; but no, she thinks dice is low and a mere coloured person's game. So then he says to set down to the card table and play this here Canfield solitaire; she's to be paid five dollars for every card she gets up and a whole thousand if she gets 'em all up. That listens good to her till she finds she has to give fifty-two dollars for the deck first. She says she knew there must be some catch about it. Still, she tries out a couple of deals just to see what would happen, and on the first she would have won thirteen dollars and on the second eight dollars. She figures then that by all moral rights Cousin Egbert owes her twenty-one dollars, and at least eight dollars to a certainty, because she was really playing for money the second time and merely forgot to mention it to him.

And while they sort of squabble about this, with Cousin Egbert very pig-headed or adamant, who should come in but this Sandy Sawtelle, that's now sobbing out his heart in song down there; and with him is Buck Devine. It seems they been looking for a game, and they give squeals of joy when they see this one. In just two minutes Sandy is collecting thirty-five dollars for one that he had carefully placed on No. 11. He gives a glad shout at this, and Leonard Wales and lady move over to see what it's all about. Sandy is neatly stacking his red chips and plays No. 11 once more, but No. 22 comes up.

"Gee!" says Sandy. "I forgot. Twenty-two, of course, and likewise 33."

So he now puts dollar bets on all three numbers, and after a couple more turns he's collecting on 33, and the next time 22 comes again. He don't hardly have time to stack his chips, they come so fast; and then it's No. 11 once more, amid rising excitement from all present. Cora Wales is panting like the Dying Gamekeeper I once saw in the Eden Musée in New York City. Sandy quits now for a moment.

"Let every man, woman, and child, come one, come all, acrost the room and crook the convivial elbow on my ill-gotten gains!" he calls out.

So everybody orders something, Tim Mahoney going in behind the bar to help out. Even Cora Wales come over when she understood no expense was attached to so doing, though taking a plain lemonade, because she said alcohol would get one's vibrations all fussed up, or something like that.

Cousin Egbert was still chipper after this reverse, though it had swept away about all he was to the good up to that time.

"Three rousing cheers!" says he. "And remember

the little ball still rolls for any sport that thinks he can Dutch up the game!"

While this drink is going on amid the general glad feeling that always prevails when some spendthrift has ordered for the house, Leonard Wales gets Buck Devine to one side and says how did Sandy do it? So Buck tells him and Cora that Sandy took eleven stitches in Jerry's hide yesterday afternoon and he was playing this hunch, which he had reason to feel was a first-class one.

"If I could only feel it was a cosmic certainty——" says Cora.

"Oh, she's cosmic, all right!" says Buck. "I never seen anything cosmicker. Look what she's done already, and Sandy only begun! Just watch him! He'll cosmic this here game to a standstill. He'll have Sour Dough there touching him for two-bits breakfast money—see if he don't."

"But eleven came only twice," says the conservative Cora.

"Sure! But did you notice Nos. 22 and 33?" says Buck. "You got to humour any good hunch to a certain extent, cosmic or no cosmic."

"I see," says Cora with gleaming eyes; "and No. 33 is not only what drew our beautiful building lot but it is also the precise number of my years on the earth plane."

Cousin Egbert overheard this and snorted like no gentleman had ought to, even in the lowest gambling den.

"Thirty-three!" says he to me.   "Did you hear the big cheat? Say! No gambling house on earth would have the nerve to put her right age on a wheel! The chances is ruinous enough now without running 'em up to forty-eight or so.   I bet that's about what you'd find if you was to tooth her."

Sandy has now gone back, followed by the crowd, and wins another bet on No. 11. This is too much for Cora's Standard Oil instincts. She never trusts Leonard with any money, but she goes over into a corner, hikes the flag of her country up over one red stocking for a minute, and comes back with a two-dollar bill, which she splits on 22 and 33; and when 33 wins she's mad clean through because 22 didn't also win, and she's wasted a whole dollar, like throwing it into the Atlantic Ocean.

"Too bad, Pettie!" says Leonard, who was crowded in by her.   "But you mustn't expect to have all the luck"—which is about the height of Leonard's mental reach.

"It was not luck; it was simple lack of faith," says Cora. "I put myself in tune with the Infinite and make my claim upon the all-good—and then I waver. The loss of that dollar was a punishment to me."

Now she stakes a dollar on No. 33 alone, and when it comes double-o she cries out that the man had leaned his hand on the edge of the table while the ball was rolling and thereby mushed up her cosmic vibrations, even if he didn't do something a good deal more crooked.   Then she switches to No. 22, and that wins.

She now gets suspicious of the chips and has 'em
turned into real money, which she stuffs into her
consort's pockets for the time being, all but two dollars that go on Nos. 11 and 33. And No. 22 comes
up again. She nearly fainted and didn't recover in
time to get anything down for the next roll—and I'm
darned if 11 don't show! She turns savagely on her
husband at this. The poor hulk only says:

"But, Pettie, you're playing the game—I ain't."

She replies bitterly:

"Oh, ain't that just like a man! I knew you were
going to say that!"—and seemed to think she had
him well licked.

Then the single-o come. She says:

"Oh, dear! It seems that, even with the higher
consciousness, one can't be always certain of one's
numbers at this dreadful game."

And while she was further reproaching her husband,
taking time to do it good and keeping one very damp
dollar safe in her hand, what comes up but old 33
again!

It looked like hysterics then, especially when she
noticed Buck Devine helping pile Sandy's chips up in
front of him till they looked like a great old English
castle, with towers and minarets, and so on, Sandy
having played his hunch strong and steady. She
waited for another turn that come nothing important
to any of 'em; then she drew Leonard out and made
him take her for a glass of lemonade out where Aggie
Tuttle was being Rebekkah at the Well, because they

charged two bits for it at the bar and Aggie's was only a dime. The sale made forty cents Aggie had took in on the evening.

Racing back to Ye Olde Tyme Gambling Denne, she gets another hard blow; for Sandy has not only win another of his magic numbers but has bought up the bar for the evening, inviting all hands to brim a cup at his expense, whenever they crave it—nobody's money good but his; so Cora is not only out what she would of made by following his play but the ten cents cash she has paid Aggie Tuttle. She was not a woman to be trifled with then. She took another lemonade because it was free, and made Len take one that he didn't want. Then she draws three dollars from him and covers the three numbers with reckless and noble sweeps of her powerful arms. The game was on again.

Cousin Egbert by now was looking slightly disturbed, or *outré*, as the French put it, but tries to conceal same under an air of sparkling gayety, laughing freely at every little thing in a girlish or painful manner.

"Yes," says he coquettishly; "that Sandy scoundrel is taking it fast out of one pocket, but he's putting it right back into the other. The wheel's loss is the bar's gain."

I looked over to size Sandy's chips and I could see four or five markers that go a hundred apiece.

"I admire your roguish manner that don't fool any one," I says; "but if we was to drink the half of

Sandy's winnings, even at your robber prices, we'd all be submerged to the periscope. It looks to me," I goes on, "like the bazaar-robbing genius is not exclusively a male attribute or tendency."

"How many of them knitted crawdabs you sold out there at your booths?" he demands. "Not enough to buy a single Belgian a T-bone steak and fried potatoes."

"Is that so, indeed?" I says. "Excuse me a minute. Standing here in the blinding light of your triumph, I forgot a little matter of detail such as our sex is always wasting its energies on."

So I call Sandy and Buck away from their Belgian atrocities and speak sharply to 'em.

"You boys ought to be ashamed of yourselves," I says—"winning all that money and then acting like old Gaspard the Miser in the Chimes of Normandy! Can't you forget your natural avarice and loosen up some?"

"I bought the bar, didn't I?" asks Sandy. "I can't do no more, can I?"

"You can," I says. "Out in that big room is about eighteen tired maids and matrons of Red Gap's most exclusive inner circles yawning their heads off over goods, wares, and merchandise that no one will look at while this sinful game is running. If you got a spark of manhood in you go on out and trade a little with 'em, just to take the curse off your depredations in here."

"Why, sure!" says Sandy. He goes back to the

layout and loads Buck's hat full of red and blue chips at one and two dollars each. "Go buy the place clean," he says to Buck. "Do it good; don't leave a single object of use or luxury. My instructions is sweeping, understand. And if there's a harness booth there you order a solid gold collar for old Jerry, heavily incrusted with jewels and his initials and mine surrounded by a wreath. Also, send out a pint of wine for every one of these here maids and matrons. Meantime, I shall stick here and keep an eye on my large financial interests."

So Buck romps off on his joyous mission, singing a little ballad that goes: "To hell with the man that works!" And Sandy moves quickly back to the wheel.

I followed and found Cora barely surviving because she's lost nine of her three-dollar bets while Sandy was away, leaving her only about a hundred winner. Len was telling her to "be brave, Pettie!" and she was saying it was entirely his fault that they hadn't already got their neat little home; but she would have it before she left the place or know the reason why.

It just did seem as if them three numbers had been resting while Sandy was away talking to me. They begin to show up again the minute he resumed his bets, and Cora was crowding onto the same with a rising temperature. Yes, sir, it seemed downright uncanny or miraculous the way one or the other of 'em showed up, with Sandy saying it was a shame to

take the money, and Cora saying it was a shame she
had to bet on all three numbers and get paid only on
one.

Of course others was also crowding these numbers,
though not so many as you'd think, because every one
said the run must be at an end, and they'd be a fool
to play 'em any farther; and them that did play 'em
was mostly making ten-cent bets to be on the safe
side.   Only Sandy and Cora kept right on showing up
one Egbert Floud as a party that had much to learn
about pulling off a good bazaar.

It's a sad tale.   Cousin Egbert had to send out
twice for more cash, Cora Wales refusing to take his
check on the Farmers and Merchants National for
hers.   She said she was afraid there would be some
catch about it.   I met Egbert out in the hall after the
second time she'd made him send and he'd lost much
of his sparkle.

"I never thought it was right to strike a lady without cause," he says bitterly; "but I'd certainly hate to
trust myself with that frail out in some lonely spot,
like Price's Addition, where her screams couldn't be
heard."

"That's right," I says; "take it out on the poor
woman that's trying to win a nice bungalow with big
sawed corners sticking out all over it, when that cutthroat Sandy Sawtelle has win about twice as much!
That ain't the light of pure reason I had the right to
expect from the Bazaar King of Red Gap."

"That's neither here nor there," says he with pet-

ulance. "Sandy would of been just as happy if he'd
lost the whole eighteen dollars him and Buck come in
here with."

"Well," I warns him, "it looks to me like you'd
have to apply them other drastic methods you met
with in this deadfall at the San Francisco Fair—
strong-arm work or medicine in the drinks of the
winners, or something like that—if you want to keep
a mortgage off the old home. Of course I won't
crowd you for that two dollars you promised me for
every one that goes out of the hall. You can have
any reasonable time you want to pay that," I
says.

"That's neither here nor there," he says. "Luck's
got to turn. The wheel ain't ever been made that
could stand that strain much longer."

And here Luella Stultz comes up and says Mrs.
Wales wants to know how much she could bet all at
once if she happened to want to. I could just see
Cora having a sharp pain in the heart like a knife
thrust when she thought what she would of win by
betting ten dollars instead of one. Cousin Egbert
answers Luella quite viciously.

"Tell that dame the ceiling sets the limit now,"
says he; "but if that ain't lofty enough I'll have a sky-
light sawed into it for her."

Then he goes over to watch, himself, being all
ruined up by these plungers. Leonard was saying:
"Now don't be rash, Pettie!" And Pettie was telling
him it was his negative mind that had kept her from

betting five dollars every clip, and look what that would mean to their pile!

Cousin Egbert give 'em one look and says, right out loud, Leonard Wales is the biggest ham that was ever smoked, and he'd like to meet him, man to man, outside; then he goes off muttering that he can be pushed so far, but in the excitement of the play no one pays the least attention to him. A little later I see him all alone out in the hall again. He was scrunched painfully up in a chair till he looked just like this here French metal statue called *Lee Penser*, which in our language means "The Thinker." I let him think, not having the heart to prong him again so quick.

And the game goes merrily on, with Sandy collecting steadily on his hunch and Cora Wales telling her husband the truth about himself every time one of these three numbers didn't win; she exposed some very distressing facts about his nature the time she put five apiece on the three numbers and the single-o come up. It was a mad life, that last hour, with a lot of other enraged ladies round the layout, some being mad because they hadn't had money to play the hunch with, and others because they hadn't had the nerve.

Then somebody found it was near midnight and the crowd begun to fall away. Cousin Egbert strolls by and says don't quit on his account—that they can stick there and play their hunch till the bad place freezes over, for all he cares; and he goes over to the bar and takes a drink all by himself, which in him is a sign of great mental disturbance.

Then, for about twenty minutes, I was chatting with the Mes-dames Ballard and Price about what a grand success our part had been, owing to Sandy acting the fool with Cousin Egbert's money, which the latter ain't wise to yet. When I next notice the game a halt has been called by Cora Wales. It seems the hunch has quit working. Neither of 'em has won a bet for twenty minutes and Cora is calling the game crooked.

"It looks very, very queer," says she, "that our numbers should so suddenly stop winning; very queer and suspicious indeed!" And she glared at Cousin Egbert with rage and distrust splitting fifty-fifty in her fevered eyes.

Cousin Egbert replied quickly, but he kind of sputtered and so couldn't have been arrested for it.

"Oh, I've no doubt you can explain it very glibly," says Cora; "but it seems very queer indeed to Leonard and I, especially coming at this peculiar time, when our little home is almost within my grasp."

Cousin Egbert just walked off, though opening and shutting his hands in a nervous way, like, in fancy free, he had her out on her own lot in Price's Addition and was there abusing her fatally.

"Very well!" says Cora with great majesty. "He may evade giving me a satisfactory explanation of this extraordinary change, but I shall certainly not remain in this place and permit myself to be fleeced. Here, darling!"

And she stuffs some loose silver into darling's last pocket that will hold any more. He was already wadded with bills and sagging with coin, till it didn't look like the same suit of clothes. Then she stood there with a cynical smile and watched Sandy still playing his hunch, ten dollars to a number, and never winning a bet.

"You poor dupe!" says she when Sandy himself finally got tired and quit. "It's especially awkward," she adds, "because while we have saved enough to start our little nook, it will have to be far less pretentious than I was planning to make it while the game seemed to be played honestly."

Cousin Egbert gets this and says, as polite as a stinging lizard, that he stands ready to give her a chance at any game she can think of, from mumblety-peg up. He says if she'll turn him and Leonard loose in a cellar that he'll give her fifty dollars for every one she's winner if he don't have Len screaming for help inside of one minute—or make it fifteen seconds. Len, who's about the size of a freight car, smiles kind of sickish at this, and says he hopes there's no hard feelings among old friends and lodge brothers; and Egbert says, Oh, no! It would just be in the nature of a friendly contest, which he feels very much like having one, since he can be pushed just so far; but Cora says gambling has brutalized him.

Then she sees the cards on the table and asks again

about this game where you play cards with yourself
and mebbe win a thousand dollars cold. She wants
to know if you actually get the thousand in cash, and
Egbert says:

"Sure! A thousand that any bank in town would
accept at par."

She picks up the deck and almost falls, but thinks
better of it.

"Could I play with my own cards?" she wants to
know, looking suspicious at these. Egbert says she
sure can. "And in my own home?" asks Cora.

"Your own house or any place else," says Egbert,
"and any hour of the day or night. Just call me up
when you feel lucky."

"We could embellish our little nook with many
needful things," says Cora. "A thousand dollars
spent sensibly would do marvels." But after fiddling
a bit more with the cards she laid 'em down with a
pitiful sigh.

Cousin Egbert just looked at her, then looked
away quick, as if he couldn't stand it any more, and
says: "War is certainly what that man Sherman said
it was."

Then he watches Sandy Sawtelle cashing in his
chips and is kind of figuring up his total losses; so I
can't resist handing him another.

"I don't know what us Mes-dames would of done
without your master mind," I says; "and yet I'd
hate to be a Belgian with the tobacco habit and have
to depend on you to gratify it."

"Well," he answers, very mad, "I don't see so many of 'em getting tobacco heart with the proceeds of your fancy truck out in them booths either!"

"Don't you indeed?" I says, and just at the right moment, too. "Then you better take another look or get your eyes fixed or something."

For just then Sandy stands up on a chair and says:

"Ladies and gents, a big pile of valuable presents is piled just at the right of the main entrance as you go out, and I hope you will one and all accept same with the welcome compliments of me and old Jerry, that I had to take eleven stitches in the hide of. As you will pass out in an orderly manner, let every lady help herself to two objects that attract her, and every gent help himself to one object; and no crowding or pulling I trust, because some of the objects would break, like the moustache cup and saucer, or the drainpipe, with painted posies on it, to hold your umbrels. Remember my words—every lady two objects and every gent one only. There is also a new washboiler full of lemonade that you can partake of at will, though I guess you won't want any—and thanking you one and all!"

So they cheer Sandy like mad and beat it out to get first grab at the plunder; and just as Cousin Egbert thinks he now knows the worst, in comes the girls that had the booths, bringing all the chips Buck Devine had paid 'em—two hundred and seventy-eight dollars' worth that Egbert has to dig down for after he thinks all is over.

"Ain't it jolly," I says to him while he was writing another check on the end of the bar. "This is the first time us ladies ever did clean out every last object at a bazaar. Not a thing left; and I wish we'd got in twice as much, because Sandy don't do things by halves when his money comes easy from some poor dub that has thought highly of himself as a thinker about money matters." He pretends not to hear me because of signing his name very carefully to the check. "And what a sweet little home you'll build for the Wales family!" I says. "I can see it now, all ornamented up, and with one of these fancy bungalow names up over the front gate—probably they'll call it The Breakers!"

But he wouldn't come back; so I left him surrounded by the wreck of his former smartiness and went home. At the door where the treasures had been massed not a solitary thing was left but a plush holder for a whisk broom, with hand-painted pansies on the front; and I decided I could live without that. Tim Mahoney was there, grouching round about having to light up the hall next night for the B'nai B'rith; and I told him to take it for himself. He already had six drawnwork doilies and a vanity box with white and red powder in it.

As I go by the Hong Kong Quick Lunch, Sandy and three or four others is up on stools; the Chinaman, cooking things behind the counter, is wearing a lavender-striped silk dressing sacque and a lace boudoir cap with pink ribbons in it. Yes; we'd all had a purple night of it!

Next day about noon I'm downtown and catch sight of Cousin Egbert setting in the United States Grill having breakfast; so I feel mean enough to go in and gloat over him some more. I think to find him all madded up and mortified; but he's strangely cheerful for one who has suffered. He was bearing up so wonderful that I asked why.

"Ain't you heard?" says he, blotting round in his steak platter with a slice of bread. "Well, I got even with that Wales outfit just before daylight—that's all!"

"Talk on," I beg, quite incredulous.

"I didn't get to bed till about two," he says, "and at three I was woke up by the telephone. It's this big stiff Len Wales, that had ought to have his head taken off because it only absorbs nourishment from his system and gives nothing in return. He's laughing in a childish frenzy and says is this me? I says it is, but that's neither here nor there, and what does he want at this hour? 'It's a good joke on you,' he says, 'for the little woman got it on the third trial.' 'Got what?' I wanted to know. 'Got that solitaire,' he yells. 'And it's a good joke on you, all right, because now you owe her the thousand dollars; and I hate to bother you, but you know how some women are that have a delicate, high-strung organization. She says she won't be able to sleep a wink if you don't bring it up to her so she can have all our little treasure under her pillow; and I think, myself, it's better to have it all settled and satisfactory while the iron's hot, and you'd probably prefer it that way, too; and she says she won't mind, this time, taking your check, though the actual money would be far more satisfactory, because you know what women are——'

"Say! He raves on like this for three minutes, stopping to laugh like a maniac about every three words, before I can get a word in to tell him that I'm a delicate, high-strung organization myself, if you come right down to it, and I can't stand there in my nightgown listening to a string of nonsense. He chokes and says: 'What nonsense?' And I ask him does he think I'd pay a thousand dollars out on a game I hadn't overlooked? And he says didn't I agree to in the presence of witnesses, and the cards is laid out right there now on the dining-room table if I got the least suspicion the game wasn't played fair, and will I come up and look for myself! And I says 'Not in a thousand years!' Because what does he think I am!

"So then Mis' Wales she breaks in and says: 'Listen, Mr. Floud! You are taking a most peculiar attitude in this matter. You perhaps don't understand that it means a great deal to dear Leonard and me—try to think calmly and summon your finer instincts. You said I could not only play with my own cards at any hour of the night or day, but in my own home; and I chose to play here, because condi-

tions are more harmonious to my psychic powers——'
And so on and so on; and she can't understand my
peculiar attitude once more, till I thought I'd bust.

"It was lucky she had the telephone between us
or I should certainly of been pinched for a crime of
violence. But I got kind of collected in my senses
and I told her I already had been pushed as far as I
could be; and then I think of a good one: I ask her
does she know what General Sherman said war was?
So she says, 'No; but what has that got to do with
it?' 'Well, listen carefully!' I says. 'You tell
dear Leonard that I am now saying my last word in
this matter by telling you both to go to war—and
then ask him to tell you right out what Sherman said
war was.'

"I listened a minute longer for her scream, and
when it come, like sweet music or something, I went
to bed again and slept happy. Yes, sir; I got even
with them sharks all right, though she's telling all
over town this morning that I have repudiated a debt
of honour and she's going to have that thousand if
there's any law in the land; and anyway, she'll get
me took up for conducting a common gambling house.
Gee! It makes me feel good!"

That's the way with this old Egbert boy; nothing
ever seems to faze him long.

"How much do you lose on the night?" I ask him.

"Well, the bar was a great help," he says, very
chipper; "so I only lose about fourteen hundred
all told. It'll make a nice bunch for the Belgians,

and the few dollars you ladies made at your cheap booths will help some."

"How will your fourteen hundred lost be any help to the Belgians?" I wanted to know; and he looked at me very superior and as crafty as a fox.

"Simple enough!" he says in a lofty manner. "I was going to give what I win, wasn't I? So why wouldn't I give what I lose? That's plain enough for any one but a woman to see, ain't it? I give Mis' Ballard, the treasurer, a check for fourteen hundred not an hour ago. I told you I knew how to run one of these grafts, didn't I? Didn't I, now?"

Wasn't that just like the old smarty? You never know when you got him nailed. And feeling so good over getting even with the Wales couple that had about a thousand dollars of his money that very minute!

Still from the dimly lighted bunk house came the wail of Sandy Sawtelle to make vibrant the night. He had returned to his earlier song after intermittent trifling with an extensive repertoire:

There's a broken heart for every light on Broadway,
A million tears for every gleam, they say.
Those lights above you think nothing of you;
It's those who love you that have to pay.   .   .   .

It was the wail of one thwarted and perishing. "Ain't it the sobbing tenor?" remarked his employer. "But you can't blame him after the killing he made before. Of course he'll get to town sooner or later and play this fourteen number, being that the new reform administration, with Lon Price as Mayor, is now safely elected and the game has opened up again. Yes, sir; he's nutty about stitches in a mule. I wouldn't put it past him that he had old Jerry kicked on purpose to-day!"

VII

KATE; OR, UP FROM THE DEPTHS

THIS day I fared abroad with Ma Pettengill over wide spaces of the Arrowhead Ranch. Between fields along the river bottom were gates distressingly crude; clumsy, hingeless panels of board fence, which I must dismount and lift about by sheer brawn of shoulder. Such gates combine the greatest weight with the least possible exercise of man's inventive faculties, and are named, not too subtly, the Armstrong gate. This, indeed, is the American beauty of ranch humour, a flower of imperishable fragrance handed to the visitor—who does the lifting—with guarded drollery or triumphant snicker, as may be. Buck Devine or Sandy Sawtelle will achieve the mot with an aloof austerity that abates no jot unto the hundredth repetition; while Lew Wee, Chinese cook of the Arrowhead, fails not to brighten it with a nervous giggle, impairing its vocal correctness, moreover, by calling it the "Armcatchum" gate.

Ma Pettengill was more versatile this day. The first gate I struggled with she called Armstrong in a manner dryly descriptive; for the second she managed a humorous leer to illumine the term; for the third, secured with a garland of barbed wire that must be painfully untwisted, she employed a still broader humour. Even a child would then have known that calling this criminal device the Armstrong gate was a joke of uncommon richness.

As I remounted, staunching the inevitable wound from barbed wire, I began to speak in the bitterly superior tones of an efficiency expert as we traversed a field where hundreds of white-faced Herefords were putting on flesh to their own ruin. I said to my hostess that I vastly enjoyed lifting a hundred-pound gate—and what was the loss of a little blood between old friends, even when aggravated by probable tetanus germs? But had she ever paused to compute the money value of time lost by her henchmen in dismounting to open these clumsy makeshifts? I suggested that, even appraising the one reliable ranch joke in all the world at a high figure, she would still profit considerably by putting in gates that were gates, in place of contrivances that could be handled ideally only by a retired weight lifter in barbed-wire-proof armour.

I rapidly calculated, with the seeming high regard for accuracy that marks all efficiency experts, that these wretched devices cost her twenty-eight cents and a half each *per diem*. Estimating the total of them on the ranch at one hundred, this meant to her a loss of twenty-eight dollars and a half *per diem*. I used *per diem* twice to impress the woman. I added that it was pretty slipshod business for a going concern, supposing—sarcastically now—that the Arrowhead was a going concern. Of course, if it were merely a toy for the idle rich——

She had let me talk, as she will now and then, affecting to be engrossed with her stock.

"Look at them white-faced darlings!" she murmured. "Two years old and weighing eleven hundred this minute if they weigh a pound!"

Then I saw we approached a gate that amazingly was a gate. Hinges, yes; and mechanical complications, and a pendant cord on each side. I tugged at one and the gate magically opened. As we passed through I tugged at the other and it magically closed. This was luxury ineffable to one who had laboured with things that seemed to be kept merely for the sake of a jest that was never of the best and was staling with use. It would also be, I hoped, an object lesson to my hostess. I performed the simple rite in silence, yet with a manner that I meant to be eloquent, even provocative. It was.

"Oh, sure!" spoke Ma Pettengill. "That there's one of your *per-diem* gates; and there's another leading out of this field, and about six beyond—all of 'em just as *per diem* as this one; and, also, this here ranch you're on now is one of your going concerns." She chuckled at this and repeated it in a subterranean rumble: "A going concern—my sakes, yes! It moved so fast you could see it go, and now it's went." Noisily she relished this bit of verbal finesse; then permitted her fancy again to trifle

with it.   "Yes, sir; this here going concern is plumb
gone!"

With active malice I asked no question, maintain-
ing a dignified silence as I lightly manipulated a second paragon of gates. The lady now rumbled confidentially to herself, and I caught piquant phrases;
yet still I forbore to question, since the woman so
plainly sought to intrigue me. Even when we
skirted a clump of cottonwoods and came—through
another perfect gate—upon a most amazing small collection of ranch buildings, dying of desertion, I retained perfect control of a rising curiosity.

By unspoken agreement we drew rein to survey
a desolation that was still immaculate. Stables
and outbuildings were trim and new, and pure with
paint. All had been swept and garnished; no un-
sightly litter marred the scene. The house was a
suburban villa of marked pretension and would have
excited no comment on Long Island.   In this valley
of the mountains it was nothing short of spectacular.
Only one item of decoration hinted an attempt to
adapt itself to environment: in the noble stone
chimney that reared itself between two spacious
wings a branding iron had been embedded. Thus
did it proclaim itself to the incredulous hills as a
ranch house.

Flowers had been planted along a gravelled walk.
While I reminded myself that the gravel must have
been imported from a spot at least ten miles distant,
I was further shocked by discovering a most improb-

able golf green, in gloomy survival. Then I detected a series of kennels facing a wired dog run. This was overwhelming in a country of simple, steadfast devotion to the rearing of cattle for market.

Ma Pettengil now spoke in a tone that, for her, could be called hushed, though it reached me twenty feet away.

"An art bungalow!" she said, and gazed upon it with seeming awe. Then she waved a quirt to indicate this and the painfully neat outbuildings. "A toy for the idle rich—was that it? Well, you said something. This was one little *per-diem* going concern, all right. They even had the name somewhere round here worked out in yellow flowers— Broadmoor it was. You could read it for five miles when the posies got up There it is over on that lawn. You can't read it now because the letters are all overgrown. My Chinaman got delirious about that when he first seen it and wanted me to plant Arrowhead out in front of our house, and was quite hurt when I told him I was just a business woman— and a tired business woman at that. He done what he could, though, to show we was some class. The first time these folks come over to our place to lunch he picked all my pink carnations to make a mat on the table, and spelled out Arrowhead round it in ripe olives, with a neat frame of celery inclosing same. Yes, sir!"

This was too much. It now seemed time to ask questions, and I did so in a winning manner; but so

deaf in her backward musing was the woman that
I saw it must all come in its own way.

"We got to make up over that bench yet," she
said at last; and we rode out past the ideal stable—
its natty weather vane forever pointing the wind to
the profit of no man—through another gate of superb cunning, and so once more to an understandable
landscape, where sane cattle grazed. Here I threw
off the depression that comes upon one in places
where our humankind so plainly have been and are
not. Again I questioned of Broadmoor and its vanished people.

The immediate results were fragmentary, serving
to pique rather than satisfy; a series of *hors d'oeuvres*
that I began to suspect must form the whole repast.
On the verge of coherence the woman would break
off to gloat over a herd of thoroughbred Durhams
or a bunch of sportive Hereford calves or a field
teeming with the prized fruits of intermarriage
between these breeds. Or she found diversion in
stupendous stacks of last summer's hay, well fenced
from pillage; or grounds for criticising the sloth of
certain of her henchmen, who had been told as plain
as anything that "that there line fance" had to be
finished by Saturday; no two ways about it! She
repeated the language in which she had conveyed
this decision. There could have been no grounds
for misunderstanding it.

And thus the annals of Broadmoor began to dribble to me, overlaid too frequently for my taste with

philosophic reflections at large upon what a lone, defenceless woman could expect in this world— irrelevant, pointed wonderings as to whether a party letting on he was a good ranch hand really expected to perform any labour for his fifty a month, or just set round smoking his head off and see which could tell the biggest lie; or mebbe make an excuse for some light job like oiling the twenty-two sets of mule harness over again, when they had already been oiled right after haying. Furthermore, any woman not a born fool would get out of the business the first chance she got, this one often being willing to sell for a mutilated dollar, except for not wishing financial ruin or insanity to other parties.

Yet a few details definitely emerged. "Her" name was called Posnett, though a party would never guess this if he saw it in print, because it was spelled Postlethwaite. Yes, sir! All on account of having gone to England from Boston and found out that was how you said it, though Cousin Egbert Floud had tried to be funny about it when shown the name in the Red Gap *Recorder*. The item said the family had taken apartments at Red Gap's premier hotel *de luxe*, the American House; and Cousin Egbert, being told a million dollars was bet that he never could guess how the name was pronounced in English, he up and said you couldn't fool him; that it was pronounced Chumley, which was just like the old smarty—only he give in that he was surprised when told how it really was pronounced; and he said if a party's name was Postlethwaite why couldn't they come out and say so like a man, instead of beating round the bush like that? All of which was promising enough; but then came the Hereford yearlings to effect a breach of continuity.

These being enough admired, I had next to be told that I wouldn't believe how many folks was certain she had retired to the country because she was lazy, just keeping a few head of cattle for diversion—she that had six thousand acres of land under fence, and had made a going concern *per diem* of it for thirty years, even if parties did make cracks about her gates; but hardly ever getting a good night's sleep through having a "passel" of men to run it that you couldn't depend on—though God only knew where you could find any other sort—the minute your back was turned.

A fat, sleek, prosperous male, clad in expensive garments, and wearing a derby hat and too much jewellery, became somehow personified in this tirade. I was led to picture him a residuary legatee who had never done a stroke of work in his life, and believed that no one else ever did except from a sportive perversity. I was made to hear him tell her that she, Mrs. Lysander John Pettengill, was leading the ideal life on her country place; and, by Jove! he often thought of doing the same thing himself—get a nice little spot in this beautiful country, with some green meadows, and have bands of large handsome cattle strolling about in the sunlight, so he could forget the world and its strife in the same idyllic peace she must be finding. Or if he didn't tell her this, then he was sure to have a worthless son or nephew that her ranch would be just the place for; and, of course, she would be glad to take him on and make something of him— that is, so the lady now regrettably put it, as he had shown he wasn't worth a damn for anything else, why couldn't she make a cattleman of him?

"Yes, sir; that's what I get from these here visitors that are enchanted by the view. Either they think my ranch is a reform school for poor chinless Chester, that got led away by bad companions and can't say no, or they think, like you said, that it's just a toy for the idle rich. Show 'em a shoe factory or a steel works and they can understand it's a business prop-osition; but a ranch—— Shucks! They think I've done my day's work when I ride out on a gentle horse and look pleased at the landscape."

Again were we diverted. A dozen alien beeves fed upon the Arrowhead preserves. Did I see that wattle brand—the jug-handle split? That was the Timmins brand—old Safety First Timmins. There must be a break in his fence at the upper end of the field. Made it himself likely. Wouldn't she give the old penny-pincher hell if she had him here? She would, indeed! Continuous muttering of a rugged character for half a mile of jog trot.

Then again:

"Cousin Egbert got all fussed up in his mind about the name and always called her Postle-nut. He don't seem to have a brain for such things. But she didn't

mind. I give her credit for that. She was fifty
if she was a day, but very, very blond; laboratory
stuff, of course. You'd of called her a superblonde,
I guess. And haggard and wrinkled in the face; but
she took good care of that, too—artist's materials.

"You know old Pete—that Indian you see cutting
up wood back on the place. Pete took a long look
at her and named her the Painted Desert. You always hear say an Indian hasn't got any sense of
humour. I don't know; Pete was sure being either a
humourist or a poet. However, this here lady handed
me a new one about my business. She thought it
was merely an outdoor sport. I never could get
that out of her head. Even when she left she says
she knows it's ripping good sport, but it's such a
terrific drain on one's income, and I must be quite
mad about ranching to keep it up. I said, yes; I
got quite mad about it sometimes, and let it go at
that. What was the use?"

A voiceless interval while we climbed a trail to the
timbered bench where fence posts were being cut by
half a dozen of the Arrowhead forces. Two of these
were swiftly detached and bade to repair the break
in the fence by which one Timmins was now profiting,
the entire six being first regaled with a brief but
pithy character analysis of the offender, portraying
him as a loathsome biological freak; headless, I
gathered, and with the acquisitive instincts of a trade
rat.

Then we rounded back on our way to the Arrowhead ranch house. Five miles up the narrowing valley we could see its outposts and its smoke. Far below us the spick-and-span buildings of deserted Broadmoor glittered newly, demanding that I be told more of them. Yet for the five-mile ride I added, as I thought, no item to my slender stock. Instead, when we had descended from the bench and were again in fields where the gates might be opened only by galling effort, I learned apparently irrelevant facts concerning Egbert Floud's pet kitten.

"Yes, sir; he's just like any old maid with that cat. 'Kitty!' here and 'Kitty!' there; and 'Poor Kitty, did I forget to warm its milk?' And so on. It was give to him two years ago by Jeff Tuttle's littlest girl, Irene; and he didn't want it at first, but him and Irene is great friends, so he pretended he was crazy about it and took it off in his overcoat pocket, thinking it would die anyway, because it was only skin and bones. Whenever it tried to purr you'd think it was going to shake all its timbers loose. His house is just over on the other side of Arrowhead Pass there, and I saw the kitten the first day he brought it up, kind of light brown and yellow in colour, with some gray on the left shoulder.

Well, the minute I see these markings I recognized 'em and remembered something, and I says right off that he's got some cat there; and he says how do I know? And I tell him that there kitten has got at least a quarter wildcat in it. Its grandmother, or mebbe its great-grandmother, was took up to the

Tuttle Ranch when there wasn't another cat within forty miles, and it got to running round nights; and quite a long time after that they found it with a mess of kittens in a box out in the harness room. One look at their feet and ears was all you'd want to see that their pa was a bobcat. They all become famous fighting characters, and was marked just like this descendant of theirs that Cousin Egbert has. And, say, I was going on like this, not suspecting anything except that I was giving him some interesting news about the family history of this pet of his, when he grabs the beast up and cuddles it, and says I had ought to be ashamed of myself, talking that way about a poor little innocent kitten that never done me a stroke of harm   Yes, sir; he was right fiery.

"I don't know how he come to take it that cross way, for he hadn't thought highly of the thing up to that moment. But some way it seemed to him I was talking scandal about his pet—kind of clouding up its ancestry, if you know what I mean. He didn't seem to get any broad view of it at all. You'd almost think I'd been reporting an indiscretion in some member of his family. Can you beat it? Heating up that way over a puny kitten, six inches from tip to tip, that he'd been thinking of as a pest and only taken to please Irene Tuttle! So he starts in from that minute to doctor it up and nurture it with canned soup and delicacies; and every time I see him after that he'd look indignant and say what great hands for spreading gossip us women are, and his kitten ain't got no more bobcat in its veins than what I have.

"He's a stubborn old toad. Irene had told him the kitten's name was Kate; so he kept right on calling it that even after it become incongruous, as you might say. Judge Ballard was up here on a fishing trip one time and heard him calling it Kate, and he says to Egbert: Why call it Kate when it ain't? Egbert says that was the name little Irene give it and it's too much trouble to think up another. The Judge says, Oh, no; not so much trouble, being that he could just change the name swiftly from Kate to Cato, thus meeting all conventional requirements with but slight added labour. But Egbert says there's the sentiment to think of—whatever he meant by that; and if you was to go over there to-day and he was home you'd likely hear him say: 'Yes; Kate is certainly some cat! Why, he's at least half bobcat— mebbe three-quarters; and the fightingest devil!' What's that? Yes; he's changed completely round about the wildcat strain. He's proud of it. If I was to say now it was only a quarter bob he'd be as mad as he was at first; he says anybody can see it's at least half bob. What changed him? Oh, well, we're too near home. Some other time."

So it befell that not until we sat out for a splendid sunset that evening did I learn in an orderly manner of Postlethwaite vicissitudes. Ma Pettengill built her first cigarette with tender solicitude; and this, in consideration of her day's hard ride, I permitted her to burn in relaxed silence. But when her trained fingers began to combine paper and tobacco for the second I mentioned Broadmoor, Postlethwaite, Posnett, and parties in general that come round the tired business woman, harassed with the countless vexations of a large cattle ranch, telling her how wise she has been to retire to this sylvan quietude, where she can dream away her life in peace. She started easily:

"That's it; they always intimate that running a ranch is mere cream puffs compared to a regular business, and they'd like to do the same thing to-morrow if only they was ready to retire from active life. Mebbe they get the idea from these here back-to-nature stories about a brokendown bookkeeper, sixty-seven years old, with neuritis and gastric complications and bum eyesight, and a wife that ain't ever seen a well day; so they take every cent of their life savings of eighty-three dollars and settle on an abandoned farm in Connecticut and clear nine thousand dollars the first year raising the Little Giant caper for boiled mutton. There certainly ought to be a law against such romantic trifling. In the first place, think of a Connecticut farmer abandoning anything worth money! Old Timmins comes from Connecticut. Any time that old leech abandons a thing, bookkeepers and all other parties will do well to ride right along with him. I tell you now——"

The second cigarette was under way, and suddenly,

without modulation, the performer was again on the theme, Posnett *née* Postlethwaite.

"Met her two years ago in Boston, where I was suffering a brief visit with my son-in-law's aunts. She was the sole widow of a large woolen mill. That's about all I could ever make out—couldn't get any line on him to speak of. The first time I called on her—she was in pink silk pyjamas, smoking a perfecto cigar, and unpacking a bale of lion and tiger skins she'd shot in Africa, or some place—she said she believed there would be fewer unhappy marriages in this world if women would only try more earnestly to make a companion of their husbands; she said she'd tried hard to make one of hers, but never could get him interested in her pursuits and pastimes, he preferring to set sullenly at his desk making money. She said to the day of his death he'd never even had a polo mallet in his hand. And wasn't that pitiful!

"And right now she wanted to visit a snappy little volcano she'd heard about in South America—only she had a grown son and daughter she was trying to make companions of, so they would love and trust her; and they'd begged her to do something nearer home that was less fatiguing; and mebbe she would. And how did I find ranching now? Was I awfully keen about it and was it ripping good sport? I said yes, to an extent. She said she thought it must be ripping, what with chasing the wild cattle over hill and dale to lasso them, and firing off revolvers in company with lawless cowboys inflamed by drink. She went on to give me some more details of ranch life, and got so worked up about it that we settled things right there, she being a lady of swift decisions. She said it wouldn't be very exciting for her, but it might be fine for son and daughter, and bring them all together in a more sacred companionship.

"So I come back and got that place down the creek for her, and she sent out a professional architect and a landscape gardener, and some other experts that would know how to build a ranch *de luxe*, and the thing was soon done. And she sent son on ahead to get slightly acquainted with the wild life. He was a tall bent thing, about thirty, with a long squinted face and going hair, and soft, innocent, ginger-coloured whiskers, and hips so narrow they'd hardly hold his belt up. That rowdy mother of his, in trying to make a companion of him, had near scared him to death. He was permanently frightened. What he really wanted to do, I found out, was to study insect life and botany and geography and arithmetic, and so on, and raise orchids, instead of being killed off in a sudden manner by his rough-neck parent. He loved to ride a horse the same way a cat loves to ride a going stove.

"I started out with him one morning to show him over the valley. He got into the saddle all right and he meant well, but that don't go any too far with a horse. Pretty soon, down on the level here, I started to canter a bit. He grabbed for the saddle horn and caught a handful of bunch grass fifteen feet to the left of the trail. He was game enough. He found his glasses and wiped 'em off, and said it was too bad the mater couldn't have seen him, because it would have been a bright spot in her life.

"Then he got on again and we took that steep trail up the side of the cañon that goes over Arrowhead, me meaning to please him with some beautiful and rugged scenery, where one false step might cause utter ruin. It didn't work, though. After we got pretty well up to the rim of the cañon he looks down and says he supposes they could recover one if one fell over there. I says: 'Oh, yes; they could recover one. They'd get you, all right. Of course you wouldn't look like anything!'

"He shudders at that and gets off to lead his horse, begging me to do the same. I said I never tried to do anything a horse could do better, and stayed on. Then he got confidential and told me a lot of interesting crimes this mater of his had committed in her mad efforts to make a companion of him. Once she'd tramped on the gas of a ninety-horsepower racer and socked him against a stone wall at a turn some fool had made in the road; and another time she near drowned him in the Arctic Ocean when she was off there for the polar-bear hunting; and she'd got him well clawed by a spotted leopard in India, that was now almost the best skin in her collection; and once in Switzerland he fell off the side of an Alp she was making him climb, causing her to be very short

with him all day because it delayed the trip. Tied to
a rope he was and hanging out there over nothing for
about fifteen minutes—he must have looked like a
sash weight.

"Then he told about learning to run a motor car
all by himself, just to please the mater. The first
time he made the sharp turns round their country
house he took nine shingles off the corner and crumpled a fender like it was tissue paper; but he stuck to
it till he got the score down to two or three shingles
only. He seemed right proud of that, like it was
bogey for the course, as you might say. He wasn't
the greatest humourist in the world, being too high-
minded, but he appealed to all my better instincts; he
was trying so hard to make the grade out of respect
for his bedizened and homicidal mother.

"And his poor sister, that come along later, was
very much like him, being severe of outline and wearing the same kind of spectacles, and not fussing much
about the fripperies of dress that engross so many of
our empty-headed sex and get 'em the notice of the
male. Her complexion was brutally honest, which
was about all her very best-wishers could say for it,
but she was kind-hearted and earnest, and thought a
good deal about the real or inner meaning of life.
What she really yearned for was to stay in Boston
and go to concerts, holding the music on her lap and
checking off the notes with a gold pencil when the
fiddlers played them. I watched her do it one night.
I don't know what her notion was, keeping cases on

the orchestra that way; but it seemed to give her a secret satisfaction. She was also interested in bird life and other studies of a high character, and she didn't want to be made a companion of by her rabid parent any more than brother did. They was just a couple of lambkins born to a tiger.

"Pretty soon the ranch buildings was all complete and varnished and polished, like you seen to-day, and the family moved in with all kinds of uniformed servants that looked unhappy and desperate. They had a pained butler in a dress suit that never once set foot outside the house the whole five months they was here. He'd of been thought too gloomy for good taste, even at a funeral. He had me nervous every time I went there, thinking any minute he was going to break down and sob.

"And this lady loses no time making companions of her children that didn't want to be. First she tried to make 'em chase steers on horseback. A fact! That was one of her ideas of ranch life. When I asked her what she was going to stock her ranch with she said didn't I have some good heads of stock I could sell her? And I said yes, I had some good heads, and showed her a bunch of my thoroughbreds, thinking none but the best would satisfy her. She looked 'em over with a glittering eye and said they was too fat to run well. I didn't get her. I said it was true; I hadn't raised 'em for speed. I said I didn't have an animal on the place that could hit better than three miles an hour, and not that for

long. I cheerfully admitted I didn't have a thoroughbred on the place that wouldn't be a joke on any
track in the country; but I wanted to know what of it.

"'How do you get any sport out of them,' demands the lady, 'if they can't give you a jolly good
chase?'

"That's what she asked me in so many words. I
says, does she aim to breed racing cattle? And she
says, where will the sport be with creatures all out of
condition with fat, like mine are? It took me about
ten minutes to get her idea, it was that heinous or
criminal. When I did get it I sent her to old Safety
First; and what does she do but buy a herd of twenty
yearling steers from the old crook! Scrubby little
runts that had been raised out in the hills and was all
bone and muscle, and any one of 'em able to do a mile
in four minutes flat, I guess.

"Old Safety was tickled to death at first when he
put off this refuse on her at a price not much more than
double what they would have brought in a tanyard,
which was all they'd ever be good for except bone fer-
tilizer, mebbe; but he was sick unto death when he
found they was just what she wanted, the skinnier the
better and he could have got anything he asked for
'em. He says to me afterward why don't I train
some of mine and trim her good? But I told him
I'm cinched for hell, anyway, and don't have to make
it tighter by torturing poor dumb brutes.

"That's what it amounted to. Having got Angora
chaps and cowboy hats for herself and offsprings,

what do they do but get on ponies and chase this herd all over creation, whirling their ropes, yelling, shooting in the air—just like you see on any well-conducted ranch. Once in a while the old lady herself, being a demon rider, would rope an animal and fetch it down; but brother and sister was very careful not to tangle their own ropes on anything. They didn't shoot their guns with any proper spirit, either; and when they tried to yip like cowboys they sounded like rabbits. And brother having to smoke brown-paper cigarettes, which he hated like poison and had trouble in rolling!

"Mother could roll 'em, all right—do it with one hand. And she urged sister to; but sister rebelled for once. The old lady admitted this was due to a fault in her early training. It seems her grandmother had been one of the old-fashioned sort; and, having studied the modern young woman of society in Boston and New York, she'd promised sister a string of pearls if she didn't either smoke or drink till her twenty-first birthday. Sister had not only won the pearls but had come on to twenty-eight without being like other young girls of the day, and wasn't going to begin now. So ma and brother had to do all the smoking.

"After a fine morning's run following the steers they'd like as not have a little branding in the afternoon, the old-fashioned kind that ain't done in the higher ranch circles any more, where a couple of silly punchers rope an animal fore and aft and throw it, thereby setting it back at least four months in its growth. The old lady was puzzled again by me having my branding done in a chute, where the poor things ain't worried more than is necessary. I bet she thought I was a short sport, not doing a thing on my place that would look well in a moving picture. She got a lot of ripping sport out of this branding. Made no difference if they was already branded, they got it again; she'd brand 'em over and over. Two or three of that herd got it so often that they looked like these leather suitcases parties bring back from Europe stuck all over with hotel labels.

"Well, this branch of sport lasted quite a while, with them steers developing speed every day till they got too fast for any one but the old lady. Brother and sister would be left far behind, or mebbe get stacked up and discouraged or sprained for the day. The old dame said it was disheartening, indeed, trying to make companions of one's children when they showed such a low order of intelligence for it. Still, she was fair-minded; so she had a golf links made, and put 'em at that. She wouldn't play herself, saying it was an effeminate game, good for fat old men or schoolboys, but mebbe her chits would benefit by it and get a taste for proper sports, where you can break a bone now and then by not using care.

"But golf wasn't much better. Sister would carry a book of poetry with her and read it as she loafed from one hit to another. The old lady near shed tears at the sight. And brother was about as bad, getting hypnotized by passing insect life and forgetting his score while prodding some new kind of bug.

"The old lady said I'd never believe what a care and responsibility children was. She had wanted 'em to go in for ranching and be awfully keen about it, and look how they acted! Still, she wouldn't give up. She suggested polo next; but sister said it wasn't a lady's game, making no demand upon the higher attributes of womanhood, and brother said he might go in for it if she'd let him play his on a bicycle, as being more reliable or stauncher than a pony.

"So she throws up her hands in despair, but thinks hard again; and at last she says she has the right sport for 'em and why didn't she think of it before! This new idea is to bring up her pack of prize-winning beagles, the sport being full of excitement, and yet safe enough for all concerned if they'll look where they walk and not stop to read slushy poems or collect insect life. Sister and brother said beagles, by all means, like drowning sailors clutching at a straw or something; and the old lady sent off a telegram.

"I admit I didn't know what kind of a game beagles was, but I didn't betray the fact when she told me about it. I was over to Egbert Floud's place next day and I asked him. But he didn't know and he couldn't even get the name right. He says: 'You mean beetles.' I says, 'Not at all'; that it's beagles. Then he says I must of got the name twisted, and

probably it's one of these curly horns. That's as
close as he ever did come to the name; and until he
actually saw the things he insisted they was either
something to blow on or something that crawled.
'Mark my words,' he says, 'they're either a horn or a
bug; and I wonder what this here blond guy will be
doing next.' So I saw nothing sensible was to be
had out of him, and I left him there, doddering.

"Then in about ten days, which was days of peace
for brother and sister, because they didn't have to go
in keenly for any new way of killing themselves off,
what comes up but several crates of beagles, in charge
of their valet or tutor! I'd looked forward to something of a thrilling or unknown character, and they
turned out to be mere dogs; just little brown-and-
white dogs that you wouldn't notice if you hadn't
been excited by their names; kind of yapping mutts
that some parties would poison off if they lived in the
same neighbourhood with' em. They all had names
like Rex II and Lady Blessington, and so on; and
each one had cost more than any three steers I had
on the place. What do you think of that? They
was yapping in their kennels when I first seen 'em,
with the old lady as excited as they was, and brother
and sister trying to look excited in order to please
mother, and at least looking relieved because no fatal-
ities was in immediate prospect.

"I listened to the noise a while and acted nice by
saying they was undoubtedly the very finest beagles
I'd ever laid eyes on—which was the simple God's

truth; and then I says won't she take one out of the
cage and let him beagle some, me not having any idea
what it would be like? But the old lady says not
yet, because the costumes ain't come. I thought at
first it was the pups that had to be dressed up, but it
seems it was costumes for her and brother and sister
to wear; so I asked a few more silly questions and
found out the mystery. It seemed the secret of a
beagle's existence was rabbits. Yes, sir; they was
mad about rabbits and went in keenly for 'em. Only
they wouldn't notice one, I gathered, if the parties
that followed 'em wasn't dressed proper for it.

"Then we went in where we could hear each other
without screaming, and the lady tells me more about
it, and how beagles is her last hope of her chits ever
amounting to anything in the great world of sport.
If they don't go in keenly for beagles she'll just have
to give up and let Nature take its course with the
poor things. And she said these was A-Number-
One beagles, being sure to get a rabbit if one was in
the country. She'd just had 'em at a big fashionable country resort down South, some place where
the sport attracted much notice from the simple-
minded peasantry, and it hadn't been a good country
for rabbits; so the beagles had trooped into a backyard and destroyed a Belgian hare that had belonged
to a little boy, whose father come out and swore at
the costumed hunters in a very common manner, and
offered to lick any three of 'em at once.

"And in hurrying acrost a field to get away from

this rowdy, that seemed liable to forget himself and do something they'd all regret later, they was put up a tree by a bull that was sensitive about costumes, and had to stay there two hours, with the bull trying to grub up the tree, and would of done so if his owner hadn't come along and rescued 'em.

"She made it sound like an exciting sport, all right, yet nothing I thought I'd ever go in keenly for. It didn't seem like anything I'd get up in the night to indulge myself in. And I agreed with her that if her chits found beagling too adventurous, then all hope was gone and she might as well let 'em die peacefully in their beds.

"Two days later the costumes come along and I was kindly sent word to show up the next morning if I wanted to see some ripping sport that I'd be quite mad about and go in for keenly, and all that sort of thing, by Jove! Of course I go over, on account of this dame's atrocities never yet having failed to interest me, and I didn't think she'd fall down now. I felt strangely out of it, though, when I seen the costumes. Ma and sister had, from the top down, black velvet jockey caps; green velvet coats with gold buttons; white pique skirts, coming to the knee; black silk stockings; and neat black shoes with white spats. Brother had been abused the same, barring the white skirt, which left him looking like something out of a collection called The Dolls of All Nations.

"I saw right off that all these clothes must be

necessary—they looked so careful and expensive.
Yes, sir; that lady would no more of went out beagling without being draped for it than she'd of gone
steer hunting without a vanity-box lashed to her saddle
horn.

"I sort of hung back with the awe-stricken help
when the start was made. They was all out in front
except the butler, who lurked in the entry looking
like he'd passed a night of grief at the new-made grave
of his mother.

"The beagles surged all over the place the minute
they was let loose, and then made for down in the
willows below the house. And, sure enough, they
started a cottontail down there and went in for him
keenly, followed by ma and brother and sister.
Brother started to yell 'Yoicks! Yoicks!' But ma
shut him off with a good deal of severity that caused
him to blush at his words. It seems Yoicks is a cry
you give at some other critical juncture in life.
When beagles start you must yell 'Gone away!' in
a clear, ringing voice. Brother meant well, but didn't
know.

"Anyhow, they followed those pups, and I trailed
along at a decent distance on my horse; and pretty
soon they got the rabbit which had been fool enough
to come round in a wide circle back to where it
started from. Say! It was mere child's play for
that plucky little band of nine dogs to clean up that
rabbit. They never had a minute's fear of it and the
rabbit didn't have the least chance of winning the

fight, not at any stage. Yes, sir! any time you see
nine beagles setting on a tuckered rabbit—I don't
care how wild he is—you'll know how to put your
money down.

"I never did see a rabbit put up a worse fight than
that one did. I rode up to its fragments, and the
old lady was saying how ripping it was and calling
sister a mollycoddle, because here was sister crying
like a baby over the rabbit's fate—a rabbit she'd
never set eyes on before in her life. Brother didn't
look like he had gone in keenly for the sport, either.
He was kind of green and yellow, like one of these
parties on shipboard about the time he's saying he
don't feel the boat's motion the least bit; and, anyway, he's got a sure-fire remedy for it if anything does
happen. I just kind of stood around, neutral and
revolted.

"Pretty soon the pack beagles off again with glad
cries; and this time, up on the hillside, what do they
start but a little spike buck that has been down to a
salt lick on the creek flat! They wasn't any more
afraid of him than they had been of the rabbit and
started to chase him out of the country. Of course
they didn't do well after they got him interested.
The last I saw of the race he was making 'em look
like they was in reverse gear and backing up full
speed. Anyway, that seemed to end the sport for
the day, because the dogs and the buck must of been
over near the county line in ten minutes. The old
lady was mad and blamed it on the valet, who come

up and had to take as sweet a roasting as you ever
heard a man get from a lady word painter. It seems
he'd ought to have taught 'em to ignore deer.

"Then I lied like a lady and said it was a ripping
sport that I would sure go in keenly for if I had time;
and we all went back to the house and sat down to
what they called a hunt breakfast. Ma said at last
her chits could hold up their heads in the world of
sport and not be a reproach to her training. The
chits looked very thoughtful, indeed. Sister still
had red eyes and couldn't eat a mouthful of hunt
breakfast, and brother just toyed with little dabs
of it.

"Next day I learned the pack didn't get back till
late that evening, straggling in one by one, and the
valet having to go out and look for the last two with
a lantern. Also, these last two had been treated
brutally by some denizen of the wildwood. Rex II
had darn near lost his eyesight and Lady Blessington was clawed something scandalous. Brother
said mebbe a rabbit mad with hydrophobia had turned
on 'em. He said it in hopeful tones, and sister
cheered right up and said if these two had it they
would give it to the rest of the pack, and shouldn't
they all be shot at once?

"Mother said what jolly nonsense; that they'd
merely been scratched by thorns. I thought, myself, that mebbe they'd gone out of their class and
tackled a jack rabbit; but I didn't say it, seeing that
the owner was sensitive. Afterward she showed me

a lot of silver things her pets had won—eyecups and custard dishes, and coffee urns and things, about a dozen, with their names engraved on 'em. She said it was very annoying to have 'em take after deer that way. What she wanted 'em to do was to butcher rabbits where parties in the right garments could stand and look on.

"Next day they tried again; and one fool rabbit was soon gone in for keenly to the renewed sound of sister's bitter sobs, and brother looking like he'd been in jail two years—no colour left at all in his face. But pretty soon the pack took up the scent of a deer again, and that was the end of another day's sport. Brother and sister looked glad and resumed their peaceful sports. He hunted butterflies with a net, and she set down and looked at birds through an opera glass and wrote down things about their personal appearance in a notebook. The old lady changed to her cowboy suit and went out and roped three steers—just to work her mad off, I guess.

"Well, this time the beagles not only limped in at a shocking hour of the night but three of the others had had their beauty marred by a demon rabbit or something. They had been licked very thoroughly, indeed; and the old lady now said it must be a grizzly bear, and brother and sister beamed on her and said: 'What a shame!' And would they hunt again next day? For the first time they seemed quite mad about the sport. Mother said they better wait till she went out and shot the grizzly, but I told her we hadn't had any grizzlies round here for years; so she said, all right, they could lick anything less than a grizzly. And they beagled again next day, with terrible and inspiring results, not only to Rex II and Lady Blessington again, but to two of the others that hadn't been touched before.

"This left only two of the pack that hadn't been horribly abused by some unknown varmint; so a halt had to be called for three days while Red Cross work was done. Brother and sister tried to look regretful and complained about this break in the ripping sport; but their manner was artificial. They spent the time riding peacefully round up in the cañon, pretending to look for the wild creature that had chewed their little pets. They come back one day and cheered their mother a whole lot by telling her the pack had been over the pass as far as the house of a worthy rancher, Mr. Floud by name. They said Mr. Floud didn't believe there was any bears round, and further said he greatly admired the beagles, even though at first they seriously annoyed his pet kitten.

"The old lady said this was ripping of Mr. Floud, to take it in such a sporting way, because many people in the past had tried to make all sorts of nasty rows when her pets had happened to kill their kittens. Brother said, yes; Mr. Floud took the whole thing in a true sporting way, and he hoped the pack would soon be well enough to hunt again. Right then I detected falsity in his manner; I couldn't make out what it was, but I knew he was putting something over on mother.

"Two days later the dogs was fit again, and another gay hunt was had, with a rabbit to the good in the first twenty minutes, and then the usual break, when they struck a deer scent. Brother said he'd follow on his horse this time and try to get whatever was bothering 'em. He didn't. He said he lost 'em. They crawled back at night, well chewed; and mother was now frantic.

"There had to be another three days in bed for the cunning little murderers, after which brother and sister both went out with 'em on horseback, with the same mysterious results—except that Rex II didn't get in till next day and looked like he'd come through a feed chopper. For the next hunt, four days after that, the old lady went, too, all of 'em on horseback; but the same slinking marauder got at the pack before they could come up with it, and two of 'em had to be brought back in arms. They all stopped here on the way home to tell about the mystery. Brother and sister was very cheerful and mad about the sport, but their manner was falser than ever. Mother says the pack is being ruined, and she wouldn't continue the sport, except it has roused the first gleam of interest her chits has ever showed in anything worth while. I caught the chits looking at each other in a guilty manner when she says this, and my curiosity wakes up. I says next time they go out I will be pleased to go with 'em; and the old lady thanks me and says mebbe I can solve this reprehensible mystery.

"In another three days they come by for me. The beagles was looking an awful lot different from what I had first seen 'em. They was not only beautifully scarred but they acted kind of timid and reproachful, and their yapping had a note of caution in it that I hadn't noticed before. So I got on my pony and went along to help probe the crime. We worked up the cañon trail and over the pass, with the pack staying meekly behind most of the time. Just the other side of the pass they actually got a rabbit, though not working with their old-time recklessness, I thought. Of course we had to stop and watch this. Brother looked the other way and sister just set there biting her lips, with an evil gleam in her pale-blue eyes. Not a beagle in the pack would have trusted himself alone with her at that minute if he'd known his business.

"Then we rode on down toward Cousin Egbert's shack, with nothing further happening and the pups staying back in a highly conservative manner. Brother says that yonder is the Mr. Floud's place he had spoken of, and ma wants to know if he, too, goes in for ranching, and I says yes, he's awfully keen about it; so she says we'll ride over and chat with him and perhaps he can suggest some solution of the mystery in hand. I said all right, and we ride up.

"Cousin Egbert is tipped back in a chair outside the door, reading a Sunday paper. Whenever he gets one up here he always reads it clean through, from murders to want ads. And he'd got into this about as far as the beauty hints and secrets of the toilet. Well, he was very polite and awkward, and asked us into his dinky little shack; and the old lady says she hears he is quite mad about ranching, and he says, Oh, yes—only it don't help matters any to get mad; and he finds a chair for her, and the rest of us set on stools and the bed; and just then she notices that the beagle pack has halted about thirty feet from the door, and some of 'em is milling and acting like they think of starting for home at once.

"So out she goes and orders the little pets up. They didn't want to come one bit; it seemed like they was afraid of something, but they was well disciplined and they finally crawled forward, looking like they didn't know what minute something cruel might happen.

"The old lady petted 'em and made 'em lie down, and asked Cousin Egbert if he'd ever seen better ones, or even as good; and he said No, ma'am; they was sure fine beetles. Then she begun to tell him about some wild animal that had been attacking 'em, a grizzly, or mebbe a mountain lion, with cubs; and he is saying in a very false manner that he can't think what would want to harm such playful little pets, and so on. All this time the pets is in fine attitudes of watchful waiting, and I'm just beginning to suspect a certain possibility when it actually happens.

"There was an open window high up in the log wall acrost from the door, and old Kate jumps up onto the sill from the outside. He was one fierce object, let me tell you; weighing about thirty pounds, all muscle, with one ear gone, and an eye missing that a porcupine quill got into, and a lot of fresh new battle scars. We all got a good look at him while he crouched there for a second, purring like a twelve-cylinder car and twitching his whiskers at us in a lazy way, like he wanted to have folks make a fuss over him. And then, all at once, catching sight of the dogs, he changed to a demon; his back up, his whiskers in a stiff tremble, and his half of a tail grown double in girth.

"I looked quick to the dogs, and they was froze stiff with horror for at least another second. Then they made one scramble for the open door, and Kate made a beautiful spring for the bunch, landing on the back of the last one with a yell of triumph. Mother shrieked, too, and we all rushed to the door to see one of the prettiest chases you'd want to look at, with old Kate handing out the side wipes every time he could get near one of the dogs. They fled down over the creek bank and a minute later we could see the pack legging it up the other side to beat the cars, losing Kate—I guess because he didn't like to get his hide wet.

"When the first shock of this wore off, here was silly old Egbert, in a weak voice, calling: 'Kitty, Kitty, Kitty! Here, Kitty! Here, Kitty!' Then

we notice brother and sister. Brother is waving
his hat in the air and yelling 'Yoicks!' and 'Gone
away!' and 'Fair sport, by Jove!'—just like some
crazy man; and sister, with her chest going up and
down, is clapping her hands and yelling 'Goody!
Goody! Goody!' and squealing with helpless
laughter. Mother just stood gazing at 'em in horrible silence. Pretty soon they felt it and stopped,
looking like a couple of kids that know it's spanking
time.

"'So!' says mother. That's all she said—just,
'So!'

"But she stuffed the simple word with eloquence;
she left it pregnant with meaning, as they say.
Then she stalked loftily out and got on her horse,
brother and sister slinking after her. I guess I
slunk, too, though it was none of my doings. Cousin
Egbert kind of sidled along, mumbling about Kitty:

"'Kitty was quite frightened of the pets first time
he seen 'em; but someway to-day it seemed like he
had lost much of his fear—seemed more like he had
wanted to play with 'em, or something.'

"Nobody listened to the doddering old wretch,
but I caught brother winking at him behind mother's
back. Then we all rode off in lofty silence, headed
by mother, who never once looked back to her late
host, even if he was mad about ranching. We got
up over the pass and the pack of ruined beagles
begun to straggle out of the underbrush. A good
big buck rabbit with any nerve could have put 'em

all on the run again. You could tell that. They slunk along at the tail of the parade. I dropped out informally when it passed the place here. It seemed like something might happen where they'd want only near members of the family present.

"I don't hear anything from Broadmoor next day; so the morning after that I ride over to Cousin Egbert's to see if I couldn't get a better line on the recent tragedy. He was still on his Sunday paper, having finished an article telling that man had once been scaly, like a fish; and was just beginning the fashion notes, with pictures showing that the smart frock was now patterned like an awning. Old Kate was lying on a bench in the sun, trying to lick a new puncture he'd got in his chest.

"I started right in on the old reprobate. I said it was a pretty how-de-do if a distinguished lady amateur, trying to raise ranching to the dignity of a sport, couldn't turn loose a few prize beagles without having 'em taken for a hunt breakfast by a nefarious beast that ought to be in a stout cage in a circus this minute! I thought, of course, this would insult him; but he sunned right up and admitted that Kate was about half to three-quarters bobcat; and wasn't he a fine specimen? And if he could only get about eight more as good he'd have a pack of beagle-cats that would be the envy of the whole sporting world.

"'It ain't done!' I remarked, aiming to crush him.

"'It is, too!' Egbert says. 'I did it myself. Look what I already done, just with Kitty alone!'

"'How'd it start?' I asked him.

"'Easy!' says he. 'They took Kate for a rabbit and Kate took them for rabbits. It was a mutual error. They found out theirs right soon; but I bet Kate ain't found out his, even to this day. I bet he thinks they're just a new kind of rabbit that's been started. The first day they broke in here he was loafin' round out in front, and naturally he started for 'em, though probably surprised to see rabbits travelling in a bunch. Also, they see Kate and start for him, which must of startled him good and plenty. He'd never had rabbits make for him before. He pulled up so quick he skidded. I could see his mind working. Don't tell me that cat ain't got brains like a human! He was saying to himself: "Is this here a new kind of rabbits, or is it a joke—or what? Mebbe I better not try anything rash till I find out."

"'They was still coming for him acrost the flat, with their tongues out; so he sooped himself up a bit with a few jumps and made for that there big down spruce. He lands on the trunk and runs along it to where the top begins. He has it all worked out. He's saying: "If this here is a joke, all right; but if it ain't a joke I better have some place back of me for a kind of refuge."

"'So up come these strange rabbits and started to jump for him on the trunk of the spruce; but it's pretty high and they can't quite make it. And in a minute they sort of suspicion something on their part, because Kate has rared his back and is giving 'em a line of abuse they never heard from any rabbit yet. Awful wicked it was, and they sure got puzzled. I could hear one of 'em saying: "Aw, come on! That ain't no regular rabbit; he don't look like a rabbit, and he don't talk like a rabbit, and he don't act like a rabbit!" Then another would say: "What of it? What do we care if he's a regular rabbit or not? Let's get him, anyway, and take him apart!"

"'So they all begin to jump again and can't quite make it till their leader says he'll show 'em a real jump. He backs off a little to get a run and lands right on the log. Then he wished he hadn't. Old Kate worked so quick I couldn't hardly follow it. In about three seconds this leader lands on his back down in the bunch, squealing like one of these Italian sopranos when the flute follows her up. He crawls off on his stomach, still howling, and I see he's had a couple of wipes over the eye, and one of his ears is shredded.

"'A couple of the others come over to ask him how it happened, and what he quit for, and did his foot slip; and he says: "Mark my words, gentlemen; we got our work cut out for us here. That animal is acting less and less like a rabbit every minute. He's more turbulent and he's got spurs on." He goes on talking this way while the others bark at Kate, and Kate dares any one of 'em to come on up there and have it out, man to man. Finally another lands on the tree trunk and gets what the first one got. I could see it this time. Kate done some dandy short-arm work in the clinches and hurled him off on his back like the other one; then he stands there sharpening his claws on the bark and grinning in a masterful way. He was saying: "You will, will you?"

"'Then one of these beetles must of said, "Come on, boys—all together now!" for four of 'em landed up on the trunk all to once. And Kate wasn't there. He'd had the top of this fallen tree at his back, and he kites up a limb about ten feet above their heads and stretches out for a rest, cool as anything, licking his paws and purring like he enjoyed the beautiful summer day, and wasn't everything calm and lovely? It was awful insulting the way he looked down on 'em, with his eyes half shut. And you never seen beetles so astonished in your life. They just couldn't believe their eyes, seeing a rabbit act that way! The leader limps over and says: "There! What did I tell you, smarties? I guess next time you'll take my word for it. I guess you can see plain enough now he ain't no rabbit, the way he skinned up that tree."

"'They calm down a mite at this, and one or two says they thought he was right from the first; and some others says: "Well, it wouldn't make no difference what he was, rabbit or no rabbit, if he'd just come down and meet the bunch of us fair and square; but the dirty coward is afraid to fight us, except one at a time." The leader is very firm, though. He tells 'em that if this here object ain't a rabbit they got no right to molest him, and if he is a rabbit he's gone crazy, and wouldn't be good to eat, anyway; so they

better go find one that acts sensible. And he gets
'em away, all talking about it excitedly.

"'Well, sir, you wouldn't believe how tickled Kate
was all that day. It was like he'd found a new interest in life. And next time these beetles come up
they pull off another grand scrap. Kate laid for 'em
just this side of the creek and let 'em chase him back to
his tree. He skun up three others that day, still pur-
suin' his cowardly tactics of fighting 'em one at a
time, and retirin' to his perch when three or four
would come at once. Also, when they give him up
again and started off he come down and chased 'em to
the creek bank, like you seen the other day, telling
'em to be sure and not forget the number, because he
ain't had so much fun since he met up with a wood-
chuck. The next time they showed up he'd got so
contemptuous of 'em that he'd leap down and engage
one that had got separated from the pack. He had
two of 'em darn' near out before they was rescued by
their friends.

"'Then, a few days later, along comes the pack
again—only this time they're being herded by the
lad with the ginger-coloured whiskers. He gets off
his horse and says how do I do, and what lovely
weather, and how bracing the air is; and I says what
pretty beetles he has; and he says it's ripping sport;
and I says, yes; Kate has ripped up a number of 'em,
but I hope he don't blame me none, because my Kitty
has to defend himself. Say, this guy brightened up
and like to took me off my feet! He grabs both my

hands and shakes 'em warmly for a long time and says do I think my cat can put the whole bunch on the blink?—or words to that effect.   And I says it's the surest thing in the world; but why?   And he says, then the sooner the better, because it's a barbarous sport and every last beetle ought to be thoroughly killed; and when they are, in case his mother don't find out the crooked work, mebbe he'll be let to raise orchids or do something useful in the world, instead of frittering his life away in the vain pursuit of pleasure.

"'Oh, he was the chatty lad, all right!   And I felt kind of sorry for him; so I says Kate would dearly love to wipe these beetles out one by one; and he says: "Capital, by Jove!"   And I call Kitty and we pull off another nice little scrap on the fallen tree, though it's hard to make the beetles take much interest in it now, except in the way of self-defense.   Even at that, they're kept plenty occupied.

"'Say, this guy is the happiest you ever see one when Kate has about four more of 'em licked to a standstill in jigtime.   He says he has one more favour to ask of me: Will I allow his sister to come up some day and see the lovely carnage?   And I says, Sure! Kate will be glad to oblige any time.   He says he'll fetch her up the first time the pack is able to get out again, and he keeps on chattering like a child that's found a new play-pretty.

"'I can't hardly get him off the place, he's so greatful to me.   He tells me his biography and about how

this here blond guy has been roughing him all over
Europe and Asia, and how it had got to stop right
here, because a man has a right to live his own life,
after all; and then he branches off in a nutty way to
tell me that he always takes a cold shower every
morning, winter and summer, and he never could read
a line of Sir Walter Scott, and why don't some genius
invent a fountain pen that will work at all times? and
so on, till it sounded delirious.   But he left at last.

"'And we had some good ripping sport when
him and sister come up.   I never seen such a blood-
thirsty female.   She'd nearly laugh her head off when
Kitty was gouging the eye out of one of these cunning
little scamps.   She said if I'd ever seen the nasty
curs pile on to one poor defenseless little bunny I'd
understand why she was so keen about my beetle-
cat.   That's what she called Kate.

"'Kate, he got kind of bored with the whole business after that.   He hadn't actually eat one yet, and
mebbe that was all that kept him going—wanting to
see if they'd taste any better than regular rabbits.
But you bet they knew now that Kate wasn't any
kind of a rabbit.   They didn't have any more argu-
ments on that point—they knew darn' well he didn't
have a drop of rabbit blood in his veins.   Oh, he's
some beetle-cat, all right!'

"That's Cousin Egbert for you!   Can you beat
him—changing round and being proud of this mixed
marriage that he had formerly held to be a scandal!

"Well, I go back home, and here is mother waiting

for me. And she's a changed woman. She's actually give up trying to make anything out of her chits, because after considerable browbeating and third-degree stuff, they've come through with the whole evil conspiracy—how they'd got her prize-winning beagles licked by a common cat that wouldn't be let into any bench show on earth! Her spirit was broke.

"'My poor son,' she says, 'I shall allow to go his silly way after this outrageous bit of double-dealing. I think it useless to strive further with him. He has not only confessed all the foul details, but he came brazenly out with the assertion that a man has a right to lead his own life—and he barely thirty!'

"She goes on to say that it's this terrible twentieth-century modernism that has infected him. She says that, first woman sets up a claim to live her own life, and now men are claiming the same right, even one as carefully raised and guarded as her boy has been; and what are we coming to? But, anyway, she did her best for him.

"Pretty soon Broadmoor was closed like you seen it to-day. Sister is now back in Boston, keeping tabs on orchestras and attending lectures on the higher birds; and brother at last has his orchid ranch somewhere down in California. He's got one pet orchid that I heard cost twelve thousand dollars—I don't know why. But he's very happy living his own life. The last I heard of mother she was exploring the headwaters of the Amazon River, hunting crocodiles and jaguars and natives, and so on.

"She was a good old sport, though. She showed that by the way she simmered down about Cousin Egbert's cat before she left. At first, she wanted to lay for it and put a bullet through its cowardly heart. Then she must of seen the laugh was on her, all right; for what did she do? Why, the last thing she done was to box up all these silver cups her beagles had won and send 'em over to Kate, in care of his owner—all the eye-cups and custard bowls, and so on. Cousin Egbert shows 'em off to every one.

"'Just a few cups that Kate won,' he'll say. 'I want to tell you he's some beetle-cat! Look what he's come up to—and out of nothing, you might say!'"

VIII

PETE'S B'OTHER-IN-LAW

ON THE Arrowhead Ranch it was noon by the bell that Lew Wee loves to clang. It may have been half an hour earlier or later on other ranches, for Lew Wee is no petty precisian. Ma Pettengill had ridden off at dawn; and, rather than eat luncheon in solitary state, I joined her retainers for the meal in the big kitchen, which is one of my prized privileges. A dozen of us sat at the long oilcloth-covered table and assuaged the more urgent pangs of hunger in a haste that was speechless and far from hygienic. No man of us chewed the new beef a proper number of times; he swallowed intently and reached for more. It was rather like twenty minutes for dinner at what our railway laureates call an eating house. Lew Wee shuffled in bored nonchalance between range and table. It was an old story to him.

The meal might have gone to a silent end, though moderating in pace; but we had with us to-day—as a toastmaster will put it—the young veterinary from Spokane. This made for talk after actual starvation had been averted—fragmentary gossip of the great city; of neighbouring ranches in the valley, where

318

professional duty had called him; of Adolph, our milk-strain Durham bull, whose indisposition had brought him several times to Arrowhead; and then of Squat, our youngest cowboy, from whose fair brow the intrepid veterinary, on his last previous visit, had removed a sizable and embarrassing wen with what looked to me like a pair of pruning shears.

The feat had excited much uncheerful comment among Squat's *confrères*, bets being freely offered that he would be disfigured for life, even if he survived; and what was the sense of monkeying with a thing like that when you could pull your hat down over it? Of course you couldn't wear a derby with it; but no one but a darned town dude would ever want to wear a derby hat, anyway, and the trouble with Squat was, he wished to be pretty. It was dollars to doughnuts the thing would come right back again, twice as big as ever, and better well enough alone. But Squat, who is also known as Timberline, and is, therefore, a lanky six feet three, is young and sensitive and hopeful, and the veterinary is a matchless optimist; and the thing had been brought to a happy conclusion.

Squat, being now warmly urged, blushingly turned his head from side to side that all might remark how neatly his scar had healed. The veterinary said it had healed by first intention; that it was as pretty a job as he'd ever done on man or beast; and that Squat would be more of a hit then ever with the ladies because of this interesting chapter in his young life.

Then something like envy shone in the eyes of those who had lately disparaged Squat for presuming to thwart the will of God; I detected in more than one man there the secret wish that he had something for this ardent expert to eliminate. Squat continued to blush pleasurably and to bolt his food until another topic diverted this entirely respectful attention from him.

The veterinary asked if we had heard about the Indian ruction down at Kulanche last night—Kulanche Springs being the only pretense to a town between our ranch and Red Gap—a post-office, three general stores, a score of dwellings, and a low drinking place known as The Swede's. The news had not come to us; so the veterinary obliged. A dozen Indians, drifting into the valley for the haying about to begin, had tarried near Kulanche and bought whiskey of the Swede. The selling of this was a lawless proceeding and the consumption of it by the purchasers had been hazardous in the extreme. Briefly, the result had been what is called in newspaper headlines a stabbing affray. I quote from our guest's recital:

"Then, after they got calmed down and hid their knives, and it looked peaceful again, they decided to start all over; but the liquor was out, so that old scar-faced Pyann jumps on a pony and rides over from the camp for a fresh supply. He pulled up out in front of the Swede's and yelled for three bottles to be brought out to him, pronto! If he'd sneaked round to the back door and whispered he'd have got it all right, but this was a little too brash, because there were about a dozen men in the bar and the Swede was afraid to sell an Injin whiskey so openly. All he could do was go to the door and tell this pickled aborigine that he never sold whiskey to Injins and to get the hell out of there! Pyann called the Swede a liar and some other things, mentioning dates, and started to climb off his pony, very ugly.

"The Swede wasn't going to argue about it, because we'd all come out in front to listen; so he pulled his gun and let it off over Pyann's head; and a couple of the boys did the same thing, and that started the rest—about six others had guns—till it sounded like a bunch of giant crackers going off. Old Pyann left in haste, all right. He was flattened out on his pony till he looked like a plaster.

"We didn't hear any more of him last night, but coming up here this morning I found out he'd done a regular Paul Revere ride to save his people; he rode clear up as far as that last camp, just below here, on your place, yelling to every Injin he passed that they'd better take to the brush, because the whites had broken out at Kulanche. At that, the Swede ought to be sent up, knowing they'll fight every time he sells them whiskey. Two of these last night were bad cut in this rumpus."

"Yes; and he'd ought to be sent up for life for selling it to white men, too—the kind he sells."

This was Sandy Sawtelle, speaking as one who knew
and with every sign of conviction. "It sure is enterprising whiskey. Three drinks of it make a decent
man want to kill his little golden-haired baby sister
with an axe. Say, here's a good one—lemme tell you!
I remember the first time, about three, four years
ago——"

The speaker was interrupted—it seemed to me with
intentional rudeness. One man hurriedly wished to
know who did the cutting last night; another, if the
wounded would recover; and a third, if Pete, an
aged red vassal of our own ranch, had been involved.
Each of the three flashed a bored glance at Sandy as
he again tried for speech:

"Well, as I was saying, I remember the first time,
about three, four years ago——"

"If old Pete was down there I bet his brother-in-
law did most of the knifework," put in Buck Devine
firmly.

It was to be seen that they all knew what Sandy
remembered the first time and wished not to hear it
again. Others of them now sought to stifle the
memoir, while Sandy waited doggedly for the tide to
ebb. I gathered that our Pete had not been one of
the restive convives, he being known to have spent a
quiet home evening with his mahala and their numerous descendants, in their camp back of the wood lot;
I also gathered that Pete's brother-in-law had committed no crime since Pete quit drinking two years
before. There was veiled mystery in these allusions

to the brother-in-law of Pete. It was almost plain that the brother-in-law was a lawless person for whose offenses Pete had more than once been unjustly blamed. I awaited details; but meantime——

"Well, as I was saying, I remember the first time, about three, four years ago——"

Sandy had again dodged through a breach in the talk, quite as if nothing had happened. Buck Devine groaned as if in unbearable anguish. The others also groaned as if in unbearable anguish. Only the veterinary and I were polite.

"Oh, let him get it offen his chest," urged Buck wearily. "He'll perish if he don't—having two men here that never heard him tell it." He turned upon the raconteur, with a large sweetness of manner: "Excuse me, Mr. Sawtelle! Pray do go on with your thrilling reminiscence. I could just die listening to you. I believe you was wishing to entertain the company with one of them anecdotes or lies of which you have so rich a store in that there peaked dome of yours. Gents, a moment's silence while this rare personality unfolds hisself to us!"

"Say, lemme tell you—here's a good one!" resumed the still placid Sandy. "I remember the first time, about three, four years ago, I ever went into The Swede's. A stranger goes in just ahead of me and gets to the bar before I do, kind of a solemn-looking, sandy-complected little runt in black clothes.

" 'A little of your best cooking whiskey,' says he to

the Swede, while I'm waiting beside him for my own drink.

"The Swede sets out the bottle and glass and a whisk broom on the bar. That was sure a new combination on me. 'Why the whisk broom?' I says to myself. 'I been in lots of swell dives and never see no whisk broom served with a drink before.' So I watch. Well, this sad-looking sot pours out his liquor, shoots it into him with one tip of the glass; and, like he'd been shot, he falls flat on the floor, all bent up in a convulsion—yes, sir; just like that! And the Swede not even looking over the bar at him!

"In a minute he comes out of this here fit, gets on his feet and up to the bar, grabs the whisk broom, brushes the dust off his clothes where he's rolled on the floor, puts back the whisk broom, says, 'So long, Ed!' to the Swede—and goes out in a very business-like manner.

"Then the Swede shoves the bottle and a glass and the whisk broom over in front of me, but I says: 'No, thanks! I just come in to pass the time of day. Lovely weather we're having, ain't it?' Yes, sir; down he goes like he's shot, wriggles a minute, jumps up, dusts hisself off, flies out the door; and the Swede passing me the same bottle and the same broom, and me saying: 'Oh, I just come in to pass the time of——' "

The veterinary and I had been gravely attentive. The faces of the others wore not even the tribute of pretended ennui. They had betrayed an elaborate

deafness. They now affected to believe that Sandy
Sawtelle had not related an anecdote. They spoke
casually and with an effect of polished ease while yet
here capitulated, as tale-tellers so often will.

"I remember a kid, name of Henry Lippincott, used
to set in front of me at school," began Buck Devine,
with the air of delicately breaking a long silence;
"he'd wiggle his ears and get me to laughing out
loud, and then I'd be called up for it by teacher and
like as not kept in at recess."

"You ought to seen that bunch of tame alligators
down to the San Francisco Fair," observed Squat
genially. "The old boy that had 'em says 'Oh, yes,
they would make fine pets, and don't I want a couple
for ten dollars to take home to the little ones?'
But I don't. You come right down to household
pets—I ruther have me a white rabbit or a canary
bird than an alligator you could step on in the dark
some night and get all bit up, and mebbe blood
poison set in."

"I recollect same as if it was yesterday," began
Uncle Abner quickly. "We was coming up through
northern Arizona one fall, with a bunch of longhorns,
and we make this here water hole about four P. M.—
or mebbe a mite after that or a little before; but, anyway, I says to Jeff Bradley, 'Jeff,' I says to him, 'it
looks to me almighty like——' "

Sandy Sawtelle savagely demanded a cup of coffee,
gulped it heroically, rose in a virtuous hurry, and at
the door wondered loudly if he was leaving a bunch of

rich millionaires that had nothing to do but loaf in
their club all the afternoon and lie their heads off, or
just a passell of lazy no-good cowhands that laid
down on the job the minute the boss stepped off the
place. Whereupon, it being felt that the rabid
anecdotist had been sufficiently rebuked, we all
went out to help the veterinary look at Adolph for
twenty minutes more.

Adolph is four years old and weighs one ton. He
has a frowning and fearsome front and the spirit of a
friendly puppy. The Arrowhead force loafed about
in the corral and imparted of its own lore to the
veterinary while he took Adolph's temperature.
Then Adolph, after nosing three of the men to have
his head rubbed, went to stand in the rush-grown
pool at the far end of the corral, which the gallery
took to mean that he still had a bit of fever, no matter
what the glass thing said.

The veterinary opposed a masterly silence to this
majority diagnosis, and in the absence of argument
about it there seemed nothing left for the Arrowhead
retainers but the toil for which they were paid.
They went to it lingeringly, one by one, seeming to
feel that perhaps they wronged the ailing Adolph
by not staying there to talk him over.

Uncle Abner, who is the Arrowhead blacksmith,
was the last to leave—or think of leaving—though
he had mule shoes to shape and many mules to shoe.
He glanced wistfully again at Adolph, in cool water
to his knees, tugged at his yellowish-white beard,

said it was a dog's life, if any one should ask me, and
was about to slump mournfully off to his shop—when
his eye suddenly brightened.

"Will you look once at that poor degraded red
heathen, acting like a whirlwind over in the woodlot?"

I looked once. Pete, our Indian, was apparently
the sole being on the ranch at that moment who was
honestly earning his wage. No one knows how many
more than eighty years Pete has lived; but from where
we stood he was the figure of puissant youth, rhythmi-
cally flashing his axe into bits of wood that flew apart
at its touch. Uncle Abner, beside me, had again
shrugged off the dread incubus of duty. He let himself go restfully against the corral bars and chuckled a
note of harsh derision.

"Ain't it disgusting! I bet he never saw the boss
when she rode off this A. M. Yes, sir; that poor
benighted pagan must think she's still in the house—
prob'ly watching him out of the east winder this very
minute."

"What's this about his brother-in-law?" I asked.

"Oh, I dunno; some silly game he tries to come the
roots over folks with. Say, he's a regular old murderer, and not an honest hair in his head! Look at
the old cheat letting on to be a good steady worker
because he thinks the boss is in the house there, keeping an eye on him. Ain't it downright disgusting!"

Uncle Abner said this as one supremely conscious
of his own virtue. He himself was descending to no
foul pretense.

"A murderer, is he?"

I opened my cigarette case to the man of probity. He took two, crumpled the tobacco from the papers and stuffed it into his calabash pipe.

"Sure is he a murderer!   A tough one, too."

The speaker moved round a corner of the barn and relaxed to a sitting posture on the platform of the pump.   It brought him into the sun; but it also brought him where he could see far down the road upon which his returning employer would eventually appear.   His eyes ever haunted the far vistas of that road; otherwise he remained blissfully static.

It should perhaps be frankly admitted that Uncle Abner is not the blacksmith of song and story and lithographed art treasure, suitable for framing.   That I have never beheld this traditional smith—the rugged, upstanding tower of brawn with muscles like iron bands—is beside the point.   I have not looked upon all the blacksmiths in the world, and he may exist.   But Uncle Abner can't pose for him.   He weighs a hundred and twenty pounds without his hammer, is lean to scrawniness, and his arms are those of the boys you see at the track meet of Lincoln Grammar School Number Seven.   The mutilated derby hat he now wore, a hat that had been weathered from plum colour to a poisonous green—a shred of peacock feather stuck in the band—lent his face no dignity whatever.

In truth, his was not an easy face to lend dignity to.   It would still look foolish, no matter what was

lent it. He has a smug fringe of white curls about
the back and sides of his head, the beard of a prophet,
and the ready speech of a town bore. The blacksmith we read of can look the whole world in the face,
fears not any man, and would far rather do honest
smithing any day in the week—except Sunday—
than live the life of sinful ease that Uncle Abner was
leading for the moment.

Uncle Abner may have feared no man; but he feared
a woman. It was easy to see this as he chatted the
golden hours away to me. His pale eyes seldom left
the road where it came over a distant hill. When the
woman did arrive—— Oh, surely the merry clang
of the hammer on the anvil would be heard in Abner's shop, where he led a dog's life. But, for a
time at least——

"So he's one of these tough murderers, is he?"

"You said it! Always a-creating of disturbances
up on the reservation, where he rightly belongs.
Mebbe that's why they let him go off. Anyway,
he never stays there. Even in his young days they
tell me he wouldn't stay put. He'd disappear for
a month and always come back with a new wife.
Talk about your Mormons! One time they sent out
a new agent to the reservation, and he hears talk
back and forth of Pete philandering thisaway; and
he had his orders from the Gov'ment at Washington,
D. C., to stamp out this here poly-gamy—or whatever you call it; so he orders Pete up on the carpet
and says to him: 'Look here now, Pete! You got

a regular wife, ain't you?' Pete says sure he has;
and how could he say anything else—the old liar!
'Well,' says Mr. Agent, 'I want you to get this one
regular wife of yours and lead a decent, orderly home
life with her; and don't let me hear no more scandalous reports about your goings on.'

"Pete says all right; but he allows he'll have to
have help in getting her back home, because she's
got kind of antagonistic and left him. The agent
says he'll put a stop to that if Pete'll just point her
out. So they ride down about a mile from the
agency to a shack where they's a young squaw out
in front graining a deerhide and minding her own
business. She looked up when they come and started
to jaw Pete something fierce; but the agent tells
her the Gov'ment frowns on wives running off, and
Pete grabbed her; and the agent he helps, with her
screeching and biting and clawing like a female
demon. The agent is going to see that Pete has
his rights, even if it don't seem like a joyous household; and finally they get her scrambled onto Pete's
horse in front of him and off they go up the trail.
The agent yells after 'em that Pete is to remember
that this is his regular wife and he'd better behave
himself from now on.

"And then about sunup next morning this agent
is woke up by a pounding on his door. He goes
down and here's Pete clawed to a frazzle and whim-
pering for the law's protection because his squaw
has chased him over the reservation all night trying

to kill him. She'd near done it, too. They say old Pete was so scared the agent had to soothe him like a mother."

Uncle Abner paused to relight his pipe, meantime negotiating a doubly vigilant survey of the distant road. But I considered that he had told me nothing to the discredit of Pete, and now said as much.

"You couldn't blame the man for wanting his wife back, could you?" I demanded. "Of course he might have been more tactful."

"Tactful's the word," agreed Uncle Abner cordially. "You see, this wasn't Pete's wife at all. She was just a young squaw he'd took a fancy to."

"Oh!" Nothing else seemed quite so fitting to say.

"'Nother time," resumed the honest blacksmith, "the Gov'ment at Washington, D. C., sent out orders for all the Injun kids to be sent off to school. Lots of the fathers made trouble about this, but Pete was the worst of all—the old scoundrel! The agent said to him would Pete send his kids peaceful; and Pete said not by no means. So the agent says in that case they'll have to take 'em by force. Pete says he'll be right there a-plenty when they're took by force. So next day the agent and his helper go down to Pete's tepee. It's pitched up on a bank just off the road and they's a low barrier of brush acrost the front of it. They look close at this and see the muzzle of a rifle peeking down at 'em; also, they can hear little scramblings and squealings of about a dozen or fourteen kids in the tepee that was likely nestled up round the old murderer like a bunch of young quail.

"Well, they was something kind of cold and cheerless about the muzzle of this rifle poked through the brush at 'em; so the agent starts in and makes a regular agent speech to Pete. He says the Great White Father at Washington, D. C., has wished his children to be give an English education and learnt to write a good business hand, and all like that; and read books, and so on; and the Great White Father will be peeved if Pete takes it in this rough way. And the agent is disappointed in him, too, and will never again think the same of his old friend, and why can't he be nice and submit to the decencies of civilization—and so on—a lot of guff like that; but all the time he talks this here rifle is pointing right into his chest, so you can bet he don't make no false motions.

"At last, when he's told Pete all the reasons he can think up and guesses mebbe he's got the old boy going, he winds up by saying: 'And now what shall I tell the Great White Father at Washington you say to his kind words?' Old Pete, still not moving the rifle a hair's breadth, he calls out: 'You tell the Great White Father at Washington to go to hell!' Yes, sir; just like that he says it; and I guess that shows you what kind of a murderer he is. And what I allus say is, 'what's the use of spending us taxpayers' good money trying to educate trash like that, when they ain't got no sense of decency in the first place, and the minute they learn to talk English they begin to curse and swear as bad as a white man? They got no wish. to improve their condition, which is what I allus have said and what I allus will say.

"Anyway, this agent didn't waste no more time on Pete's brats. He come right away from there, though telling his helper it was a great pity they couldn't have got a good look into the tepee, because then they'd have known for the first time just what kids round there Pete really considered his. Of course he hadn't felt he should lay down his life in the interests of this trifling information, and I don't blame him one bit. I wouldn't have done it myself. You can't tell me a reservation with Pete on it would be any nice place. Look at the old crook now, still lamming that axe round to beat the cars because he thinks he's being watched! I bet he'll be mad down to his moccasins when he finds out the Old Lady's been off all day."

Uncle Abner yawned and stretched his sun-baked form with weary rectitude. Then he looked with pleased dismay into the face of his silver watch.

"Now, I snum! Here she's two-thirty! Don't it beat all how time flits by, as it were, when you meet a good conversationalist and get started on various topics! Well, I guess like as not I better amble along over toward the little shop and see if they ain't some little thing to be puttered at round

there. Yes, sir; all play and no work makes Jack
a dull boy, as the saying is."

The honest fellow achieved a few faltering paces
in the general direction of his shop. Then he turned
brightly.

"A joke's a joke, all right; but, after all, I hate to
see old Pete working hisself into the grave that way,
even if he ain't a regular human being. Suppose
you loaf over there and put him wise that the Madam's been off the place since sunup. The laugh's
on him enough already."

Which showed that Uncle Abner had not really a
bad heart. And I did even as he had said.

Pete was instantly stilled by my brief but informing speech. He leaned upon his axe and gazed
at me with shocked wonder. The face of the
American Indian is said to be unrevealing—to be a
stoic mask under which his emotions are ever hidden.
For a second time this day I found tradition at fault.
Pete's face was lively and eloquent under his shock
of dead-black hair—dead black but for half a dozen
gray or grayish strands, for Pete's eighty years have
told upon him, even if he is not yet sufficiently gray
at the temples to be a hero in a magazine costing over
fifteen cents. His face is a richly burnished mahogany and tells little of his years until he smiles; then
from brow to pointed chin it cracks into a million
tiny wrinkles, an intricate network of them framing
his little black eyes, which are lashless, and radiating

from the small mouth to the high cheek bones of his race.

His look as he eyed me became utter consternation; then humour slowly lightened the little eyes. He lifted the eyes straight into the glare of the un-dimmed sun; nor did they blink as they noted the hour. "My good gosh!" he muttered; then stalked slowly round the pile of stove wood that had been spreading since morning. He seemed aggrieved— yet humorously aggrieved—as he noted its noble dimensions. He cast away the axe and retrieved some outflung sticks, which he cunningly adjusted to the main pile to make it appear still larger to the casual eye.

"My good gosh!" he muttered again. "My old mahala she tell me Old Lady Pettengill go off early this morning; but I think she make one big mistake. Now what you know about that?" He smiled win-ningly now and became a very old man indeed, the smile lighting the myriad minute wrinkles that in-stantly came to life. Again he ruefully surveyed the morning's work. "I think that caps the cli-max," said he, and grimanced humorous dismay for the entertainment of us both.

I opened my cigarette case to him. Like his late critic, Pete availed himself of two, though he had not the excuse of a pipe to be filled. One he coyly tucked above his left ear and one he lighted. Then he sat gracefully back upon his heels and drew smoke into his innermost recesses, a shrunken little figure of

a man in a calico shirt of gay stripes, faded blue overalls, and shoes that were remarkable as ruins.   With
a pointed chip in the slender fingers of one lean brown
hand—a narrow hand of quite feminine delicacy—he
cleared the ground of other chips and drew small
figures in the earth.

"Some of your people cut up in a fight down at
Kulanche last night," I remarked after a moment of
courteous waiting.

"Mebbe," said Pete, noncommittal.

"Were you down there?"

"I never kill a man with a knife," said Pete; "that
ain't my belief."

He left an opening that tempted, but I thought it
wise to ignore that for the moment.

"You an old man, Pete?"

"Mebbe."

"How old?"

"Oh, so-so."

"You remember a long time ago—how long?"

He drew a square in his cleared patch of earth, sub-
divided it into little squares, and dotted each of these
in the centre before he spoke.

"When Modocs have big soldier fight."

"You a Modoc?"

"B'lieve me!"

"When Captain Jack fought the soldiers over in
the Lava Beds?"

"Some fight—b'lieve me!" said Pete, erasing his
square and starting a circle.

"You fight, too?"

"Too small; I do little odd jobs—when big Injin kill soldier I skin um head."

I begged for further items, but Pete seemed to feel that he had been already verbose. He dismissed the historic action with a wise saying:

"Killing soldiers all right; but it don't settle nothing." He drew a triangle.

Indelicately then I pried into his spiritual life.

"You a Christian, Pete?"

"Injin-Christian," he amended—as one would say "Progressive-Republican."

"Believe in God?"

"Two." This was a guarded admission; I caught his side glance.

"Which ones?" I asked it cordially; and Pete smiled as one who detects a brother liberal in theology.

"Injin God; Christian God. Injin God go like this——" He brushed out his latest figure and drew a straight line a foot long. And Christian God go so —he drew a second straight line perpendicular to the first. I was made to see the line of his own God extending over the earth some fifty feet above its surface, while the line of the Christian God went straight and endlessly into the heavens. "Injin God stay close—Christian God go straight up. Whoosh!" He looked toward the zenith to indicate the vanishing line. "I think mebbe both O. K. You think both O. K.?"

"Mebbe," I said.

Pete retraced the horizontal line of his own God and the perpendicular line of the other.

"Funny business," said he tolerantly.

"Funny business," I echoed. And then—the moment seeming ripe for intimate personal research: "Pete, how about that brother-in-law of yours? Is he a one-God Christian or a two-God, like you?"

He hurriedly brushed out his lines, flashed me one of his uneasy side glances, and seemed not to have heard my question. He sprang lightly from his heels, affected to scan a murky cloud-bank to the south, ignited his second cigarette from the first, and seemed relieved by the actual diversion of Laura, his present lawful consort, now plodding along the road just outside the fence.

Laura is ponderous and billowy, and her moonlike face of rusty bronze is lined to show that she, too, has gone down a little into the vale of years. She was swathed in many skirts, her shoulders enveloped by a neutral-tinted shawl, and upon her head was a modish toque of light straw, garlanded with pink roses. This may have been her hunt constume, for the carcasses of two slain rabbits swung jauntily from her girdle. She undulated by us with no sign. Pete's glistening little eyes lingered in appraisal upon her noble rotundities and her dangling quarry. Then, with a graceful flourish of the new cigarette, he paid tribute to the ancient fair.

"That old mahala of mine, she not able to chew

much now; but she's some swell chicken—b'lieve
me!"

I persisted in the impertinence he had sought to
turn.

"How about this brother-in-law of yours, Pete?"

Again he was deaf. He picked up his axe, appear-
ing to weigh the resumption of his task against a reply
to this straight question. He must have found the
alternative too dreadful; he leaned upon the axe, thus
winning something of the dignity of labour, with none
of its pains, and grudgingly asked:

"Mebbe some liars tell you in conversation about
that old b'other-in-law?"

"Of course! Many nice people tell me every day.
They tell me all about him. I rather hear you tell
me. Is he a Christian?"

"He's one son-of-gun, pure and simple—that old
feller. He caps the climax."

"Yes; I know all about that. He's a bad man. I
hear everything about him. Now you tell me again.
You can tell better than liars."

"One genuine son-of-gun!" persisted Pete, shrewdly
keeping to general terms.

"Oh, very well!" I rose from the log I was sitting on, yawning my indifference. "I know everything he ever did. Other people tell me all the
time."

I moved off a few steps under the watchful side
glance. It worked. One of Pete's slim, womanish
hands fluttered up in a movement of arrest.

"Those liars tell you about one time he shoot white man off horse going by?"

"Certainly!"

"That white man still have smallpox to give all Injins he travel to; so they go 'n' vote who kill him off quick, and my b'other-in-law he win it."

I tried to look as if this were a bit of stale gossip.

"Then whites raise hell to say Pete he do same. What you know about that? My old b'other-in-law send word he do same—twenty, fifty Injin witness tell he said so—and now he gon' hide far off. Dep'ty sheriff can't find him. That son-of-gun come back next year, raise big fight over one span mules with Injin named Walter that steal my mules out of pasture; and Walter not get well from it—so whites say yes, old Pete done that same killing scrape to have his mules again; plain as the nose on the face old Pete do same. But I catch plenty Injin witness see my b'other-in-law do same, and I think they can't catch him another time once more, because they look in all places he ain't. I think plenty too much trouble he make all time for me—perform something not nice and get found out about it; and all people say, Oh, yes—that old Pete he's at tricks again; he better get sent to Walla Walla, learn some good trade in prison for eighteen years. That b'other-in-law cap the climax! He know all good place to hide from dep'ty sheriff, so not be found when badly wanted—the son-of-gun!"

Pete's face now told that, despite the proper loath-

ing inspired by his misdeeds, this brother-in-law compelled a certain horrid admiration for his gift of
elusiveness.

"What's your brother-in-law's name?"

Pete deliberated gravely.

"In my opinion his name Edward; mebbe Sam,
mebbe Charlie; I think more it's Albert."

"Well, what about that next time he broke out?"

"Whoosh! Damn no-good squaw man get all Injins drunk on whiskey; then play poker with four aces.
'What you got? No good—four aces—hard luck—
deal 'em up!'" Pete's flexible wrists here flashed
in pantomime. "Pretty soon Injin got no mules, no
blanket, no spring wagon, no gun, no new boots, no
nine dollars my old mahala gets paid for three bushel
wild plums from Old Lady Pettengill to make canned
goods of—only got one big sick head from all night;
see four aces, four kings, four jacks. 'What you got,
Pete? No good. Full house here. Hard luck—my
deal. Have another drink, old top!'"

"Well, what did your brother-in-law do when he
heard about this?"

"Something!"

"Shoot?"

"Naw; got no gun left. Choke him on the neck—
I think this way."

The supple hands of Pete here clutched his corded
throat, fingertips meeting at the back, and two po-
tent thumbs uniting in a sinister pressure upon his
Adam's apple. To further enlarge my understanding

he contorted his face unprettily. From rolling eyes
and outthrust tongue it was apparent that the squaw
man had survived long enough to regret the in-
veteracy of his good luck at cards.

"Then what?"

"Man tell you before?" He eyed me with frank
suspicion.

"Certainly; you tell, too!"

"That b'other-in-law he win everything back this
poor squaw man don't need no more, and son-of-gun
beat it quick; so all liars say Old Pete turn that trick,
but can't prove same, because my b'other-in-law
do same in solitude. And old judge say: 'Oh, well,
can't prove same in courthouse, and only good squaw
man is dead squaw man; so what-the-bad-place!' I
think mebbe."

"Go on; what about that next time?"

"You know already," said Pete firmly.

"You tell, too."

He pondered this, his keen little eyes searching my
face as he pensively fondled the axe.

"You know about this time that son-of-gun go 'n'
kill a bright lawyer in Red Gap? I think that cap
the climax!"

"Certainly, I know!" This with bored impatience.

"I think, then, you tell me." His seamed face
was radiant with cunning.

"What's the use? You know it already."

He countered swiftly:

"What's use I tell you—you know already."

I yawned again flagrantly.

"Now you tell in your own way how this trouble first begin," persisted Pete rather astonishingly. He seemed to quote from memory.

Once more I yawned, turning coldly away.

"You tell in your own words," he was again gently urging; but on the instant his axe began to rain blows upon the log at his feet.

Sounds of honest toil were once more to be heard in the wood lot; and, though I could not hear the other, I surmised that the sledge of Uncle Abner now rang merrily upon his anvil. Both he and Pete had doubtless noted at the same moment the approach of Mrs. Lysander John Pettengill, who was spurring her jaded roan up the long rise from the creek bottom.

My stalwart hostess, entirely masculine to the eye from a little distance, strode up from the corral, waved a quirt at me in greeting, indicated by another gesture that she was dusty and tired, and vanished briskly within the ranch house. Half an hour later she joined me in the living-room, where I had trifled with ancient magazines and stock journals on the big table. Laced boots, riding breeches, and army shirt had gone for a polychrome and trailing tea gown, black satin slippers, flashing rhinestone rosettes, and silk stockings of a sinful scarlet. She wore a lace boudoir cap, plenteously beribboned, and her sunburned nose had been lavishly powdered. She looked now merely like an indulged matron whose most poignant worry would be a sick Pomeranian or overnight losses at bridge. She wished to know whether I would have tea with her. I would.

Tea consisted of bottled beer from the spring house, half a ham, and a loaf of bread. It should be said that her behaviour toward these dainties, when they had been assembled, made her seem much less the worn social leader. There was practically no talk for ten active minutes. A high-geared camera would have caught everything of value in the scene. It was only as I decanted a second bottle of beer for the woman that she seemed to regain consciousness of her surroundings. The spirit of her first attack upon the food had waned. She did fashion another sandwich of a rugged pattern, but there was a hint of the dilettante in her work.

And now she spoke. Her gaze upon the magazines of yesteryear massed at the lower end of the table, she declared they must all be scrapped, because they too painfully reminded her of a dentist's waiting-room. She wondered if there mustn't be a law against a dentist having in his possession a magazine less than ten years old. She suspected as much.

"There I'll be sitting in Doc Martingale's office waiting for him to kill me by inches, and I pick up a magazine to get my mind off my fate and find I'm reading a timely article, with illustrations, about Cervera's fleet being bottled up in the Harbour of Santiago. I bet he's got *Godey's Lady's Book* for 1862 round there, if you looked for it."

Now a brief interlude for the ingestion of malt liquor, followed by a pained recital of certain complications of the morning.

"That darned one-horse post-office down to Kulanche! What do you think? I wanted to send a postal card to the North American Cleaning and Dye Works, at Red Gap, for some stuff they been holding out on me a month, and that office didn't have a single card in stock—nothing but some of these fancy ones in a rack over on the grocery counter; horrible things with pictures of brides and grooms on 'em in coloured costumes, with sickening smiles on their faces, and others with wedding bells ringing out or two doves swinging in a wreath of flowers—all of 'em having mushy messages underneath; and me having to send this card to the North American Cleaning and Dye Works, which is run by Otto Birdsall, a smirking old widower, that uses hair oil and perfumery, and imagines every woman in town is mad about him.

"The mildest card I could find was covered with red and purple cauliflowers or something, and it said in silver print: 'With fondest remembrance!' Think of that going through the Red Gap post-office to be read by old Mis' Terwilliger, that some say will even open letters that look interesting—to say nothing of its going to this fresh old Otto Birdsall, that tried to hold my hand once not so many years ago.

"You bet I made the written part strong enough not to give him or any other party a wrong notion of my sentiments toward him. At that, I guess Otto wouldn't make any mistake since the time I give him hell last summer for putting my evening gowns in his show window every time he'd clean one, just to show off his work. It looked so kind of indelicate seeing an empty dress hung up there that every soul in town knew belonged to me.

"What's that? Oh, I wrote on the card that if this stuff of mine don't come up on the next stage I'll be right down there, and when I'm through handling him he'll be able to say truthfully that he ain't got a gray hair in his head. I guess Otto will know my intentions are honest, in spite of that 'fondest remembrance.'

"Then, on top of that, I had a run-in with the Swede for selling his rotten whiskey to them poor Injin boys that had a fight last night after they got tight on it. The Swede laughs and says nobody can prove he sold 'em a drop, and I says that's probably true. I says it's always hard to prove things. 'For instance,' I says, 'if they's another drop of liquor sold to an Injin during this haying time, and a couple or three nights after that your nasty dump here is set fire to in six places, and some cowardly assassin out in the brush picks you off with a rifle when you rush out—it will be mighty hard to prove that anybody did that, too; and you not caring whether it's proved or not, for that matter.

"'In fact,' I says, 'I don't suppose anybody would take the trouble to prove it, even if it could be easy proved. You'd note a singular lack of public inter-

est in it—if you was spared to us. I guess about as
far as an investigation would ever get—the coroner's
jury would say it was the work of Pete's brother-in-
law; and you know what that would mean.' The
Swede bristles up and says: 'That sounds like fighting talk!' I says: 'Your hearing is perfect.' I left
him thinking hard."

"Pete's brother-in-law? That reminds me," I
said. "Pete was telling me about him just—I mean
during his lunch hour; but he had to go to work again
just at the beginning of something that sounded
good—about the time he was going to kill a bright
lawyer. What was that?"

The glass was drained and Ma Pettengill eyed
the inconsiderable remains of the ham with something like repugnance. She averted her face from
it, lay back in the armchair she had chosen, and
rolled a cigarette, while I brought a hassock for the
jewelled slippers and the scarlet silken ankles, so
ill-befitting one of her age. The cigarette was presently burning.

"I guess Pete's b'other-in-law, as he calls him,
won't come into these parts again. He had a kind
of narrow squeak this last time. Pete done something pretty raw, even for this liberal-minded community. He got scared about it himself and left the
country for a couple of months—looking for his
brother-in-law, he said. He beat it up North and
got in with a bunch of other Injins that was being
took down to New York City to advertise a railroad,

Pete looking like what folks think an Injin ought to look when he's dressed for the part. But he got homesick; and, anyway, he didn't like the job.

"This passenger agent that took 'em East put 'em up at one of the big hotels all right, but he subjects 'em to hardships they ain't used to. He wouldn't let 'em talk much English, except to say, 'Ugh! Ugh!'—like Injins are supposed to—with a few remarks about the Great Spirit; and not only that, but he makes 'em wear blankets and paint their faces—an Injin without paint and blanket and some beadwork seeming to a general passenger agent like a state capitol without a dome. And on top of these outrages he puts it up with the press agent of this big hotel to have the poor things sleep up on the roof, right in the open air, so them jay New York newspapers would fall for it and print articles about these hardy sons of the forest, the last of a vanishing race, being stifled by walls—with the names of the railroad and the hotel coming out good and strong all through the piece.

"Three of the poor things got pneumonia, not being used to such exposure; and Pete himself took a bad cold, and got mad and quit the job. They find him a couple of days later, in a check suit and white shoes and a golf cap, playing pool in a saloon over on Eighth Avenue, and ship him back as a disgrace to the Far West and a great common carrier.

"He got in here one night, me being his best friend, and we talked it over. I advised him to go down and give himself up and have it over; and he agreed, and went down to Red Gap the next day in his new clothes and knocked at the jail door. He made a long talk about how his brother-in-law was the man that really done it, and he's been searching for him clear over to the rising sun, but can't find him; so he's come to give himself up, even if they ain't got the least grounds to suspect him—and can he have his trial for murder over that afternoon, so he can come back up here the next day and go to work?

"They locked him up and Judge Ballard appointed J. Waldo Snyder to defend him. He was a new young lawyer from the East that had just come to Red Gap, highly ambitious and full of devices for showing that parties couldn't have been in their right mind when they committed the deed—see the State against Jamstucker, New York Reports Number 23, pages 19 to 78 inclusive.

"Oh, he told me all about it up in his office one day —how he was going to get Pete off. Ain't lawyers the goods, though! And doctors? This J. W. Snyder had a doctor ready to swear that Pete was nutty when he fired the shot, even if not before nor after. When I was a kid at school, back in Fredonia, New York State, we used to have debates about which does the most harm—fire or water? Nowadays I bet they'd have: Which does the most harm— doctors or lawyers? Well, anyway, there Pete was in jail——"

"Please tell in your own simple words just how this

trouble began," I broke in. "What did Pete fire
the shot for and who stopped it? Now then!"

"What! Don't you know about that? Well,
well! So you never heard about Pete sending this
medicine man over the one-way trail? I'll have to
tell you, then. It was three years ago. Pete was
camped about nine miles the other side of Kulanche,
on the Corporation Ranch, and his little year-old
boy was took badly sick. I never did know with
what. Diphtheria, I guess. And I got to tell you
Pete is crazy about babies. Always has been.
Thirty years ago, when my own baby hadn't been
but a few weeks born, Lysander John had to be in
Red Gap with a smashed leg and arm, and I was here
alone with Pete for two months of one winter. Say,
he was better than any trained nurse with both of us,
even if my papoose was only a girl one! Folks used
to wonder afterward if I hadn't been afraid with just
Pete round. Good lands! If they'd ever seen him
cuddle that mite and sing songs to it in Injin about
the rain and the grass! Anyway, I got to know Pete
so well that winter I never blamed him much for
what come off.

"Well, this yearling of his got bad and Pete was
in two minds. He believed in white doctors with
his good sense, but he believed in Injin doctors with
his superstition, which was older. So he tried to
have one of each. There was an old rogue of a
medicine man round here then from the reservation
up north. He'd been doing a little work at haying

on the Corporation, but he was getting his main graft selling the Injins charms and making spells over their sick; a crafty old crook playing on their ignorance —understand? And Pete, having got the white doctor from Kulanche, thought he'd cinch matters by getting the medicine man, too. At that, I guess one would of been about as useful as the other, the Kulanche doctor knowing more about anthrax and blackleg than he did about sick Injin babies.

"The medicine man sees right off how scared Pete is for his kid and thinks here's a chance to make some big money. He looks at the little patient and says yes, he can cure him, sure; but it'll be a hard job and he can't undertake it unless Pete comes through with forty dollars and his span of mules. But Pete ain't got forty dollars or forty cents, and the Kulanche doctor has got to the mules already, having a lien on 'em for twenty-five.

"Pete hurried over and put the proposition up to me. He says his little chief is badly sick and he's got a fine white doctor, but will I stake him to enough to get this fine Injin doctor?—thus making a cure certain. Well, I tore into the old fool for wanting to let this depraved old medicine man tamper with his baby, and I warned him the Kulanche doctor probably wasn't much better. Then I tell him he's to send down for the best doctor in Red Gap at my expense and keep him with the child till it's well. I tell him he can have the whole ranch if it would cure his child, but not one cent for the Injin.

"Well, the poor boy is about half convinced I'm right, but he's been an Injin too long to believe it all through. He went off and sent for the Red Gap doctor, but he can't resist making another try for the Injin one; and that old scoundrel holds out for his price. Pete wants him to wait for his pay till haying is over; but he won't because he thinks Pete can get the money from me now if he really has to have it. Pete must of been crazy for fair about that time.

" 'All right,' says he; 'you can cure my little chief?'

"The crook says he can if the money is in his hand.

" 'All right,' says Pete again; 'but if my little chief dies something bad is going to happen to you.'

"That's about all they ever found out concerning this threat of Pete's, though another Injin who heard it said that Pete said his brother-in-law would make the trouble—not Pete himself. Which was likely true enough.

"Pete's little chief died the night the Red Gap doctor got up here. Ten minutes later this medicine man had hitched up his team, loaded his plunder into a wagon, and was pouring leather into his horses to get back home quick. He knew Pete never talks just to hear himself talk. They found him about thirty miles on his way—slumped down in the wagon bed, his team hitched by the roadside. There had been just one careful shot. As he hadn't been robbed—he had over a hundred dollars in gold on him—it pointed a mite too strong at Pete after his threat.

"A deputy sheriff come up.   Pete said his brother-in-law had been hanging round lately and had talked very dangerous about the medicine man.   He said the brother-in-law had probably done the job.   But Pete had pulled this too often before when in difficulties.   The deputy said he'd better come along down to Red Gap and tell the district attorney about it.   Pete said all right and crawled into his tepee for his coat and hat—crawled right on out the back and into the brush while the deputy rolled a cigarette.

"That was when he joined this bunch of noble redmen to advertise the vanishing romance of the Great West—being helped out of the country, I shouldn't wonder, by some lawless old hound that had feelings for him and showed it when he come along in the night to the ranch where he'd nursed her and her baby.   They looked for him a little while, then dropped it; in fact, everybody was kind of glad he'd got off and kind of satisfied that he'd put this bad Injin, with his skull-duggery, over the big jump.

"Then he got homesick, like I told you, and showed up here at the door; and I saw it was better for him to give himself up and get out of it by fair and legal means.   Now!   You got it straight that far?"

I nodded.

"So Pete took my advice, and a couple days later I hurried down to Red Gap and had a talk with Judge Ballard and the district attorney.   The judge said it had been embarrassing to justice to have my

old Injin walk in on 'em, because every one knew he
was guilty. Why couldn't he of stayed up here where
the keen-eyed officers of the law could of pretended
not to know he was? And the old fool was only making things worse with his everlasting chatter about
his brother-in-law, every one knowing there wasn't
such a person in existence—old Pete having had
dozens of every kind of relation in the world but a
brother-in-law. But they're going to have this
bright young lawyer defend him, and they have
hopes.

"Then I talked some. I said it was true that everybody knew Pete bumped off this old crook that had it
coming to him, but they could never prove it, because
Pete had come to my place and set up with me all
night, when I had lumbago or something, the very
night this crime was done thirty-odd miles distant
by some person or persons unknown—except it could
be known they had good taste about who needed
killing.

"At this Judge Ballard jumps up and calls me an
old liar and shook hands warmly with me; and Cale
Jordan, that was district attorney then, says if Mrs.
Pettengill will give him her word of honour to go on
the witness stand and perjure herself to this effect
then he don't see no use of even putting Kulanche
County, State of Washington, to the expense of a
trial, the said county already being deep in the hole
for its new courthouse—but for mercy's sake to stop
the old idiot babbling about his brother-in-law, that

every one knows he never had one, because such a joke
is too great an affront to the dignity of the law in such
cases made and provided—to wit: tell the old fool to
say nothing except 'No, he never done it.'   And he
shakes hands with me, too, and says he'll have an
important talk with Myron Bughalter, the sheriff.

"I says that's the best way out of it, being myself
a heavy taxpayer; and I go see this Snyder lawyer,
and then over to the jail and get into Pete's cell,
where he's having a high old time with a sack of peppermint candy and a copy of the *Scientific American.*
I tell him to cut out the brother-in-law stuff and just
say 'No' to any question whatever.   He said he would,
and I went off home to rest up after my hard ride.

"Judge Ballard calls that night and says everything is fixed.   No use putting the county to the
expense of a trial when Pete has such a classy per-
jured alibi as I would give him.   Myron Bughalter
is to go out of the jail in a careless manner at nine-
thirty that night, leaving all cells unlocked and the
door wide open so Pete can make his escape without
doing any damage to the new building.   It seems the
only other prisoner is old Sing Wah, that they're
willing to save money on, too.   He'd got full of per-
fumed port and raw gin a few nights before, announced himself as a prize-hatchet man, and started
a tong war in the laundry of one of his cousins.
But Sing was sober now and would stay so until the
next New Year's; so they was going to let him walk
out with Pete.   The judge said Pete would probably

be at the Arrowhead by sunup, and if he'd behave
himself from now on the law would let bygones be
bygones. I thanked the judge and went to bed feeling easy about old Pete.

"But at seven the next morning I'm waked up by
the telephone—wanted down to the jail in a hurry.
I go there soon as I can get a drink of hot coffee and
find that poor Myron Bughalter is having his troubles.
He'd got there at seven, thinking, of course, to find
both his prisoners gone; and here in the corridor is
Pete setting on the chest of Sing Wah, where he'd
been all night, I guess! He tells Myron he's a fool
sheriff to leave his door wide open that way, because
this bad Chinaman tried to walk out as soon as he'd
gone, and would of done so it Pete hadn't jumped him.

"It leaves Myron plenty embarrassed, but he finally says to Pete he can go free, anyway, now, for
being such an honest jailbird; and old Sing Wah can
go, too, having been punished enough by Pete's
handling. Sing Wah slides out quickly enough at
this, promising to send Myron a dozen silk hand-
kerchiefs and a pound of tea. But not Pete. No,
sir! He tells Myron he's give himself up to be tried,
and he wants that trial and won't budge till he gets
it.

"Then Myron telephoned for the judge and the
district attorney, and for me. We get there and tell
Pete to beat it quick. But the old mule isn't going
to move one step without that trial. He's fled back
to his cell and stands there as dignified as if he was

going to lay a cornerstone. He's a grave rebuke to
the whole situation, as you might say. Then the
Judge and Cale go through some kind of a hocus-
pocus talk, winding up with both of them saying
'Not guilty!' in a loud voice; and Myron says to
Pete: 'There! You had your trial; now get out of
my jail this minute.'

"But canny old Pete is still balking. He says
you can't have a trial except in the courthouse, which
is upstairs, and they're trying to cheat a poor old
Injin. He's talking loud by this time, and Judge
Ballard says, all right, they must humour the poor
child of Nature. So Myron takes Pete by the wrist
in a firm manner—though Pete's insisting he ought
to have the silver handcuffs on him—and marches
him out the jail door, round to the front marble
steps of the new courthouse, up the steps, down the
marble hall and into the courtroom, with the judge
and Cale Jordan and me marching behind.

"We ain't the whole procession, either. Out in
front of the jail was about fifteen of Pete's friends
and relatives, male and female, that had been hanging round for two days waiting to attend his coming-
out party. Mebbe that's why Pete had been so
strong for the real courthouse, wanting to give these
friends something swell for their trouble. Anyway,
these Injins fall in behind us when we come out and
march up into the courtroom, where they set down
in great ecstasy. Every last one of 'em has a sack
of peppermint candy and a bag of popcorn or peanuts,

and they all begin to eat busily. The steam heat had been turned on and that hall of justice in three minutes smelt like a cheap orphan asylum on Christmas morning.

"Then, before they can put up another bluff at giving Pete his trial, with Judge Ballard setting up in his chair with his specs on and looking fierce, who rushes in but this J. Waldo person that is Pete's lawyer. He's seen the procession from across the street and fears some low-down trick is being played on his defenseless client.

"He comes storming down the aisle exclaiming: 'Your Honour, I protest against this grossly irregular proceeding!' The judge pounds on his desk with his little croquet mallet and Myron Bughalter tells Snyder, out of the corner of his mouth, to shut up. But he won't shut up for some minutes. This is the first case he'd had and he's probably looked forward to a grand speech to the jury that would make 'em all blubber and acquit Pete without leaving the box, on the grounds of emotional or erratic insanity—or whatever it is that murderers get let off on when their folks are well fixed. He sputters quite a lot about this monstrous travesty on justice before they can drill the real facts into his head; and even then he keeps coming back to Pete's being crazy.

"Then Pete, who hears this view of his case for the first time, begins to glare at his lawyer in a very nasty way and starts to interrupt; so the judge has to knock wood some more to get 'em all quiet. When they do get still—with Pete looking blacker than ever at his lawyer—Cale Jordan says: 'Pete, did you do this killing?' Pete started to say mebbe his brother-in-law did, but caught himself in time and said 'No!' at the same time starting for J. Waldo, that had called him crazy. Myron Bughalter shoves him back in his chair, and Cale Jordan says: 'Your Honour, you have heard the evidence, which is conclusive. I now ask that the prisoner at the bar be released.' Judge Ballard frowns at Pete very stern and says: 'The motion is granted. Turn him loose, quick, and get the rest of that smelly bunch out of here and give the place a good airing. I have to hold court here at ten o'clock.'

"Pete was kind of convinced now that he'd had a sure-enough trial, and his friends had seen the marble walls and red carpet and varnished furniture, and everything; so he consented to be set free—not in any rush, but like he was willing to do 'em a favour.

"And all the time he's keeping a bad little eye on J. Waldo. The minute he gets down from the stand he makes for him and says what does he mean by saying he was crazy when he done this killing? J. Waldo tries to explain that this was his only defense and was going on to tell what an elegant defense it was; but Pete gets madder and madder. I guess he'd been called everything in the world before, but never crazy; that's the very worst thing you can tell an Injin.

"They work out toward the front door; and then I hear Pete say: 'You know what? You said I'm crazy. My b'other-in-law's going to make something happen to you in the night.' Pete was seeing red by that time. The judge tells Myron to hurry and get the room cleared and open some windows. Myron didn't have to clear it of J. W. Snyder. That bright young lawyer dashed out and was fifty feet ahead of the bunch when they got to the front door.

"So Pete was a free man once more, without a stain on his character except to them that knew him well. But the old fool had lost me a tenant. Yes, sir; this J. W. Snyder young man, with the sign hardly dry on the glass door of his office in the Pettengill Block, had a nervous temperament to start with, and on top of that he'd gone fully into Pete's life history and found out that parties his brother-in-law was displeased with didn't thrive long. He packed up his law library that afternoon and left for another town that night.

"Yes, Pete's a wonder! Watch him slaving away out there. And he must of been working hard all day, even with me not here to keep tabs on him. Just look at the size of that pile of wood he's done up, when he might easy of been loafing on the job!"

LITTLE OLD NEW YORK

MONDAY'S mail for the Arrowhead was brought in by the Chinaman while Ma Pettengill and I loitered to the close of the evening meal: a canvas sack of letters and newspapers with three bulky packages of merchandise that had come by parcels post. The latter evoked a passing storm from my hostess. Hadn't she warned folks time and again to send all her stuff by express instead of by parcels post, which would sure get her gunned some day by the stage driver who got nothing extra for hauling such matter? She had so!

We trifled now with a fruity desert and the lady regaled me with a brief exposure of our great parcels-post system as a piece of the nerviest penny pinching she had ever known our Government guilty of. Because why? Because these here poor R. F. D. stage drivers had to do the extra hauling for nothing.

"Here's old Harvey Steptoe with the mail contract for sixty dollars a month, three trips a week between Red Gap and Surprise Valley, forty-five miles each way, barely making enough extra on express matter and local freight to come out even after buying horse-feed. Then comes parcels post, and parties that had had to pay him four bits or a dollar for a large package, or two bits for a small one, can have 'em brought in by mail for nothing. Of course most of us eased up on him after we understood the hellish injustice of it. We took pains not to have things sent parcels post and when they come unbeknown to us, like these here to-night, we'd always pay him anyway, just like they was express. It was only fair and, besides, we would live longer, Harvey Steptoe being morose and sudden.

"Like when old Safety First Timmins got the idea he could have all his supplies sent from Red Gap for almost nothing by putting stamps on 'em. He was tickled to death with the notion until, after the second load of about a hundred pounds, some cowardly assassin shot at him from the brush one morning about the time the stage usually went down past his ranch. The charge missed him by about four inches and went into the barn door. He dug it out and found a bullet and two buckshot. Old Safety First ain't any Sherlock Holmes, but even Doctor Watson could of solved this murderous crime. When Harvey come by the next night he went out and says to him, 'Ain't you got one of them old Mississippi Yaegers about seventy-five years old that carries a bullet and two buckshot?' Harvey thought back earnestly for a minute, then says, 'Not now I ain't. I used to have one of them old hairlooms around the house but I found they ain't reliable when you want to do fine work from a safe distance; so I threw her

away yesterday morning and got me this nice new
30-30 down to Goshook & Dale's hardware store.'

"He pulled the new gun out and patted it tenderly
in the sight of old Timmins. 'Ain't it a cunning
little implement?' he says; 'I tried it out coming up
this afternoon. I could split a hair with it as far,
say, as from that clump of buck-brush over to your
barn. And by the way, Mr. Timmins,' he says, 'I
got some more stuff for you here from the Square
Deal Grocery—stuff all gummed up with postage
stamps.' He leans his new toy against the seat
and dumps out a sack of flour and a sack of dried
fruit and one or two other things. 'This parcels
post is a grand thing, ain't it?' says he.

"'Well—yes and no, now that you speak of it,'
says old Safety First. 'The fact is I'm kind of
prejudiced against it; I ain't going to have things
come to me any more all stuck over with them
trifling little postage stamps. It don't look dignified.' 'No?' says Harvey. 'No,' says Safety First
in a firm tone. 'I won't ever have another single
thing come by mail if I can help it.' 'I bet you're
superstitious,' says Harvey, climbing back to his
seat and petting the new gun again. 'I bet you're so
superstitious you'd take this here shiny new implement off my hands at cost if I hinted I'd part with
it.' 'I almost believe I would,' says Safety First.
'Well, it don't seem like I'd have much use for it after
all,' says Harvey. 'Of course I can always get a
new one if my fancy happens to run that way again.'

"So old Safety First buys a new loaded rifle that he ain't got a use on earth for. It would of looked to outsiders like he was throwing his money away on fripperies, but he knew it was a prime necessity of life all right. The parcels post ain't done him a bit of good since, though I send him marked pieces in the papers every now and then telling how the postmaster general thinks it's a great boon to the ultimate consumer. And I mustn't forget to send Harvey six bits for them three packages that come to-night. That's what we do. Otherwise, him being morose and turbulent, he'd get a new gun and make ultimate consumers out of all of us. Darned ultimate! I reckon we got a glorious Government, like candidates always tell us, but a postmaster general that expected stage drivers to do three times the hauling they had been doing with no extra pay wouldn't last long out at the tail of an R. F. D. route. There'd be pieces in the paper telling about how he rose to prominence from the time he got a lot of delegates sewed up for the people's choice and how his place will be hard to fill. It certainly would be hard to fill out here. Old Timmins, for one, would turn a deaf ear to his country's call."

Lew Wee having now cleared the table of all but coffee, we lingered for a leisurely overhauling of the mail sack. Ma Pettengill slit envelopes and read letters to an accompanying rumble of protest. She several times wished to know what certain parties took her for—and they'd be fooled if they did; and

now and again she dwelt upon the insoluble mystery
of her not being in the poorhouse at that moment;
yes, and she'd of been there long ago if she had let
these parties run her business like they thought they
could. But what could a lone defenceless woman
expect? She'd show them, though! Been showing
'em for thirty years now, and still had her health,
hadn't she?

Letters and bills were at last neatly stacked and
the poor weak woman fell upon the newspapers.
The Red Gap *Recorder* was shorn of its wrapper.
Being first a woman she turned to the fourth page to
flash a practised eye over that department which is
headed "Life's Stages—At the Altar—In the Cradle!—To the Tomb." Having gleaned recent vital
statistics she turned next to the column carrying
the market quotations on beef cattle, for after being
a woman she is a rancher. Prices for that day must
have pleased her immensely for she grudgingly
mumbled that they were less ruinous than she had
expected. In the elation of which this admission
was a sign she next refreshed me with various personal items from a column headed "Social Glean-
ings—by Madame On Dit."

I learned that at the last regular meeting of the
Ladies' Friday Afternoon Shakespeare Club, Mrs.
Dr. Percy Hailey Martingale had read a paper en-
titled "My Trip to the Panama-Pacific Exposition,"
after which a dainty collation was served by mine
hostess Mrs. Judge Ballard; that Miss Beryl Mae

Macomber, the well-known young society heiress, was visiting friends in Spokane where rumour hath it that she would take a course of lessons in elocution; and that Mrs. Cora Hartwick Wales, prominent society matron and leader of the ultra smart set of Price's Addition, had on Thursday afternoon at her charming new bungalow, corner of Bella Vista Street and Prospect Avenue, entertained a number of her inmates at tea. Ma Pettengill and I here quickly agreed that the proofreading on the *Recorder* was not all it should be. Then she unctuously read me a longer item from another column which was signed "The Lounger in the Lobby":

"Mr. Benjamin P. Sutton, the wealthy capitalist of Nome, Alaska, and a prince of good fellows, is again in our midst for his annual visit to His Honour Alonzo Price, Red Gap's present mayor, of whom he is an old-time friend and associate. Mr. Sutton, who is the picture of health, brings glowing reports from the North and is firm in his belief that Alaska will at no distant day become the garden spot of the world. In the course of a brief interview he confided to ye scribe that on his present trip to the outside he would not again revisit his birthplace, the city of New York, as he did last year. 'Once was enough, for many reasons,' said Mr. Sutton grimly. 'They call it "Little old New York," but it isn't little and it isn't old. It's big and it's new—we have older buildings right in Nome than any you can find on Broadway. Since my brief sojourn there last year

I have decided that our people before going to New York should see America first.' "

"Now what do you think of that?" demanded the lady. I said I would be able to think little of it unless I were told the precise reasons for this rather brutal abuse of a great city. What, indeed, were the "many reasons" that Mr. Sutton had grimly not confided to ye scribe?

Ma Pettengill chuckled and reread parts of the indictment. Thereafter she again chuckled fluently and uttered broken phrases to herself. "Horsecar" was one; "the only born New Yorker alive" was another. It became necessary for me to remind the woman that a guest was present. I did this by shifting my chair to face the stone fireplace in which a pine chunk glowed, and by coughing in a delicate and expectant manner.

"Poor Ben!" she murmured—"going all the day down there just to get one romantic look at his old home after being gone twenty-five years. I don't blame him for talking rough about the town, nor for his criminal act—stealing a street-car track."

It sounded piquant—a noble theft indeed! I now murmured a bit myself, striving to convey an active incredulity that yet might be vanquished by facts. The lady quite ignored this, diverging to her own opinion of New York. She tore the wrapper from a Sunday issue of a famous metropolitan daily and flaunted its comic supplement at me. "That's how I always think of New York," said she—"a kind of a comic supplement to the rest of this great country. Here—see these two comical little tots standing on their uncle's stomach and chopping his heart out with their axes—after you got the town sized up it's just that funny and horrible. It's like the music I heard that time at a higher concert I was drug to in Boston—ingenious but unpleasant."

But this was not what I would sit up for after a hard day's fishing—this coarse disparagement of something the poor creature was unfitted to comprehend.

"Ben Sutton," I remarked firmly.

"The inhabitants of New York are divided fifty-fifty between them that are trying to get what you got and them that think you're trying to get what they got."

"Ben Sutton," I repeated, trying to make it sullen.

"Ask a man on the street in New York where such and such a building is and he'll edge out of reaching distance, with his hand on his watch, before he tells you he don't know. In Denver, or San Francisco now, the man will most likely walk a block or two with you just to make sure you get the directions right."

"Ben Sutton!"

"They'll fall for raw stuff, though. I know a slick mining promoter from Arizona that stops at the biggest hotel on Fifth Avenue and has himself paged by the boys about twenty times a day so folks will know how important he is. He'll get up from his table in the restaurant and follow the boy out in a way to make 'em think that nine million dollars is at stake. He tells me it helps him a lot in landing the wise ones."

"Stole a street-car track," I muttered desperately.

"The typical New Yorker, like they call him, was born in Haverhill, Massachusetts, and sleeps in New Rochelle, going in on the 8:12 and coming out on the——"

"I had a pretty fight landing that biggest one this afternoon, from that pool under the falls up above the big bend. Twice I thought I'd lost him, but he was only hiding—and then I found I'd forgotten my landing net. Say, did I ever tell you about the time I was fishing for steel head down in Oregon, and the bear——" The lady hereupon raised a hushing hand.

Well, as I was saying, Ben Sutton blew into town early last September and after shaking hands with his old confederate, Lon Price, he says how is the good wife and is she at home and Lon says no; that Pettikins has been up at Silver Springs resting for a couple weeks; so Ben says it's too bad he'll miss the little lady, as in that case he has something good to suggest, which is, what's the matter with him and Lon taking a swift hike down to New York which Ben ain't seen since 1892, though he was born there, and he'd now like to have a look at the old home in Lon's company.

Lon says it's too bad Pettikins ain't there to go along, but if they start at once she wouldn't have time to join them, and Ben says he can start near enough at once for that, so hurry and pack the suitcase. Lon does it, leaving a delayed telegram to Henrietta to be sent after they start, begging her to join them if not too late, which it would be.

While they are in Louis Meyer's Place feeling good over this coop, in comes the ever care-free Jeff Tuttle and Jeff says he wouldn't mind going out on rodeo himself with 'em, at least as far as Jersey City where he has a dear old aunt living—or she did live there when he was a little boy and was always very nice to him and he ain't done right in not going to see her for thirty years—and if he's that close to the big town he could run over from Jersey City for a look—see.

Lon and Ben hail his generous decision with cheers and on the way to another place they meet me, just down from the ranch. And why don't I come along with the bunch? Ben has it all fixed in ten seconds, he being one of these talkers that will odd things along till they sound even, and the other two chiming in with him and wanting to buy my ticket right then. But I hesitated some. Lon and Ben Sutton was all right to go with, but Jeff Tuttle was a different kittle of fish. Jeff is a decent man in many respects and seems real refined when you first meet him if it's in some one's parlour, but he ain't one you'd care to follow step by step through the mazes and pitfalls and palmrooms of a great city if you're sensitive to public notice. Still, they was all so hearty in their urging, Ben saying I was the only lady in the world he could travel that far with and not want to strangle, and Lon says he'd rather have me than most of the men he knew, and Jeff says if I'll consent to go he'll take his full-dress suit so as to escort me to operas and lectures in a classy manner, and at last I give up. I said I'd horn in on their party since none of 'em seemed hostile.

I'd meant to go a little later anyway, for some gowns I needed and some shopping I'd promised to do for Lizzie Gunslaugh. You got to hand it to New York for shopping. Why, I'd as soon buy an evening gown in Los Angeles as in Portland or San Francisco. Take this same Lizzie Gunslaugh. She used to make a bare living, with her sign reading "Plain and Fashionable Dressmaking." But I took that girl down to New York twice with me and showed her how and what to buy there, instead of going to Spokane for her styles, and to-day she's got a thriving little business with a bully sign that we copied from them in the East —"Madame Elizabeth, Robes et Manteaux." Yes, sir; New York has at least one real reason for taking up room. That's a thing I always try to get into Ben Sutton's head, that he'd ought to buy his clothes down there instead of getting 'em from a reckless devil-dare of a tailor up in Seattle that will do anything in the world Ben tells him to—and he tells him a plenty, believe me. He won't ever wear a dress suit, either, because he says that costume makes all men look alike and he ain't going to stifle his individuality. If you seen Ben's figure once you'd know that nothing could make him look like any one else, him being built on the lines of a grain elevator and having individuality no clothes on earth could stifle. He's the very last man on earth that should have coloured braid on his check suits. However!

My trunk is packed in a hurry and I'm down to the 6:10 on time. Lon is very scared and jubilant over deserting Henrietta in this furtive way, and Ben is all ebullient in a new suit that looks like a lodge regalia and Jeff Tuttle in plain clothes is as happy as a child. When I get there he's already begun to give his imitation of a Sioux squaw with a hare lip reciting "Curfew Shall Not Ring To-night" in her native language, which he pulls on all occasions when he's feeling too good. It's some imitation. The Sioux language, even when spoken by a trained elocutionist, can't be anything dulcet. Jeff's stunt makes it sound like grinding coffee and shovelling coal into a cellar at the same time. Anyway, our journey begun happily and proved to be a good one, the days passing pleasantly while we talked over old times and played ten-cent limit in my stateroom, though Jeff Tuttle is so untravelled that he'll actually complain about the food and service in a dining-car. The poor puzzled old cow-man still thinks you ought to get a good meal in one, like the pretty bill of fare says you can.

Then one morning we was in New York and Ben

Sutton got his first shock. He believed he was still
on the other side of the river because he hadn't rid in a
ferryboat yet. He had to be told sharply by parties
in uniform. But we got him safe to a nice tall hotel
on Broadway at last. Talk about your hicks from
the brush—Ben was it, coming back to this here
birthplace of his. He fell into a daze on the short
ride to the hotel—after insisting hotly that we
should go to one that was pulled down ten years ago—
and he never did get out of it all that day.

Lon and Jeff was dazed, too. The city filled 'em
with awe and they made no pretense to the contrary.
About all they did that day was to buy picture cards
and a few drinks. They was afraid to wander very
far from the hotel for fear they'd get run over or
arrested or fall into the new subway or something
calamitous like that. Of course New York was looking as usual, the streets being full of tired voters
tearing up the car-tracks and digging first-line trenches
and so forth.

It was a quiet day for all of us, though I got my
shopping started, and at night we met at the hotel
and had a lonesome dinner. We was all too dazed
and tired to feel like larking about any, and poor Ben
was so downright depressed it was pathetic. Ever
read the story about a man going to sleep and waking
up in a glass case in a museum a thousand years later?
That was Ben coming back to his old town after only
twenty-five years. He hadn't been able to find a
single old friend nor any familiar faces. He ordered

a porterhouse steak, family style, for himself, but he was so mournful he couldn't eat more than about two dollars' worth of it. He kept forgetting himself in dismal reminiscences. The onlysright thing he'd found was the men tearing up the streets. That was just like they used to be, he said. He maundered on to us about how horse-cars was running on Broadway when he left and how they hardly bothered to light the lamps north of Forty-second Street, and he wished he could have some fish balls like the old Sinclair House used to have for its free lunch, and how in them golden days people that had been born right here in New York was seen so frequently that they created no sensation.

He was feeling awful desolate about this. He pointed out different parties at tables around us, saying they was merchant princes from Sandusky or prominent Elks from Omaha or roystering blades from Pittsburgh or boulevardeers from Bucyrus—not a New Yorker in sight. He said he'd been reading where a wealthy nut had sent out an expedition to the North Pole to capture a certain kind of Arctic flea that haunts only a certain rare fox—but he'd bet a born New Yorker was harder to find. He said what this millionaire defective ought to of done with his inherited wealth was to find a male and female born here and have 'em stuffed and mounted under glass in a fire-proof museum, which would be a far more exciting spectacle than any flea on earth, however scarce and arctic. He said he'd asked at least forty

men that day where they was born—waiters, taxi-
drivers, hotel clerks, bartenders, and just anybody
that would stop and take one with him, and not a
soul had been born nearer to the old town than
Scranton, Pennsylvania. "It's heart-rending," he
says, "to reflect that I'm alone here in this big city of
outlanders. I haven't even had the nerve to go down
to West Ninth Street for a look at the old home that
shelters my boyhood memories. If I could find only
one born New Yorker it would brace me up a whole
lot."

It was one dull evening, under this cloud that enveloped Ben. We didn't even go to a show, but
turned in early. Lon Price sent a picture card of the
Flatiron Building to Henrietta telling her he was having a dreary time and he was now glad he'd been disappointed about her not coming, so love and kisses
from her lonesome boy. It was what he would of
sent her anyway, but it happened to be the truth so
far.

Well, I got the long night's rest that was coming to
me and started out early in the A. M. to pit my cunning against the wiles of the New York department
stores, having had my evil desires inflamed the day
before by an afternoon gown in chiffon velvet and
Georgette crêpe with silver embroidery and fur trim-
ming that I'd seen in a window marked down to
$198.98. I fell for that all right, and for an all-silk
jersey sport suit at $29.98 and a demi-tailored walk-
ing suit for a mere bagatelle, and a white corduroy

sport blouse and a couple of imported evening gowns they robbed me on—but I didn't mind. You expect to be robbed for anything really good in New York, only the imitation stuff that's worn by the idle poor being cheaper than elsewhere. And I was so busy in this whirl of extortion that I forgot all about the boys and their troubles till I got back to the hotel at five o'clock.

I find 'em in the palm grill, or whatever it's called, drinking stingers. But now they was not only more cheerful than they had been the night before but they was getting a little bit contemptuous and Western about the great city. Lon had met a brother real estate shark from Salt Lake and Jeff had fell in with a sheep man from Laramie—and treated him like an equal because of meeting him so far from home in a strange town where no one would find it out on him— and Ben Sutton had met up with his old friend Jake Berger, also from Nome. That's one nice thing about New York; you keep meeting people from out your way that are lonesome, too. Lon's friend and Jeff's sheep man had had to leave, being encumbered by watchful-waiting wives that were having 'em paged every three minutes and wouldn't believe the boy when he said they was out. But Ben's friend, Jake Berger, was still at the table. Jake is a good soul, kind of a short, round, silent man, never opening his head for any length of time. He seems to bring the silence of the frozen North down with him except for brief words to the waiter ever and anon.

As I say, the boys was all more cheerful and contemptuous about New York by this time. Ben had
spent another day asking casual parties if they was
born in New York and having no more luck than a
rabbit, but it seemed like he'd got hardened to these
disappointments. He said he might leave his own
self to a museum in due time, so future generations
would know at least what the male New Yorker
looked like. As for the female, he said any of these
blondes along Broadway could be made to look near
enough like his mate by a skilled taxidermist. Jeff
Tuttle here says that they wasn't all blondes because
he'd seen a certain brunette that afternoon right in
this palm grill that was certainly worth preserving for
all eternity in the grandest museum on earth—which
showed that Jeff had chirked up a lot since landing in
town. Ben said he had used the term "blonde"
merely to designate a species and they let it go at
that.

Lon Price then said he'd been talking a little himself to people he met in different places and they
might not be born New Yorkers but they certainly
didn't know anything beyond the city limits. At
this he looks around at the crowded tables in this
palm grill and says very bitterly that he'll give any of
us fifty to one they ain't a person in the place that ever
so much as even heard of Price's Addition to Red
Gap. And so the talk went for a little, with Jake
Berger ever and again crooning to the waiter for another round of stingers. I'd had two, so I stayed out

on the last round. I told Jake I enjoyed his hospi-
tality but two would be all I could think under till
they learned to leave the dash of chloroform out of
mine. Jake just looked kindly at me. He's as
chatty as Mount McKinley.

But I was glad to see the boys more cheerful, so I
said I'd get my lumpiest jewels out of the safe and put
a maid and hairdresser to work on me so I'd be a
credit to 'em at dinner and then we'd spend a jolly
evening at some show. Jeff said he'd also doll up in
his dress suit and get shaved and manicured and
everything, so he'd look like one in my own walk of
life. Ben was already dressed for evening. He had
on a totally new suit of large black and white checks
looking like a hotel floor from a little distance, bound
with braid of a quiet brown, and with a vest of wide
stripes in green and mustard colour. It was a suit
that the automobile law in some states would have
compelled him to put dimmers on; it made him look
egregious, if that's the word; but I knew it was no
good appealing to his better nature. He said he'd
have dinner ordered for us in another palm grill that
had more palms in it.

Jake Berger spoke up for the first time to any one
but a waiter. He asked why a palm room neces-
sarily? He said the tropic influence of these palms
must affect the waiters that had to stand under 'em
all day, because they wouldn't take his orders fast
enough. He said the languorous Southern atmosphere give 'em pellagra or something. Jeff Tuttle

says Jake must be mistaken because the pellagra is a
kind of a Spanish dance, he believes. Jake said
maybe so; maybe it was tropic neurasthenia the
waiters got. Ben said he'd sure look out for a fresh
waiter that hadn't been infected yet. When I left
'em Jake was holding a split-second watch on the
waiter he'd just given an order to.

By seven P. M. I'd been made into a work of
art by the hotel help and might of been observed progressing through the palatial lobby with
my purple and gold opera cloak sort of falling away
from the shoulders. Jeff Tuttle observed me for one.
He was in his dress suit all right, standing over in a
corner having a bell-hop tie his tie for him that he
never can learn to do himself. That's the way with
Jeff; he simply wasn't born for the higher hotel life.
In his dress suit he looks exactly like this here society
burglar you're always seeing a picture of in the papers. However, I let him trail me along into this
jewelled palm room with tapestries and onyx pillars
and prices for food like the town had been three years
beleagured by an invading army. Jake Berger is
alone at our table sipping a stinger and looking embarrassed because he'll have to say something. He
gets it over as soon as he can. He says Ben has ordered dinner and stepped out and that Lon has
stepped out to look for him but they'll both be back
in a minute, so set down and order one before this new
waiter is overcome by the tropic miasma. We do
the same, and in comes Lon looking very excited

in 'the¯ dress suit he was married in back about
1884.

"Ben's found one," he squeals excitedly—"a real
genuine one that was born right here in New York
and is still living in the same house he was born in.
What do you know about that? Ben is frantic with
delight and is going to bring him to dine with us as
soon as he gets him brushed off down in the wash room
and maybe a drink or two thrown into him to revive
him from the shock of Ben running across him.
Ain't it good, though! Poor old Ben, looking for a
born one and thinking he'd never find him and now he
has!"

We all said how glad we was for Ben's sake and
Lon called over a titled aristocrat of foreign birth
and ordered him to lay another place at the table.
Then he tells us how the encounter happened. Ben
had stepped out on Broadway to buy an evening
paper and coming back he was sneaking a look at his
new suit in a plate-glass window, walking blindly
ahead at the same time. That's the difference between the sexes in front of a plate-glass window. A
woman is entirely honest and shameless; she'll stop
dead and look herself over and touch up anything
that needs it as cool as if she was the last human
on earth; while man, the coward, walks by slow and
takes a long sly look at himself, turning his head
more and more till he gets swore at by some one he's
tramped on. This is how Ben had run across the
only genuine New Yorker that seemed to be left.

He'd run across his left instep and then bore him to
the ground like one of these juggernuts or whatever
they are. Still, at that, it seemed kind of a romantic
meeting, like mebbe the hand of fate was in it. We
chatted along, waiting for the happy pair, and Jake
ordered again to be on the safe side because the
waiter would be sure to contract hookworm or sleeping sickness in this tropic jungle before the evening
was over. Jeff Tuttle said this was called the Louis
Château room and he liked it. He also said, looking
over the people that come in, that he bet every dress
suit in town was hired to-night. Then in a minute
or two more, after Jake Berger sent a bill over to the
orchestra leader with a card asking him to play all
quick tunes so the waiters could fight better against
jungle fever, in comes Ben Sutton driving his captive
New Yorker before him and looking as flushed and
proud as if he'd discovered a strange new vest pattern.

The captive wasn't so much to look at. He was
kind of neat, dressed in one of the nobby suits that
look like ninety dollars in the picture and cost
eighteen; he had one of these smooth ironed faces
that made him look thirty or forty years old, like
all New York men, and he had the conventional
glue on his hair. He was limping noticeably where
Ben had run across him, and I could see he was highly
suspicious of the whole gang of us, including the man
who had treated him like he was a cockroach. But
Ben had been persuasive and imperious—took him

off his feet, like you might say—so he shook hands all around and ventured to set down with us. He had the same cold, slippery cautious hand that every New York man gives you the first time so I says to myself he's a real one all right and we fell to the new round of stingers Jake had motioned for, and to the nouveaux art-work food that now came along.

Naturally Ben and the New Yorker done most of the talking at first; about how the good old town had changed; how they was just putting up the Cable Building at Houston Street when Ben left in '92, and wasn't the old Everett House a good place for lunch, and did the other one remember Barnum's Museum at Broadway and Ann, and Niblo's Garden was still there when Ben was, and a lot of fascinating memories like that. The New Yorker didn't relax much at first and got distinctly nervous when he saw the costly food and heard Ben order vintage champagne which he always picks out by the price on the wine list. I could see him plain as day wondering just what kind of crooks we could be, what our game was and how soon we'd spring it on him—or would we mebbe stick him for the dinner check? He didn't have a bit good time at first, so us four others kind of left Ben to fawn upon him and enjoyed ourselves in our own way.

It was all quite elevating or vicious, what with the orchestra and the singers and the dancing and the waiters with vitality still unimpaired. And New York has improved a lot, I'll say that. The time I was there before they wouldn't let a lady smoke except in the very lowest table d'hotes of the underworld at sixty cents with wine. And now the only one in the whole room that didn't light a cigarette from time to time was a nervous dame in a high-necked black silk and a hat that was never made farther east than Altoona, that looked like she might be taking notes for a club paper on the attractions or iniquities of a great metropolis. Jeff Tuttle was fascinated by the dancing; he called it the "tangle" and some of it did look like that. And he claimed to be shocked by the flagrant way women opened up little silver boxes and applied the paints, oils, and putty in full view of the audience. He said he'd just as lief see a woman take out a manicure set and do her nails in public, and I assured him he probably would see it if he come down again next year, the way things was going—him talking that way that had had his white tie done in the open lobby; but men are such. Jake Berger just looked around kindly and didn't open his head till near the end of the meal. I thought he wasn't noticing anything at all till the orchestra put on a shadow number with dim purple lights.

"You'll notice they do that," says Jake, "whenever a lot of these people are ready to pay their checks. It saves fights, because no one can see if they're added right or not." That was pretty gabby for Jake. Then I listened again to Ben and his little pet. They was talking their way up the Bowery from

Atlantic Garden and over to Harry Hill's Place which it seemed the New Yorker didn't remember, and Ben then recalled an old leper with gray whiskers and a skull cap that kept a drug store in Bleecker Street when Ben was a kid and spent most of his time watering down the sidewalk in front of his place with a hose so that ladies going by would have to raise their skirts out of the wet. His eyes was quite dim as he recalled these sacred boyhood memories.

The New Yorker had unbent a mite like he was going to see the mad adventure through at all costs, though still plainly worried about the dinner check. Ben now said that they two ought to found a New York club. He said there was all other kinds of clubs here—Ohio clubs and Southern clubs and Nebraska societies and Michigan circles and so on, that give large dinners every year, so why shouldn't there be a New York club; maybe they could scare up three or four others that was born here if they advertised. It would of course be the smallest club in the city or in the whole world for that matter. The New Yorker was kind of cold toward this. It must of sounded like the scheme to get money out of him that he'd been expecting all along. Then the waiter brought the check, during another shadow number with red and purple lights, and this lad pulled out a change purse and said in a feeble voice that he supposed we was all paying share and share alike and would the waiter kindly figure out what his share was. Ben didn't even hear him. He peeled

a large bill off a roll that made his new suit a bad
fit in one place and he left a five on the plate when
the change come. The watchful New Yorker now
made his first full-hearted speech of the evening. He
said that Ben was foolish not to of added up the
check to see if it was right, and that half a dollar tip
would of been ample for the waiter. Ben pretended
not to hear this either, and started again on the dear
old times. I says to myself I guess this one is a real
New Yorker all right.

Lon Prince now says what's the matter with going
to some corking good show because nothing good has
come to Red Gap since the Parisian Blond Widows
over a year ago and he's eager for entertainment.
Ben says "Fine! And here's the wise boy that will
steer us right. I bet he knows every show in town."

The New Yorker says he does and has just the
play in mind for us, one that he had meant to see
himself this very night because it has been endorsed
by the drama league of which he is a regular member.
Well, that sounded important, so Ben says "What did
I tell you? Ain't we lucky to have a good old New
Yorker to put us right on shows our first night out.
We might have wasted our evening on a dead one."

So we're all delighted and go out and get in a
couple of taxicabs, Ben and this city man going in the
first one. When ours gets to the theatre Ben is
paying the driver while the New Yorker feebly protests that he ought to pay his half of the bill, but
Ben don't hear him and don't hear him again when

he wants to pay for his own seat in the theatre. I got my first suspicion of this guy right there; for a genuine New Yorker he was too darned conscientious about paying his mere share of everything. You can say lots of things about New Yorkers, but all that I've ever met have been keenly and instantly sensitive to the presence of a determined buyer. Still I didn't think so much about it at that moment. This one looked the part all right, with his slim clothes and his natty cloth hat and the thin gold cigarette case held gracefully open. Then we get into the theatre. Of course Ben had bought a box, that being the only place, he says, that a gentleman can set, owing to the skimpy notions of theatre-seat builders. And we was all prepared for a merry evening at this entertainment which the wise New Yorker would be sure to know was a good one.

But that curtain hadn't been up three minutes before I get my next shock of disbelief about this well-known club man. You know what a good play means in New York: a rattling musical comedy with lively songs, a tenor naval lieutenant in a white uniform, some real funny comedians, and a lot of girls without their stockings on, and so forth. Any one that thinks of a play in New York thinks of that, don't he? And what do we get here and now? Why, we get a gruesome thing about a ruined home with the owner going bankrupt over the telephone that's connected with Wall Street, and a fluffy wife that has a magnetic gentleman friend in a sport suit,

and a lady crook that has had husband in her toils,
only he sees it all now, and tears and strangulations
and divorce, and a faithful old butler that suffers
keenly and would go on doing it without a cent of
wages if he could only bring every one together again,
and a shot up in the bathroom or somewhere and
gripping moments and so forth—I want to tell you
we was all painfully shocked by this break of the
knowing New Yorker. We could hardly believe
it was true during the first act. Jeff Tuttle kept
wanting to know when the girls was coming on, and
didn't they have a muscle dancer in the piece. Ben
himself was highly embarrassed and even suspicious
for a minute. He looks at the New Yorker sharply
and says ain't that a crocheted necktie he's wearing,
and the New Yorker says it is and was made for him
by his aunt. But Ben ain't got the heart to question
him any further. He puts away his base suspicions
and tries to get the New Yorker to tell us all about
what a good play this is so we'll feel more entertained. So the lad tells us the leading woman is a
sterling actress of legitimate methods—all too hard
to find in this day of sensationalism, and the play is a
triumph of advanced realism written by a serious
student of the drama that is trying to save our stage
from commercial degradation. He explained a lot
about the lesson of the play. Near as I could make
out the lesson was that divorce, nowadays, is darned
near as uncertain as marriage itself.

"The husband," explains the lad kindly, "is suspected by his wife to have been leading a double life, though of course he was never guilty of more than an indiscretion——"

Jake Berger here exploded rudely into speech again. "That wife is leading a double chin," says Jake.

"Say, people," says Lon Price, "mebbe it ain't too late to go to a show this evening."

But the curtain went up for the second act and nobody had the nerve to escape. There continued to be low murmurs of rebellion, just the same, and we all lost track of this here infamy that was occurring on the stage.

"I'm sure going to beat it in one minute," says Jeff Tuttle, "if one of 'em don't exclaim: 'Oh, girls, here comes the little dancer!'"

"I know a black-face turn that could put this show on its feet," says Lon Price, "and that Waldo in the sport suit ain't any real reason why wives leave home—you can't tell me!"

"I dare say this leading woman needs a better vehicle," says the New Yorker in a hoarse whisper.

"I dare say it, too," says Jeff Tuttle in a still hoarser whisper. "A better vehicle! She needs a motor truck, and I'd order one quick if I thought she'd take it."

Of course this was not refined of Jeff. The New Yorker winced and loyal Ben glares at all of us that has been muttering, so we had to set there till the curtain went down on the ruined home where all

was lost save honour—and looking like that would
have to go, too, in the next act. But Ben saw it
wasn't safe to push us any further so he now said this
powerful play was too powerful for a bunch of low-
brows like us and we all rushed out into the open
air. Everybody cheered up a lot when we got there
—seeing the nice orderly street traffic without a gripping moment in it. Lon Price said it was too late to
go to a theatre, so what could we do to pass the time
till morning? Ben says he has a grand idea and we
can carry it out fine with this New York man to guide
us. His grand idea is that we all go down on the
Bowery and visit tough dives where the foul creatures of the underworld consort and crime happens
every minute or two. We was still mad enough
about that play to like the idea. A good legitimate
murder would of done wonders for our drooping
spirits. So Ben puts it up to the New Yorker and
he says yes, he knows a vicious resort on the Bowery,
but we'd ought to have a detective from central office
along to protect us from assault. Ben says not at
all—no detective—unless the joints has toughened
up a lot since he used to infest 'em, and we all said
we'd take a chance, so again we was in taxicabs.
Us four in the second cab was now highly cynical
about Ben's New Yorker. The general feeling was
that sooner or later he would sink the ship.

Then we reach the dive he has picked out; a very
dismal dive with a room back of the bar that had a
few tables and a piano in it and a sweet-singing

waiter. He was singing a song about home and mother, that in mem-o-ree he seemed to see, when we got to our table. A very gloomy and respectable haunt of vice it was, indeed. There was about a dozen male and female creatures of the underworld present sadly enjoying this here ballad and scowling at us for talking when we come in.

Jake Berger ordered, though finding you couldn't get stingers here and having to take two miner's inches of red whiskey, and the New Yorker begun to warn us in low tones that we was surrounded by danger on every hand—that we'd better pour our drink on the floor because it would be drugged, after which we would be robbed if not murdered and thrown out into the alley where we would then be arrested by grafting policemen. Even Ben was shocked by this warning. He asks the New Yorker again if he is sure he was born in the old town, and the lad says honest he was and has been living right here all these years in the same house he was born in. Ben is persuaded by these words and gives the singing waiter a five and tells him to try and lighten the gloom with a few crimes of violence or something. The New Yorker continued to set stiff in his chair, one hand on his watch and one on the pocket where his change purse was that he'd tried to pay his share of the taxicabs out of.

The gloom-stricken piano player now rattled off some ragtime and the depraved denizens about us got sadly up and danced to it. Say, it was the most

formal and sedate dancing you ever see, with these
gun men holding their guilty partners off at arm's
length and their faces all drawn down in lines of
misery.   They looked like they might be a bunch of
strict Presbyterians that had resolved to throw all
moral teaching to the winds for one purple moment
let come what might.   I want to tell you these depraved creatures of the underworld was darned near
as depressing as that play had been.   Even the second round of drinks didn't liven us up none because
the waiter threw down his cigarette and sung another
tearful song.   This one was about a travelling man
going into a gilded cabaret and ordering a port wine
and a fair young girl come out to sing in short skirts
that he recognized to be his boyhood's sweetheart
Nell; so he sent a waiter to ask her if she had forgot
the song she once did sing at her dear old mother's
knee, or knees, and she hadn't forgot it and proved
she hadn't, because the chorus was "Nearer My God
to Thee" sung to ragtime; then the travelling man
said she must be good and pure, so come on let's
leave this place and they'd be wed.

   Yes, sir; that's what Ben had got for his five, so
this time he give the waiter a twenty not to sing any
more at all.   The New Yorker was horrified at the
sight of a man giving away money, but it was well
spent and we begun to cheer up a little.   Ben told
the New Yorker about the time his dog team won the
All Alaska Sweepstake Race, two hundred and six
miles from Nome to Candle and back, the time being

76 hours, 16 minutes, and 28 seconds, and showed him the picture of his lead dog pasted in the back of his watch. And Jake Berger got real gabby at last and told the story about the old musher going up the White Horse Trail in a blizzard and meeting the Bishop, only he didn't know it was the Bishop. And the Bishop says, "How's the trail back of you, my friend?" and the old musher just swore with the utmost profanity for three straight minutes. Then he says to the Bishop, "And what's it like back of you?" and the Bishop says, "Just like that!" Jake here got embarrassed from talking so much and ordered another round of this squirrel poison we was getting, and Jeff Tuttle begun his imitation of the Sioux squaw with a hare lip reciting "Curfew Shall Not Ring To-night." It was a pretty severe ordeal for the rest of us, but we was ready to endure much if it would make this low den seem more homelike. Only when Jeff got about halfway through the singing waiter comes up, greatly shocked, and says none of that in here because they run an orderly place, and we been talking too loud anyway. This waiter had a skull exactly like a picture of one in a book I got that was dug up after three hundred thousand years and the scientific world couldn't ever agree whether it was an early man or a late ape. I decided I didn't care to linger in a place where a being with a head like this could pass on my diversions and offenses so I made a move to go. Jeff Tuttle says to this waiter, "Fie, fie upon you, Roscoe! We shall go to some re-

spectable place where we can loosen up without being called for it." The waiter said he was sorry,
but the Bowery wasn't Broadway. And the New
Yorker whispered that it was just as well because we
was lucky to get out of this dive with our lives and
property—and even after that this anthropoid
waiter come hurrying out to the taxis after us with
my fur piece and my solid gold vanity-box that I'd
left behind on a chair. This was a bitter blow to
all of us after we'd been led to hope for outrages of an
illegal character. The New Yorker was certainly
making a misdeal every time he got the cards. None
of us trusted him any more, though Ben was still
loyal and sensitive about him, like he was an only
child and from birth had not been like other children.

The lad now wanted to steer us into an Allied
Bazaar that would still be open, because he'd promised to sell twenty tickets to it and had 'em on
him untouched. But we shut down firmly on this.
Even Ben was firm. He said the last bazaar he'd
survived was their big church fair in Nome that
lasted two nights and one day and the champagne
booth alone took in six thousand dollars, and even
the beer booth took in something like twelve hundred,
and he didn't feel equal to another affair like that
just yet.

So we landed uptown at a very swell joint full of
tables and orchestras around a dancing floor and more
palms—which is the national flower of New York—
and about eighty or a hundred slightly inebriated

débutantes and well-known Broadway social favourites and their gentlemen friends. And here everything seemed satisfactory at last, except to the New
Yorker who said that the prices would be something
shameful. However, no one was paying any attention to him by now. None of us but Ben cared a
hoot where he had been born and most of us was sorry
he had been at all.

Jake Berger bought a table for ten dollars, which
was seven more than it had ever cost the owner, and
Ben ordered stuff for us, including a vintage champagne that the price of stuck out far enough beyond
other prices on the wine list, and a porterhouse steak,
family style, for himself, and everything seemed on a
sane and rational basis again. It looked as if we
might have a little enjoyment during the evening
after all. It was a good lively place, with all these
brilliant society people mingling up in the dance in
a way that would of got 'em thrown out of that gangsters' haunt on the Bowery. Lon Price said he'd
never witnessed so many human shoulder blades in
his whole history and Jeff Tuttle sent off a lot of
picture cards of this here ballroom or saloon that
a waiter give him. The one he sent Egbert Floud
showed the floor full of beautiful reckless women in
the dance and prominent society matrons drinking
highballs, and Jeff wrote on it, "This is my room;
wish you was here." Jeff was getting right into the
spirit of this bohemian night life; you could tell that.
Lon Price also. In ten minutes Lon had made the

acquaintance of a New York social leader at the next table and was dancing with her in an ardent or ribald manner before Ben had finished his steak.

I now noticed that the New Yorker was looking at his gun-metal watch about every two minutes with an expression of alarm. Jake Berger noticed it, too, and again leaned heavily on the conversation. "Not keeping you up, are we?" says Jake. And this continual watch business must of been getting on Ben's nerves, too, for now, having fought his steak to a finish, he says to his little guest that they two should put up their watches and match coins for 'em. The New Yorker was suspicious right off and looked Ben's watch over very carefully when Ben handed it to him. It was one of these thin gold ones that can be had any place for a hundred dollars and up. You could just see that New Yorker saying to himself, "So this is their game, is it?" But he works his nerve up to take a chance and gets a two-bit piece out of his change purse and they match. Ben wins the first time, which was to of settled it, but Ben says right quick that of course he had meant the best two out of three, which the New Yorker doesn't dispute for a minute, and they match again and Ben wins that, too, so there's nothing to do but take the New Yorker's watch away from him. He removes it carefully off a leather fob with a gilt acorn on it and hands it slowly to Ben. It was one of these extra superior dollar watches that cost three dollars. The New Yorker looked very stung, indeed. You

could hear him saying to himself, "Serves me right
for gambling with a stranger!" Ben feels these
suspicions and is hurt by 'em so he says to Jeff, just
to show the New Yorker he's an honest sport, that
he'll stake his two watches against Jeff's solid silver
watch that he won in a bucking contest in 1890.
Jeff says he's on; so they match and Ben wins again,
now having three watches. Then Lon Price comes
back from cavorting with this amiable jade of the
younger dancing set at the next table and Ben makes
him put up his gold seven-jewelled hunting-case
watch against the three and Ben wins again, now
having four watches.

Lon says "Easy come, easy go!" and moves over
to the next table again to help out with the silver
bucket of champagne he's ordered, taking Jeff Tuttle
with him to present to his old friends that he's known
for all of twenty minutes. The New Yorker is now
more suspicious then ever of Ben; his wan beauty
is marred by a cynical smile and his hair has come
unglued in a couple of places. Ben is more sensitive
than ever to these suspicions of his new pal so he calls
on Jake Berger to match his watch against the four.
Jake takes out his split-second repeater and him and
Ben match coins and this time Ben is lucky enough
to lose, thereby showing his dear old New Yorker
that he ain't a crook after all. But the New Yorker
still looks very shrewd and robbed and begins to gulp
the champagne in a greedy manner. You can hear
him calling Jake a confederate. Jake sees it plain

enough, that the lad thinks he's been high-graded, so he calls over our waiter and crowds all five watches onto him. "Take these home to the little ones," says Jake, and dismisses the matter from his mind by putting a wine glass up to his ear and listening into it with a rapt expression that shows he's hearing the roar of the ocean up on Alaska's rockbound coast.

The New Yorker is a mite puzzled by this, but I can see it don't take him long to figure out that the waiter is also a confederate. Anyway, he's been robbed of his watch forever and falls to the champagne again very eager and moody. It was plain he didn't know what a high-powered drink he was trifling with. And Ben was moody, too, by now. He quit recalling old times and sacred memories to the New Yorker. If the latter had tried to break up the party by leaving at this point I guess Ben would of let him go. But he didn't try; he just set there soggily drinking champagne to drown the memory of his lost watch. And pretty soon Ben has to order another quart of this twelve-dollar beverage. The New Yorker keeps right on with the new bottle, daring it to do its worst and it does; he was soon speaking out of a dense fog when he spoke at all.

With his old pal falling into this absent mood Ben throws off his own depression and mingles a bit with the table of old New York families where Lon Price is now paying the checks. They was the real New Yorkers; they'd never had a moment's distrust of Lon after he ordered the first time and told the waiter

to keep the glasses brimming. Jeff Tuttle was now
dancing in an extreme manner with a haggard society
bud aged thirty-five, and only Jake and me was left
at our table. We didn't count the New Yorker any
longer; he was merely raising his glass to his lips
at regular intervals. He moved something like an
automatic chess player I once see. The time passed
rapidly for a couple hours more, with Jake Berger
keeping up his ceaseless chatter as usual. He did
speak once, though, after an hour's silence. He said
in an audible tone that the New Yorker was a human
hangnail, no matter where he was born.

And so the golden moments flitted by, with me
watching the crazy crowd, until they began to fall
away and the waiters was piling chairs on the naked
tables at the back of the room. Then with some
difficulty we wrenched Ben and Lon and Jeff from
the next table and got out into the crisp air of dawn.
The New Yorker was now sunk deep in a trance
and just stood where he was put, with his hat on the
wrong way. The other boys had cheered up a lot
owing to their late social career. Jeff Tuttle said it
was all nonsense about its being hard to break into
New York society, because look what he'd done in
one brief evening without trying—and he flashed
three cards on which telephone numbers is written
in dainty feminine hands. He said if a modest and
retiring stranger like himself could do that much,
just think what an out-and-out social climber might
achieve!

Right then I was ready to call it an absorbing and instructive evening and get to bed. But no! Ben Sutton at sight of his now dazed New Yorker has resumed his brooding and suddenly announces that we must all make a pilgrimage to West Ninth Street and romantically view his old home which his father told him to get out of twenty-five years ago, and which we can observe by the first tender rays of dawn. He says he has been having precious illusions shattered all evening, but this will be a holy moment that nothing can queer—not even a born New Yorker that hasn't made the grade and is at this moment so vitrified that he'd be a mere glass crash if some one pushed him over.

I didn't want to go a bit. I could see that Jeff Tuttle would soon begin dragging a hip, and the streets at that hour was no place for Lon Price, with his naturally daring nature emphasized, as it were, from drinking this here imprisoned laughter of the man that owned the joint we had just left. But Ben was pleading in a broken voice for one sight of the old home with its boyhood memories clustering about its modest front and I was afraid he'd get to crying, so I give in wearily and we was once more encased in taxicabs and on our way to the sacred scene. Ben had quite an argument with the drivers when he give 'em the address. They kept telling him there wasn't a thing open down there, but he finally got his aim understood. The New Yorker's petrified remains was carefully tucked into the cab with Ben.

And Ben suffered another cruel blow at the end of the ride. He climbed out of the cab in a reverent manner, hoping to be overcome by the sight of the cherished old home, and what did he find? He just couldn't believe it at first. The dear old house had completely disappeared and in its place was a granite office building eighteen stories high. Ben just stood off and looked up at it, too overcome for words. Up near the top a monster brass sign in writing caught the silver light of dawn. The sign sprawled clear across the building and said PANTS EX-CLUSIVELY. Still above this was the firm's name in the same medium—looking like a couple of them hard-lettered towns that get evacuated up in Poland.

Poor stricken Ben looked in silence a long time. We all felt his suffering and kept silent, too. Even Jeff Tuttle kept still—who all the way down had been singing about old Bill Bailey who played the Ukelele in Honolulu Town. It was a solemn moment. After a few more minutes of silent grief Ben drew himself together and walked off without saying a word. I thought walking would be a good idea for all of us, especially Lon and Jeff, so Jake paid the taxi drivers and we followed on foot after the chief mourner. The fragile New Yorker had been exhumed and placed in an upright position and he walked, too, when he understood what was wanted of him; he didn't say a word, just did what was told him like one of these boys that the professor hypno-tizes on the stage. I herded the bunch along about half a block back of Ben, feeling it was delicate to let him wallow alone in his emotions.

We got over to Broadway, turned up that, and worked on through that dinky little grass plot they call a square, kind of aimless like and wondering where Ben in his grief would lead us. The day was well begun by this time and the passing cars was full of very quiet people on their way to early work. Jake Berger said these New Yorkers would pay for it sooner or later, burning the candle at both ends this way—dancing all night and then starting off to work.

Then up a little way we catch sight of a regular old-fashioned horse-car going crosstown. Ben has stopped this and is talking excitedly to the driver so we hurry up and find he's trying to buy the car from the driver. Yes, sir; he says its the last remnant of New York when it was little and old and he wants to take it back to Nome as a souvenir. Anybody might of thought he'd been drinking. He's got his roll out and wants to pay for the car right there. The driver is a cold-looking old boy with gray chin whiskers showing between his cap and his comforter and he's indignantly telling Ben it can't be done. By the time we get there the conductor has come around and wants to know what they're losing all this time for. He also says they can't sell Ben the car and says further that we'd all better go home and sleep it off, so Ben hands 'em each a ten spot, the driver lets off his brake, and the old ark rattles on while Ben's eyes is suffused with a suspicious moisture, as they say.

Ben now says we must stand right on this corner to watch these cars go by—about once every hour. We argued with him whilst we shivered in the bracing winelike air, but Ben was stubborn. We might of been there yet if something hadn't diverted him from this evil design. It was a string of about fifty Italians that just then come out of a subway entrance. They very plainly belonged to the lower or labouring classes and I judged they was meant for work on the up-and-down street we stood on, that being already torn up recklessly till it looked like most other streets in the same town. They stood around talking in a delirious or Italian manner till their foreman unlocked a couple of big piano boxes. Out of these they took crowbars, adzes, shovels, and other instruments of their calling. Ben Sutton has been standing there soddenly waiting for another dear old horse-car to come by, but suddenly he takes notice of these bandits with the tools and I see an evil gleam come into his tired eyes. He assumes a businesslike air, struts over to the foreman of the bunch, and has some quick words with him, making sweeping motions of the arm up and down the cross street where the horse-cars run. After a minute of this I'm darned if the whole bunch didn't scatter out and begin to tear up the pavement along the car-track on this cross street. Ben tripped back to us looking cheerful once more.

"They wouldn't sell me the car," he says, "so I'm going to take back a bunch of the dear old rails. They'll be something to remind me of the dead past.

Just think! I rode over those very rails when I was a tot."

We was all kind of took back at this, and I promptly warned Ben that we'd better beat it before we got pinched. But Ben is confident. He says no crime could be safer in New York than setting a bunch of Italians to tearing up a street-car track; that no one could ever possibly suspect it wasn't all right, though he might have to be underhanded to some extent in getting his souvenir rails hauled off. He said he had told the foreman that he was the contractor's brother and had been sent with this new order and the foreman had naturally believed it, Ben looking like a rich contractor himself.

And there they was at work, busy as beavers, gouging up the very last remnant of little old New York when it was that. Ben rubbed his hands in ecstasy and pranced up and down watching 'em for awhile. Then he went over and told the foreman there'd be extra pay for all hands if they got a whole block tore up by noon, because this was a rush job. Hundreds of people was passing, mind you, including a policeman now and then, but no one took any notice of a sight so usual. All the same the rest of us edged north about half a block, ready to make a quick getaway. Ben kept telling us we was foolishly scared. He offered to bet any one in the party ten to one in thousands that he could switch his gang over to Broadway and have a block of that track up before any one got wise. There was no takers.

Ben was now so pleased with himself and his little band of faithful workers that he even begun to feel kindly again toward his New Yorker who was still standing in one spot with glazed eyes. He goes up and tries to engage him in conversation, but the lad can't hear any more than he can see. Ben's efforts, however, finally start him to muttering something. He says it over and over to himself and at last we make out what it is. He is saying: "I'd like to buy a little drink for the party m'self."

"The poor creature is delirious," says Jake Berger.

But Ben slaps him on the back and tells him he's a good sport and he'll give him a couple of these rails to take to his old New York home; he says they can be crossed over the mantel and will look very quaint. The lad kind of shivered under Ben's hearty blow and seemed to struggle out of his trance for a minute. His eyes unglazed and he looks around and says how did he get here and where is it? Ben tells him he's among friends and that they two are the only born New Yorkers left in the world, and so on, when the lad reaches into the pocket of his natty topcoat for a handkerchief and pulls out with it a string of funny little tickets—about two feet of 'em. Ben grabs these up with a strange look in his eyes

"Bridge tickets!" he yells. Then he grabs his born New Yorker by the shoulders and shakes him still further out of dreamland.

"What street in New York is your old home on?"

he demands savagely. The lad blinks his fishy eyes and fixes his hat on that Ben has shook loose.

"Cranberry Street," says he.

"Cranberry Street! Hell, that's Brooklyn, and you claimed New York," says Ben, shaking the hat loose again.

"Greater New York," says the lad pathetically, and pulls his hat firmly down over his ears.

Ben looked at the imposter with horror in his eyes. "Brooklyn!" he muttered—"the city of the un-buried dead! So that was the secret of your strange behaviour? And me warming you in my bosom, you viper!"

But the crook couldn't hear him again, having lapsed into his trance and become entirely rigid and foolish. In the cold light of day his face now looked like a plaster cast of itself. Ben turned to us with a hunted look. "Blow after blow has fallen upon me to-night," he says tearfully, "but this is the most cruel of all. I can't believe in anything after this. I can't even believe them street-car rails are the originals. Probably they were put down last week."

"Then let's get out of this quick," I says to him. "We been exposing ourselves to arrest here long enough for a bit of false sentiment on your part."

"I gladly go," says Ben, "but wait one second." He stealthily approaches the Greater New Yorker and shivers him to wakefulness with another hearty wallop on the back. "Listen carefully," says Ben as the lad struggles out of the dense fog. "Do you see those workmen tearing up that car-track?"

"Yes, I see it," says the lad distinctly. "I've often seen it."

"Very well. Listen to me and remember your life may hang on it. You go over there and stand right by them till they get that track up and don't you let any one stop them. Do you hear? Stand right there and make them work, and if a policeman or any one tries to make trouble you soak him. Remember! I'm leaving those men in your charge. I shall hold you personally responsible for them."

The lad don't say a word but begins to walk in a brittle manner toward the labourers. We saw him stop and point a threatening finger at them, then instantly freeze once more. It was our last look at him. We got everybody on a north-bound car with some trouble. Lon Price had gone to sleep standing up and Jeff Tuttle, who was now looking like the society burglar after a tough night's work at his trade, was getting turbulent and thirsty. He didn't want to ride on a common street car. "I want a tashicrab," he says, "and I want to go back to that Louis Château room and dance the tangle." But we persuaded him and got safe up to a restaurant on Sixth Avenue where breakfast was had by all without further adventure. Jeff strongly objected to this restaurant at first, though, because he couldn't hear an orchestra in it. He said he couldn't eat his breakfast without an orchestra. He did, however, ordering

apple pie and ice cream and a gin fizz to come. Lon
Price was soon sleeping like a tired child over his ham
and eggs, and Jeff went night-night, too, before his
second gin fizz arrived.

Ben ordered a porterhouse steak, family style, con-
suming it in a moody rage like a man that has been
ground-sluiced at every turn. He said he felt like
ending it all and sometimes wished he'd been in the
cab that plunged into one of the forty-foot holes in
Broadway a couple of nights before. Jake Berger
had ordered catfish and waffles, with a glass of In-
valid port. He burst into speech once more, too.
He said the nights in New York were too short to get
much done. That if they only had nights as long as
Alaska the town might become famous. "As it is,"
he says, "I don't mind flirting with this city now and
then, but I wouldn't want to marry it."

Well, that about finished the evening, with Lon and
Jeff making the room sound like a Pullman palace car
at midnight. Oh, yes; there was one thing more.
On the day after the events recorded in the last chapter, as it says in novels, there was a piece in one of the
live newspapers telling that a well-dressed man of
thirty-five, calling himself Clifford J. Hotchkiss and
giving a Brooklyn address, was picked up in a dazed
condition by patrolman Cohen who had found him at-
tempting to direct the operations of a gang of workmen engaged in repairing a crosstown-car track. He
had been sent to the detention ward of Bellevue to
await examination as to his sanity, though insisting

that he was the victim of a gang of footpads who had plied him with liquor and robbed him of his watch. I showed the piece to Ben Sutton and Ben sent him up a pillow of forget-me-nots with "Rest" spelled on it— without the sender's card.

No; not a word in it about the street-car track being wrongfully tore up. I guess it was like Ben said; no one ever would find out about that in New York. My lands! here it is ten-thirty and I got to be on the job when them hayers start to-morrow A. M. A body would think I hadn't a care on earth when I get started on anecdotes of my past.

THE END

www.ingramcontent.com/pod-product-compliance
Lightning Source LLC
Chambersburg PA
CBHW071641260626
47170CB00001B/188